Dead Houses and Other Works

Edith Miniter

Edith Miniter

DEAD HOUSES
and other works

Edited by
Kenneth W. Faig, Jr.
and Sean Donnelly

Hippocampus Press
New York

Published by Hippocampus Press
P.O. Box 641
New York, NY 10156
http://www.hippocampuspress.com

Cover design by Sean Donnelly.
Hippocampus Press logo by Anastasia Damianakos.

First Edition
1 3 5 7 9 8 6 4 2

ISBN 978-0-9793806-7-9

In Memory of
Hyman Bradofsky
1906-2002

CONTENTS

FICTION

INTRODUCING EDITH MINITER

Edith (Dowe) Miniter (1867-1934) has hitherto been known to the literary world at large only for her novel *Our Natupski Neighbors* (Henry Holt, 1916), a sensitive portrayal of the difficult adjustment of Polish immigrants to life in a fictional New England town ("West Holly") in the early twentieth century. Actually, the town was Edith's own native Wilbraham, Massachusetts and the novel was as much about the adjustment of the townspeople to the immigrants as it was about the adjustment of the immigrants to the townspeople. In fact, so revealing (and sometimes unflattering) was Edith's portrayal of the residents of her native town that some of them tried to suppress the book, which allegedly had to be kept under lock and key at the town library. If this brief account of Edith's novel piques the reader's curiosity, it may be noted that Kessinger Publishers have recently reprinted *Our Natupski Neighbors* as a paperbound facsimile of the original 1916 Holt edition.

In actuality, Edith Miniter left a literary heritage far larger than her sole published novel, but it has hitherto lain neglected in forgotten amateur magazines and professional magazines and newspapers. Perhaps her richest legacy was in the domain of the short story, of which she contributed numerous examples to the amateur press from her advent to the hobby as a sixteen-year-old in 1883 through the second decade of the twentieth century. From the time of her marriage to John T. Miniter (1864?-1900) in 1887, she was also engaged in professional newspaper work, most notably with the society weekly *The Boston Home Journal* from 1893 until 1906. It is possible that the digitalization of newspaper and magazine archives will eventually reveal more as-yet unreprinted work by Edith Miniter, including her *Boston Globe* article "How To Dress on $40 A Year" (ca. 1895-98), which drew perhaps the greatest response of all the works published during her lifetime. By the second and third decades of the twentieth century, Edith was beginning to carve out a niche as an authority on ancient customs and household appurtenances of colonial New England. It is only a pity that declining health during the final years of her life cut short the development of her work in this line of writing, for which she had a definite gift. The antiques preserved by Evanore Beebe in her home Maplehurst in Wilbraham, where Edith lived in the last years of her life, and Miss Beebe's own antiquarian knowledge undoubtedly assisted Mrs. Miniter in pursuing this line of writing.

After presenting a rich selection of biographical memoirs to introduce the reader to Mrs. Miniter, we will concentrate on two aspects of Edith's work in this collection. First of all, the marvellous short stories which have lain neglected since their first publication in the amateur press. It is amazes us that a classic story like "The Emancipation of Elvira" (*The Random Amateur,* 1906) appears for the first time professionally in this collection. Edith wrote many equally good stories depicting the warp and woof of life in New England from a woman's perspective. While she had little sympathy for supernatural fiction, Edith had a deep appreciation of the darker aspects of the New England psyche—some of the blood of the Mathers definitely flowed in her veins. In the appraisal of her close friend and fellow amateur journalist W. Paul Cook, "Dead Houses" (*Leaves,* 1938)—from which this collection takes its title—was her finest work. (Cook was enraged when young R. H. Barlow first published this story—which Cook had originally reserved for his own never-published Miniter memorial volume—in a mimeographed amateur magazine.) While only a few of Edith's very early journeyman stories (not reprinted here) are explicitly ghostly, "Wonted Fires" (*Con Amore,* 1905), included in this collection, is as dark a piece of gothic fiction as the aficionado might desire—albeit pleasantly devoid of the cliched trappings of the genre. We hope that the present collection will help to secure for Edith Miniter at least a small niche in the pantheon of New England regionalism, where writers like Sarah Orne Jewett and Mary E. Wilkins-Freeman already have established places. While her friend Howard Phillips Lovecraft may have been "reaching" to compare Mrs. Miniter's fiction with Jane Austen's, we feel strongly that she merits a recognized place among the New England regionalists.

The second aspect of Edith Miniter's writing that we explore in this collection is her occasional writing for the amateur press. Edith first entered amateur journalism in 1883 in response to a twenty-five cent advertisement placed by Finlay Arnon Grant in the Worcester, Massachusetts *Spy*, but enjoyed her greatest renown in the hobby during the two decades following her arrival in Boston in 1893. The Hub Amateur Journalists' Club had been founded by Ella Maude Frye in 1890 and for nearly thirty years from 1893 onward Edith was its guiding spirit. She and her mother the poet Jennie E. T. Dowe (1840-1919) hosted many meetings of the club at their home "Stately Stairways" at 17 Akron Street in Roxbury from 1906 until 1918.

If Edith lacked anything as an amateur journalist, it was the ability to coexist with political opponents. She remained an idealist at heart and had difficulty in accepting views opposed to her own. She never forgave the New York faction which denied her close friend John Leary Peltret (1874-1938) the presidency of the National Amateur Press Association (N.A.P.A.) during its unruly convention in New York City in 1902 and unwisely continued for years her efforts to have Peltret's name substituted for that of the elected Anthony E. Wills on the N.A.P.A. presidential roll. When Edith became the first woman to be elected President of N.A.P.A. in 1909, the New York faction withheld its support from her administration, and she had to fire Official Editor George Julian Houtain and Treasurer Victor J. Singer for their non-cooperation.

When The Fossils, the alumni organization of the amateur journalism hobby, advocated the elimination of adults from active participation in the hobby, Edith and the Hub Club pressed for the expulsion of their leaders from N.A.P.A., but cooler heads prevailed. By 1914 Edith had become such a formidable figure in the hobby that young Edna von der Heide (later Edna Hyde McDonald) was somewhat intimidated when she first met Edith and her compatriots Laurie A. Sawyer and Ethel May Johnston-Myers in the parlor of the Hotel Statler at the N.A.P.A. convention in Bridgeport, Connecticut. Even her once warm relationship with her young protege Edward H. Cole eventually cooled when she concluded that his support for the revived Massachusetts Amateur Press Association was detracting from the Hub Club.

M rs. Miniter famously admitted new acquaintances within the hobby "on suspicion," but in 1920 she first met in person an amateur journalist—Howard Phillips Lovecraft—whom she grew to like very well indeed. The amateur essays reprinted here include a rich mine of information concerning Lovecraft, who was one of very few amateur journalists invited to visit Edith after she retired to the home of her remote kinswoman Evanore Beebe in Wilbraham in 1925. Lovecraft's visit, in 1928, furnished some of the local background for his famous story "The Dunwich Horror." His account of Mrs. Miniter, first published in the "Miniter Memorial" issue of Hyman Bradofsky's *The Californian* (spring 1938) is as fine a portrait as the one Mrs. Miniter drew of her mother in "My Mother—As She Seemed To Me" (*In Memoriam Jennie E. T. Dowe*, 1921). Both essays are reprinted here as well as Mrs. Miniter's delightful parody of Lovecraft and his work "Falco Ossifracus" (*The Muffin Man*, 1921).

Much more of Edith Miniter's work remains to be explored. Space limitations have not allowed us to include Edith's incomplete serial "Love Without Wings" (*The Varied Year*, 1902-10), which appears to be based largely on her troubled marriage to John T. Miniter, or her collaborative account of the summer she spent camping in Wilbraham with her mother and John Leary Peltret (*From Fireflies to Crickets*, 1905). The sequel to *Our Natupski Neighbors* mentioned by Lovecraft in his essay on Mrs. Miniter apparently does not survive except in outline form, but two unpublished novels *The Village Green* and *Lydia 'n' Gerald* survive in manuscript in the Lovecraft Collection at Brown University along with a scattering of other Miniter manuscripts. We have reprinted here only our personal favorites among Mrs. Miniter's short stories, and many fine stories remain to be reprinted. Stories from Edith's ultra-realist period in the early 1890s like "Cindy's Child" and "For a Big Roll of Money" may especially interest modern readers. The majority of Edith's professional writing also has yet to be resurrected and reprinted.

The electronic texts used for this collection derive from two archival collections published in 100-copy limited editions by co-editor Faig's Moshassuck Press—*Going Home and Other Amateur Writings* (1995) and *The Coast of Bohemia and Other Writings* (2000). "Edith Miniter: A Life" originally appeared in the second Moshassuck Press collection and has been condensed and corrected for its reprinting here.

We wish to thank Derrick Hussey and Hippocampus Press for becoming the second publisher (after Henry Holt in 1916) to place the work of Edith Miniter before a wider reading public. We hope that most of those readers will share our high opinion of her work. We believe that her work richly deserves the revival which it is here afforded.

Kenneth W. Faig, Jr.
Sean Donnelly

About Edith Miniter

EDITH MINITER: A LIFE
Kenneth W. Faig, Jr.

Edith May Dowe was born in her maternal grandfather's house in Wilbraham, Massachusetts on May 19, 1867, the daughter of William Hilton Dowe (1840-1875) and Jane Elizabeth (Tupper) Dowe (1840-1919). Edith May Dowe came from old New England stock on both sides of her family. An interjection of Irish blood came from her maternal grandmother Catherine Orpha Moore, who was born on November 30, 1812, in Enfield, Connecticut. Edith wrote of her Irish grandmother:

> Her [Jennie Dowe's] mother's maiden name was Catherine Orpha Moore, and Grandfather Moore was of a branch of the family of Thomas Moore. Catherine Orpha was a real "Irish beauty" in looks, with large blue eyes and soft dark hair. She had no poetry in her make-up, being eminently practical, but there was taste for rhyme as well as reason in the family. Several of her sisters, my mother's aunts, were addicted to the making of "varses" on local happenings. These "varses" used to be tacked up on guide posts with auction bills and other literature; they made the Moore girls quite famous.

Catherine Orpha Moore married Edwin Lombard Tupper, and they had a son Charles Edwin, born May 18, 1838, and a daughter Jane Elizabeth, born December 13, 1840. Edwin Lombard Tupper acquired a portion of the Bliss farm in 1842 and erected his own home there, the home in which Edith May Dowe was born, about 1846. Mrs. Miniter wrote of Edwin Lombard Tupper:

> Jane's father was not a money maker. He was intensely industrious and of great skill in his line of work; he built churches and beautiful houses, but when it came to collecting pay therefor he was extremely unbusinesslike. No debtor was ever pressed by him, and his partners generally benefitted at E. L. Tupper's expense. This resulted in his being famous as a kind and generous man; it also resulted in considerable stringency in his own home. He was always that way. Later, as a farmer, he would bud and graft and

sit up nights coaxing fruit trees to wonderful results, but he would not market or sell the products. Such characters have always been found in New England, despite the fame of Yankees for trading.

Of her mother's early years in Wilbraham, Edith wrote:

Jane's father built his own house on the mountain, calling it done with the upper rooms largely "not done off," as was the custom. Then he went to Brimfield to build a church, leaving his wife and two children to look after a 40-acre farm. I have in my own mind at this moment a mental picture of young Jane, her auburn hair flung to the breeze, her clear voice raised in vociferous remonstrance, while she goes "hell bent for 'lection" in response to the bad news "fence is down and cows is out." It seems that the Tupper family never had company to tea but those pesky cows got out. The pasture was part swale; Jane always prided herself on her skill in leaping lightly from bog to bog without getting bemired.

After she dissolved her own household in Worcester in 1891, Jennie Dowe went back to Wilbraham to care for her aging parents. Despite all the "improvements" which Edwin Lombard Tupper and his son Charles Edwin Tupper had installed in the home on Wilbraham Mountain, it still lacked running water, and Jane had to draw water from the well outside and lug it up a path culminating in a flight of stone steps. Wrote Edith of these difficult years in her mother's life:

For about eight years she remained there, doing a great deal of housework, which she despised above all forms of labor; living with very little congenial society, and in the midst of that butter and cheese making from which she had earlier in life asked to be excused. Perhaps because she had proven to herself that it wasn't her life work, she took it quite jauntily. She even made butter and cheese with her own hands, and was immensely tickled when the neighbors considered the results just as good as Mrs. Edwin Tupper's famed products. You see, my mother always accepted what she felt had to be, with good grace. The farm was there, it must be cultivated. Her parents were there and too old to be left alone. They refused to be coaxed from their home, even when unable to 'tend the cows and chickens or keep cobwebs away from

that part of the front windows visible to "the passing." My uncle's
wife was dead; on my mother alone depended aid in female form.

During most of the period 1891-93, Edith was engaged in newspaper work in Manchester, New Hampshire. Jennie Dowe seems to
have accompanied her daughter to Manchester to begin with; but
shortly after she went to Wilbraham to care for her aging parents
and was able only to pay occasional weekend visits to her daughter. After Edith settled permanently in Boston in December 1893,
Jennie Dowe would steal away from Wilbraham for a few weeks
at a time, to indulge with her daughter in "orgies" of theater performances and restaurant meals. Every summer, Edith would come
to visit her mother and her grandparents in Wilbraham. During
the winter of 1895-96, Jennie nursed her mother through a serious
bout of pneumonia, but when the illness recurred in the spring,
Catherine's heart was no longer equal to the struggle for breath, and
she succumbed on May 2, 1896. Later that year, Jennie turned the
family household (and the care of her surviving parent) over to her
nephew Herbert Edwin Tupper, and joined her daughter in Boston.
They were to remain together for the rest of Jennie's life, until her
death on March 6, 1919.

The difficult years 1891-96 were far in the future as Jennie Tupper
grew up into a petite and attractive young woman in Wilbraham.
She attended the town's venerable Academy, and commenced teach-
ing school even before graduation. After teaching for a time, she
overcame her mother's resistance and went to Westfield Normal to
prepare for a university career at Oberlin, one of the first colleges to
admit women. But it was not to be. While at Westfield Normal, she
met young William Hilton Dowe, an advanced student of classical
languages who had his own small private school in his native Charlton, Massachusetts. On June 29, 1864, Rev. George Booler married
William H. Dowe of Charlton and Jennie E. Tupper of Wilbraham
in Westfield. The Charlton vital record of this marriage lists William H. Dowe's occupation as millwright. The young couple went
first to live in the home of the groom's parents in Charlton. Jennie began at this time to contribute poetry to the newspaper press.
Her husband soon joined the firm of Norcross Brothers builders in
Worcester, and removed to that city, where the Universalist Church

was one of his first projects. Soon he went on to even more important building projects in Springfield. Taking after his father-in-law and brother-in-law, young William Dowe seems to have spent much of his spare time remodelling the family home at 13 Mason Street in Worcester. Jennie returned to her parents' home on Wilbraham Mountain to give birth to young Edith May Dowe on May 19, 1867. But the young family was not destined to remain together for long. William Hilton Dowe died in Worcester on February 12, 1875, a week shy of thirty-four years three months. Jennie and her young daughter, not yet eight years old, were well enough off to remain in the family home in Worcester.

Despite the early loss of her father, Edith's youth seems to have been generally quite happy. Jennie Dowe's circumstances allowed her and her daughter to remain in the family home at 13 Mason Street in Worcester, amidst the busy city life which Jennie so adored. Several friends who knew both mother and daughter commented that the pair seemed more like sisters. As an adult, Edith called her mother "Jane," and they made common household from 1896 until Jennie Dowe died in 1919. As a young widow, Jennie Dowe busied herself with her home and with her literary career, achieving some success as a poet in the periodical and newspaper press. Edith lived and breathed books and writing from her earliest years, although her own and her mother's tastes were starkly different—Jennie the optimist and romantic, Edith the pessimist and realist. Jennie's novels never attained publication, but her short stories found some success and her poetry was widely published. After her son-in-law John T. Miniter flooded their Worcester household with Irish verse, Jennie began to write in this vein. Although she had never been to Ireland, her Irish poetry rang true and found ready acceptance with Richard Watson Gilder at *Century*. Jennie loved the ocean, and she and her daughter usually spent part of July boarding near the open water, in Rhode Island, where they had relatives, or in Maine. Then they would go to Wilbraham to stay with Jennie's parents until the first frost. In later years, they would go with friends to camp on Edith's property "Meadowbeck" in Wilbraham or visit the Noyes sisters at "Breezyhurst" on the Merrimac at Methuen.

Edith was largely educated by her mother at home. She later attended a private school of elocution in Worcester. One of her par-

ticular loves was *St. Nicholas Magazine* and there in the June 1882 issue fifteen-year-old Edith read Harlan H. Ballard's lively account of
the amateur journalism hobby. What fun these young men seemed
to have with their privately printed magazines and the lively politics of their annual conventions. The National Amateur Press Association had been organized in Philadelphia in 1876 and the hobby
was in full bloom by the mid-eighties. Then, in May 1883, the
prominent amateur journalist Finlay Arnon Grant (1862-1897)
published a twenty-five cent advertisement in the *Worcester Spy*, inviting both boys and girls to inquire about the hobby. The response
from young Edith May Dowe was the only one which he received,
but he stated that he never regretted spending the money in light of
his illustrious recruit. It wasn't long before young Edith was writing away for samples of amateur magazines. By July 1883, Grant
and Frank S. C. Wicks escorted Edith to her first-ever amateur press
association convention, the meeting of the New England Amateur
Press Association (N.E.A.P.A.) held in Gardner, Massachusetts
over the Fourth of July holiday. There Edith met Gracia A. Smith,
one of her earliest and closest female confidantes in amateur journalism. On the male side, she first met at Gardner lifelong friends
like Truman J. Spencer, Willard O. Wylie, and George E. Day. At
the banquet, she was seated between Finlay Grant and Howard K.
Sanderson, just one place setting removed from Leonard E. Tilden,
who sat at the head of the banquet table across from Dennie A. Sullivan on the opposite side.

Throughout her long career in amateur journalism, Edith was
primarily a writer, rather than a publisher, although she did publish
a notable list of amateur magazines including *The Worcester Amateur*
(1884-86), *The Webster Amateur* (1887), *Aftermath* (1894-1921),
The Varied Year (1902-10), *True Blue* (1906-10), and *The Muffin
Man* (1921). In addition, she was associated with John Leary Peltret (1874-1938) as co-publisher of *Ours* (1902-03). Early in her
career, in 1885-86, she was associated with John Moody's *Bayonne
Budget* and *Rising Age*, and Moody honored her by including her
in his compilation *Men of Today* (aka *Leaders of Today*) in the latter
year. John Moody (1868-1958) went on to worldwide notoriety
as founder of Moody's Investor Services in New York City. But it
was as a writer for amateur publications that Edith found her real

metier. Her early manuscripts, written in red or violet ink in a large hand, must have consumed many pages. But amateur editors, starving for contributions, were glad to have these literate contributions from the young muse of Worcester. Beginning with "Bert Gifford's Masterpiece" in *The Cincinnati Amateur* for January 1884, she published thirteen items in the amateur press in 1884, and then eighteen in 1885. Edith's love for the cause of amateur journalism was cemented early; and when she hit her metier as a writer of fiction in the early years of this century, it was still largely to the amateur press that she directed her work. Such a classic story as "The Emancipation of Elvira"—considered by many as her finest work—first appeared in Warren J. Brodie's *Random Amateur* in March 1906 and is published here for the first time.

Edith approached the politics and conventions of the amateur press associations more cautiously, building her knowledge before she ventured very far. The N.E.A.P.A. met semiannually in those days. Since the Gardner convention in July 1883 had chosen Edith's home town of Worcester for its next meeting place, it seems likely that she was in attendance when N.E.A.P.A. assembled at Natural History Hall in Worcester on January 2, 1884 to elect Truman J. Spencer as President and George E. Day as Vice President; however, there is no proof that she attended this N.E.A.P.A. convention in her own home town. Nor is she known to have attended the next two N.E.A.P.A. conventions, in Portland, Maine on July 2, 1884 and in New Bedford, Massachusetts on January 1, 1885. A few days after the latter meet, however, she does seem to have attended the convention of the Massachusetts Amateur Press Association (M.A.P.A.) held in Worcester, Massachusetts. Of this M.A.P.A. meeting, Edith wrote twenty-five years later in "A Rearward Glance":

> It was a tame affair, with no banquet. I thought it better fun to stay
> at home writing letters than attending such stupid "meets."

In September 1884, she commenced publication of *The Worcester Amateur,* with prominent Worcester amateur journalist Frank Roe Batchelder's Go-Ahead Press as printer. Her correspondence was such that the local mail carrier complained that she received more mail than the factory in the next block. When she and Gracia Smith both boarded with relations in Wilbraham during the late August and September of 1885, the local postmaster must have been astounded by the volume of mail which accumulated for the two very active female amateur journalists. For the first time, the National Amateur Press Association invited girls to attend its national convention to be held at Quincy House in Boston on July 15, 1885. Edith attended both this convention and the N.E.A.P.A. convention which the Metcalf brothers hosted in Providence, Rhode Island, the preceding day, July 14, 1885. The two conventions together were an experience which she never forgot; while she had been to Providence numerous times to visit relatives, it was her first-ever trip to the Boston metropolis.

In Providence on July 14, she was elected to her second political office in amateur journalism, a six-month term as N.E.A.P.A. Secretary. (She had earlier been elected, apparently in absentia, to a six-month term as Second Vice President of N.E.A.P.A. at the New Bedford, Massachusetts, convention on January 1, 1885.) Finlay Arnon Grant and Bertha York married at the Boston convention. Miss Dowe's serial "Back o' the Mountain" in *The New Century* won the serial laureate, much to the distress of veteran male amateur journalist Clarence E. Stone, who had coveted the same award. At the Boston N.A.P.A. convention Miss Dowe met for the first time lifelong friends like Edwin Booth Swift and his first wife Zelda (Arlington) Swift, James H. Ives Munro, Helen G. Phillips, and Jennie M. Day. The young women, recognized for the first time at the Boston N.A.P.A. meet, soon resolved to form their own association, and in 1885-86 Edith acted as Official Editor for the short-lived Young Women's Amateur Press Association.

Miss Dowe was beginning to be an influential force in amateur journalism. Wrote her future husband John T. Miniter in *Haverhill Life* for August 1885:

> Miss Edith May Dowe of Worcester, Secretary of NEAPA, gave us lots of encouragement. We owe her much, but trust that we will sometime have an opportunity of thanking her in person.

Mrs. Miniter herself reflected in "A Rearward Glance":

> After this detour into the N.A.P.A. {the July 1885 Boston convention}, we New Englanders turned our attention back to local affairs. On returning to my home in Worcester I found a letter from

one John T. F. Miniter, asking for directions in forming an amateur club, and before long one was formed in Haverhill ⁅Massachusetts⁆ that was probably the largest on record, outside of Gardner. It published a handsome paper called *Haverhill Life,* and two of the publishers, Miniter and Chamberlain were at the New England convention in Leominster in December of 1885.

By autumn of the same year, William M. Emery and George A. Hough were touting Miss Dowe for the presidency of the Eastern Amateur Press Association. While girls had held lesser offices in amateur press associations, this was the first major campaign to elect a female to the presidency. John T. Miniter added his voice to Emery's and Hough's in *Haverhill Life* for September 20, 1885:

> *The Ephemera* ⁅Emery's and Howe's amateur magazine⁆ has nominated Miss Edith May Dowe for the presidency of the Eastern APA. We endorse the nomination, and we intend to be at Brooklyn, in January, to support Worcester's careful writer and enthusiastic amateur. The good news of Miss Dowe's acceptance came too late for us to write more this issue.

Before the campaign in the E.A.P.A. was over, however, Miss Dowe elected to withdraw. Perhaps she had other fish to fry. Writing in "Chronicle of the Year" in Virgil B. Clymer's and Eugene J. Wyckoff's *Reflector,* she closed sarcastically, "I am, and ever will be, Edith M. Dowe." Yet, she was one of the first of her group of young female friends in amateur journalism to wed. At the December 28, 1885 Leominster, Massachusetts convention, which N.E.A.P.A. shared with the smaller Massachusetts Amateur Press Association (M.A.P.A.)—there was no want for organizations in those days— Miss Dowe met for the first time in person her correspondent and future husband, John T. Miniter, then of Haverhill, Massachusetts. At this same convention, John T. Miniter was elected to a six-month term as President of M.A.P.A.

We know very little of John T. Miniter. In the information which she shared with Dowe family genealogist Robert Piercy Dow in 1904, Mrs. Miniter stated that John T. Miniter was born in Newcastle, England on May 2, 1862, the son of Milton and Bridget (Mohun) Miniter. However, when the English researcher Richard

Dalby attempted to verify this vital statistic in 1997, he found no one named John T. Miniter recorded as having been born in England between 1858 and 1865 inclusive. The Miniter name is definitely of Irish origin. The name of John T. Miniter is first found in the Haverhill, Massachusetts, city directories for 1883 and 1886, recorded as a clerk at 115 Merrimack Street. Mr. P. A. Rollins of the Special Collections of the Haverhill Public Library identified 115 Merrimack Street as the Masonic Temple Building, occupied mostly by insurance offices. By November 20, 1885, Miniter had withdrawn from the editorship of *Haverhill Life* to join the professional ranks as a reporter on the *Haverhill Gazette*. His successor Edward P. Ryan repeated Haverhill Life's endorsement of Miss Dowe for the E.A.P.A. presidency. By the time v. 1 no. 6 of *Haverhill Life* was published on March 25, 1886, John Miniter had resumed his post as editor and used the opportunity to announce Miss Dowe's candidacy for the editorship of the official organ, the *National Amateur*:

> Miss Edith May Dowe, after much hesitation, has consented to run for the official editorship of the N.A.P.A. She possesses all the ability requisite for the position, and should be unanimously elected. It is to be hoped that she will be supported for her ability alone, and that so-called false gallantry will not gain for her a single vote.

As it turned out, however, Ernest A. Edkins, who had unsuccessfully sought the N.A.P.A. official editorship at Boston in 1885, decided to seek the post again in 1886, and he soundly defeated Miss Dowe for the official editorship at the San Francisco N.A.P.A. convention in July 1886. He published but one issue of *The National Amateur* before he resigned, and President James H. Ives Munro appointed William B. Baldwin in his stead. Miss Dowe would have to wait until 1895-96 for her turn in the N.A.P.A. official editorship.

Meanwhile *Haverhill Life,* under its new editor-in-chief A. L. Sawyer, had important news relating to John T. Miniter to report in its issue dated June 1, 1886:

> Mr. Miniter, who has retired from the post of editor since the last issue, was well known in this city, and will be pleasurably remembered by all with whom he came in contact. He was devoted to the cause of amateur journalism, being the President of MAPA. For

this reason, as well as for his practical experience with one of our leading papers, we openly deplore his withdrawal from our ranks. Mr. Miniter has acquired a position on the staff of the *Worcester Telegram,* and we congratulate that paper in securing his services. We can assure our Worcester brothers in the 'dom that they will find him an enthusiastic and ready worker.

In addition, John Miniter and Edith May Dowe had the opportunity to renew their acquaintance at the joint convention of N.E.A.P.A. and M.A.P.A. held at the Windsor Hotel in Lowell, Massachusetts on July 7, 1886. Miss Dowe travelled to the convention with her friend Gracia A. Smith. Miss Dowe, Miss Smith, and Mabel F. Noyes—whom Edith met for the first time at this convention—were the only girls in attendance. Mr. Miniter handed the presidency of M.A.P.A. over to his successor. The conventioneers all seem to have had a merry time, although the girls were nearly thrown into the bear pit at Tyng's Island amusement park when a railing gave way. By that summer, rumors of the romance of Miss Dowe and Mr. Miniter had begun to spread within the small world of amateur journalism. Editor A.L. Sawyer reported in *Haverhill Life* for August 1, 1886:

> *Dixie* concludes, after perusing Miss Dowe's poem "Solitary," that she must be in love. A correct guess if report is true.

In the same issue the editor commented:

> Wedding bells will be found of use to all bachelors and maids of the 'dom who have any desire to put an end to single blessedness.

The editor does not believe that either Miss Dowe or Mr. Miniter attended the next N.E.A.P.A. convention, held in Concord, New Hampshire, on January 5, 1887. By February 1887, however, editor L. W. Chamberlain could announce in *Haverhill Life* under the heading "Dame Rumor Says":

> That Miss Edith May Dowe, the 'dom's charming young writer, is soon to be married. That accounts partially for her long silence.

The 1887 Worcester city directory recorded John T. Miniter as a reporter for the *Worcester Daily Spy* and *Sunday Telegram* at 386

Main Street, making his residence at 55 Park Street in the same city, while Jennie Dowe and her daughter continued to reside in the family home at 13 Mason Street in the same city. Edith always felt a twinge when accused of inactivity in print, which may account for the following notice under the heading "Dame Rumor Says" in *Haverhill Life* for May 1887:

> That Edith May Dowe and Mabelle F. Noyes contemplate re-issu-
> ing *The Worcester Amateur*.

Edith's *Worcester Amateur* had last appeared on July 7, 1886, in conjunction with the N.E.A.P.A. convention in Lowell, Massachusetts, and in fact made no further appearances. Edith and Miss Noyes, however, would later be involved with *Quartette*.

Edith Dowe and John Miniter were both in attendance at the next N.E.A.P.A. convention in Boston on July 6, 1887, where they sat next to each other at the banquet table. At this convention, Edith also met her longtime friend Harriet Caryl Cox (later Mrs. Albert Woodbury Dennis) for this first time. Virgil B. Clymer, who had criticized the girls for attending the banquet at the N.A.P.A. convention in Boston in 1885, made bold to shake hands with the pre-eminent female amateur of the day, Edith Dowe. The Dowe-Miniter romance had not much longer to run until its conclusion. On September 19, 1887, they were married by Rev. George Pelton at the Congregational Church in Worcester. Shortly before their marriage, Mr. Miniter had acquired *The Worcester County News*, a weekly newspaper published from Webster, Massachusetts. The Webster, Massachusetts, vital record of the Dowe-Miniter marriage gives the groom's age as twenty-three, his birthplace as England, his occupation as editor, and his parents as Milton and Bridget (Mohun) Miniter. The new couple made their home in Webster, where both labored long and hard to make their newspaper a success. Edith's incomplete novelette "Love Without Wings," serialized in *The Varied Year*, may paint a partially autobiographical portrait of their marriage. If the portrayal in "Love Without Wings" is accurate, Mr. Miniter ("David Lombard") labored over subscriptions, advertising, and collections, while Mrs. Miniter ("Ellyn Lombard") labored over the mechanical and editorial work of the newspaper. She spoke for herself in her reminiscent essay "A Rearward Glance":

In 1888, having proven the falsity of my assertion that "I am and always shall be yours very truly Edith May Dowe," I thought to embalm my new name of Edith Miniter in an amateur paper. It was called *The Webster Amateur* (I was then living in a town of central Massachusetts, Webster by name), and was notable for nothing, save the particular kobosh which it put upon the large and flourishing professional office where it was gotten out. Innocent four-by-seven, for months afterward nothing happened—a form pied, a comp. out how-come-you-so, press day late, press cranky, safety valve blown off the boiler—that the intelligent help in this establishment didn't trace the happening to "that week, you know, when we got out the amateur paper."

Edith's all-editorial *Webster Amateur* is dated November 1887, soon after the Miniter's marriage. Intended as a monthly amateur news magazine, only one issue of the journal ever appeared, perhaps because of the problems cited in "A Rearward Glance." Frank Denmark Woollen commented: "In her new publication, Mrs. Miniter calmly takes out her little yahtaghan and flays us neck to heel." Twenty years later, Mrs. Miniter was left to wonder: "what is a yagtaghan?" (*The Oxford English Dictionary* sayeth not.) Other comment came from *Haverhill Life* for December 1887:

> *The Webster Amateur* from Webster, Mass., Edith Dowe Miniter, editor, is an all-editorial sheet filled to the brim with articles that maketh the average amateur's heart glad. We wish, however, to inform Mrs. Miniter that Miss Mabelle Noyes of Lawrence, Mass., has not left the 'dom, and is as much interested as ever in amateur affairs.

The final news of the Miniters to be found in *Haverhill Life* occurs in the issue dated February 1888:

> John T. Miniter and Edith Dowe Miniter, two of our most active amateurs, are publishing a professional weekly, *The Worcester County News*.

The strain of making a success of their marriage and of their professional venture apparently began to take its toll on the Miniters during the course of the year 1888. Amateur papers began to remark Edith's inactivity—the kind of comment which always drew her resentment. Writing under the heading "Of Passing Interest" in Samuel J. Steinberg's *Dilettante* for September 1892, Harriet Caryl Cox remembered:

> There was a time during the year of '88 when Mrs. Ottinger, then Cora Lynch, and I were the only girls constantly active. The Wood-zelle sisters were heard from but occasionally, and Miss Harrison did not become active 'til the latter part of the year. Girls in A.J. became almost an unknown quantity.

After four contributions in 1887, the year of her marriage, Edith had but one contribution in the amateur press in 1888 and two in 1889. Her activity as an author did not begin to revive until 1890, when four stories from her pen appeared in amateur journals. In truth, the Miniters were deep in the struggle to succeed as marriage partners and business proprietors. Edith's dear friend Gracia Smith had married a post office employee, Mr. Woffenden, in the fall of 1887—probably the first of her friends to marry after her own wedding—but Mr. Woffenden caught cold during their wedding trip, developed consumption, and sank rapidly, dying in March 1888. Gracia (Smith) Woffenden survived her husband by only a few months, adding to Edith's grief during this difficult period of her life.

Writing in the "Miniter Memorial" which appeared in Hyman Bradofsky's amateur magazine *The Californian* in Spring 1938, Joseph Dana Miller, a poet and early contributor to *The Worcester Amateur* recalled the next stage in the struggle. In 1938, he could find but three surviving letters from his onetime voluminous correspondence with Mrs. Miniter, but two of these letters dated from the crucial period of her marriage. On February 2, 1889, Mrs. Miniter, still in Webster, wrote to advise Mr. Miller of the reprinting of one of his poems in *The Worcester County News* and to give a brief account of her reception of a party of W.C.T.U. women. Later that spring she wrote Mr. Miller again, this time from Worcester:

> You ask about our newspaper and whether it will be discontinued. No, we have moved it here [Worcester]. I have this day got out the second issue in this place. I would send you a copy but I fear you would criticize our country journal very severely. I am very tired

today, as we worked all last night, so excuse my stupidity. During the last week I have written a bushel, more or less, of copy and have fixed over as much more from our rural correspondents. Also written scores of letters, made out fifty bills, read I don't know how much proof, interviewed a girl suspected of murder, drove forty-five miles in one day, and last night sat up all night reading proofs, painting bulletins and toward early morning our printers struck and left us in the lurch, so that at 7 A.M. we were obliged to take their places. I have also been reading some of Charles Reade in my leisure time. So you can see what a variety of stupid things I spend my time doing.

How long the Miniters struggled on with *The Worcester County News* is not well-documented. No issues of this weekly newspaper from the period of their ownership (ca. 1887-90) appear to be recorded in institutional collections at the present time. Nancy E. Gaudette, librarian of the Worcester Collection at the Worcester Public Library consulted the Worcester city directories for the author and found John T. Miniter back in the directory in 1889, residing at the Dowe home at 13 Mason Street. In all of the city directories 1887-1915 which Ms. Gaudette checked for the editor, the name of Edith Miniter occurred only once, in the 1890 directory: "Miniter, Edith M., Mrs., publisher, Worcester County News, 164 Front St., bds. ⟨boards⟩ 13 Mason." So that 1890, the year after her surviving correspondence with Joseph Dana Miller, may well mark the proximate end of *The Worcester County News*. The editor last found John T. Miniter mentioned in connection with the 13 Mason Street address in *The Bay State Official* (vol. VIII no. 3) for March 1891, which listed both Edith and John at that address.

Mr. Miniter was never more to appear in amateur circles, and his name was not even spoken. When she appeared at the Boston amateur journalists' conference in February 1891 and at the Boston N.A.P.A. conventions in 1892 and 1894, Mrs. Miniter appeared without her husband. As early as 1898, Charles N. Andrews expressed curiosity about Mr. Miniter in his amateur magazine *The Smoker*:

And what a host of memories Mrs. Miniter revived! ⟨They had met again at the New York City N.A.P.A. convention in 1898.⟩ I wot not of the transition wrought in time's flight, nor the circumstances that have made little Edith May Dowe her present self. It is all sufficient to know that as Mrs. Miniter she added volumes to the convention's ensemble, her every utterance being impregnated with a repartee that positively left one jejune.

Twenty-five years after the death of Mrs. Miniter, matters were still very much in the dark as Edward H. Cole wrote in *The Fossil* for April 1961:

> Mrs. Miniter's attitude {toward Frank Roe Batchelder's divorce} occurred to me as somewhat ironic, for something of mystery always surrounded her own married life. A query frequently raised in the years when she lived in Roxbury was why she didn't marry John Leary Peltret, a well known amateur journalist from the West Coast, who lived with Mrs. Miniter and Mrs. Dowe and for whom Mrs. Miniter evidently felt considerable affection. The answer, so far as I have ever gleaned it, is that John Miniter was confined to an asylum and Mrs. Miniter was not free to remarry. So much for gossip.

George Dorr may have teased Mrs. Miniter with her famous "I am and always shall be, Edith M. Dowe" closing in *The Reflector* at the Boston N.A.P.A. convention in 1892, but those few intimate friends in amateur journalism who knew the unhappy story of her marriage weren't telling. For the simple truth was that John Miniter, that devoted amateur journalist and connoisseur of Irish poetry, destroyed his marriage and perhaps his business through his intemperate consumption of alcohol. He and Edith must have separated by 1891, probably at about the same time that Mrs. Dowe sold her home at 13 Mason Street in Worcester, where they had been living, to go to Wilbraham to care for her aged parents. Edith obtained newspaper work in Manchester, New Hampshire, where she spent a lonely exile during most of the period 1891-93, relieved by occasional visits from her mother and her dear friend Mabel F. Noyes. It seems doubtful that the Miniters ever laid eyes on each other again after separating in 1891. Mr. Peter S. Alexis of the Pollard Memorial Library in Lowell, Massachusetts found two listings of John T. Miniter as a boarder, in the 1892 and 1894 Lowell city directories, the first listing his occupation as "peddler" and the second as "extracts." Mr. Alexis also found the newspaper account of Mr. Miniter's death in the *Lowell Sun* for Tuesday, September 4, 1900. Miniter had been staying for a month at the St. Cloud Hotel (389 Middlesex Street), selling essences and a machine oil preparation during the day. He retired on the evening of Monday, September 3, after heavy drinking, and was found dead in his room the following morning at 8 A.M. There was no evidence of foul play, and John Miniter's death certificate attributed his death to alcoholism. He was buried in the Roman Catholic cemetery in Lowell. He was survived by a brother, a druggist, in Haverhill, Massachusetts. The sad story in the *Sun* concludes:

> He was a former newspaper man and a bright fellow but drink ruined him. He worked on the *Haverhill Bulletin* and other papers and married a newspaper woman, Edith Miniter, who, however, soon left him because of his intemperate habits.

Mr. Miniter's death certificate gives his age as thirty-one years nine months (i.e., born ca. December 1868) and his birthplace as Ireland. The editor, however, is skeptical that he was so young since a December 1868 date of birth would make him only fifteen when he first appeared in the Haverhill directories in 1883 and not yet nineteen when he married on September 19, 1887. The editor is inclined to favor May 2, 1864, as his most probable date of birth, since he stated his age as twenty-three for his official marriage record and likely had no cause to misstate the month and day of his birth. Whether he was born in England or Ireland remains a debatable point. He was certainly of Irish ancestry. One is inclined to favor Ireland as his place of birth since no record of his birth can be found in the official records for England for the period 1858-65. While Mrs. Miniter did not see fit to discuss the unhappy end of her marriage with anyone other than her most intimate friends in amateur journalism, she did not attempt to disguise the facts. In the information provided to Mr. Dow for the Dowe genealogy in 1904, Edith reported her husband's date and place of death accurately. Mrs. Miniter did not choose to mourn her husband, and entertained the Hub Club at her apartment at 77 Berkeley Street on September 13, 1900, just nine days after his death. It was the first meeting of the year, and the subject was vacation stories.

So, John T. Miniter passes into obscurity. In writing of her mother in "My Mother—As She Seemed To Me" in 1921, Edith had only this much to say about her own marriage:

> In 1887 I was married to John T. F. Miniter, a native of Great Britain and a special admirer of Irish literature. We lived with my mother, and she of course had to read all the volumes of Irish poetry with which he swamped the establishment. It seems to have opened a new world to her, one in which she was almost instantly at home.

She could remember a happy result attributable to the marriage—her mother's flourishing as an Irish poet—even from the remove of all of her own suffering. The brief notice of her death which appeared in the Springfield newspaper, for which Evanore Olds Beebe was probably the informant, contained the following line:

> After her marriage to John Miniter, they purchased the *Worcester County News* and published it for some years.

Edith must have loved John Miniter very dearly and mourned the affliction which destroyed their life together. She loved him enough to remain his wife throughout the decade which saw his disastrous decline as an alcoholic. Perhaps the suffering she underwent helped to hone the fine skills with which she dissected the human psyche in her mature fiction. Of her domestic life she probably chose to remain silent out of the reserve so characteristic of the New England race from which she sprang. Today we can only imagine the courtship of Edith Dowe and John Miniter and their struggle to make their marriage and their business successful. They did not succeed, but can we truly say they failed? That they did not love one another or ought not to have loved one another? John Miniter made bold to marry Edith Dowe outside his church, despite the censures this undoubtedly brought upon him. Despite the Irish branches in her own Moore and Shields ancestry, Miss Dowe chose to marry an emigrant, probably the last thing one would expect of a Yankee girl. It speaks well of Mrs. Dowe that she chose to accept the couple into her own home. Having known love herself, she must have respected her daughter's choice, whatever her own misgivings. Both William Hilton Dowe (1840-1875) and John T. Miniter (1864?-1900) lived tragically short lives. Mother and daughter thus shared not only love but loss. But with the departure of John Miniter from her life in 1891, Edith was ready to resume her work as a professional news-paper woman and as an amateur journalist. These two endeavors were to become the preoccupation of her remaining years.

By 1890, as both *The Worcester County News* and the Miniter mar-riage began to wind down, Edith once more began to engage in the amateur activity which she had largely allowed to lapse during her days of struggle in 1888-89. Ella Maude Frye had founded the Hub Amateur Journalists' Club (commonly known simply as the Hub Club) in her Maplewood kitchen on March 10, 1890. The joke was commonly told that the Hub Club never ventured very far from the kitchen, such was its determination both to be fed and to be entertained. After she settled permanently in Boston in December 1893, Edith launched fullblown into the activities of the Hub Club and became its mainstay for over thirty years, until she left Boston permanently to spend the final years of her life with Evanore Olds Beebe at "Maplehurst" in Wilbraham. Edith's first amateur fiction of 1890, "When the Fog Lifted," appeared in May 1890 in A. D. Grant's *Nugget* from New Glasgow, Nova Scotia. Even during the period of her least activity in amateur journalism (1887-89), she had continued to appear in Canadian amateur magazines.

Then, on July 20, 1890, Samuel J. Steinberg published the first of Mrs. Miniter's controversial new "realistic" stories, "For a Big Roll of Money," in *Dilettante* for the same date. The notorious "Cin-dy's Child" followed in Alson J. Brubaker's *Ink Drops* from Fargo, North Dakota in December 1891, and precipitated a months' long debate within amateur journalism over its merits and demerits. Mrs. Miniter's old rival Ernest A. Edkins was its principal detractor, while her new friend James F. Morton, Jr. was its champion. Later in life, Edkins expressed regret over the virulence of his attacks.

Sam Steinberg's sister Rose Bee Steinberg (later Mrs. David L. Hollub) followed with Edith's "Overheard on the Beach" in her own *Iris Magazine* in September 1890. And then in October 1890 Edith, still in Worcester, together with Ella Maude Frye of Maplewood and the Noyes sisters (Mabel F. and Minna B.) of Law-rence, launched upon the amateur world their *Quartette,* so called because of the number of its editors. Edith appeared with "Maggie" in the October 1890 issue. Writing under the title "The Spice Box" in the same issue, she explained her long absence from amateur journalism:

> It seems incredible to myself, but it is three years since I have written editorially for the amateur press. My thanks are due to Miss Noyes for her suggestion that I should become an associate on *Quartette,* and she could not have mentioned anything that I more desired. Amateurs frequently write to me saying "I presume you have given up all interest in amateur Journalism, but" etc., etc. Now I always feel insulted at receiving such a letter. I am just as much interested in the 'dom as ever, and I hope to remain so for many years to come. Lack of time may prevent my publishing a paper at present, but I intend to do away with that at some period not far removed into the future, and until then I am always happy when the mail brings in a batch of amateur papers. I intend, every year, (as long as there are publishers to be deluded) to write enough for the amateur press to keep technically "active," and I firmly believe that "once an amateur" is "always an amateur," in the sense of liking amateur journalists and feeling heart-affection for the welfare of the cause.

Quartette published a new issue on February 22, 1891, to coincide with the first Boston amateur journalists' conference. In its pages, Edith denied being the amateur then writing under the pseudonym "Helen Hall." She attended the amateur journalists' conference in Boston in person, with John Miniter nowhere in evidence, and presented a paper on "The Scope of Amateur Journalism," which Sam Steinberg promptly printed in *The Dilettante* for February 1891. Consistent with the position she maintained throughout the years, she maintained that amateur journalists should write from their own experience rather than from bookish models and that they should concentrate their editorial writing on amateur matters rather than national or international affairs. At this conference, Edith first met James F. Morton, Jr. who remained her friend for the rest of her life. An attorney by training, red-haired Morton contributed mightily to the amateur cause over more than fifty years of activity and served both the National (1896-97) and the Interstate (1908-09) as president. His proudest moment, however, was undoubtedly his achievement in electing his friend Edith Miniter as the first woman to occupy the presidency of the National in July 1909. Edith wrote affectionately of him in *Quartette* for June 10, 1891:

> Some call him Jimmy, some call him James,
> Some say Mister when they speak to him,
> Ma calls him Jamesey, Pa calls him Jeemes,
> But all the time he wants to be,
> > Just plain Jim.
> At least he said HE DID!

True to the promise made in *Quartette,* Edith published four strong stories in the amateur press in 1891, including one of her finest, "A Tragedy of the Hills" in Charles W. Edwards' *The Fern Leaf* in March 1891 and the notorious "Cindy's Child" in Alson J. Brubaker's *Ink Drops* in December 1891. The controversy over the latter story alone kept her name before the amateur public during the following year. In 1891 Truman J. Spencer also published his massive *Literary Cyclopedia of Amateur Journalism,* wherein he took Edith to task for the unfortunate trends in her realistic fiction while praising and reprinting some of her earlier work. Perhaps Spencer's criticism led Mrs. Miniter to reconsider her goals, for during the next several years the only fiction which she published appeared in Spencer's own *Investigator*—"Love or Ennui" in January 1892, "Wabbits" in 1893, and the lengthy "A Shadow on the Water" in 1895. After "A Shadow on the Water" appeared in *The Investigator* in 1895, Mrs. Miniter would publish no more amateur fiction until "Where Prudence Points" appeared in the Anthony E. Wills' *Fiction* in June 1902.

The reasons for Mrs. Miniter's reduced fictional output after 1891 are undoubtedly to be found at least partially in her private life during this period. Sometime during 1891, perhaps during the spring or summer, Jennie Dowe sold her home at 13 Mason Street in Worcester. If the Miniters had not already separated by this date, their separation certainly dates from no later than this time. Jennie accompanied her daughter Edith to Manchester, New Hampshire, where Edith worked for three months as a proofreader on the *Manchester Telegram.* Mabel Noyes came to visit mother and daughter several weekends during this lonely period. On July 10, 1891, Edith did manage to attend the annual N.E.A.P.A. convention in Boston. Politically, N.E.A.P.A. remained her primary identification during her first decade in amateur journalism. It is therefore some-what surprising to note that she apparently never served as President or First Vice President of this association, which flourished from 1883 until 1904. She undoubtedly held many lesser offices in N.E.A.P.A. and is known to have served as Second Vice President for the first half of 1885 (elected at the New Bedford, Massachusetts convention on January 1, 1885) and as Secretary for the second half of 1885 (elected at the Providence, Rhode Island, convention on July 14, 1885).

Then, after three months as a proofreader for the *Telegram*, Edith obtained a better newspaper job in Manchester, as city editor of a penny afternoon daily. By now the time was perhaps the fall of 1891. Then another shoe dropped, for Jennie Dowe had to go to Wilbraham to care for her aging parents, where she was to remain until after her mother's death in 1896. Far from the centers of ama-teur activity and separated both from her husband and now from her mother, Edith was doubtless quite lonely during this period, and grateful for the newspaper work which kept her busy. Perhaps her recollection of shedding tears after accidentally dropping a letter from James F. Morton, Jr. into a puddle and having it thereby ren-dered unreadable, dates from this period. During 1892, the contro-versy over "Cindy's Child" was raging in amateur journalism, and Morton was one of Edith's most loyal defenders. When Edwin Had-ley Smith and other political opponents of Mrs. Miniter threatened, in later decades, to reprint "Cindy's Child" for a new generation of amateur journalists to read, Edith's defenders, including William R. Murphy, opined that a reprinting would only enhance her liter-ary reputation. But doubtless the controversy over "Cindy's Child" made Edith feel more foresaken in her outpost in Manchester.

In July 1892, Edith did manage to attend her second N.A.P.A. convention in Boston, Massachusetts. She visited the Noyes sisters in Methuen before travelling to the convention, where she met her lifelong friends Walter H. Thorpe and Helen M. Small for the first time. In the surviving group portraits of the 1892 and 1894 Boston N.A.P.A. convention, Edith is in the center of the group and stares intently at the camera. With her curly black hair, piercing eyes and ready repartee, she was a center of attention at these conventions. Wrote Capitola L. Harrison (later Mrs. Truman J. Spencer) in "As It Seems to Me" in Sam Steinberg's *Dilettante* for September 1892:

> By the way what a sweet face Miss Morton has—next to the majestic figure of Mrs. Miniter, I think hers the most interesting face in the convention photo. Its modesty and strength are at variance and yet most deftly blended into a womanly sweetness.

Albeit a majestic figure in her womanliness and wit, there is undoubtedly a hint of loneliness in these portraits of Mrs. Miniter in her mid-twenties. In 1892, John T. Miniter, who ought to have been her proud companion at the conventions, was working as a peddler in Lowell, Massachusetts, and doubtless well on his way to ruin. What happened with her city editorship in Manchester is unknown, but from August 1892 until February 1893 Mrs. Miniter had her first period of residence in Boston, which later became her permanent home. In September, she was late to Mr. and Mrs. Frye's wooden wedding anniversary celebration in Maplewood, and some-time during the autumn she attended the first of many Hub Amateur Journalists' Club meetings. From February 1893 through December 1893, Mrs. Miniter's whereabouts are not known. It seems highly unlikely that she attempted a reconciliation with her husband dur-ing this period; perhaps she returned to newspaper work in Man-chester, New Hampshire, and perhaps she joined her mother in Wilbraham to help care for her aging grandparents. On July 17, 1893, she did manage to attend the annual N.E.A.P.A. convention held in Boston.

In December 1893, however, Edith returned permanently to Boston, to accept an editorial position with the society and literary weekly newspaper, *The Boston Home Journal*. Edith was to remain with the Home Journal for more than twelve years, finally severing her connection in January 1906, after the paper had undergone a change of ownership and transformed itself into a hotel paper. The Boston Public Library owns a file of *The Boston Home Journal* ranging from January 1, 1887 through December 28, 1895, that were once the property of the St. Botolph Club. Harvard University owns another file of the newspaper which extends through 1904. The

American Antiquarian Society owns a special issue dated October 10, 1903, which contains a photograph of the Home Journal offices at 147 Summer Street. Edith Miniter's name does not occur on the masthead in the 1893-95 issues of *The Boston Home Journal* at the Boston Public Library. Nor does the newspaper contain any articles signed by Mrs. Miniter during this period. During this period, the *Home Journal* was published every Saturday for five cents a copy or $2.50 for an annual subscription. W. Wallace Waugh was Managing Editor and Atherton Brownell, Editor, and the paper's offices were at 403 Washington Street in Boston. On April 20, 1895, the paper's offices removed to 220 Devonshire Street in the same city.

William R. Murphy later recalled that Mrs. Miniter had both book reviews and stories in the *Journal*. It is doubtful that she ever published any fiction in the *Journal* but Murphy is probably correct that she was responsible for many of the book reviews. In the same January 6, 1894 issue, "E. Valise" wrote of the work of Sarah Orne Jewett under the title "Books and Authors." Throughout 1894, staff writer "Sara Sylvester" wrote weekly on fashions and manners under the title "Fashions as They Fly," and many titles of the articles seem characteristic of Mrs. Miniter's style. For example:

February 24: Novelties in Dress Materials; Headgear Which Will Be Seen At Opera
March 10: Hints of Springtime Shopping—Sara's and Dorothy's Three Happy Hours
March 17: Dorothy Sews, Sara Talks—Bonnets, Present, to Come, and Dreams of Bonnets

The July 28 and August 11 "Fashions As They Fly," signed by Ella McKenna Friend, from Paris, were titled "Sights of Gay Paris—The Battle of Flowers—Some Elegant Gowns" and "Garden Party Gowns—A Parisian Wedding—Worth and Wire." Whether this indicates that Ella McKenna Friend was the regular "Sara Sylvester" columnist on fashions and manners, is unknown. Certainly, Mrs. Miniter never had the good fortune to travel to Paris, even in a professional capacity, or we would have had report of her travels in the amateur press.

Later in 1894, the "Sara Sylvester" columns continued under the title "Rhyme and Reason." Subjects covered included:

October 27: Sara Sylvester Applies Both to Feminine Fads and
Fashions As They Fly
November 3: The Child Told the Truth–Absent-Minded Men and
Women–A Crushable Waist
November 10: Is Crinoline en Route? Paquin's Frocks–A Gift for a
Bride–Luncheons

In the issue of December 28, 1895, "Sara Sylvester" was still
holding forth under the title "Rhyme and Reason." An unsigned
article of March 10, 1894, "Exploded Superstitions: Odd Beliefs of
Our English Ancestors Now Curious to Behold" seems very typical
of Mrs. Miniter's own interests. An unsigned article of July 7, 1894
covers the slightly racy topic "All About Bloomers: The Innovation
in Women's Dress Wrought by Athletics." An unsigned article on
"Amateur Journalists," describing the 1894 Boston N.A.P.A. convention, is most certainly attributable to Mrs. Miniter's pen. Before
one discounts entirely the possibility that Mrs. Miniter was responsible for at least some of the "Sara Sylvester" articles in the *Home
Journal,* it should be remembered that an article on "How to Dress
on $40 a Year" which appeared in *The Boston Globe* sometime in the
mid-1890s won Mrs. Miniter her greatest local newspaper fame.
The article was discussed in "Everybody's Column" in the *Globe*
for weeks after its publication.

Mabel F. Noyes's impression of Edith Miniter in her Devonshire
Street offices at *The Boston Home Journal* is worth quoting:

Of medium height, slight, with black hair and expressive black
eyes, she is a person once seen to be long remembered. Strangers
often speak of her sympathetic face, and on account of this affliction (?) many are the woeful tales poured into her ears. Add to this
the possession of exquisite tact, the happy faculty of knowing the
right word to say in the right place, and the ability to put awkward
people or strangers at once at their ease, and you have the best
description possible of the subject of our sketch. The walls of the
room we are in proof that its owner has, at some time, been afflicted
with the poster fad, and many would think themselves fortunate
to be the possessor of some of the works of art in that line, that are
hung about her desk.

As the years passed Edith doubtless grew stronger and stronger in her own identity as she flourished both in her professional work and in the amateur journalism hobby. After 1894, John T. Miniter disappears from the Lowell city directories (perhaps because he had begun travelling more as a salesman) and more and more from the independent life of his wife as she continued to flourish in all her endeavors.

Early during her residency in Boston, Mrs. Miniter boarded with her friend Ella Maude Frye, the founder of the Hub Club. It was at the Frye residence that Mrs. Miniter and Mrs. Frye jointly hosted the first of many Hub Club Halloween parties on October 31, 1894. Otherwise, Mrs. Miniter maintained her activity in N.E.A.P.A., her first love, attending its Boston conventions in the summers of 1894, 1895 and 1896. But in 1895 the N.A.P.A. finally called her to high office. Official Editor Albert Woodbury Dennis (later husband of Harriet Caryl Cox), elected to office at the Chicago N.A.P.A. convention in July 1895, after having been appointed to it by President Burger during the prior 1894-95 official year, found he could not continue in the office and resigned. President Will Hancock of Fargo, North Dakota, called upon Mrs. Miniter to undertake the completion of the 1895-96 volume of *The National Amateur*, and she accepted appointment as Official Editor despite her heavy professional commitments. With the help of Truman J. Spencer as printer, she produced a handsome four-number volume (XVIII) of *The National Amateur*. The March 1896 issue is exceedingly rare and it is possible that some kind of accident affected its distribution. When Warren J. Brodie was seeking to complete his file of The National Amateur in 1899, it was the March 1896 number from Mrs. Miniter's volume that he needed. He was somewhat reluctant to approach the "Lioness of Boston" in person with his request, after having failed to receive a response to a mailed inquiry, but once he met Mrs. Miniter, he found that she was willing to part with her last spare copy to allow him to complete his collection. While Sam Steinberg criticized both the expense ($100) and the "chattiness" of Mrs. Miniter's volume of *The National Amateur*, her volume is really quite respectable. Although hampered to some extent by a lack of cooperation from other officers, Edith managed to print the essential information and to avoid controversy. It is apparent that Edith herself wrote most of the unsigned articles in her volume of *The National Amateur*. It was Edith's unfortunate fate to hold high office in the National during the inevitable periodic low points of activity, both during her official editorship in 1895-96 and her presidency in 1909-10. It is fair to state that her performance was never perfect; she had a natural inclination to rely too heavily upon her friends and to mistrust amateurs not personally known to her. But in both cases she acquitted herself with honor and fulfilled the principal duties of her offices. What she did, she clearly did for the love of the hobby.

Happiness arrived on Mrs. Miniter's doorstep sometime during the summer or fall of 1896, when Jennie Dowe came to stay. Grandmother Catherine Orpha (Moore) Tupper had died in Wilbraham the previous May, and Jennie's nephew Herbert Edwin Tupper, the son of her unruly brother Charles, and his wife took over the management of the home which Edwin Lombard Tupper had built fifty years before. "Bert" Tupper's family of two children would grow to eight over the years. Edwin Tupper himself would survive five more years, dying just before his eighty-sixth birthday in March 1901. His was only the second wake to be held in the home which he had built. But the arrival of Jennie Dowe in Boston in 1896 was truly the beginning of Edith Miniter's golden years. They first took up residence together in an apartment at 119 Berkeley Street, but by 1897 had relocated to the famous walk-up apartment at 77 Berkeley Street where they entertained so many amateurs until their removal to 17 Akron Street in Roxbury on February 1, 1906. At Akron Street Edith and Jennie were to spend twelve and a half more happy years together, marred only by Mrs. Dowe's failing health and increased financial pressures toward the end of the World War. But it can be said without doubt that the years 1897-1919 which she spent together with her mother were truly the golden years of Edith Miniter's life. There were other achievements during these years—notably the N.A.P.A. presidency in 1909-10 and the publication of *Our Natupski Neighbors* in 1916—but it was the constant presence of Jennie Dowe which kept Edith going through thick and thin. "Lady Jane" Dowe, as she was known to several generations of Boston amateurs and visitors, was ever the gracious hostess and never at a loss for a poem to grace a special occasion, like the anniversary dinners held every March to commemorate the founding of the Hub Club on March 10, 1890. It is a pity that a collection of her charming verse has never been gathered. Supported adequately by Mrs. Dowe's capital and Edith's earnings, mother and daughter led the good life in Boston, belonging to Rev. J. Henry Wiggin's playgoers' club and of course to the Hub Club. They dined out and entertained frequently. Few amateurs visiting Boston during the years 1896-1918 could make claim to escaping without being entertained at 77 Berkeley Street or 17 Akron Street. The decade 1897-1906 spent at 77 Berkeley Street was probably Edith's and Jane's busiest. By the 1906-1918 period spent at 17 Akron Street their activity was focused more narrowly on the Hub Club and amateur journalism. Edith no longer worked downtown at *The Boston Home Journal.* Nevertheless, 17 Akron Street in Roxbury remained a mecca for visiting amateur journalists and Hub Club members during this entire period.

The outward events of the period 1897-1906 were relatively few. Edith's friend James F. Morton, Jr. held the N.A.P.A. presidency in 1896-97, elected at the 1896 Washington, D.C., convention, but he was saddled with a hostile Edwin Hadley Smith as Official Editor and proved to be an ineffective executive. The following year, N.A.P.A. went to San Francisco for its convention and elected David L. Hollub (brother-in-law of Sam Steinberg) as president for the 1897-98 term. Subsidized by the Chicago Amateur Press Club under Steinberg's leadership, Hollub had a highly successful year in office. Edith Miniter and Mabel Noyes came to New York City for the 1898 N.A.P.A. convention and a photograph of them taken on the Fall River Line steamer has been preserved. In New York Edith met for the first and only time Sam Steinberg (1870-1903), who was elected to the official editorship but shortly resigned his office after a dispute concerning the size of the official organ. More importantly, she met for the first time West Coast amateur journalist John Leary Peltret (1874-1938), who presided over the New York convention and was making plans to relocate to New York. Peltret was born in San Francisco, California on June 8, 1874, the son of Peter Clode Peltret, born in France of American parents. He was involved in West Coast amateur journalism in the 1890s and when he came East worked as a theatrical manager and representative, primarily in New York City, but also in Boston. While in Boston, he generally resided with Mrs. Dowe and Mrs. Miniter. In the early years of the century, he often shared their summertime camping trips to "Meadowbeck," Edith's property in Wilbraham, one of which was immortalized in the booklet *From Fireflies to Crickets* distributed at Christmas, 1905. A little over two years after the first meeting of Edith Miniter and John Leary Peltret in New York City in July 1898, Edith Miniter was left a widow through the death of John T. Miniter in Lowell, Massachusetts, on September 4, 1900. Many amateurs from Edward H. Cole onward have wondered why Miniter and Peltret did not marry. If a declining John T. Miniter was ever confined to an asylum during the years 1894-1900, he was nevertheless dead by September 4, 1900. The truth may be that it was Peltret who was not free to marry. Although he died in his birthplace of San Francisco, California, on October 27, 1938, he remained on the East Coast through the early thirties. His death certificate indicates that he was survived by a widow Twila Frances Peltret of 1691 Eighteenth Avenue in San Francisco. Unless he was married very late in life, it is possible that Peltret was estranged from his wife during the many years he spent in the East and only decided to rejoin her a few years before his death. Like John T. Miniter, he may have battled alcohol, for cirrhosis of the liver was the primary cause of his death in 1938. Even if Peltret was free to marry during the first decade of the century, it is possible that Edith would have spurned his offers if he already had a problem with alcohol.

We will in all probability never know the intimate history of the relationship between Edith Miniter and John Leary Peltret. That Edith loved him dearly we can tell from her outrage when political trickery (the rejection of the proxy ballots) deprived him of the N.A.P.A. presidency in favor of the local favorite son Anthony E. Wills (1879-1912) at the unruly New York City convention in 1902. The N.A.P.A. convention in Boston in 1900, which temporarily derailed the "young blood" movement marshalled behind John M. Acee and installed the relatively inexperienced Nelson G. Morton, nineteen-year-old brother of James F. Morton, Jr., in the presidency, had set an example of backroom politics, and the New Yorkers retaliated with a vengeance in 1902 to install Wills. In truth, the politics of the 1902 N.A.P.A. convention was hard-fought on all sides; before the convention, the Peltret party had solicited proxies from all the oldtimers and at the convention ruthlessly "blackballed" persons proposed for membership by the New Yorkers. Edith was ungracious in defeat in New York City in 1902, and for years fought to have Peltret's name officially added to the presidential roster. However, Wills astutely insisted that his name be removed if Peltret's were to be added, and the National never took the action proposed by Mrs. Miniter and her allies.

If she admitted new friends only with caution, Edith nevertheless made many new friends over the decade 1896-1906 which she and her mother spent at 119 and then 77 Berkeley Street. In the autumn of 1896, she first met her beloved friend Laura A. Sawyer (1865-1965) at a Hub Club theater party. "Little Laurie" and her husband Charles M. Sawyer lived in Allston, Massachusetts, where they made room for Mrs. Miniter and her mother after they removed from 17 Akron Street in Roxbury in the late fall of 1918. Laurie became widely known for her "Mrs. Dooley" sketches and was a staunch ally of Mrs. Miniter and the Hub Club in all the political battles within amateur journalism. Even so, Edith did not hesitate to kid Laurie about the Catholic scruples which forbade her to attend a Protestant church service. Laurie's Allston residence was famous for nearby "one o'clock hill," where many late-night amateur sessions ended. At the 1900 N.A.P.A. convention in Boston, Edith first met Charles A. A. Parker (1880-1965), publisher of *The Literary Gem* and later of *L'Alouette,* who became one of her closest friends and supporters. In 1901, she met William R. Murphy (1884-1936) at N.A.P.A.'s twenty-fifth anniversary banquet at Dooner's Hotel in Philadelphia, Pennsylvania. Murphy was to publish some of Mrs. Miniter's finest work in his amateur magazine *The Pioneer.* During this same period, Edith made the acquaintance of Ethel May Johnston (1882-1971) (later Mrs. Denys Peter Myers), who became one of her closest friends. The marriages of Nelson Morton and Nellie Benson (June 26, 1904), Charles A. A. Parker and Augusta L. Mueller (September 3, 1906), and Ethel May Johnston and Denys Peter Myers (January 4, 1908) gladdened the Hub Club and its members during this period. At the very end of this period, Mrs. Miniter met for the first time the youngsters Edward H. Cole (1892-1966) and Jacob Golden, who were holding forth with *The Hustler* from West Somerville. She soon graciously adopted them into the Hub Club and taught them both the ideals and the ropes of amateur journalism. Among the oldtimers, the Noyes sisters and Harriet Caryl (Cox) Dennis (Mrs. Albert Woodbury Dennis) continued to be fast friends. Edith also valued attorney Walter H. Thorpe for his undivided loyalty to the Hub Club. When he died in 1918, Edith recollected his pacing off the length of a proposed Hub Club walk on the Boston Common, so that the hikers might know whether they would have time to complete their proposed itinerary before dark. Had John Leary Peltret not emerged as the man in Edith's life during this decade, it is possible that Walter Thorpe might have taken his place; he was roughly the contemporary of Edith. During this same period, Edith's beloved N.E.A.P.A., which always had her first loyalty, wound down to its final meeting in 1904. Sectional associations and local clubs were becoming more difficult to maintain as activity flourished at the national level.

Still hurting badly from the rejection of Peltret at the New York City N.A.P.A. convention in 1902, Edith and a band of supporters met in Boston in June 1903 to form a new association, the Interstate Amateur Press Association, whose constitution required publishing activity and forbade feuding and political chicanery. While the Interstate never obtained as many as fifty members, Edith and her friends managed to attract a number of prominent amateur journalists, including Edwin B. Swift and James F. Morton, Jr. to its ranks. The Interstate scheduled its annual conventions over Labor Day, so as not to conflict with the National, which traditionally met over the Fourth of July holiday. Meeting in New Brunswick, New Jersey, in September 1904, the Interstate bestowed the presidency which the National had denied on John Leary Peltret. The presidential roster of the Interstate reads like a list of Edith's most loyal friends and supporters: 1903-04, Leston M. Ayres and William R. Murphy; 1904-05, John Leary Peltret; 1905-06, Dr. Edwin B. Swift; 1906-07, Edith Miniter; 1907-08, Charles A. A. Parker; 1908-09, James F. Morton, Jr.; 1909-10, Laura A. Sawyer. Edith served as Official Editor for I.A.P.A. under President Swift in 1905-06. The members of the Interstate participated willingly in the affairs of other associations and generated a laudable amount of activity, benefitting both the Interstate itself and its fellow associations. By 1910, especially after Edith herself attained the N.A.P.A. presidency for the 1909-10 term, the Interstate seemed obsolete. Its members celebrated the conclusion of eight years of laudable activity at a final banquet in New York City on Columbus Day, 1911.

Nevertheless, the Interstate was not uncontroversial in its birthing. Since 1895, the National had been fighting a rival association, the United, which tended to attract younger and less experienced members. Although the United was plagued with many factions, it remained a powerful rival of the National. National President Edward M. Lind, elected in San Francisco in July 1904 for the 1904-05 term, did all he could do to counteract the Interstate. Mrs. Miniter's continued efforts to add the name of John Leary Peltret to the National's presidential roster for the 1902-03 term did nothing to alleviate tensions between the two organizations. With the formation of The Fossils, the alumni association of amateur journalism, by Charles C. Heuman and associates on May 28, 1904, a potent new political force entered the amateur arena. Under the editorship of Joseph Dana Miller, The Fossils were soon publishing their own journal, *The Fossil*. In its pages, the Fossil leaders, including Heuman, Miller and Louis Kempner all advocated that mature adults be eliminated from active participation in the amateur journalism hobby and that the leadership of the hobby be returned to the adolescents they remembered from their own glory days. By the time of Mrs. Miniter's term as President of the National in 1909-10, Charles C. Heuman and other Fossils expressed the opinion that the National would have to be dissolved before it could be reconstituted on sound principles. Meanwhile, the "young blood" movement continued to flex its muscles within amateur journalism. Timothy Thrift (1905-06), William R. Murphy (1906-07), Charles W. Heins (1907-08), and William C. Ahlhauser (1908-09) shepherded the N.A.P.A. ship of state through dangerous waters while the United continued to wax strong despite divisions, and The Fossils continued to express their desire for a restoration of the "halcyon days" of yore. In support of the candidacy of her friend William R. Murphy, Mrs. Miniter travelled to the Philadelphia N.A.P.A. convention in July 1906, and this time she saw her efforts rewarded with success. President Murphy appointed Mrs. Miniter Chairman of the Bureau of Public Criticism, and throughout the 1906-07 official year she and her fellow bureau members did yeomen's work. The published official criticism of that year has likely not been exceeded in quantity or quality by any subsequent bureau. Only a few weeks later, on September 3, 1906, in Boston, she was herself honored by election as president of the Interstate Amateur Press Association. Despite all the political toils, the decade 1896-1906 was a very successful one for Edith Miniter, both in the professional and in the amateur worlds. Best of all, she had the constant companionship and love of her mother, Jennie Dowe.

In all frankness, the years at 17 Akron Street in Roxbury in 1906-1918 were more of a mixed bag for Edith and her mother. Jennie's health begin to fail, and financial difficulties increased, finally forcing mother and daughter to leave 17 Akron Street late in the fall of 1918, while the influenza epidemic was raging. The beginning of the period, on February 1, 1906, witnessed Edith's severance of her twelve-year connection with *The Boston Home Journal*. For the remainder of her life, she would struggle to make ends meet as a freelance writer and journalist. As an amateur writer and publisher, Mrs. Miniter hit her stride during the first decade of the century. *The Varied Year*, a quarterly founded in 1902 and revived in 1909-10 for Mrs. Miniter's year in the N.A.P.A. presidency, was one of the finest literary journals of its time. Mrs. Miniter also published her own best amateur fiction during this decade, capped, perhaps, by the magnificent story "The Emancipation of Elvira" in Warren J. Brodie's *Random Amateur* for March 1906. "He That Will Not While He May," originally published in Paul J. Campbell's *The Scotchman* for January 1905 was awarded the Interstate short story laureate at the Boston Interstate convention in September 1906; "Utilizing a By-Product," originally published in William R. Murphy's *The Pioneer* for February 28, 1907, was similarly honored at the July 1907 N.A.P.A. convention in Boston; and "The Emancipation of Elvira" was awarded the Interstate story laureate at the Interstate convention in September 1907 in Philadelphia.

The new home of Mrs. Dowe and Mrs. Miniter, 17 Akron Street, was built on a steep hillside in the Roxbury section of Boston. Mother and daughter named their home "Stately Stairways," for the twenty-five steps which had to be ascended to reach the door. Carved pineapples, symbols of hospitality, graced the lintel of the main entrance, and hospitality was never wanting at 17 Akron Street while Edith and Jennie resided there. From the cupola on top of the house, one had a magnificent view of Boston. The National returned to Boston for its 1907, 1912 and 1916 conventions, and 17 Akron Street served as a center of hospitality on each occasion. Few visiting "amachewers" left Boston without a taste of Edith's famed muffins, Laurie Sawyer's baked beans or Ethel May Johnston-Myers' fudge. Eugene Morrison's youthful recollections of his visit to 17 Akron Street during the 1912 convention may be typical. But if 17 Akron Street was a very successful center of amateur journalism, the success which Edith found there as a professional freelance writer was mixed. Edith placed two poems in *The New England Magazine* in 1907-08, one of which, "Goin' Way Out West" (May 1907), in the manner of Edgar A. Guest, was given a lavish illustrated multipage spread. In the February 1908 issue of the same magazine, she had a lengthy article on "The Old Scholar and His Schoolbooks," but seemingly she had not yet reached her metier as an author of such antiquarian articles, for no further placements followed in *The New England Magazine*. Then, in 1911, she cracked her mother's old market, *Century*, to place two poems. Jennie Dowe must have been quite proud to read her daughter's poetry in *Century*. Finally, on August 1, 1914, one of Edith's short stories, "Worthless Neighbors," made *Collier's*, a major potential market. But as with *The New England Magazine*, no further placements followed. Presumably, Edith was also writing for the newspaper press during this same period, to make ends meet. Writing on "Mrs. Miniter as a Parnassian" in Edward H. Cole's *The Olympian* for March 1907, William R. Murphy cited appearances of Mrs. Miniter's work in *Success, The Reader Magazine, Youth's Companion, St. Nicholas, The New England Magazine,* and *The Sunday Magazine*. Somehow, Edith managed to make ends meet as a professional writer during the years at 17 Akron Street in 1906-18. However, it seems likely that she and her mother had to dip in to their savings to maintain their standard of living during these years. Clearly, they did not spend as freely as they did during their first decade together in Boston (1896-1906), when Edith was supported by her job at *The Boston Home Journal*.

Edith and her mother maintained a close connection with their ancestral roots in Wilbraham during their residency in Boston. Each year, they spent a good portion of the summer camping on Edith's property "Meadowbeck" on Mountain Road in Wilbraham. The most famous such occasion was probably the summer of 1905, when Edith, Jennie and John Leary Peltret stayed from the emergence of the fireflies to the first pipings of the crickets, and memorialized their visit with the booklet *From Fireflies to Crickets* published at Christmas, 1905. The trio were not spartan campers, but would hike to the town center every day to receive mail and purchase both the necessities and luxuries of life. They were well supplied by butchers and other merchants on wheels. Some of the town residents thought it decadent that Edith and her guests slept under tents at "Meadowbeck" while the decrepit house on the property was used only for storage. There were doubtless whispered criticisms that Mr. Peltret and Mrs. Miniter were not known to be married. Blistering summer days were spent shaded in hammocks with the latest novels—a pursuit doubtless disapproved by hard-working neighbors. Evanore Olds Beebe, Mrs. Miniter's remote relation and the town pooh-bah, would stop by periodically to check on the campers. Other amateur journalists would frequently drop in for short visits.

Among the hardest working neighbors from 1909 forward would have been the Polish emigrant Kazmier Nietupski and his family. By the second decade of the century, Edith and Jennie had largely retired from camping in the open, and spent their summer visits with Miss Beebe at Maplehurst, immediately adjoining the Nietupski property. Here Edith and Jennie witnessed the human interactions which went into the making of Edith's novel *Our Natupski Neighbors*. Edith and Jennie discussed every aspect of the novel, except the dedication to Jennie, which Edith kept a secret from her mother. When it was published by Henry Holt in 1916, *Our Natupski Neighbors* was hardly a commercial success, although it received over two hundred professional reviews, including a favorable notice from William Lyon Phelps. However, literary tastes were changing, and Holt & Company never called upon Mrs. Miniter to complete the hoped-for sequel, notes for which survive in the Lovecraft Collection at Brown University. Just how far Edith progressed with the sequel is unknown. In a brief notice of Mrs. Miniter which he published in *Threads in Tapestry 1934: An Anthology of Verse*, Charles A. A.

Parker stated: "It is to be regretted that she left incomplete the notes of a novel commissioned by her publishers." In his 1934 memoir of Mrs. Miniter, published in *The Californian* for Spring 1938, Howard P. Lovecraft wrote: "In 1916 appeared Mrs. Miniter's novel *Our Natupski Neighbors*, the sequel to which has unfortunately never seen publication." Later in his memoir, Lovecraft writes of the final illness-plagued years of Mrs. Miniter's life: "Work, however, went bravely if intermittently on; and the unpublished novels doubtless bear myriad touches made almost at the end." With W. Paul Cook, Lovecraft assumed responsibility for the posthumous preservation and publication of Mrs. Miniter's works, and the two novel manuscripts that survive in Lovecraft's papers are *The Village Green* and the fragmentary *Lydia 'n' Gerald*. Only an outline of a potential sequel to *Our Natupski Neighbors* survives among the Lovecraft papers. The greater likelihood appears to be that the *Natupski* sequel did not progress beyond the extant fragments. Writing of Mrs. Miniter's only published novel, Lovecraft accurately assessed her mixed success in the literary world:

> Her short stories had meanwhile gained a substantial foothold in many standard magazines, while her reviews and antiquarian articles enjoyed more than a local fame. Actually, she deserved even more recognition than she received. It was her misfortune to follow a middle course in an age of abrupt transition—so that in youth her work was far in advance of its time, while in later life it failed to keep pace with the decadent and abnormal interests of modernism. It was in the "Natupski" period that she and her environment most closely coincided, and that she received the enthusiastic praise of William Lyon Phelps and other critics. At no time could she have been an idol of the masses, since her work was too honest for vitiated popular taste. Her integrity as an artist was absolute. She did not cater to the low-grade demands of the herd, and probably could not have done so had she wished.

In his memoir, Lovecraft compared Mrs. Miniter's powers of observation and description to those of Jane Austen; and even Mrs. Miniter's old nemesis, Ernest A. Edkins, writing his own memoir for *The Californian*, had to concede the justice of the comparison, while making amends for his own harsh early criticism of "Cindy's Child."

For a modern novel, *Our Natupski Neighbors,* which was probably produced in an original edition of several thousand copies, is now scarce; perhaps there may be some truth to the longstanding rumor that some of Miss Beebe's Wilbraham neighbors, finding its portrayals too close to life, chose to buy up copies to remove them from circulation. The Nietupskis themselves, if report be true, felt complimented by the attention given their brood in Edith's novel. The second generation of Nietupskis went on to become some of the most prosperous farmers and businessmen in the Wilbraham region.

In 1908, N.A.P.A. met in Milwaukee, Wisconsin, and elected William C. Ahlhauser President and Frank Austin Kendall, of *Torpedo* fame, Official Editor. President Ahlhauser named Mrs. Miniter to a second term as Chairman of the Bureau of Critics, a post which she had previously held in 1906-07. The 1908-09 bureau, however, produced far less criticism than had its 1906-07 predecessor under Mrs. Miniter's chairmanship. Kendall was an energetic, gifted editor, and aspired to the presidency in the following year. But James F. Morton, Jr. decided that Mrs. Miniter's time to be honored with this post had come. The Boston amateur journalists' conference held February 22, 1909 helped solidify support for Mrs. Miniter's candidacy. One of the challenges Morton had to face was continuing criticism of Mrs. Miniter's role in the Interstate Amateur Press Association, which many members of N.A.P.A. still perceived as a competitor. Eventually, Morton persuaded Kendall to withdraw his candidacy, and Mrs. Miniter was easily elected to the presidency for the 1909-10 term at the July 1909 N.A.P.A. convention in New York City. But New Yorkers, still stinging from Mrs. Miniter's harsh criticisms of the conduct of the 1902 New York N.A.P.A. convention which had denied John Leary Peltret the presidency, had secured control of most of the other important offices. George Julian Houtain (1884-1945) was elected official editor and Victor J. Singer was elected treasurer. Houtain offered excuse after excuse for not producing the first number of *The National Amateur* by the required date, and Mrs. Miniter finally discharged him in favor of Charles A. A. Parker in October 1909. Parker proceeded to produce a modest volume of *The National Amateur* in strict accordance with the so-called "Parker Principles," which forbade personal subsidization of the official organ. Soon after his dismissal, Houtain finally mailed his delayed *National Amateur,* and followed with one more issue containing voluminous charges against President Miniter which he filed with the Executive Judges. Singer refused outright any cooperation with President Miniter, declined to honor her invoices, and apparently advanced Houtain money for his issues of *The National Amateur.* In November, President Miniter proceeded to dismiss Singer and appointed Amanda (Frees) Thrift (Mrs. Timothy Burr Thrift) as his successor. In retaliation for her actions, New York lapsed into nearly complete inactivity for the remainder of the official year. The Fossils rose up with new criticism of the role played by mature adults in the amateur journalism hobby. Mrs. Miniter struggled boldly on, and not only oversaw the executive responsibilities to the best of her ability but also provided a distinguished record of personal activity in publishing *The Varied Year* and *True Blue.* She was delighted when her many friends surprised her with an honorary dinner at the United States Hotel in Boston on April 30, 1910, near the end of her demanding term. In July 1910, she travelled all the way to Cleveland, Ohio, to attend the N.A.P.A. convention which elected Edward F. Suhre as her successor. Only fifteen members attended in person, perhaps commencing in earnest the so-called "weary years" of which Burton Crane wrote so tellingly in his projected history of amateur journalism. The Cleveland convention granted outgoing President Miniter the traditional honor of election as one of the three Executive Judges called upon to resolve constitutional disputes, her second round in N.A.P.A. office which she had also occupied during the 1907-08 official year.

No more was Edith successfully out of a demanding year in office than criticism from The Fossils waxed even more intense. In addition, during her presidential year, Joseph Lane and other adherents of the "young blood" movement had reorganized the long-dormant Massachusetts Amateur Press Association as a rival to the more staid Hub Amateur Journalists' Club. Mrs. Miniter was hurt by the energies which young Edward H. Cole devoted to the M.A.P.A. cause, and their once-cordial relationship visibly cooled. The criticism of The Fossils waxed so vehement that Nelson G. Morton finally filed charges against their leaders—Charles C. Heuman and Louis Kempner—with the N.A.P.A. executive judges on February 11,

1911. The 1910-11 Board of Executive Judges consisted of Mrs. Miniter, Chair, Irving MacD. Sinclair, and Walter E. ("Pop") Mellinger. Judges Miniter and Sinclair reported in favor of the suspension of Messrs. Heuman and Kempner, but Judge Mellinger opined more moderately:

> In re the charges presented against Messrs. Heuman and Kempner, I believe that the accused have been sufficiently punished by the discussions their actions have occasioned; I believe that said actions were ill-advised, but not worthy either of suspension or expulsion, and I recommend that the entire matter be dropped.

When the National met for its annual convention in June 1911 in Chicago, the convention refused to sustain the action of the majority of the Executive Judges, and Messrs. Heuman and Kempner remained life members of N.A.P.A. Here again Edith in her staunch adherence to ideals and principles may have missed an opportunity to bury the political ax. It seems clear in retrospect that Judge Mellinger and the 1911 convention acted wisely in rejecting the majority report of the Executive Judges. The 1911 convention elected Walter F. Zahn to the N.A.P.A. presidency and Mrs. Miniter's erstwhile protege Edward H. Cole to the official editorship. The stage was set for Cole to advance to the presidency at the 1912 N.A.P.A. convention in his home town of Boston, which duly occurred. Mrs. Miniter must have been proud of the accomplishments of young Cole, despite their differences over the "young blood" movement.

After an exhausting term as President of N.A.P.A., there remained for Mrs. Miniter the loyal friends of the Hub Club who had always supported her. In 1908 and subsequent years, Mrs. Miniter and her mother began to spend part of their summers with the Noyes sisters at their home in Methuen on the Merrimack River, which the visitors named "Breezyhurst." After the Noyes sisters had relocated to Westfield, Mrs. Miniter and her mother continued to pay them summertime visits in 1914-16. Mrs. Miniter, Laura Sawyer, and Ethel May Johnston-Myers constituted themselves an "Old Lady's Sewing Circle" and published an occasional journal using that name. They enjoyed social events like cruises on the Charles River on the *Barnacle* under the command of "Skipper" Denys Peter Myers. After the Myers' son Denys Peter Jr. arrived in April

1916, he rapidly displaced Marshall Sawyer as the darling of the Hub Amateur Journalists' Club. New faces in the Hub Club during this decade included Winifred Virginia (Jordan) Jackson (1876-1959) and Elise Dorothy (Grant) MacLaughlin (Mrs. David S. MacLaughlin, 1889-1980). In the summer of 1913, Mrs. Miniter and her mother travelled to Wilbraham to participate in the town's sesquicentennial. Mrs. Dowe composed a poem for the occasion. Mrs. Miniter and her mother spent part of their summer in 1914 with Miss Beebe in Wilbraham, and doubtless continued their close observation of the Nietupski neighbors which finally resulted in the publication of *Our Natupski Neighbors* in October 1916.

Mrs. Miniter did attend the July 1914 N.A.P.A. convention in Bridgeport, Connecticut, which elevated Leston M. Ayres, brother-in-law of Ethel May Johnston-Myers, to the presidency. At this convention Mrs. Miniter met for the first time Edna von der Heide (later Mrs. Edna Hyde McDonald, 1893-1962), who was to become one of the leading female amateurs of the next generation. Miss von der Heide was charmed if somewhat intimidated by the Boston ladies. Defeated by Hubert A. Reading for the official editorship at Bridgeport in 1914, Miss von der Heide was nevertheless appointed to the office by President Ayres after Reading resigned. But Miss von der Heide was not to be the second female to be elected president of N.A.P.A. George Julian Houtain re-emerged with a vengeance at the Brooklyn convention in July 1915 and was elected to the presidency. When N.A.P.A. returned to Boston for its annual convention in July 1916, Houtain was elected to an unprecedented second term; Edith's New York friend Hazel Bosler Pratt (later Mrs. A. M. Adams) was elected official editor. President Houtain named Mrs. Miniter Chairman of the Bureau of Critics for the 1916-17 official year and his successor Harry E. Martin reappointed her for the 1917-18 term, but she seems to have published little criticism during these terms. She and her colleagues may have continued to criticize manuscripts submitted to them privately through correspondence. Mrs. Miniter attended the July 1917 N.A.P.A. convention in New York City which elected Mr. Martin to the presidency. It was to be the last convention outside Boston that she would attend.

Sadly, Mrs. Miniter began to lose beloved colleagues in amateur journalism during this decade. Susan Brown Robbins died in Biddeford, Maine, on January 10, 1910. Will S. Dunlop, who had published her *Phillis, the Fair* in Dunlop's *Amateur Library*, died just a few days later, in Milwaukee, Wisconsin, on January 28, 1910. Will R. Antisdel, who had questioned Mrs. Miniter's authorship of her early work, died on February 8, 1916. Brainerd Prescott Emery followed him in death on March 12, 1917. James H. Ives Munro died on January 16, 1918, and Walter H. Thorpe on April 5, 1918. George Edward Day died in April 1919, and Albert Woodbury Dennis also died in that year. Clearly, the ranks of amateur journalists of Mrs. Miniter's generation were beginning to thin as the decade concluded. Even the younger generation was not preserved from loss. Helen (Hoffman) Cole (Mrs. Edward H. Cole) died in the bloom of her youth in March 1919, the same month that Mrs. Miniter lost her mother.

Mrs. Dowe's health began to decline during the decade. In the summer of 1917, she and Edith spent a month with Nelson and Nellie Morton at Melrose, Massachusetts, while Mrs. Dowe recuperated from a serious illness. Then, in September 1917, Mrs. Miniter and Mrs. Dowe, Laurie Sawyer, and Mr. and Mrs. Denys Peter Myers and their baby Peter spent a month in Onset, Massachusetts, where they received many visitors. Jennie had her wish and was able to spend the final vacation of her life at the ocean. During 1918, Mrs. Dowe began to fail visibly and financial pressures on the household at 17 Akron Street in Roxbury increased. One cheering note was the election of W. Paul Cook to the N.A.P.A. official editorship at the Chicago convention in July 1918. Cook published a lavish volume of *The National Amateur* in 1918-19 and printed some of Mrs. Miniter's finest work therein. Cook was honored with the presidency of the National for the 1919-20 term at the July 1919 convention in Newark, New Jersey. But by then Mrs. Dowe was no more. In 1918, Edith had had to sell her property "Meadowbeck" in Wilbraham, the site of so many happy summer camps during the prior decade. Then in the autumn, Jennie and Edith had to sell their home at 17 Akron Street. While the influenza epidemic raged, Charles and Laura Sawyer took Mrs. Dowe and Mrs. Miniter into their home in Allston, Massachusetts. Mrs. Dowe had a bright, cheery bedroom of her own. But nevertheless she continued to fail, and died on the morning of March 6, 1919. One may say that the happiest years of

Mrs. Miniter's life ended with the death of her mother. Mrs. Dowe had wished for a funeral service comprised of friends' recollections and that was what she received; many, like Nelson G. Morton, felt honored to be asked to speak. Just four days after the death of Mrs. Dowe, the Hub Club met for its annual anniversary dinner at the Cambridge home of Mr. and Mrs. Denys Peter Myers. Mrs. Dowe's body was cremated but her ashes remained unscattered until after her daughter's death in 1934. In September 1935, Edward H. Cole and Howard P. Lovecraft undertook this melancholy duty in Wilbraham.

For the many Eastern amateur journalists who could not attend that year's N.A.P.A. convention in Cleveland, Ohio, Boston hosted an amateur journalists' conference in July 1920. It was at this conference that Howard P. Lovecraft of Providence met Mrs. Miniter for the first time. During the conference, the joyous news of the election of Boston's Marjorie H. Outwater to the N.A.P.A. official editorship at the Cleveland convention was received. Boston was chosen for the next meeting place at the Cleveland convention, and the Hub Club hosted yet another amateur journalists' conference over Labor Day in 1920 in preparation for the "big event" in July 1921. George Julian Houtain was much in evidence at these conferences, attempting to ingratiate himself with the Boston amateurs and to advise Howard Lovecraft to perk up. That he managed to charm at least one of Boston's "galled jades" is evident from the fact Boston's E. Dorothy (Grant) MacLaughlin married him on August 31, 1921, just a few weeks after her election as N.A.P.A. president at the Boston convention in July 1921. In September 1921, Michael White and W. Paul Cook published their magnificent tribute to Mrs. Miniter's mother, *In Memoriam: Jennie E. T. Dowe,* of which Mrs. Miniter's long memoir "My Mother—As She Seemed To Me" is the centerpiece. Also in September, Mrs. Miniter and Laura Sawyer visited Wellesley College with their young friend Lillian Crane. They were pleased to find a copy of *Our Natupski Neighbors* in the town library.

The Hub Club had lapsed into an unusual period of inactivity in 1921-22. Perhaps many of its members were exhausted by the work of hosting the July 1921 N.A.P.A. convention. But Mrs. Miniter spearheaded a reorganization with many new members in the fall of 1922. On November 30, 1922, Howard P. Lovecraft, the quintessential United man, had accepted appointment by the Executive Judges as successor to N.A.P.A. President William Dowdell, who had resigned after completing only a few months of his term. Lovecraft attended the Hub Club meeting on February 8, 1923, in Huntington Chambers and heard the address by Maitland Chambers, editor of Boston's *National Magazine,* where he himself had published verse during the prior decade. On March 10, 1923, he returned to Boston to attend the anniversary dinner of the Hub Club, celebrated that year at the Hotel Hemenway. After dinner, President Lovecraft addressed the guests. In June 1923, Lovecraft returned again to Boston to hear the address of George Brinton Beal, editor of the *Sunday Post Magazine,* to the Hub Club in Huntington Chambers. Mrs. Miniter's final political cause in the National association was the election of her friend Hazel Bosler (Pratt) Adams to the presidency in 1923. This aim was achieved at the Cleveland convention in July 1923, which also elevated Clyde G. Townsend to the official editorship and named Boston as the next meeting place. The July 1924 N.A.P.A. convention held at the Hotel Vendome in Boston was fated to be Edith's last. Clyde G. Townsend, elevated to the N.A.P.A. presidency, named Mrs. Miniter Chairman of the Bureau of Critics for the 1924-25 official year.

During the period following her mother's death, Edith lived with Charles and Laura Sawyer in Allston and with Charles and Augusta Parker in Malden. From these two homes, she made a valiant effort to support herself by literary endeavor. There were a few cheering developments. The prestigious journal *Poetry* accepted two poems by Mrs. Miniter which it published under the collective title "Confidences" in its October 1923 issue. Even more encouragingly, *The New York Times* published Mrs. Miniter's poem "Kerry Dancing" in its issue dated September 1, 1924. "Weeping Heroines of Yesteryear" followed in *The New York Times Book Review* on March 8, 1925, and "As A Man Courted A Maid 100 Years Ago" in *The New York Times Magazine* on February 21, 1926. "An Elmer Gantry of '82" followed in *The New York Times Magazine* for August 5, 1928. In addition, Mrs. Miniter's essays on antiquarian topics began to appear with some regularity in the Boston and Springfield newspapers and in the journal *Antiques.* While she never again attained the public attention she had received for her article "How to Dress on $40 a Year" in *The Boston Globe* in the 1890s, she began during the 1920s to be recognized as a reliable author on anything relating to the customs, dress and domestic furnishings of oldtime New England. During this period, she also continued work on her novels *The Village Green* and *Lydia 'n' Gerald*. The former exists entire as a holograph manuscript in the Lovecraft Collection at Brown University but the latter is incomplete. It is possible that Mrs. Miniter attempted to market some of the chapters separately as short stories. Two such chapters were recovered by Mr. R. Alain Everts from Tupper family sources in Wilbraham when he was researching Lovecraft and his associates in the 1960s and 1970s.

The shared living arrangements with the Sawyers and the Parkers proved in the end to be unsatisfactory. Perhaps Edith needed more privacy than she could obtain in either household. In the fall of 1923, the Hub Club hosted yet another amateur journalists' conference at the United States Hotel. On April 23, 1924, the Hub Club sat down to dinner in Chinatown to mark the one hundredth anniversary of the death of Byron. It was one of the very last meetings of the club as an active entity. Perhaps the effort of hosting the Boston N.A.P.A. convention in July 1924 was the penultimate nail in the Club's coffin. Edith's health and dwelling place no longer permitted her to undertake a lion's share of the hospitality work, which inevitably fell on shoulders less willing or able to accept the load. The final blow, of course, was Mrs. Miniter's permanent removal to Wilbraham to reside with Evanore Olds Beebe at "Maplehurst." The N.A.P.A. membership lists appear to indicate that Mrs. Miniter remained with the Sawyers at 21 Imrie Road in Allston over the winter of 1925-26, but Lovecraft states that her removal to Wilbraham was permanent by 1925. In 1924, Charles Parker had appointed Mrs. Miniter the first contributing editor of his small literary magazine *L'Alouette* and Mrs. Miniter's work continued to appear there occasionally. In the 1930s, Parker reprinted some of Mrs. Miniter's poems in his *Threads in Tapestry* anthologies. However, he apparently never achieved publication of Jennie Dowe's *Five Little Gossoons and Other Irish Verses* as announced in *L'Alouette* in 1924. Mrs. Miniter's final appearance in an amateur magazine during her lifetime appears to have been with "Cuddley Music" in

Mary Morgan Ware's *Pot Pourri* published from Brattleboro, Vermont in July 1929.

Lovecraft provides an admirable portrait of life at Maplehurst in the late 1920s in his memoir "Mrs. Miniter—Estimates and Recollections." He was the invited guest of Mrs. Miniter and Miss Beebe for a week during the month of July 1928. W. Paul Cook and H. Warner Munn accompanied him from Cook's home in Athol, Massachusetts, with Cook doing the driving. Cook and Munn stayed only for the first night, while Lovecraft stayed the entire week. Cook later recalled that Miss Beebe was fit to be tied on account of the massive sugar residues Lovecraft left in her antique coffee service. But Mrs. Miniter and Miss Beebe proved to be gracious hostesses, and Lovecraft spent a memorable week amongst the plentiful household pets and antiques which filled Maplehurst to the brim. Mrs. Miniter accompanied him on shorter expeditions, and provided instructions for longer ones. She shared with him the folklore of the region, including the legend of whippoorwills' waiting for the souls of the departed, which he adapted for his famous story "The Dunwich Horror." The few letters of Mrs. Miniter to Lovecraft preserved in the Lovecraft Collection at Brown University address him as "Mr. Goodguile," in memory of the name given to him in Mrs. Miniter's parody "Falco Ossifracus" as published in *The Muffin Man* of April 1921. Lovecraft chose to quote from the poem "A.D. 1921" which originally appeared in that scarce publication at the end of his own memoir.

Lovecraft was one of few amateur journalists to be invited into the very private world of Mrs. Miniter's retirement years at Maplehurst. It was hoped that she would be able to attend the Boston N.A.P.A. convention in July 1930, but her health prohibited the trip. Asthma combined with heart disease often left her as short of breath as her grandmother Catherine Orpha (Moore) Tupper had been during her final days in 1895-96, when she was nursed by Jennie Dowe. As the 1930s arrived in the midst of the Depression, such were Mrs. Miniter's straitened circumstances that her dear friend W. Paul Cook would often send her small donations of household necessities or cash. In 1931, Mrs. Miniter suffered a new reversal when Evanore Olds Beebe suffered a stroke. Now, more of the household responsibilities fell on Mrs. Miniter's shoulders, despite her own weakness. Lovecraft recorded that she suffered several painful fractures as a result of falls during this period. Illness forbade any work, literary or otherwise, although Lovecraft believed that Mrs. Miniter continued to touch-up her novel manuscripts even toward the end of her life. The death of Capitola L. (Harrison) Spencer (Mrs. Truman J. Spencer) on January 29, 1933 removed another beloved friend from Mrs. Miniter's life. But she was not herself to bear many more losses. On Memorial Day, 1934, she felt well enough to attend the local celebrations in Glendale, where she had helped dedicate the memorial stone in 1913. However, she died suddenly on the evening of June 4, 1934, at Maplehurst and was buried in the Tupper lot at Woodland Dell Cemetery in Wilbraham on June 6, 1934.

A short obituary appeared in the local Springfield, Massachusetts newspaper on June 5, 1934. Edward H. Cole wrote a fuller obituary for *The National Amateur* dated September 1934. Charles W. "Tryout" Smith and Laura A. Sawyer, two of Edith's closest friends in the amateur journalism hobby, got out a small memorial booklet entitled *In Memory of Edith May Miniter: A Coworker in Amateur Journalism 1884-1934*. The July 1934 N.A.P.A. convention held in Chicago, Illinois took little notice of Mrs. Miniter's passing despite her fifty-year career in the hobby. In truth, her own heyday in the hobby had long passed. After a period of lax activity which lasted through the 1920s (which Burton Crane dubbed "the weary years"), the National was once more in the throes of the "young blood" revolution during the 1930s. Mrs. Miniter left no will, but Howard P. Lovecraft and W. Paul Cook took charge of her literary papers. Lovecraft's portion of the Miniter papers is preserved in the Lovecraft Collection at Brown University. The fate of Cook's portion is not known. Evanore Olds Beebe did not long survive her friend Edith Miniter, dying on May 29, 1935, of a cerebral hemorrhage. Miss Beebe did not join Edith Miniter in Woodland Dell Cemetery but was buried in the quaint little Glendale Cemetery near her beloved home Maplehurst. In September 1935, Edward H. Cole and Howard P. Lovecraft recovered the ashes of Jennie Dowe from a Boston funeral director and scattered them according to her direction in Wilbraham, Massachusetts.

Posthumous recognition of Mrs. Miniter's work was slow in coming. Hyman Bradofsky published a generous sampling of surviving Miniter manuscripts culled from Messrs. Lovecraft and Cook in his amateur magazine *The Californian*, in issues dated between Winter 1935 and Autumn 1937. Cook had long been considering the idea of publishing a Miniter memorial more substantial than the small chapbook issued by Charles W. "Tryout" Smith and Laura A. Sawyer in 1934, but because of the disorder in his own living arrangements in the wake of the death of his wife in 1930, could not bring his ideas to fruition. After living alone in Boston in 1930-35, Cook lived with Mr. and Mrs. Paul J. Campbell in East Saint Louis, Illinois in 1935-37, before joining Walter John Coates's Driftwind Press in North Montpelier, Vermont in 1937. His co-trustee Lovecraft had died on March 15, 1937, leaving behind his own generous memoir of Mrs. Miniter written for the hoped-for memorial volume. When in 1938, Lovecraft's young friend Robert H. Barlow published Mrs. Miniter's story "Dead Houses"—considered by Cook to be Mrs. Miniter's finest—in his mimeographed magazine *Leaves* issued from Lakeport, California, Cook was enraged and felt that his plans for the memorial volume had been spoiled. In fact, Barlow's amateur magazine probably reached fewer than sixty persons. But Cook decided to release the essays written for the Miniter memorial to Hyman Bradofsky, who published them in a special "Miniter Memorial" edition of *The Californian* dated Spring 1938. Mr. Bradofsky had a plate of Mrs. Miniter's portrait cut specially for this special number of his amateur magazine.

By the late 1930s the amateurs of Mrs. Miniter's generation had begun to pass from the scene in droves. William R. Murphy, Edwin Booth Swift, and Harriet Caryl (Cox) Dennis all died in April 1936. Charles E. Wilson died a few weeks later on July 9, 1936. John Leary Peltret, the second man in Edith's life, died in San Francisco on October 27, 1938. The editor does not know whether he lived to see the "Miniter Memorial" issue of *The Californian* (Spring 1938). Ralph Metcalf, who hosted the N.E.A.P.A. in Providence on July 14, 1885, died on April 14, 1939, and Joseph Dana Miller, one of the earliest contributors to Miss Dowe's own *Worcester Amateur*, followed him in death on May 8, 1939. John G. Kugler died on June 26, 1939, and Alfred H. Nash in November 1939. Tragically, both Minna B. Noyes, aged eighty-two, and Mabel F. Noyes, aged seventy-two, and twenty of their beloved cats died in a fire in their home in Westfield, Massachusetts on January 19, 1941. Mrs. Miniter's foes as well as her friends passed away: Charles Robert Burger died on May 31, 1939; Charles C. Heuman ("to err is Heuman"), on June 20, 1940; David L. Hollub, on January 25, 1942; Edwin Hadley Smith, on March 22, 1944; Louis Kempner, on July 6, 1944; George Julian Houtain, on August 21, 1945. Many old friends also passed away during the decade of the forties: James F. Morton, Jr., on October 7, 1941; Truman J. Spencer, on September 28, 1944; Willard O. Wylie, on November 30, 1944; Warren J. Brodie, on August 5, 1945; Paul J. Campbell, on August 16, 1945; Bertha York Grant Avery (widow of Finlay Arnon Grant), on December 23, 1945; Ernest A. Edkins, on July 3, 1946; Frank Roe Batchelder, on February 5, 1947; Timothy Burr Swift, on April 12, 1947; W. Paul Cook, on January 22, 1948; Charles W. ("Tryout") Smith, on February 17, 1948; Leston M. Ayres, on February 24, 1948; Will Hancock, in 1949. Yet more colleagues followed in death during the 1950s: Alson J. Brubaker, on October 18, 1950; A. M. Adams, on February 7, 1952; Joseph Bernard Lynch, on August 27, 1952; Frank S. C. Wicks (who escorted Miss Dowe to the Gardner convention with Finlay A. Grant in July 1883), on December 22, 1952; Augusta L. (Mueller) Parker, in 1953; Walter E. Mellinger, on October 12, 1954; George A. Hough (who boosted Miss Dowe for the presidency of E.A.P.A. in 1885-6), on October 13, 1955; Frank E. Schermerhorn, on December 14, 1957; John Moody, in his ninetieth year, in 1958; Winifred Virginia Jordan, in 1959; Michael White, on September 11, 1959. In the sixties and seventies fell silent the last remaining contemporaries of Edith Miniter: Edna Hyde McDonald ("Vondy"), on March 2, 1962; Laura A. Sawyer, just short of her one hundredth birthday, in March 1965; Charles A. A. Parker, on June 1, 1965; Edward H. Cole, in June 1966; Charles W. Heins, on October 19, 1967; Nelson G. Morton, in November 1968; Ethel May Johnston-Myers, in 1971; Denys Peter Myers, in February 1972.

What has been done to date to preserve her memory is modest, but nevertheless worthy of note. Were it not for Hyman Bradofsky's determination to preserve her memory, Mrs. Miniter would likely be completely forgotten today. The standard bibliographies would list her novel *Our Natupski Neighbors* (Holt, 1916) and nothing more. As a result of the wealth of information which Mr. Bradofsky published in his amateur magazine *The Californian* between 1935 and 1938, the memory of Mrs. Miniter and her work was effectively preserved for new generations of amateur journalists. W. Paul Cook did not let either Bradofsky or Barlow have the final word in the posthumous publication of Mrs. Miniter's work, and published her story "Whom We Call Dead" in the Spring 1943 issue of his amateur periodical *The Ghost,* issued from North Montpelier, Vermont, where he continued to assist the widow of Walter John Coates with the operation of the Driftwind Press until his own death in 1948. In Autumn 1945, Ernest A. Edkins and Timothy Burr Thrift reprinted Mrs. Miniter's story "Nobody Home" in their fine amateur journal *The Aonian.* This reprinting marked the final appearance of Mrs. Miniter's work in an amateur magazine. It is fitting that Mrs. Miniter's old foe Ernest A. Edkins, near the end of his own life, saw that one of Mrs. Miniter's finest stories was reprinted in the beautiful *Aonian.* Truman J. Spencer's *History of Amateur Journalism* (The Fossils, 1957) contained a generous discussion of Mrs. Miniter and her work. Nelson G. Morton also remembered his dearly beloved friend in an article in *The Fossil* in 1954. But it took the determination of Hyman Bradofsky and Victor Moitoret to supply the writer with the necessary raw material for his first collection of Edith Miniter's work, *Going Home And Other Amateur Writings,* published in an edition of one hundred copies on June 18, 1995. A second collection, *The Coast of Bohemia and Other Writings* (Moshassuck Press, 2000), relied as well on the contributions of Messrs. Bradofsky and Moitoret, although it also drew on additional sources such as the wonderful collections of nineteenth-century amateur journals at the American Antiquarian Society in Worcester, Massachusetts, the Western Reserve Historical Society in Cleveland, Ohio, and the New York Public Library in New York City, New York, which enabled the writer to recover many of Mrs. Miniter's "missing" early pieces.

The writer hopes that *Dead Houses and Other Works* will help to bring Mrs. Miniter's fine works to the attention of a wider public. May it be worthy of W. Paul Cook's vision of a "Miniter Memorial" planned so many years ago.

MRS. MINITER—
ESTIMATES AND RECOLLECTIONS
H. P. Lovecraft

I

It would be an interesting if invidious task to attempt a classification of amateur journalists past and present on a basis of sheer quality. The process would not be simple; for to be a "great amateur" one must not only possess absolute intellectual or aesthetic talent, and excellence in scholarship and letters, but must successfully devote a substantial part of his energies to the furtherance of what is really best in the amateur cause. Fame founded on political prowess and purely social activity in amateurdom, or on triumphs—literary or otherwise—in the outside world, would not count. Only high-grade thinkers and creators serving amateurdom in a high-grade way would be eligible for exaltation. The number of the "great" as reckoned by such a standard would probably be smaller than we like to think—but in their very front rank, acclaimed without a dissenting voice, would undoubtedly be placed the late Edith Miniter.

Mrs. Miniter was the daughter of a poetess and a mathematician, and in her own personality and work as a fiction-writer the diverse strains clearly showed. She had, while disavowing poetry as a major interest, a sense of the soil, and of the pageantry of life and visible forms, which amounted to a poet's symbolism. Yet at the same time her keen faculty for observation, analysis, and comparison forbade her to view mankind and the world through a poet's sentimental haze. Her eye for the minutiae of human conduct, speech, and manners was almost preternaturally sharp; and this, coupled with her extreme sensitiveness to incongruities and comic contrasts, marked her out early as a natural humorist and ironist. She was a sworn and consistent foe of the pompous, the extravagant, and the romantic. A born deflater, she scorned the stupid optimisms, violent, over-coloured situations, false emotions and motivations, and artificial "happy endings" which cluttered up the dominant fiction of her earlier years.

In short stories and novels alike she chose to draw the ordinary people she knew in the ordinary situations most common to them.

With her tremendous command of detail, she built up characters so lifelike that our memories confuse them with persons we have met. All their traits and foibles stand out before us, and we watch their groping progress through the familiar, everyday world toward that impasse of unsatisfying inconclusiveness which forms the goal of most human pilgrimages. We see their fatuous, practical, or greedy springs of action without the varnish of conventional sentiment and mendacious melodrama; we follow their gestures, idioms, accents, and typical absurdities till each figure becomes utterly individualised and unforgettable. The satire is never heavy or violent. Always subtle, it peeps forth slyly as an integral part of the description and perspective. Addison and Jane Austen, especially the latter, are comparisons which naturally occur to one. And yet there is at times a certain grim realism which vaguely suggests something more—perhaps the objective school of Flaubert and de Maupassant, despite Mrs. Miniter's conscious rejection of all influences and subjects outside her own ancestral stream.

For above all things, Mrs. Miniter was an unalloyed outgrowth of her hereditary soil. It was supremely appropriate that, though her childhood home was in Worcester and the scene of her mature activities as writer and newspaper woman was Boston, she chanced to be born in her grandfather's farmhouse on Wilbraham Mountain in central Massachusetts, amidst fields and groves that her forbears had known for generations. New England's rock-strewn countryside, its great elms, its stone walls and winding roads, its white-steepled villages, and its curious moods, phrases, and folkways formed the core of her inheritance; and upon this most of her interests and art was built.

The books, records, and tangible objects connected with the long continuous stream of local life fascinated her profoundly, so that eventually her antiquarianism reached a professional status. As a collector of old china she was notable, and readers of the Boston Transcript and Springfield Republican will not soon forget her articles on antiques, old school-books, local history, and bygone customs of which she was almost the last first-hand reporter. Her zeal in research and her memory for ancient things were fully as sharp as her observation of details around her. No more indefatigable collector of quaint epitaphs ever lived.

Nor was she ever long out of touch with the ancestral scene. Nearly every summer or autumn found her in the shadow of Wilbraham Mountain—while, with a symbolic aptness rivalling that of her birth, the last nine years of her life were spent on the ancient soil, in the rambling, antique-filled farmhouse of a close friend and extremely distant cousin. With such a programme, her detailed, coordinated knowledge and basic, sympathetic comprehension of Central New England character, speech, legends, manners, and customs became those of a profound specialist. The field was worthy of her devotion, for the Connecticut Valley's backwaters present typical and tenacious phases of life not to be found elsewhere; phases contrasting sharply with the brisk, well-ordered, seaward-gazing and often adventurous life of coastal New England and its vivid old ports.

In the first Puritan days this region was a trackless wilderness covered with black woods whose depths the settlers' fancy peopled with unknown horrors and evil shadows. Then the Bay Path was hewn through to the settlements on the Connecticut, and after King Philip's War thin streams of pioneers began to trickle along it and branch off from it: cutting faint roadways and clearing meagre farmsteads on the silent rocky hillsides. Grim, low-pitched, unpainted farmhouses sprang up in the lee of craggy slopes, their dim, small-paned windows looking secretively off across leagues of loneliness. Life was hard and practical, and contact with the world very slight. Old tales and thoughts and words and ways persisted, and people remembered odd fancies which others had forgotten. There was less breadth and changing of ideas; less response to new times; than on the coast, where links with Europe were many, and where prosperity and "book-l'arnin'" had fostered a more flexible mentality.

The years passed, and modern influences stole into the Wilbraham country. Springfield's proximity began to be felt, and a stately brick academy arose in the village on fields above the sleepy, elm-shaded street. Farmers throve in a modest way, and took on a literacy and taste clearly reflected in the general life. Finer houses were built. But always the undercurrent of isolation and ancient whispers persisted. One of Mrs. Miniter's ancestresses in the early nineteenth century was a suspected witch; and people talked about the queer sounds in the air each evening at the pasture bars where the road bends north of the mountain.

Then the cityward tide set in, and some of the most vigorous stock vanished—to return only for burial in the spectral cemeteries near the village. Funerals, Mrs. Miniter once wrote, came to form Wilbraham's chief industry. Deserted houses grew common, and some of the humbler farmers began to show queer softenings of morale and queer vagaries in their standards. Foreigners appeared—the typical Connecticut Valley Poles whom the keen realist so faithfully depicted in her novel *Our Natupski Neighbors*. A new element of sombreness was added to the old background of persistent legend— the sombreness of decay, desolation, and impending change. Even in its late phases the ancient land cannot lose its distinctiveness! All this Mrs. Miniter caught as clearly as she caught the ancestral heritage. She was, from first to last, a realist; and in her the brooding countryside had a voice and an historian.

But in no sense was Mrs. Miniter a rustic, provincial, or one-sided artist. Side by side with her reflection of old backgrounds was a mature, cosmopolitan scholarship and general culture which always made her see her chosen field in its true perspective. Her interests were as wide as those of any other urban literateur, as all who knew her stories, book reviews, and brilliant conversation can well attest. In taste she followed the nineteenth-century mainstream, though constantly transcending it in unexpected ways. None excelled her in social accomplishments and organising genius; qualities which made her for over thirty years the natural leader of Boston amateurdom and the originator of the most typical touches of wit and distinctiveness in the Hub Club's programmes and publications. No mere coincidence caused the death of the club only a few months after her final departure from Boston.

II

The details of Mrs. Miniter's long career—a career inseparable from amateur journalism after her sixteenth year—will doubtless be covered by writers well qualified to treat of them. Reared in Worcester, taught by her poet-mother and at a private school, and given to solid reading and literary attempts from early childhood onward, the erstwhile Edith May Dowe entered amateurdom in 1883 and was almost immediately famous in our small world as a fiction realist. Controversies raged over her stories—so different from the saccharine froth of the period—but very few failed to recognize her importance. After 1890 she was engaged in newspaper and magazine work in the larger outside world, though her interest in amateur matters increased rather than diminished.

From 1894 onward she dominated the historic Hub Club of Boston, and was foremost in ensuring the success of amateur conventions in her city. In 1895 she was Official Editor of the National, and in 1909 she became its President. Her occasional editorship of *The Hub Club Quill*, and of various individual papers, gave repeated proof of her peculiar charm as a humorous commentator, and her skill and effectiveness in meeting amateurdom's diverse issues. Especially famous was her *Aftermath*, published after the conventions she attended and touching on their salient features with inimitable humour and acuteness. The same qualities of wit and observation animated all her letters, so that she was highly valued as a correspondent. Her home, whatever its location, was always a recognised headquarters of amateurs—its charm enhanced by the presence of her gifted mother, Mrs. Jennie E. T. Dowe, from 1896 until Mrs. Dowe's death in 1919.

In 1916 appeared Mrs. Miniter's novel *Our Natupski Neighbors*, the sequel to which has unfortunately never seen publication. Her short stories had meanwhile gained a substantial foothold in many standard magazines, while her reviews and antiquarian articles enjoyed more than a local fame. Actually, she deserved even more recognition than she received. It was her misfortune to follow a middle course in an age of abrupt transition—so that in youth her work was far in advance of its time, while in later life it failed to keep pace with the decadent and abnormal interests of modernism. It was in the "Natupski" period that she and her environment most closely coincided, and that she received the enthusiastic praise of William Lyon Phelps and other critics. At no time could she have been an idol of the masses, since her work was too honest for vitiated popular taste. Her integrity as an artist was absolute. She did not cater to the low-grade demands of the herd, and probably could not have done so had she wished.

My own direct acquaintance with Mrs. Miniter dates only from the summer of 1920, when I first attended gatherings of the Boston amateurs. She was then inhabiting the memorable halls of 20 Web-ster Street in Allston—"Epgephian Temple" of cryptic amateur lore—and was, as always, surrounded by a homelike array of antiques and family possessions, and attended by a faithful feline bearing the various names of "Grey Brother," "Grey Bother," and "Tat."

The festive July conclave marking my introduction is still fresh in memory. Though of diminutive stature, and given to choosing a low and inconspicuous seat amidst an assembly, Mrs. Miniter did not fail to dominate more or less imperceptibly every event at which she was present. Her piquant conversation and constant humour gave a vividness to the most ordinary happenings, and vastly enlivened an all-day trip to Castle Island. My own bias toward the archaic made me especially appreciative of her interests in that direction. Later I enjoyed the spirited and hilarious comments on the gathering which she published—both under her own name and as the amanuensis of "Tat"—in that short-lived but unforgettable journal *Epgephi*.

For the next few years I saw Mrs. Miniter quite often at meetings and festivals of the Hub Club, and always admired the effectiveness with which she devised entertainment and maintained interest. In April, 1921, her quaintly named and edited paper *The Muffin Man* contained a highly amusing parody of one of my weird fiction at-tempts—"Falco Ossifracus, by Mr. Goodguile"—though it was not of a nature to arouse hostility. Notwithstanding her saturation with the spectral lore of the countryside, Mrs. Miniter did not care for stories of a macabre or supernatural cast; regarding them as hope-lessly extravagant and unrepresentative of life. Perhaps that is one reason why, in the early Boston days, she had declined a chance to revise a manuscript of this sort which later met with much fame—the vampire novel *Dracula*, whose author was then touring America as manager for Sir Henry Irving.

It was in September, 1921, that W. Paul Cook issued his ample brochure in memory of Mrs. Dowe, for which Mrs. Miniter fur-nished a magnificent tribute in the form of a biographical sketch of her mother. This sketch, in which the ancestral Wilbraham back-ground is desribed with great piquancy and detail, and in whose later parts the fortunes of the household are traced with keen dra-matic humour, contains not a little self-revelation, and forms one of the most adequate records of its writer's personality now available.

Throughout the N. A. P. A.'s Boston convention of 1921 Mrs. Miniter's guidance and inspiration were manifest. In the breezy *Aftermath* describing this event I was quite overwhelmed to find the chapter headings dedicated to me—each being a quotation from Dr. Samuel Johnson, as was fitting in commemorating an eighteenth-century devotee. Late in 1922 Mrs. Miniter was prominent in reorganising the Hub Club and broadening its personnel. Her abode was the the pleasant white house in Maplewood where the still-flourishing *L'Alouette* held forth. Here her library and her many antiques were displayed to especial advantage. Throughout 1923 she stood behind the club, aiding in its expansion campaign, and lending her wit to its banquet and convention programmes, and to its official organ.

At this period a heated controversy regarding schools of poetry was raging in amateurdom—the disciples of Victorian placidity being arrayed against the followers of Swinburne, Baudelaire, and the Symbolists. As an anti-Victorian, I published among other things an editorial with distinctly cool references to the soulful Messrs. Longfellow and Tennyson. Mrs. Miniter, on the other side, countered with a long column of comment whose paragraphs were separated by alternate quotations from the two gentlemanly versifiers in question.

This, too, was the time when explorers of the old Massachusetts coast towns had the benefit of Mrs. Miniter's antiquarian knowledge. I recall a trip to old Marblehead with its tangled ways and brooding gambrel roofs, in which Edward H. Cole also participated. Mrs. Miniter supplied many legends and particulars which no guidebook could furnish—and it was on this occasion that I first heard of the rustic superstition which asserts that window-panes slowly absorb and retain the likeness of those who habitually sit by them year after year. To Boston also Mrs. Miniter was an ideal guide. All the historic sites and literary landmarks were at her tongue's tip—including many which would otherwise have been very difficult to find. No one could surpass her in explaining the various minor domestic objects of the past—betty lamps, sausage-guns, potato-boilers, tinder-wheels, clock-jacks, plate-warmers, smoking-tongs, and the like—which are found in such abundance in antique collections and around the kitchen fireplaces of old houses open as museums.

III

1924 and 1925 brought many changes, and before the close of the latter year Mrs. Miniter's permanent return to her native countryside was effected. The seat of her residence was Maplehurst, "back of the mountain" in North Wilbraham; a large, rambling farmhouse, once an inn, which lies just across the marsh-meadows from Wilbraham Mountain, at a bend and dip of the road where giant maples form a green, mystical arcade. This is the ancestral domain of the Beebes—with whose surviving representative, the locally famous antiquarian and antique collector Miss Evanore Olds Beebe, Mrs. Miniter combined household forces.

Miss Beebe—now unfortunately an invalid—was then virtually the leading spirit of Wilbraham; a kind of feminine village Pooh-Bah who held, among numberless other offices, the posts of Superintendent of Schools and member of the Town Council. She was a stout, capable, kindly, and quietly humorous gentlewoman then about seventy years of age, and was looked up to as an oracle by all the surrounding population. Her telephone rang constantly with requests for information and advice—political, social, historical, domestic, or otherwise—from citizens and town officials, and her voice in civic affairs was one of almost supreme authority. Though of straitened finances, she was the owner of most of the land in sight, including a goodly part of Wilbraham Mountain. An old friend of the family, and distant kinswoman in the Olds line, she had been Mrs. Miniter's hostess on many a summer sojourn; so that the returning native's immediate milieu was by no means a strange one.

The house, of early nineteenth century date, was spacious and attractive; and was literally choked to repletion with the rare antiques inherited or assembled by its owner. The ancient tables, secretaries, and chests which crowded the large rooms were covered and piled high with lesser antiques of every conceivable sort—china, glassware, candlesticks, snuffers, sand-boxes, whale-oil lamps, and all the other typical legacies of the past. Venerable paintings and samplers in close array all but hid the centuried paper of the walls, while the archaic fireplaces formed a setting for innumerable warming-pans, foot-stoves, sets of bellows and fire-irons, and less recognisable household appliances of yore. Amidst this antiquarian's

paradise there moved—with a truly miraculous lack of evil consequences—a retinue of seven cats and two dogs, each with a distinct
personality of his own.

Printer (whose name was a corruption of "Prince of Orange"—
this in turn based on the colour of his eyes) was the dean of the
felidae, and had seen nearly seventeen winters in this world. He
was a tiger of friendly disposition, and last of the Beebe mousers to
know or avail himself of the old-fashioned "cat ladder"—a series of
brick steps inside the great chimney—which led from the ground
floor to the realms above. Old Fats was a bluff, brusque, plumpish,
outdoor cat of golden hue and great martial prowess, whose primary
ambition seemed to be to become a dog. He would curl up beside
the dogs as if one of their clan, and would follow his human friends
all over the farm—trotting caninely at their heels. His three brothers Tardee, Pettie, and Prince of Wails (so named for his vocal at-
tainments) were likewise of aureate colouring. Pettie was the most
affectionate and gentlemanly of the household, while the Prince's
chief fame arose from his ability to thread his way among and over
the furniture without the least damage or even peril to the laby-
rinth of fragile antiques. Their sister Little Bit was a tiger, and fond
of sleeping in a tripod-suspended kettle on the lawn. Her young
daughter Tiger Ann (later renamed Marcelle) completed the feline
roster at the period of the present writer's census. Of the two dogs
Stitchie was an aged collie of aristocratic lineage and impeccable
courtesy, beginning to suffer from deafness and dim sight, while
Donny was a boisterous and clumsy puppy in the process of growing to Gargantuan proportions.

The farm still existed as such, though operated on a reduced scale
by the time of Mrs. Miniter's advent. Very little ground was really
cultivated, but haying was conducted with local talent seasonally
engaged—and with the more or less languid cooperation of the one
hired boy, a sentimental vocalist whose melodic enthusiasm rivaled
that of the Prince of Wails. Of livestock there remained some poul-
try, two lowing kine, and two patriarchal equines. The barn was a
huge, spectral place with an immense hayloft. Picturesque sloping
meadows stretched off in every direction, and just down hill at the
road's bend there brooded the pasture bars where strange noctur-
nal influences were said to linger. Between the highway and the

mountain the marsh spread out—half-traversed by the grass-grown remnants of a never-finished road. On summer nights the throngs of dancing fireflies above the marsh—and above the pasture of the haunted bars—were of a strange multitudinousness and brilliancy which well justified the rustic whisperings attached to them.

Into this congenial environment Mrs. Miniter fitted admirably and instantaneously. It was her own country, and here she remained till the end; though a vague idea of a possible return to Boston caused her to keep some of her possessions stored there. More and more of her articles dealt with Wilbraham folklore—articles which she wrote at intervals between work on two still unpublished novels. Material was plentiful at hand, and not far away dwelt the colourful Polish family around which her "Natupski" novel had been written. Through her pen the reading public came to know of Lieutenant Mirick, whose killing by a "pizen sarpient" in a hayfield on Wilbra'm Mountain in 1761 gave rise to the name "Rattlesnake Peak" as applied to the principal summit. In other articles she told of the mysterious murders of travellers, of the man who moved a schoolhouse to his own neighborhood to accommodate his children, of the inn whose floor shows the marks of stacked Revolutionary muskets, of the ensign who in 1744 could carry six bushels of salt on his back all at one time, and of kindred choice bits from Wilbraham's long annals.

An eight-day visit to the household at Maplehurst in July, 1928, formed my last personal glimpse of Mrs. Miniter. I had never seen the Wilbraham region before, and was charmed by the vivid vistas of hills and valleys, and the remote winding roads so redolent of other centuries. No better hierophants of the local arcana than Mrs. Miniter and Miss Beebe could possibly have been found, and my knowledge of Central New England lore was virtually trebled during my short stay.

I saw the ruinous, deserted old Randolph Beebe house where the whippoorwills cluster abnormally, and learned that these birds are feared by the rustics as evil psychopomps. It is whispered that they linger and flutter around houses where death is approaching, hoping to catch the soul of the departed as it leaves. If the soul eludes them, they disperse in quiet disappointment; but sometimes they set up a chorused clamour of excited, triumphant chattering which makes the watchers turn pale and mutter—with that air of hushed, awestruck portentousness which only a backwoods Yankee can assume—"They got 'im!" On another day I was taken to nearby Monson to see a dark, damp street in the shadow of a great hill, the houses on the hillward side of which are whispered about because of the number of tenants who have gone mad or killed themselves.

I saw the haunted pasture bars in the spectral dusk, and one evening was thrilled and amazed by a monstrous saraband of fireflies over marsh and meadow. It was as if some strange, sinister constellation had taken on an uncanny life and descended to hang low above the lush grasses. And one day Mrs. Miniter showed me a deep, mute ravine beyond the Randolph Beebe house, along whose far-off wooded floor an unseen stream trickles in eternal shadow. Here, I am told, the whippoorwills gather on certain nights for no good purpose.

I was taken over the sightly Beebe acres by my hostess, Old Fats trotting doglike at our heels; and beheld some of the silent, uncommunicative, slowly retrograding yokelry of the region. Later the aged, courtly Stitchie and Mrs. Miniter were my joint guides to neighboring Glendale and its ancient church and churchyard. Still another trip was up old Wilbr'm Mountain, where the road winds mystically aloft into a region of hushed skyey meadowland seemingly half-apart from time and change, and abounding in breathtaking vistas. Through the haze of distance other mountains loom purple and mysterious. A line of fog marks the great Connecticut, and the smoke of Springfield clouds the southwestern horizon. Sometimes even the golden dome of the Hartford state house, far to the south, can be discerned. Though the slopes were much as Lieutenant Mirick must have known them in his day, I saw no "pizen sarpients." On the way Mrs. Miniter pointed out the home of the "Natupskis" immortalised in her novel.

A subsequent day was devoted to a long walk around the mountain, over roads which included some of quite colonial primitiveness. On this occasion, for the only time in my life, I saw a wild deer in its native habitat. Wilbraham village, under the mountain's southern edge, is a drowsy, pleasant town with a quiet main street and great elms. Mrs. Miniter displayed the moss-grown graveyards of the place—one of which, The Dell, includes a dank wooded declivity beside a stream that is said to wash away the earth and expose curious secrets at times. The old brick Academy, built in 1825 and still surviving after many vicissitudes, was another interesting sight. The return trip, beginning in the wild and picturesque woodlands behind the Academy, led over unspoiled colonial roads on the mountain's side, and revealed many of the brooding, unpainted houses of other generations. At one stage of the journey I saw the house where Mrs. Miniter was born—built in 1842 by her grandfather, Edwin Lombard Tupper, and still inhabited by his direct descendants. Among the varied and exquisite prospects along this route is one of a strangely blasted slope where grey, dead trees claw at the sky with leafless boughs amidst an abomination of desolation. Vegetation will grow here no longer—why, no one can tell.

Toward the end of my walk, Mrs. Miniter gave directions for a walk too long for her to attempt, and I followed an ancient road—full of striking vistas—to the pleasant village of Hampden. The town lies at the bend of a stream, and all the houses are strung at length along a road winding up the side of a mountain from the valley. Here the traditional white-steepled church building shelters a thriving grocery store—one of those humour-fraught contrasts in which Mrs. Miniter always delighted. Here, also, stands a World War memorial in the most flamboyant taste (or lack of taste) of Civil War times—the gift of an aged local magnate who remembered the past and knew what he wanted!

The hours spent at Maplehurst among the old books and antiques, with Pettie and Tardee and the Prince weaving dexterously through the narrow lanes of navigation, and venerable Printer often drowsing, purring or sneezing in my lap, will not soon be forgotten. Mrs. Miniter and Miss Beebe formed unsurpassable hosts, and the impromptu course in folklore which they gave me was illustrated at every turn by volumes, pictures, and actual objects from the local past. The fireflies at evening—the distant wind-borne strains of melodious Chauncey tramping homeward across the fields—the delightful agricultural-pedagogical household next door, whose kindly-proferred Model T helped to solve many problems of distance—the tales of other days brought forth by Mrs. Miniter from her inexhaustible store of erudition—all these varied recollections spring up at mention of the name of Wilbraham.

During the final years Mrs. Miniter was harassed by illness—largely an increase of the asthmatic tendency which had long troubled her. Letters, though always cheerful and overflowing with wit, became fewer and fewer. It was hoped that she might attend the Boston convention of the National in 1930, but her health was unequal to the trip.

After 1931 came the illness and ultimate invalidism of Miss Beebe, which placed upon Mrs. Miniter new burdens and responsibilities. There were likewise accidents—two falls involving fractures—affecting Mrs. Miniter herself. And always the anxieties and retrenchments attendant upon the depression hung in the offing. Work, however, went bravely if intermittently on; and the unpublished novels doubtless bear myriad touches made almost at the last.

Messages from the outside world shed many a heartening beam—and the familiar countryside itself, of which she was so wholly and innately a part, must have been a potent balm in its way. Never was she separated from the old things and ancestral influences that she loved so well. Her health gave way bit by bit; but the cherished books and favourite china and homelike confusion of andirons and crickets and warming-pans were always around her, while from her front windows age-old Wilbra'm Mountain always loomed up across the eerie marsh-meadows. She died on June 4, 1934—late enough, perhaps, to have seen the year's first fireflies dancing over the pasture grasses. And now she rests among the time-crumbled headstones of her forefathers in the old graveyard below the mountain—The Dell, with its trees, its shadows, and its spectral stream.

It is difficult to realise that Mrs. Miniter is no longer a living presence; for the sharp insight, subtle wit, rich scholarship, and vivid literary force so fresh in one's memory are things savouring of the eternal and the indestructible. Of her charm and kindliness many will write reminiscently and at length. Of her genius, skill, courage, and determination, her work and career eloquently speak. Though a lifelong antiquarian, she was not one to yearn vainly for the past or bewail the present and future—her staunch mood of acceptance being admirably summed up in one of her rather infrequent specimens of verse; a sonnet entitled "1921," appearing in the pages of the clever *Muffin Man*. There is no better way of closing this tribute than to quote that sonnet complete—for in it so much of its author stands revealed:

"Dear dreams of youth—could one seek your return,
Ask glamour of an earlier spring to glow,
Or clothe in verdure trees now lying low,
In ashes dull cause wonted fires to burn,
Still life's best lessons would be left to learn.
Of many brooks is made one river's flow;
From yesteryears tomorrows thrive and grow;
The future nothing of the past may spurn.

"Nor is aught forfeit. In its course the stream
Denotes accretion, gain for evermore;
So ripples life with joy beyond the dream,
When mellow hues of autumn tinge the shore.
I would not call you back, dear dreams of youth,
So much you're bettered by the present truth!"

Providence, R.I., October 16, 1934

(*The Californian*, Spring 1938)

EDITH MINITER
Edward H. Cole

Edith Miniter was one of the first with whom I became acquainted after I entered amateur journalism in 1905. Mere mention of that date reminds me how little fitted I am to write a biographical memoir of her, for at that time she was already one of the Old Timers whose very existence the Fossils were to thunder against within five years. I cannot attempt to write of her earlier years, despite knowing somewhat and having heard much; but from 1906 on, I came to know very intimately her admirable qualities, and later, too, to feel the lash of her criticism. Amateur journalism, indeed, was the greatest passion of her life. Life, I know, had hurt her. She received new acquaintances "on suspicion." Once they proved to share her love for our world of letters she gathered them to her heart and gradually admitted them to her circle of friends and opened to them a joyousness of conversation and companionship rare and precious. She seemed to find that Jacob Golden and I, who together made her acquaintance as the young publishers of *The Hustler*, were worthy of the privilege; and, neither of us, I am certain, will ever lose from his heart the glorious days of the following five years. Her home at 17 Akron Street, Roxbury, was a Mecca to which came every amateur journalist visiting Boston. Together with her gracious and lovable mother, Lady Jane Dowe, Edith Miniter presided over a salon whose hospitality and brilliance were unforgettable.

She had created the Hub Amateur Journalists' Club in the nineties. That she was the heart which pulsated its life blood is obvious from the fact that although it lived to be one of the oldest organizations of amateur journalists, it ceased to exist after her departure from Boston, approximately ten years ago.

Edith Miniter became president of the National Amateur Press Association at the New York Convention in 1909. Unfortunately, her administration marks the transition from a somewhat Golden Age; and it is the unhappy fact that the convention at which she was chosen, and, indeed, the very fact of her election, gave rise to a bitter attack by the Old Guard (the Olympian Council) of the Fossils upon the participation of mature men and women in amateur affairs. Regardless of the merits of the case, it was indeed one of the ironies of life that the attack should have come in the administration of the one woman to whom amateur journalism was life itself and whose elevation to the presidency was a reward richly deserved and too long delayed. Though friendships of long standing were strained or destroyed, Edith Miniter met attack with ridicule and brilliant wit that kept many of the honors of the combat on her side. Nevertheless, from that day there has been a cloud over anyone who has ventured to remain active, especially politically, in the National Amateur Press Association beyond the period of youth. Although the New York convention of 1933 rather dissipated that cloud into nothing more than thin mist, and although, too, several of those who, over twenty years previously, had attacked her took occasion to mitigate their earlier severity, I feel certain that the injustices of the Young Blood Movement hurt Edith Miniter keenly.

The years that swiftly followed brought other unhappy consequences. Although there was the successful novel, or rather series of sketches, *Our Natupski Neighbors,* to mark the height of her professional success, there came with the World War a changed literary taste that prevented publication of the sequel upon which she was working. There came, too, the death of her loved mother, the breakup of her home, and several unsatisfactory attempts to live with one friend or another. Then, too, there was constantly the increase of asthma. So far as amateur journalism went, these years were marked by her unfailing efforts to keep alive the Hub Club, from which had departed, for one reason or another, most of the older members.

Ultimately she retired to Wilbraham, not far from Springfield, Massachusetts. There her family had property. There her relatives lived. There, in the happier days of her mother's life, there had been an annual vacation, shared infrequently but memorably by such amateur journalists as had the opportunity to make the trip. In the last years of her life she became a semi-invalid. At such times as she was able (infrequent, however) she welcomed short visits from friends; nevertheless, even writing letters became a task almost beyond her strength. She was compelled by reason of ill health to reject an opportunity to attend the convention in New York in 1933. For all that, she retained her lively interest in the affairs of our small world, and several who were fortunate to receive word from her in the past year will cherish the flashes of wit and the occasionally caustic comment on current affairs as well as the kindly and friendly interest and sympathy which characterized them.

Years ago, in the Akron Street days, a happy idea received animated discussion—the establishing of a Haven for amateur journalists, a colony to which we could retreat and hold communion with those we loved and with those, too, whom we fought but really cherished. We all realized, even as we painted the glad picture, how unlikely of realizations it was in this mortal world. But none of us, I know, has ever quite despaired of the hope that in the world to which we shall go, each in his time, there will be a little corner apart where we who have shared bright golden hours in the fellowship of amateur journalism shall come together again for unending days. Should such a dream come true, every one who knew her will look forward to joining that band and finding Edith Miniter as Presiding Genius.

(*National Amateur,* September 1934)

MY RECOLLECTIONS
William R. Murphy

Edith Miniter had many distinct tones. Endeavors to recall these to mind out of the years bring a flood of memories, too numerous and some too fleeting to encompass within the space of a necessarily short memorial tribute to her career in Amateur Journalism. Her personality combined in a rare degree the unusual attributes of efficiency and charm. She was one of the first women to attend a convention of the National Amateur Press Association. It was as Edith May Dowe, that she was the very youthful belle of the 1885 Boston convention. She was the second woman to hold the official editorship, filling out a term in 1895. She was the first woman to serve as president of the NAPA, being elected at the New York 1909 convention, and bringing her unusual power and vast energy to a rehabilitation of the association which had a couple of years previously entered a slump, following the unique and impressive activity which characterized the first half decade of the new century which seemed to culminate in the auspicious circumstances that made my administration (1906-07) the weak peak since the early '90s and the late '70s.

I was her historian and was amazed in compiling the records of her term at how much she had achieved. She gave a new impetus which afforded momentum for several years.

She had distinctions as an author, first of all. As editor, as organizer, as executive, as hostess. She was the focus of Boston's prolonged activity over several decades. She was the inspiration which kept the Hub Club alive through prosperous amateur journalistic years and equally through depressions. To her more than to any other was due the success of the numerous Boston conventions of 1892, 1894, 1900, 1907, 1916, and 1921, as well as many Boston conferences. Increasing infirmities and taxing duty of caring for an aged invalid relative kept her from the 1930 meeting. Her home in Boston was a mecca for amateur journalists. Open house prevailed. At nearly every convention the party which she gave for the delegates was one of the most enjoyable of the entertainment features.

I first met her at the silver anniversary of the NAPA at Dooner's Hotel, Philadelphia, 1901. I last met her, and her charm remained undiminished, at a Boston conference at the United States Hotel, rallying place for Boston conventions, in 1923. In the interim I was frequently her guest at the home of her mother, the poet, Jennie E. T. Dowe, and herself, both delightfully hospitable. I met her many times at conventions and with others enjoyed her keen intellect, her brilliant wit, her well-stored memory of amateur journalism. She made any gathering vital.

As an editor she was effective. Her volumes of *Hub Club Quill, Aftermath,* with classic reports of conventions, and its distinguished editorial and critical comment, and other papers, including the Official Organ, are a monument that will survive. She was ever ready to aid the young editor with contributions, many of them far exceeding in merit the vehicle in which they appeared. Her fiction and essays were particularly good and won her more than one laureate award. She was a master of telling, vivid and happy phrase, she had convincing characterizations and veracious observations of life.

Only briefly can be mentioned her professional work. For many years she was editor of the *Boston Home Journal,* a weekly widely known. Her book reviews were much quoted. In it, too, she published considerable fiction of genuine merit, as she did in other magazines. Her novel *Our Natupski Neighbors* told with insight and sympathy and knowledge a story of modern New England. She wrote much on antiques and New England archaeology, and as an authority. In later years she contributed many reviews to the *New York Times Review of Books.*

Over the thirty odd years I have known her, none went without the interchange of correspondence between us; the last as recently as this spring. A longtime and valued friendship is terminated by her passing, which has saddened me, as I shall know no more her fine spirit, her fine wit and wisdom.

(*In Memory of Edith May Miniter,* 1934)

MEMORIES AND IMPRESSIONS
Ernest A. Edkins

"And did you once see Shelley plain?"— Browning's *Memorabilia*.

In the golden summer of 1885 I journeyed across the pleasant countryside from Hartford to Boston. It must have been a golden summer because I was in my seventeenth year. The thrill of discovery that struck "stout Cortez" silent upon a peak in Darien could scarcely have equalled the less restrained delight with which I had but recently hailed my own discovery of Amateur Journalism. Moreover, I was going to my first convention. It was, if my memory is not at fault, the tenth annual meeting of the National Amateur Press Association.

My travelling companion was Brainerd Prescott Emery—then a tall and somewhat drooping young man with a lackadaisical air, a pince-nez dangling on a black cord, and a thin volume of Rossetti's Blessed Damosel in his pocket—but already beginning to reveal indications of that literary preciosity which later was to label him as the most passionate aesthetician of his period. We were embarking on what seemed to us a great adventure, and beguiled the tedium of travel with callow causeries and ingenuous revelations of those literary idolatries and prejudices which are (or were) the meat and drink of amateur adolescence. Fragments of conversation come back to me, fixed in my memory by the curious fact that it was Emery who introduced me to Swinburne.

"The author of 'Laus Veneris'," he declared, with oracular severity, "is a moral leper—but what a supreme master of imagery and rhythm! Do you remember the glorious surge and swing of his `Hesperia'?" Whereupon he declaimed:

> Out of the golden remote wild west where the sea without shore is,
> Full of the sunset and sad, if at all, with the fulness of joy,
> As a wind sets in with the Autumn that blows from the region of
> stories,
> Blows with the perfume of songs and of memories beloved from a
> boy—

No, I had to admit that I did not remember, and for an excellent reason; but he recited the lines with such gusto that I made a mental note to look up Mr. Swinburne. Meanwhile, and not to be out-done, did Emery recall Lanier's "Marshes of Glyn," written in almost the identical pattern and meter? Ah, there was music for you! And so on, and so on. Finally, and in a most exalted spiritual glow, we alighted in Boston, where an amazing two-wheeled vehicle known locally as a herdic conveyed us to our hotel.

It was at this convention that I met Edith May Dowe.

The year 1885 marked the end of a glamorous lustrum and perhaps the turn of a much longer romantic period in American letters, politics and social affairs. Grover Cleveland had just defeated Blaine for the Presidency. Crude arc lamps were beginning to sputter on Main Street. A few of the new-fangled telephones were in use. William Dean Howells had written *A Modern Instance* three years earlier and was about to earn new laurels with the publication of his *Rise of Silas Lapham*. Henry James was achieving a narrower recognition as the author of *Portrait of A Lady*. The reverberations of Oscar Wilde's lecture tour in the United States had not wholly subsided. MacDowell's first concert in A Minor, presented at Weimar in 1882, was still scarcely known in his own country. Whistler was signalizing his "middle period" with such important paintings as Sarasate and Lady Archibald Campbell, but it is doubtful if the natives of Lowell, where he was born, or of Stonington and Springfield, where he spent some of his youth, were particularly interested. Art had not yet become very important in America. The smug obscurantism of the preceding "long, dark night" was soon to be harried by new and arrogant schools of thought, but only a few heard or heeded the mutterings of thunder on the left. Meanwhile, little was recked of these dire portents in the happy valley of enchantment wherein the naive young scribblers of amateur journalism pursued their mimic affairs, so serenely oblivious of the world of hard realities just beyond their horizon.

On the night of our arrival a group of young people were seated on some red-carpeted stairs leading down to a reception room. In their midst I noted a shy-looking little girl in a white dress and high buttoned shoes. "A little white flower on a crimson background," thought I, being in those days addicted to impressions which I fondly imagined to be poetic. When I was duly presented, she seemed to be both frightened and defiant; the hand she offered me was cold and, I thought, slightly trembling. We exchanged some nervous banalities about the convention but there was a sense of strain.

"Are you a realist or an idealist?" she suddenly demanded, out of the blue.

"A little of both," I confided, diplomatically.

"Idealism," she declared scornfully, "is untrue to Life!"

I pondered this one, but could find nothing more apposite to offer than the feeble Pilatean paraphrase, "what is Life?" Her hands, I noted, were very slender and never still. "She is scared of me," I reflected—"but hang it all, I am scared of her!"

"Who is your favorite poet?" I probed, intent on carrying the war into Africa.

"My favorite poet?" she echoed, vaguely. "Why, my favorite poet is—" but I was never to hear the confession. At that moment a radiant young vision of blonde loveliness in a cascading party dress and blue ribbons came floating down the stairs. More introductions, and this time no cold hands but a pair of devastating blue eyes and a smile of such lethal sweetness that I was slain on the spot. At this far cry her name eludes me, but I have the vaguest sort of notion that she was George Day's sister—or was that a later episode? It is curious that I cannot recall her name, though I never spoke to her again; it might seem more curious that I can recall my brief encounter with Edith Dowe so vividly; but the truth is that the frightened little Dowe girl had something more than mere girlish charm; to borrow Pater's phrase, an intense spirit seemed to burn within her, with a hard, gem-like flame. Soon there was a general movement in the direction of the meeting room, and Edith Dowe passed out of my ken—but not without accolade. Metcalf the Magnificent tossed a remark over his shoulder to another Pontifical Personage (how thrilling, just to be near those great men and hear them talk!)—something about "that queer, clever little girl" and a reference to "Emily Brontë," but it was too deep for my juvenile comprehension. It amuses me now to recall how we of the fledgling brood stood around, dumbly adoring those sophisticated Big Shots—the Metcalf brothers, Dennis Sullivan, Finlay Grant, Antisdel, a dozen others. I remember Antisdel scribbling a ribald note and passing it to me during a nominating speech. It was like being admitted to the Fellowship! I must have almost passed out with delight, and I know that I treasured the note for years. Still, silly as it sounds, I might well be pardoned for my hero-worship. Antisdel was a darling of the gods, as charming as a young prince in a fairy tale, a prodigy of learning, a linguist whose French and German was as fluent as his English and who read Aeschylus and Petronius Arbiter in their original texts....But that is another story.

In venturing a contribution to this Memorial I am handicapped by my unfamiliarity with Mrs. Miniter's later work. When she published "Cindy's Child," the ensuing discussion was as furious as that provoked by Zola's *La Terre*. I did not like her sordid little story and said so with such unnecessary frankness, if not brutality, as to arouse James Morton to majestic wrath. Mrs. Miniter did not lack for champions, and before the rumpus was over I had been expertly drawn and quartered. Undoubtedly the honors were with Mr. Morton, to whom at this late date I tender the broken lance of the vanquished. But Mrs. Miniter was then only experimenting with media and methods; within a few years she developed an authoritative technique and became a master of her particular genre.

In 1916 her narrative entitled *Our Natupski Neighbors* was published by Henry Holt and Company. It was a penetrative analysis of the reactions of first and second generation Polish immigrants to the fatalistic immobility of a decadent New England community. With typical stupidity the book cover blurb recommended *Our Natupski Neighbors* to readers "who care for country characters and like a good laugh." Thus the publishers described a book wherein tragedy and irony mingle in a social pattern too sardonic for tears but certainly too poignant for laughter, unless it be the laughter of insensate clowns. It seems scarcely necessary to add that the book was not a "best seller," but perhaps accomplished its author's purpose in becoming a *sucès d'estime*. Objective in treatment, it presents a loosely woven series of episodes with almost complete authorial detachment. Here, one observes, the method exemplifies the Flaubert-Maupassant canon that an artist should stand outside his work—observing and recording, but without the slightest attempt to rationalize or synthesize, save by the most delicate indirection; if the reader is not intelligent enough to do his own rationalizing, let him stew in his own juice! But is the method really deliberate? Is it not rather the result of Mrs. Miniter's own ineluctable spiritual heritage—that tight-lipped New England reticence, that almost fantastic parsimony of verbal commitment symbolized by the Yankee's eternally sautious "seems as if"? Like her own deliciously drawn characters, Mr. and Mrs. Slocumb, the author leaves most of her deeper reflections implicit. The technique is surgical, the style reportorial, and the product a work of austere art for the particular few; in short, for those penetrative minds capable of grasping all that Mrs. Miniter has so delicately (and perhaps inevitably) left unsaid. For it is profoundly true that had she moralized and rationalized over the disturbing social and economic implications of her story until all who can might read, the story would not have been worth reading.

My friend Lovecraft, in a recent letter, expressed the opinion that "Mrs. Miniter was a quiet, ironic, unemotional realist, perhaps closer akin to Jane Austen than to any other well-known writer." Well, the suggested parallel is somewhat startling at first, but only because we are apt to think of the tremendous gulf of times, manners and *mise en scène* which yawns between the *Mansfield Park* or *Pride and Prejudice* of 1816 and the *Natupski Neighbors* of a century later—instead of seeing, as Mr. Lovecraft does with his unerring instinct for fundamentals, their essential congruity of treatment. I think, however, that Mrs. Miniter may have been more consciously influenced by the contemporary reclame of those remarkable stories of the Tennessee mountains written by Charles Egbert Craddock (Mary Noailles Murfree) which were published in the middle eighties—*Down the Ravine* and *The Prophet of the Great Smoky Mountains*. It is not at all certain, on the other hand, that she was conscious of any external influence. She knew her New England people down to the tap roots of their strangely tangled ancestry. She may have read Craddock's dialect stories and Sally Pratt McLean's satirical chronicles of Cape Cod folks, but it is improbable that they had much effect on her predestined work, which was to observe and describe, with ironical economy of phrase and with consummate sense of drama, the simple lives of an inarticulate and bewildered people. Yet, even as they fell forever short of adequate self-expression, so too did Mrs. Miniter, and in the end she died with her message still locked in her heart.

In my youth I was frequently moved to lament the futility of amateur journalism; this arose from my inability to perceive or my reluctance to admit the basic object of the movement, which was, of course, to print little papers, and not to produce literature. It seemed to me nothing short of tragic that this fascinating field of amateur letters should fail to turn out brilliant future novelists, essayists and poets, instead of producing a crop of mediocre scribblers and "mute, inglorious Miltons." Scribner, it is true, became a great publisher, and Beck a great publicist but what other graduates have attained any distinction in the field to which their amateur efforts pointed? I can recall but few whose names are even remembered today. And even in the annals of amateur journalism they are practically forgotten, for that fluid and unstable institution has little pride of tradition. Fanny Kemble Johnson published a notable book of poems, and later wrote a novel of Virginian manners; Mack contributed some sparkling but ephemeral criticism; Spencer browsed learnedly in Shakespearean fields; but what has become of them? O'Connell, meditating cynically on the mistakes of a contemporary, bequeathed an epigram too good to die, though it lives only in the memory of a few old timers. And perhaps only a few of his readers knew that he was paraphrasing Pope when he said, "To err is Heuman!" But after all, we were momentarily happy in our fool's paradise; we loved, and fought, and scribbled the most delightfully pretentious nonsense, before the turbid tide of life bore us away to our prosaic destinies. We did not realize our dreams of distinction in the field of letters, but we took with us many beautiful and precious "memories beloved from a boy." And so, musing rather sadly over that Golden Age of Innocence, and my failure to make the most of its fleeting hours, I find myself wishing that I had been less censorious, a little more kind, in my earlier priggish criticisms of Mrs. Miniter's work, and hoping that she may have long since forgiven me—for Pope, who said so many wise things, said nothing truer than "To err is human—to forgive, divine."

October 3, 1934

(*The Californian,* Spring 1938)

AS I KNEW HER
Arthur H. Goodenough

It seems no more than yesterday that Edith Miniter was in our midst, showing like a bright candle in our little circle of patient plodders. Leadership seemed to come naturally to her, and her spirit seemed to permeate the National.

And now the bright candle has been quenched forever, so far as this world is concerned. While it was never my lot to know Mrs. Miniter personally—through correspondence and the medium of her literary work, and incidentally her political activities, I felt that I knew her fairly well.

Her delightful social side, of which others have often made mention, was not for me to share; but her mental likeness, as conveyed by her enchanting stories, her delicate and graceful poems, and her pungent and pithy editorials, is to my mind both clear and vivid.

Although successful in entering that wider professional sphere which lies beyond our little republic of letters, she never disdained nor disregarded her first love, and continued her amateur activities until acute physical infirmity stayed her hand.

In her death Amateur Journalism suffers a blow that can scarcely be repaired, and the world is poorer by the loss of one more brave, bright and gifted spirit!

November 6, 1934

(*The Californian*, Spring 1938)

SOME THOUGHTS OF EDITH MINITER

James F. Morton

The thought of Edith Miniter is inconceivably precious to me, calling up, as it does, the memory of an unbroken friendship of some forty-five years. Her name was among the first brought to my attention upon my entry into amateur journalism in the early part of 1889; and my admiration for her brilliant and original mind has never waned. My first meeting with her came not many months later, though the preservation of precise chronological remembrance has never been one of my strong points. According to my best recollection, her removal from Worcester to Boston came shortly after the organization of the Hub Club in early 1890. Credit for this organization belongs almost entirely to the true-hearted and energetic worker of the best type in Amateur Journalism, whom we then knew as Mrs. Ella Maud Frye, now still living under her maiden name of Murray. Willard O. Wylie, Charles E. Wilson and I were among her assistants, present at the birth of the club, which had at the time of its demise the longest record of continuous existence ever achieved by any local organization associated with Amateur Journalism, and in later years rivaled or excelled only by the Blue Pencil Club. Edith Miniter, however, from the moment of her arrival in Boston, became a prominent figure in the Club, and proved by far its greatest asset. The time was to come, in later years, when its very existence, to say nothing of its more brilliant achievements, might with entire justice be claimed to be almost wholly due to her untiring vigilance in its interests, as well as to her acute and versatile mind.

Who among us, that was Boston in the latter nineties, or even of those who, though residing elsewhere, enjoyed the privilege of occasional visits to the Hub, with admission to the charmed circle of Hub Club devotees, can forget the delight of those intimate little gatherings in the dainty Roxbury home, where Edith Miniter and her equally gifted mother, Jennie T. Dowe, kept open house for their Amateur Journalism friends? Zeal for Amateur Journalism was the one indispensable passport to the hearts of these most perfect hostesses and delightful companions. Sparkling wit, penetrating comment, incisive but not unkindly satire, thoughtful and serious discussion of plans for the good of the amateur fraternity and its organizations, made the hours pass all too swiftly. Nor was the culinary art forgotten. My deepest pity is offered to the epicure who has gone through life without once tasting those inimitable pop-overs which Edith insisted on calling by the humbler name of muffins. And if trouble beset any member of the Amateur Journalist fold, nowhere more readily than in that same little household were sympathy and practical helpfulness more speedily at hand. Truly, those were unforgettable days.

Accustomed to heavy and often painful responsibilities, Edith Miniter was always game to the core, and always strong to meet whatever fate had to offer. She had more than her share of bitter trials; and it is hard for her friends to know that her last years were those of suffering and ill health, just when her talents had won her a wider recognition, and when the road before her seemed to stretch clearly and uninterruptedly toward a high rank in American letters. Had she not been thus stricken down, she would have gone far. Her passage from amateur journalist literary activity and from professional editorial labors to the larger field of American fiction and humor, with the registration of her keen and sympathetic observation of humans and their manners, met with instant and ungrudging acceptance by the competent spokesmen of the literary world; and a brilliant future was promised and assured, which could have been thwarted only by what actually happened, in the breakdown of her physical powers.

Her entire connection with Amateur Journalism, which was at all times her chief non-professional activity and something more than what we commonly term a hobby, was that of constructive leadership. Never, till the summons came to lay down the task of life, did her love for the institution flag. While her vital interest was in the development of the literature of Amateur Journalism, and in raising the standards and keeping them high, she did not hesitate nor fear to enter into the political arena, when volunteers were needed to defend the better principles of its leading organization. But she never stooped to seek victory by underhanded means, nor to consent to the slightest deviation from the path of openness and unwavering integrity. She cherished no ill will against honorable opponents. If, however, there was a weak spot in her makeup, it consisted of an inability to forgive and forget, where she had once detected plainly dishonorable conduct. Even the passage of long years left her unconvinced of the reform of one who had once gone definitely wrong. There was nothing personal in this sternness of attitude, the one remnant of Puritanism which always clung to her; it was rather an innate feeling that honor among human beings was so sacred a thing that they who tampered with it must evermore be excluded from complete confidence. Some of the most important passages in her amateur career can be understood only by comprehending her point of view in this regard.

It was at a comparatively early period in my own career that I reached the conviction that the unlimited male ascendancy in the control of the National Amateur Press Association was not altogether wholesome; and that the presidency of the organization should be recognized as an honor to which the female members might as fittingly aspire as their brethren. Several years passed before the opportunity came to do anything about it. Meanwhile, I began to lay a foundation for the presentation of the name of Edith Miniter, whom I recognized as best deserving and best fitted to break the ice in this respect. When, in due course, the time seemed ripe, it was not an easy matter to secure her consent, since service, rather than the satisfaction of personal ambition, formed the key to her entire amateur activities. After she had reluctantly given permission, the campaign was not an easy one. There was the usual ultra conservative hostility to innovation. There were those who were embittered against her on account of her unyielding attitude toward what she had forcefully condemned as unallowable trickery. There were impatient ambitions to be quieted or thwarted. All these obstacles were eventually overcome; and it was one of my proudest moments, when I saw our labors crowned with triumph, and was enabled to greet her as the first of her sex to be elected president of the Association, which she had served so long and faithfully in a humbler capacity.

In spite of unusual difficulties and of unforseeable betrayals, her administration was able and efficient; and it ended forever the tradition that the highest official position within our gift was earmarked "For Men Only." With the later distinguished careers of Jennie

Kendall Plaisier and Hazel Pratt Adams in memory, no Amateur Journalist of the present or the future will venture to stand forth as an apostle of masculine monopoly of office in our honored organization. The administration of Edith Miniter thus marks one of the epochal events in Amateur Journalism as a progressive institution.

As a friend, she was staunch and true, being loyal to the core. Her natural acuteness was not the mark of a cold nature. On warrantable occasion, her tongue or pen could be as caustic as witty; but these occasions were few. Her humor was intense, but stingless, except when employed against disloyalty or dishonor. With all her powers of discernment, she was not infrequently imposed on by those who knew how to play on her warmly sympathetic nature. Could all her unobtrusive acts of simple kindness be made known, they would fill a volume of no mean proportions. We who knew her best, loved her most. It is hard for us to think of her as gone; and we shall never cease to miss her. Her parting has left a gap in the ranks, which can never be quite filled.

(*Californian*, Spring 1938)

MY FRIEND EDITH MINITER
Nelson Glazier Morton

To me Edith Miniter always was the embodiment of Amateur Journalism. That I was privileged to count her as a friend for more than thirty years is a memory I shall always cherish.

When after my schooldays in New Hampshire I came to Boston to work, the hospitable apartment at 77 Berkeley Street was one of the first places where I was made to feel thoroughly at home. In the years that followed that feeling steadily increased, thanks to the unfailing friendliness and hospitality of Edith and her wonder-ful mother, the never to be forgotten Jennie E. T. Dowe. After my marriage the same friendship was extended to my wife and in later years to my daughter Dorothy. One of our pleasantest recollections is the summer when we were afforded the happiness of repaying in some small measure our friendly debt by having Edith and her mother stay for a period in our home at a time when Mrs. Dowe was in poor health.

At the very first, when I was a boy of nineteen, I was a little in awe of Edith Miniter. My brother James and sister Mary had known her well for some years. I had been poring over amateur papers for four years and was well acquainted with Edith's record in Amateur Journalism and with her reputation for a rather biting satire. But after I came to know her I soon found that the satire was chiefly an intellectual pastime and that she was one of the most kindly and warm-hearted of women.

It was to her friendly interest in me, I believe, that I chiefly owed my election as president of the N. A. P. A. in 1900. The old-timers who remember the campaign and Boston convention of that year will recall the strenuous efforts of Edwin Hadley Smith to engineer into office what he called a "Young Blood" ticket and the fruitless attempts of the more conservative element to persuade Warren J. Brodie to accept the presidency which could have been his for the mere nod of his head.

It was not until Brodie, after repeated refusals to run, gave his final emphatic "No" at the convention that the necessity of seeking another candidate became wholly apparent. I have never known just what went on behind the scenes at that time. All I know is that Edith Miniter and Frank S. C. Wicks asked me to accept the nomination, Wicks promising to help me out in the publication of a regular paper as required in the constitution—a promise which he faithfully kept. Of course I was flattered and with little realization of the tremendous burden involved in the presidency I accepted. I don't know how many other possibilities were canvassed in that hurried caucus before the leaders settled on my name, but I am inclined to attribute to Edith Miniter the strategy which suggested the naming of a slightly known boy of nineteen rather than one of the older and prominent members, so as to spike Smith's guns and kill his claim to sponsorship of the only "Young Blood" available for the presidency. Well, I was elected and in the strenuous year that followed Edith was one of my most helpful supporters.

In the next few years I took a pretty active part in political affairs in the N. A. P. A. and the tickets which Charlie Parker and I sponsored in the old *Literary Gem* met with a considerable degree of success. Edith Miniter was always with us in these efforts. Toward the end of her own year as president, when from no fault of her own she was suffering the keen disappointments of an administration made unsuccessful by lack of support and the machinations of her political enemies, Charlie and I took keen delight in giving her a genuine surprise by arranging a banquet in her honor which was a huge success. I have always felt that this helped a little to brighten those unhappy days of her amateur journalistic career.

As the years went by and the disparity in our ages became less noticeable we came more and more on the same intellectual footing. We didn't always agree in our ideas of Amateur Journalism or of other things, but we always respected each other's opinions. In the N. A. P. A. and more intimately in the Hub Amateur Journalists' Club we worked hand in hand.

There have been several instances in the history of the N. A. P. A. of the able litterateur and the shrewd politician combined in one person. Of these I believe Edith Miniter to have been pre-eminent. She delighted in far-seeing political combinations which in most cases were highly successful. Notwithstanding the imputations of her opponents on many occasions, I am absolutely certain that she always made a fair fight. Moreover, she never felt any personal animosity toward those whom she opposed, and often she entertained them in her home with the same cordiality that she extended to all other Amateur Journalists.

Her literary talent was of a high order. She was mistress of the mordant phrase but she was no less skillful in evoking by a happily chosen word the spirit of pure fun. In her more serious writings she showed a depth of thought and an insight into the comedy and tragedy of human affairs rare among the imaginative writers of Amateur Journalism. These same qualities appeared in her professional writings, notably her book, *Our Natupski Neighbors*. Had her health not failed her in her later years, I am convinced that she would have made even more notable contributions to professional letters.

But it is as friends and hostesses that the inseparable names of Edith Miniter and "Lady Jane" Dowe stand out in the memory of those who knew and loved them. The hospitality of the apartment on Berkeley Street and afterwards of the rambling old house at 17 Akron Street in the Roxbury district of Boston was nothing short of amazing. Visiting amateur journalists from all parts of the country invariably were entertained there and it was an unfailing rendezvous of the old Hub Club and of its individual members. The atmosphere was that of the genuine old New England home, with its unfailing good cheer, informality and abundance of delicious food and drink. No one who was a constant participant in those delightful affairs will ever forget Edith Miniter's muffins or the punch which she served in the huge bowl which belonged to the Hub Club.

Edith Miniter had her full share of disappointments and sorrows. Yet she was not embittered and always she would put her personal troubles in the background to extend a word of cheer or to do a deed of kindness to someone else in need. Hers was a life of loving service. In her very last months, when she herself was half crippled with asthma, deafness and eye trouble, she was caring for a cousin who had been stricken with a shock. Yet she sounded a cheery note in the last letter I received from her, in March, 1934.

"I get out of the house about twice a season," she wrote, "but we have heaps of company and going on, so I'm not lonesome."

Edith and her mother were more like sisters than mother and daughter. Edith called her mother "Jane" and was never failing in her devotion to her. The most touching recognition of our friendship came when Edith asked me to say a few words at the funeral of Mrs. Dowe. I was glad to pay tribute to the mother. Now the daughter is only a memory and I can but add this small leaf to her laurels.

(*The Californian,* Spring 1938)

MY ASSOCIATION WITH EDITH MAY MINITER
Truman J. Spencer

Iknew Edith May Dowe, later Mrs. Miniter, for many years, and by reason of this my life has been richer and more enjoyable. It is hard, almost impossible in fact, to express Mrs. Miniter's personality in words; it was unique. Shrewd and incisive in intellectual energy, she was kind and sincere in her emotional reactions, a devoted and loyal friend. To use a Shakespearean phrase, she was "as witty a piece of Eve's flesh as any," but there was no malice in the flashes of her merriment. I remember that she wrote me regarding some paragraphs she sent me for publication in the 1894 Convention Number of *The Investigator*: "I think that there is nothing ill-natured in them, certainly nothing I mean so—just a little fun." This was characteristic and true.

I met her many times at National and New England conventions, Hub Club meetings and picnics, and other social gatherings. I had a correspondence with her covering more than a quarter of a century. She contributed stories, excellent stories, to my papers, beginning with her "Dot" in my Farewell *Sphinx,* and notable stories in the Midwinter, Christmas, New Year's and Farewell issues of my *Investigator*. We worked together over the selection of stories for publication in my *Literary Cyclopedia*. I printed issues of her *Aftermath*, and the *National Amateur* when she was Official Editor. In all these years, and in all this personal intercourse and correspondence I never knew her to utter an unkind word or express one unworthy thought, even under the severest provocation. And she had, at times, much to provoke one. She was always courteous and unusually appreciative of the slightest service. This was especially brought home to me during the many trying incidents in connection with printing the *National Amateur*. Officers hindered her by delaying reports, mails carried proofs astray, and types cut strange capers at times, but her temper was ever serene, and her spirit was ever that shown by the characteristic twist with which she closed one of her letters: "All's well that doesn't end otherwise."

I first knew of the existence of Miss Dowe through the receipt of the following letter in April, 1883: "Will you please send a copy of the *Sphynx* containing the last paper of J. D. Miller's `Essay on Poetry' to E. M. Dowe." I first met her at the New England convention at Gardner that year, but did not really make her acquaintance until the Boston convention of the National in 1885, where she was one of the first young ladies to attend a convention of that organization of which she was later President. For many years thereafter she was one of the outstanding personalities of the conventions I attended. Her flashes of wit, her kindly solicitude, her unfailing good-nature, her flow of anecdote and reminiscence, all combined to make her company not only enjoyable, but one to be looked back to with delight.

I remember, as one example of the richness of her humor, her saying of the writing of many amateurs that it was "like the woman who made the pudding all out of her own head."

There have been few among those whom I have met in life's career, whose friendship I valued more or whose personality I admired more.

(*The Californian*, Spring 1938)

EDITH MINITER
In Memory of Edith May Miniter, 1934

Born on Wilbraham Mountain, Massachusetts, May 5, 1869.
Died at North Wilbraham, Massachusetts, June 8, 1934.

Through her the hills their age-long memories told;
Their centuried heritage unmixed she bore;
And now those rock-strewn slopes at last enfold
Her kindred dust—a child come home once more.

She knew the lore of distant, crowded ways,
The sights and language of the market place,
But deep within, there flowed through all her days
The currents of New England's changeless race.

No lyric lay of golden dreams was hers;
She held a mirror to the world she saw,
Vain hopes she left to fools and flatterers,
Content with what a truthful pen could draw.

Others might sing of heroes, pomps and powers—
For her the quiet substance of the age,
She caught the faint, dull tones of common hours
Till living figures thronged each vital page.

Mankind she studied with a searching sight;
Folly she pictured with a smiling mind;
Whilst over all she felt the hovering light
Of brooding years and what they leave behind.

Always she dwelt amidst the ancient things;
The household relique and the crumbling tome;
Her ears could catch the beat of hidden wings
By moss-grown grave, and lonely hillside home.

Wit, learning, art, were hers in amplitude,
And kindliness that helped the loyal friend,
And charm and skill that fostered and renewed
Parnassian dreams in others without end.

Merged with the meadows where her fathers sleep,
The weary clay has come into its own;
The mind, too keen for any tomb to keep,
Lives in the fruits and memories it has sown.

—H. P. Lovecraft, Providence, R I., September 10, 1934

Amateur Journalism

The Aftermath

(N. A. P. A., 1909.)

The clans they came together,
  Far out from north an' south;
Those prolific in pen an' print,
  In thought an' in word o' mouth.

An' they came from where the sun doth set,
  An' far from the golden east;
An' the small were like unto the greatest,
  An' the greatest like unto the least.

An' they worked for the love o' the work—
  Untouched by the golden rod—
An' that is the nearest the earth-man
  Can come to the one called God.

—J. E. T. D.

This Number is the work of
EDITH MINITER
JENNIE E. T. DOWE
MINNA B. NOYES
MABEL F. NOYES
ETHEL MAY JOHNSTON-MYERS
LAURIE A. SAWYER
HELEN M. SMALL

SALUTATORY

It is with a feeling much akin to timidity that we enter the arena wherein are gathered so many of the bright youth of the country, and join the galaxy of "new recruits." We will only say that our utmost labor shall be for the good of Amateurdom and our own self-improvement, that we shall endeavor to make each issue somewhat ahead of its predecessor, and certainly shall not belong to the coterie of "Vol. I No. 1, never-seen-henceforth" amateur journals.

We hope our contemporaries will be lenient towards our failings, and that our faults may be such as can be eradicated by time and experience. When we first entered the outskirts of the 'Dom, we had not the slightest intention of ever becoming an amateur editor, feeling neither ambition nor capability. But during a year we have learned much. We have become aware that amateur journals lose their interest, that the editorials seem alienated to your mind, unless you are yourself a full-fledged amateur, and an editor likewise. To fully appreciate and enjoy the publications of the 'Dom, one must unite themselves to the institution in its fullest sense, and, wholly realizing this, we join the fraternity, and hope that our lack of experience has not already condemned this first fledgling sent forth into the amateur world.

(*The Worcester Amateur*, September 1884)

EDITORIAL

To an individual easily astonished Amateurdom offers continual opportunities for wonderment. Why, oh why, may we inquire, are so many laudable plans and schemes allowed to pass by undebated?

The Amateur Authors' Association; the Amateur Alumni; the grand fraternity magazine; and the especially practical idea of establishing a series of sizes and forms for amateur journals to be issued in; are only a few of the 'dom's various unfruitful schemes.

It is a surprise that Truax's proposal with regard to amateur departments in reading rooms and libraries has been so cordially received. Judging from other examples the very goodness of the idea should have condemned it. However, the plan is now in full practical working; and, as far as we can see, is certainly productive of nothing but good.

One reason for not forming an amateur authors' association may be the small number of amateurs who are authors alone. And with the Amateur Alumni, amateurs of the present have nothing to do. It is solely the fossils—the old-timers—who would be benefited by such an institution, and it therefore remains for them to agitate the subject and form the association.

The majority of fossils are scattered in their places of residence, while their business and social interests are diverse. They left Amateurdom at different times, not quitting it simultaneously, as does a graduating class at school or college. Many of them, when they left, intended to return to the ranks; to have joined an alumni association would have seemed like bidding farewell forever to all hopes of activity. These reasons seem to us amply sufficient to show why the alumni will probably long remain a scheme to be fulfilled only by the future.

Amateurdom lacks strict organization, its number of members constantly changes, while its leaders are often those incapable of commanding even themselves. A table containing estimates of the present life and occupations of old-timers might be of interest to tyros, as showing them what their future would most likely be; and we should presume the fossils themselves would enjoy meeting each other at stated periods, and discussing the "halcyon days"—otherwise than this the alumni association would be of but little use.

Next on our list comes the fraternity magazine. At first we thought this plan failed for lack of necessary funds; but when Koch, after establishing the unparalleled *Telephone* on a paying basis, and making it a true representative of the 'dom, could not arouse the Napa out of its apathy sufficient to accept the fruit of his unprecedented labor, we wonder not that, sick and heartless, he gave up his unappreciated toil, and, too disgusted to even rail or argue, quietly quitted the lists. Others have been treated likewise, before his time, and after reading of Grant's failure of 18–, and musing over Koch's of 1884, what amateurs of the present instant will dare attempt to awake the Napa from its blind sleep?

The establishing of a scale of sizes for journals is a comparatively new scheme, and seems to be debated only by such editors as go to the trouble and expense of binding their exchanges. We scarcely believe this plan will ever become a reality, as the unwritten motto of Young America is "Absolute Independence," and no one cares to be ruled in even so unimportant a matter as the size of his journalistic publication.

When we are a member of the Napa, a committee shall be formed, comprising all the acknowledged leaders, and those considering themselves leaders—which is about equivalent to saying "a committee of the whole"—and before this body shall be laid all plans and schemes, emanating from no matter what the source; and they, after voting on each plan, shall report at each National convention; when if the vote is a yea vote, the scheme shall immediately be put into working order, and if a nay vote, it shall be forever dropped. And a special stipulation should be that no scheme could be presented more than once, and thus would we do away with all "periodical discussions." However, this would deprive Amateurdom of several truly interesting subjects, and each recruit would not have the chance—as he does now—of trying his skill in debating the several tough questions which have agitated the 'dom for the last decade. After all, there is nothing new the world over, our most original writers only view old subjects from new standpoints. But the majority of amateur editors seem to be massed on the same standpoint; for, as each scheme is proposed, one and all pronounce it "splendid," "first-rate," "just the thing to place the 'dom on a firmer basis," "fine," "ne plus ultra," and just as regularly is each proven to be unpractical.

(*The Worcester Amateur,* October-November 1884)

DEFINITIONS DEFINITELY DEFINED

Recruit—One who has published a paper, but never attended a convention.

Amateur Journalist—One who has attended a convention and had a paper "in press" two and a half years.

Fossil—Anyone who has seen two campaigns.

Convention—An excuse for eating.

Conference—Ditto.

Friend—An amateur whom we have never met.

Correspondent—A girl amateur to whom we write letters signed "Yours fraternally."

Acquaintance—An amateur whom we address as "Dear Old George" on postals, and as "Mr. Jones" in the convention hall.

Enemy—Any amateur to whom we write notes beginning "Dear Sir."

Vacation—An occurrence simultaneous with conventions.

Banquet—A good "chaser" for a sirloin steak and accompaniments.

Paper—What our friends get out.

Publication—What we get out ourselves.

Proxy—Another way of saying "If."

Quotation—What we call into requisition when we are afraid to use our own language.

Apostrophe—Something the average amateur printer never heard of.

Work—What we put in when we run for office.

Pernicious Activity—What our opponent exhibits when he runs for office.

Critic—An amateur who lacks means to publish a paper and brains to write stories of his own.

Shakespeare—Otherwise Bacon, a man who lived in order that Truman J. Spencer might have something to quote.

Speech—What an amateur says at a banquet when he is called to respond to a toast for which someone else is slated.

A few extemporaneous remarks—Reading, at a banquet, of an essay covering six sheets of foolscap and worn round the edges from being conned over.

(*The Aftermath*, December 1894)

SOME BENEFITS OF AMATEUR JOURNALISM

"Will it pay?" is a perfectly right and legitimate question to be asked when about to enter upon any new undertaking. This question is as pertinent in regard to Amateur Journalism as in regard to anything else. In order, however, to candidly weigh the matter, one must have clearly in mind the benefits which may be derived from a connection with Amateur Journalism. To have a clear knowledge of what may be gained from Amateurdom, several have been asked to tell of the benefits which have accrued to them.

To one who has remained in connection with Amateur Journalism for a period of years, the woof of life becomes so interwoven with the pursuit that it is easier to tell what Amateur Journalism has not done for the individual than what it has. I have Amateur Journalism to thank for many happy hours, for many sincere friends, and for much experience in the line of work which is now my profession. Although Amateur Journalism differs in many ways from Professional, yet the one is the only practical school where one can be educated for the other. The kindly criticism of my friends helped me to do away with some of the crudities of early days, and what small successes have been mine in later years I feel are due more to my amateur training than to aught else. One learns in no way to write except by seeing one's writings in print, and to the young author, whose work is not adapted to see the light of publicity in professional papers, the world of Amateurdom is open. But beyond giving me a profession, Amateur Journalism has given me friends whom I prize above all others. I am sure that in making this statement I am only echoing that made by many other old-timers. To a true Amateur Journalist the friendship of one who is not connected with the dear old cause is soon forgotten, and I know of several amateurs who even now affect to despise Amateur Journalism, and call it useless and mere "boy's play," yet who make the paradoxical boast that the only friends for whom they care were first met in the ranks of Amateur Journalism. Many a boy and girl whose early life has been spent amid environment not wholly congenial has eagerly greeted the friends made in amateur circles, where a common ambition animates all real workers, and they, like me, can say of

Amateur Journalism, "What has it done for me?" It has brought me appreciative friends of the truest character, and hours of the happiest kind.

(*The Monthly Visitor,* January 1896)

A HALLOWE'EN INVITATION

¶ Your presence is requested at an observance of Hallowe'en, at eight-thirty o'clock, Friday, October thirty-first, at seventy-seven Berkeley Street. ¶ As a condition of admittance, please bring a stick of wood that you have stolen, and be prepared to tell the story of the theft while it burns.

Sincerely,
Edith Miniter.

(Excerpt from "Chiquita's Comment" in *The Literary Gem*, January 1903)

HALLOWE'EN HAPPENINGS

It is always a pleasure to recall happiness—yes, despite that pessimistic poet who wrote that "sorrow's crown of sorrow" was recalling happier things. For myself I find it agreeable, as October comes around, to remember the numerous last days of that month, when, with a few "Hub Clubbers" around me, I have watched the night die.

My first Hallowe'en party was a product of bad weather, and occurred on the proper date in 1894. Mrs. Ella Maude Frye and myself just then lived in the same house, and at about five p.m., remarked on what a very, very stormy evening it was, and how impossible for anyone to be abroad, in such weather, who was not compelled to be out by important business. Having settled this we at once hied us to telephone booths and began to arrange to get out as many people as we could, for an impromptu celebration of the eve. Whether or not this could be called "important business," I don't know, at any rate eight o'clock found Mr. and Mrs. N. W. Small, E. T. Capen, James F. Morton, Jr., and heaps of other Hub Club members, assembled in our humble home, and we repaid them for their bravery by giving them apples to "bob," flour and soot to smudge their faces with, nuts to name, and all the necessary paraphernalia for rank foolishness. In my memory the only important event of the evening was James F. Morton's allowing some lady who was present (I can't now recall who) to cut off a lock of his luxuriant hair, the deed being accomplished with the largest possible shears. I have somehow always fancied, since, that the J. F. Morton hair looked thinner on one side than the other—but I have never been able to decide which side.

Having started the ball rolling, the next Hallowe'en party, given two years later, at 119 Berkeley Street, Boston, was somewhat more formally arranged for. Its chief feature was a toasted marshmallow eating contest, in which Mrs. E. M. Frye, who never could bear to be beaten by anyone, and Miss Mary E. Wynne, then president of the Hub Club, soon distanced all competitors. Mrs. Frye was bound to win, but finally was forced to give Miss Wynne the lead, by a single marshmallow. To tell the truth, the affair was decidedly unfair to Mrs. Frye, as Mr. Capen, who officiated as toaster for her, burned the marshmallows disgracefully, while Miss Wynne's toaster served her with delicious lumps delicately browned. Besides, the two ate so much that marshmallows really ran out at the end, and Mrs. Frye was fed by "ringers" of Turkish delight, furnished by Mrs. H. M. Small.

For the nine years of my living at 77 Berkeley Street (up three flights) I think only one year (1904) missed a Hallowe'en observance. At that of 1897 we first told ghost stories for prizes, the best prizes (the tales themselves) going to John L. Wright, who was caught red handed taking notes of everyone's story on his cuffs, for presumable future use in the "literary skindicate" which he hadn't then formed, but was going to. It was for this party, too, that I recollect providing mince pie as fit stuff to give weird Hallowe'en dreams, and remembering, about five minutes before the first guest yelled up the speaking tube, that the flat boasted only six forks. Like the famous Peterkins who once didn't have teacups enough to go round at a tea party, I was saved by recollecting that the Lady from Philadelphia had telegraphed "In Philadelphia when we haven't enough of anything we borrow from the neighbors." In flatland one is supposed to have no neighbors, but there was a newcomer to the house who had broken the ice by asking for the loan of a mop, and the day—or rather the evening—was saved.

I think it was the guests to the party of 1898 who refused to go home at all. I remember seeing various people coming out of cat naps to listen to John L. Wright and James F. Morton, who considered 3:30 a.m. a fit hour to start a discussion on literature vs. social reform, and Mrs. L. A. Sawyer has always recalled this as the year when she walked to Allston with those two (they still discussing) and arrived just in time to be taken in at her own door along with the day's supply of milk.

By 1899 most of the old games had become stale and in trying to strike out in a new line I made a "Jack Horner" pie, with foolish gifts at the end of each string; I also provided "prophesying quotations" for everyone to take away, and was afterward told that some of these hit of unknown but interesting anticipations to the life. Indeed, my bewildered guests gave me credit for occult powers of the highest sort, when really I owed all my success to "Bartlett's

Familiar Quotations." A portion of this evening, too, was spent by each and every one going about with the name of some famous "spook" pinned on his or her back, and trying to guess, from the conversations of others, what spook he or she was supposed to be. And you would never realize, until you tried to provide a sufficiency of ghosts for a large party, how scant is their number in legend and fiction.

In 1900 we tried the same thing over again, only the names this time applied to people supposed to reside in Hades. And the affair broke up with a couple of solid phalanxes claiming (1) that Catherine of Russia did belong there, and (2) that she didn't.

In 1902, as Boston was suffering from a fuel famine, it was suggested by some kind soul, like John Gilpen's wife,

"Although she was on pleasure bent, she had a frugal mind"

that each guest should fetch a stick of wood, to keep the open fire a-going. This was later amended so that each was obliged to steal a stick of wood, bring it, and tell the story of the theft while the stick burned. Well, C. A. A. Parker slid in with a slab pulled from the fence of the Misses Fitz-Gerald's home, after an evening call upon those young ladies; Miss Ethel May Johnston brought a huge lump of well-seasoned hardwood which with great trouble she had abstracted from the woodbox during a visit at the home of the Mortons in Andover, N. H.; and Frank S. Morton almost brought down the house (literally) by attaching a cord to a great piece of maple and dragging it up all three flights of stairs to the flat. Perhaps the best stories, however, were told by four residents of the Sawyer home in Allston, every one of whom had employed the youngster Marshall Sawyer to "swipe" the wood, bewildering that youth to such an extent that he actually proposed giving up school and getting a job to caddy at a nearby golf links—as he supposed the fuel was intended for home use, and that somehow the family fortunes were at too low an ebb for any to be purchased during the ensuing winter.

So attractive had dishonesty become that the next year people were told to "just steal" and tell the story of it. The prize went to Walter H. Thorpe, who stole a beautiful box of stuffed dates, and had an attendant yarn of how he ordered $4.98 worth of fancy groceries in order to get the clerk in the rear of the store changing a $5 bill while the "kleptomaniac" stunt should be done.

It was this same year that a fortune teller was introduced. Swathed in white garments, veiled and gloved, she sat in a dimly lighted apartment, and from time to time called for those in the parlor to listen to her lore. She had all the pasts and presents down so fine that everyone implicitly credited her prophesies for the future, but no one was able to solve her identity, since no one was missing of those usually guests at these affairs. Finally, however, she was unmasked and discovered to be Miss Bertha A. Johnston (now Mrs. Franklin Ayres). Her clever ability as a seeress provided a refreshing variation on the programme, which it must be remembered invariably included such time-worn features as bobbing for apples—Thorpe always beating out—blowing out candles held at arm's length, the number of whiffs necessary indicating the number of years one must wait to find a life partner (and those who were to wed within the coming year generally couldn't extinguish it at all); floating candles in nut shells on pans of water, dropping melted lead through the handle of a doorkey, throwing apple peelings, and so on. Several years we had great fun with "invisible letters" written in lemon juice, and only readable after application to the heat of the fire. And speaking of refreshing things brings to mind refreshments—and the year I tried to have a "harvest home" table, decorated with pumpkins and cabbages, and having the salad and olives in pepper cups. As a consequence everyone took a mouthful, yelled, "Gee, it's hot!" and afterward refused everything but cold drinks. Then there was the year Laurie Sawyer confessed she was "dying for big, puffy home-made doughnuts," and I planned to make some, but being somehow delayed didn't, and palmed off on her those from a common, everyday bakeshop—and she wouldn't stop complimenting me for a whole year.

Last year (1905) the party was not so violently novel, but I recollect that everyone was supposed to steal something from some other guest, and then answer twenty questions as to what it might be. And, strange to say, nearly everyone present chose Mr. James Thomas Kirby as a victim, and denuded him of handkerchiefs, newspapers, souvenior postals, hats, etc. at such a rate that he actually went out before the refreshments came in, saying angrily, "If I don't go now, I shall be obliged to return home al fresco." It took us most of the rest of the evening to try and make out what we thought he thought he meant.

The greatest pleasure of these little affairs has been the abandonment of care, and also of any personal prejudices which might interfere with perfect comradeship. To just be jolly, sit in the firelight and give the best of oneself in song or story for the benefit of the rest—such has been our endeavor always, and success has crowned our effortless effort. It is on occasions such as these—and on similar social occasions to be described by other hostesses later—that the Hub Club comes to be a compact unity. Made up as it is of the most individual of folk, they are united in a desire to get from life the good cheer which alone makes life worth living—and amateur journalist clubs worth while.

(*The Olympian*, January 1907)

THE AFTERMATH

Near-Fossils and the like perchance remember
How in the dear dead days beyond recall
A paper used to come—about November—
Bringing the genial July into Fall.

The years swerve on—the swerves they number 'leven,
Since Aftermath was last upon the scene,
A sudden leap from commonplace to "Heaven"—
Brings resurrection from what once has been.

With the best intentions we, of 20 Webster Street, Allston, (next door to No. 36), welcomed the coming guest on July the second. It is now noon of the 10th, full time, one might think, to speed the parting. But what are the evidences of speed?

Echo, (clever guy) answers "None!" So likewise answer L. Sawyer and W. V. Jordan, unrefreshed even after the unparalleled indulgence of two hours of sleep in a real bed. So repeats M. O. White, out all night, and killing time so that the neighbors may see him coming in at 1 p. m., and believing he has been with his "folks" in the country. So might have replied the writer, who feared to close her eyes at 5 a. m. lest she miss the ice cart at noon.

Of the guests, one greeted the rising sun in rapturous terms as "a beautiful red high ball." What more need be said?

We have informed them there won't be any luncheon either, but at that the best they offer is 5 p. m., the 11th. A three-dollar bill has just passed for the sixth time from Conserve to Splinter No. 2, their performances reminding us of those characters in some Dickens novel who eked out an existence solely by selling fried fish to one another.

A truce to mere jesting—we know we're not wittiest
Nor highbrow nor lowbrow, so let us be serious,
Nor had Cleveland "exclusives" on these—or the prettiest—
And if pleasure's a lunacy, we were delirious.

(We assure you this weggery is quite "in the light of a friend." And if W. Paul Cook's linotyper makes that waggery there'll be murder in Athol. He may save all he likes on the United by "absolutely cutting out proofreading," but our instinct for Thrift runs not such ways.)

The first that I remember, after digesting the 'phone girl's very lucid explanation of Conserve's first telegram ("Lady, I think he's so darn fond of you that he ain't even waiting to get his hair cut nor nothing") was going out with Ouija to buy supplies. They were the last. Not that we lacked credit, but grocers in Allston do not keep open between midnight and early bed time. Besides, during conventions, one exists always on that which supported David Copperfield in Chapter XXVIII.

Saturday night, July 2nd, shines out in memory. Mark it with a white stone. Some beauty sleep was secured.

Dawned Sunday, departed some for auto trips to Salem, N. H., arrived local ams. in "clean bib and tucker," arose loud shouts. "Paul Cook is came." A chicken dinner was served, and they were not ALL seated round the festal board either.

Sunday night was born the Epgephi. The birth sadly hindered by the progenitor, who would insist on going back to first principles and rolling unctuously each luscious sentence with which said "poiposes" were promulgated. (Yes, L. Theobald, Jr., came next day. We are now meditating an essay on the influence of bagwigs upon hair nets.)

Dawned Monday and arrived Splinter No. 2 and 54 and 7-8ths. The first-named was greeted vociferously because he was a friend both old and tried (that is we often try him). The last mentioned was also greeted vociferously because he had not come before. Arrived Alcalde once again from where he had been (no place in particular) to see what was doing (and nothing was) and was greeted vociferously because he hadn't been to breakfast (with us). And whatever he'd had it couldn't have been of the correct component parts because he at once retired to a couch on the back porch and called for Ouija to bring forth the Royal Pill Box.

Descended the Orb of Day (thank goodness we're done for the time with that Dawn thing) and arrived all the Hub Club and people from Malden. Then did each shine forth in characteristic manner. L. Sawyer pridefully inviting guests to stroll on One O'Clock Hill, and Lovecraft sonorously inquiring "With what objective?"

Mrs. Thompson asserting in the manner of modernity, "Associating as I do with actors, actresses and singers I need not waste time in acquiring knowledge in the old-fashioned manner, but go all of *The Tale of Two Cities* in two hours, when it took Alice three weeks to read it," and Niece Alice making a worse of bad enough by exclaiming, "Yes, and I've read it three times." Mrs. Parker accepting private invitations to observe various bits of house handicraft, and Charles A. A. Parker qualifying for the Saga class and as for the young blood flooring of 'em flat with his magnificent past in A. J. (And how else, quo' Some of the Quotables, may one judge of the future but by the past?) Houtain, as may have been mentioned, made the welkin ring (poetic license, we never have such a thing in the house except on Tuesday), and M. Oscar White took up the Negro ʃQuestionʅ and argued either pro or con, we forget which, and proved it, too. And Mesdames Fairbanks and Lane (the last named coming all the way from Iowa—especially?—well, why not?) brought forth real conversation and considered it not thrown away. And R. Kleiner discovered the prettiest and the wittiest—though a poet and slightly near-sighted at that—and never wandered far from E. Dorothy MacLaughlin, W. V. Jordan, "the golden girl," and "Sumac," the winsome product of Gallic-best. And Cook oft chortled in his glee, and Lynch enjoyed himself fairly well e'en while he

"Saw a hand we could not see
That beckoned him away."

And Orville and Flora Fuller were unwelcome only because they came so late, while Mrs. Jackson with her sweet silences often

"Healed the blows of sounds,"

and the one who made the punch, "Aunt Edith," was so fully at home that hardly anyone noted her presence (particularly when saying good night).

Miss Alice Hamlet and H. P. Lovecraft went to Dorchester, chaperoned by Mrs. Thompson and escorted by Mr. White, some then draped their forms on ancient relics (Amateur Journalese for couches on which have slept the best ex-presidents in the history of the N. A. P. A.), while others used stores of yet untapped conversation until the 4.30 car left at half after three.

Dawned Tuesday, with excursions to City Point, Castle Island, South Boston, and a lunch for which the check had to be 85 cents, "because," quo' the waitress, "it adds up to 83, but we ain't got no place for pennies on the printed part." It was an extraordinary lunch, forcefully enjoyed by Chesterfield-Lovecraft. His comments at a later hour, while he playfully brushed the snuff from his gold brocade waistcoat (not the silver tissue) bear expurgation.

So sweet its memory that he could not bear to erase it from the tablets of time (whatever they be). At the door of the Quincy House he quit us cold. "It is the hour of 7.30," saith he, "and even at this moment the 7.30 train leaves the South Station, an mile away. The co-incidence is too valuable to leave go unmarked." We should think so!

A fine dinner, marked by one untoward incident. L. Sawyer fell in love with the Jazz band and G. J. Houtain neglected buying it until he had spent all his money buying a lot of other things.

The next dawn would appear to be Wednesday. We are sure of this because up to now Wednesday seems to have always followed Tuesday. It is one of the few manners and customs remaining untouched by the war. I believe we went to a place called Nantasket where we ate several times also several clams. As most of the visitors did not like clams the home folks had a good feed! (Note to remember for 1921 convention.) Telegrams came from Cleveland, and shouts of joy followed the name of Marjorie. On arriving home we may have sat up or gone to bed. I think it was one or the other.

Thursday—dawned. A trip was taken to Mount Auburn, City of the Dead. So different from our city. They could sleep. And did. We could, but—inference too obvious. On the way home Kleiner was violently anxious to waste two dollars and a half of his own money on something which he wanted for himself. Such selfishness! Of course it was not permitted.

Friday dawned with general relaxation in vogue, but the arrival of M. Oscar White with a "let's do something" air, revived all the guests "and everything" and taking our second wind in our teeth we went to Revere Beach where were done all the conventional things undone to date, such as dancing on the sands and thinking of buying Houtain a ten-cent souvenir to keep forever in memory of the evening, and finally deciding not to spend all that money on just one mere man.

After Revere a Symposium was held. The one great feature of a Symposium is that while on other nights one goes to bed in the morning on a Symposium night one does not go to bed at all.

This brings me to the beginning, when M. O. White proved to his own absolute satisfaction that the sun actually does rise as poets and milkmen tell and see. Have I exceeded my 100 words? Have I?

> Farewell, dear friends, a pleasant melancholy
> Dwells with me when you're far who once were near—
> Yet not too sad am I, soon we'll be jolly
> In July just another little year.

—Planchette

(*Epgephi*, September 1920)

EPGEPHI MAISUINGS

Let me introduce myself. My full name is Lord High Bother, House Tat, of 20 Webster Street, Allston, Mass. Once it was just Gray Brother, out of something Mr. Kipling wrote (I mean the one who sent *Barrack Room Ballads* from a place called India, "tied round the stomach with a piece of red string like a fat brown baby," he says, though for the nine lives o' me I can't see what that has to do with it) —not the man who was here Epgephi week, and called "Rudyard" because one of my mothers never could remember his name was "Rheinhart." The one who named me Gray Brother was the lady part of "50-50," but some time last winter it was changed to "Gray Bother." Winifred Virginia Jordan did it, just for why? She seemed to think I was a bother when I went up two flights of stairs and asked her to come down 'em and open a door for me. And it was twice as much work for me as for she, seeing's I had four feet to manage, and anyhow I meant it as a compliment. Otherwise there were plenty of folks right on the first floor to do it.

She wrote a verse about it, too, which I might as well put in here. She's always writing verses when I want her to be doing something else.

If G. Brother had a Mother,
Who took more care of He,
Less of yowling, less of prowling,
In Tip-Top house would be.

Little Winny is grown skinny,
G. Brother sees to that!
She's always chasing, down stairs racing,
Jest waiting on that Kat!

—Little Winny,
Secretary and Lady in Waiting to Lord High Gray Bother, House Tat.

You see, I haven't a "mother," because I'm owned in partnership. One-half belongs to Ouija and the other half to Planchette. As one or the other is forever going away I'm half orphan most of the time. My color is maltese, and any punning reference to a "Maltese cross" make me like that. Even Planchette never said anything so bad, though an amateur named Truman J. Spencer once gave her the "worst punny record," for remarking, "Praise Dodd from whom all pleasings flow" when an amateur named Dodd sent a chest of Tea to the Hub Club.

You see how truthful I am. I own right up I'm of catty disposition, instead of hiding the fact, as did Mrs. Ethel Myers' "Hortense" way back in 1914. That creature wrote a great deal for the amateur press, pretending to be a human girl, and got mash notes and everything. Even Edward H. Cole sent her a lovely letter beginning,

"Horty, Horty, hear my plea,
I's in love with little thee,"

and when he found out the truth he must have felt 'twas an awful catastrophe.

The first I heard of Epgephi week was one day when Planchette was serving coffee to Ouija and Mis' Jordan in what they call the "Green T. Room," which is just any place where they set out some green-colored cups and saucers and her grandmother's spoons. The last two was sitting on a dreadful old piece of furniture, a lounge that is just "the shadow ot its former self," like the one the amateur Mr. Wills spoke of long time ago in a book called "Mons. Paul de Fere." Its name now is "The Ancient Relic," and they are going to have a bronze plate put on it, they say, naming the long list of worthy presidents of the N. A. P. A., who have reposed thereon. (Only if they include that man Houtain, who was re-elected, I guess he'll complain. Anyhow, he complained of the Relic. Said he hadn't no repose at all the time he tried it, it was "concave," whatever that is. I guess he meant conVEXED.)

"We positively can't go to Cleveland," says they, "let's get up a consolation party."

So they named a lot of nice people, only discounting by saying before each name, "Of course it won't be possible to get HIM," or "but HE won't want to waste the holiday visiting US."

However, it's a long way to Ohio, and letters of acceptance cheered us all up. The first arrival came in a thunder storm, and a taxicab the very day our Boston contingent, Mrs. and Miss Outwater, started for Cleveland. He's always in a hurry, that man Houtain, as you may believe when I say he beat his own telegram saying he was at the station and would we summon band. Planchette and Ouija were out at the stores buying things to eat, and after a few hours they decided not to waste any money on music. They'd need it all to satisfy his demand for food. They say in 1902 he had a "hearty laugh," but now it's a "hearty appetite." Why, he even complained because they gave me a few giblets from Sunday's fowl! Think of a lawyer "who makes a hundred dollars every time he crosses the street" (as they said in 1917) bregrudging a paltry chicken heart to a little cat!

Although the affair hadn't properly started they were awful hilarious Saturday evening, especially after my "pa," C. M. Sawyer, came home. The others made him and company go out in the kitchen and prepare toast and coffee, and company would show his ignorance of latest improvements by lighting the gas with a match every time, and then "pa" would put it out and show him how to light it properly by the pilot that they keep always burning just to save matches. They wasted a whole box of matches saving 'em that way. Men are SO economical.

It was the next evening, Sunday, the 4th, that this Epgephi thing was invented. They were all sitting round the table in Ouija's dining room. Some more of the Boston amateurs had come to join in, and W. Paul Cook had arrived from the Athol of America and Winifred V. Jordan named him "The Dependable." She's great for calling names, is that girl. She even called George Houtain "Early."

First they made the man from Athol "Alcalde," I suppose because he was sitting at the head of the table in the largest arm chair. And he laughs just as much as George, even if not quite as loud. Next, instead of a "Vice-President" they had a "Virtue Alcalde," because, they said, there was no taint of "Vice" anywhere about this organization—at least then, when it was just five minutes of age. I hung around a while, waiting for an office, but I presume they didn't "smell" any "mice," so finally I went off to bed.

The next morning there was a great deal of discussion as to when two others would arrive from Providence. They had sent a message saying it would be "in the early afternoon," which sounds plain enough, but that bunch can discuss hours and hours over just anything—whether or not to let me get on intimate terms with next door's hens for instance. They were still discussing when the two rang the door bell, and some weren't half dressed (hadn't got their earrings on).

The two who came were Mr. Lovecraft of Providence, who has so many other names there would be more than enough had he as many lives as I, and Mr. R. Kleiner of New York. They had been quoting each other's poetry to each other and taking each other's pictures doing it for two days, and I guess were pretty glad to see US.

That evening a whole lot more folks came, and everybody had to sit down and write something for this paper. I tell you it was some literary sight. Winny Jordan was dictating and Mike White was being dictated to, being informed he had just "got to" get to work, and all the fountain pens had been borrowed. The refreshments wasn't much. Some kind of purple punch and crackers and stuffed dates and the like. Why don't they serve fried liver or canned salmon?

An elegant telegram was sent to those folks in Cleveland, with most of the names signed (not mine—I'm a little careful where I put my paws). It would show, they said, how our hearts and thoughts was way off in Ohio, even though, as Mr. J. Bernard Lynch (other half of 50-50) kept singing, "'Twas a starry night" in Allston.

Well, talk about Cats being "night owls." I was tucked up in my crib hours before the house was still. Mrs. Thompson and her niece, Miss Hamlet, took Mr. Lovecraft home with them to Dorchester, 'cause he said he'd just go to have a "quiet room to himself," and there was no such thing here, though there's 18 rooms and 6 halls in this establishment. They even put "Alcalde" on the back porch to sleep, but I guess he didn't sleep much, owing to that "Milkman's matinee" which my Ma Ouija got up, and which she attended wearing the beautiful gown she had made for my little brother Marshall Sawyer's wedding and had considered too elegant to wear to anything since.

Says she, "Mr. Milkman, what's the matter the milk being stole every day lately?"

Says he, "Well, Lady, if you'll always be up like this to take it in it won't be no trouble."

'Twas about 4 A. M., Ouija says his politeness was due to the fact that once in his life milkman seen her dressed up. But I don't think any of it made much of a hit with Alcalde, 'cause next morn-

ing he left town at a very early hour. He didn't even wait for breakfast, which was probably a good thing, as they had scarcely enough
for Conserve, though nobody else wanted much. I think it was this
morning they put up an awful bluff on that man. He said he would
have "bacon and EGGS" and by making the last into an omelette
they put him off with one instead of two.

The very first thing they 'phoned over to Dorchester and found
the man who is in a class by himself was up and ready for some
more fun, so they decided to take him to City Point. I can't say anything about the day, as I was left at home. When they left the house
he was assuring Ouija he "was quite willing to be a regular Hooli-
gan—for the day," and I guess he was. They came back without him,
and found a queer-sounding message on a piece of paper:

"Moitoret......Outwater Boston."

There were a lot of other names which I can't remember. Anyhow when they read it they began to laugh, and shout "Three
cheers for Marge," which I didn't understand, no such object being mentioned. Then they would laugh some more, that is Ouija
and Planchette and Conserve would, while that man they named
"Splinter" just sat with his arms folded and looked disgusted. Finally they compared themselves to melancholy Jacques in the Shakespeare play, who laughed an hour by the clock, and, out of consideration for the neighbors, went into the house.

I seem to remember the next day was awful hot, and they kept
me company some of the time, only going out for lunch, and to see a
graveyard and to a Bahai meeting. This last I suppose had something
to do with Baa-Lamb, but they never fetched me home so much
as a bone. And coming back from the Graveyard Splinter lost the
streetcar transfers and saw a pipe he wanted to buy, though he has
about 26 now. He claims to be a poet, but I have my opinion of one
who talks more of a cheap $2.75 pipe than of the last resting places
of Holmes, Longfellow, Lowell and Kate Field. Says the pipe was
"perfect"—how could he know that until he'd smoked it a while?
And he didn't like Lowell's gravestone a bit. Well, perhaps the
great man himself would just as soon not have to have it.

The day after they got up early and telling me to be a nice Tat
and not have words with that horrid yallar cat from up the street

they went to a place called Nantasket. Mis' Jordan's mother Munsey Jackson had to feed me, and I kept her pretty busy, but I should
judge they was about as busy eating themselves. They had clams,
with so much melted butter that Conserve was able to conserve a lot
and bring it home on his white flannel clothes. And they had club
sandwiches and when the waitress didn't know what A La Mode
was Conserve went to work and took some cake and put the ice
cream on it and said that was it. Most as clever cooking as he was in
our kitchen. I understand it was such a cheerful day that they were
even able to listen to a reading of one of Mr. Lovecraft's stories—that
one about a likely boy who grew up looking into a tomb.

All this while, remember, Conserve was either typewriting this
paper, or eating, or going out to lunch, or suggesting a snack or saying, "When is dinner?" And Splinter, too, even though he is a poet,
was always what he called "A Bite."

Ouija said this was only a NEAR convention, but they acted
about as it 'twas a real one.

Friday morning that jolly man named Mike White called over
and asked them all to go out to Revere and ride on flying horses and
shoot the chutes and get washed in the Human Laundry and fall
off the Roulette Wheel. Of course they accepted, and called on the
'phone to a lot of other people, but when he was gone they said,
"We will not fly on horses nor shoot any chutes nor enter any Human Laundry nor will they get us on to any Roulette Wheel." But,
they added, "All the rest of you may do these things if you want
to."

I don't know what they did or didn't, but they came home about
midnight and kept ME awake till morning. They sat round in that
same room where Epgephi was organized, only Planchette sat in
Alcalde's chair and held me so I could listen and learn. The subject seemed to start with something Splinter had said on the Beach
about "Love minus Emotion," whatever that is, all the rest seemed
to think peculiar if not impossible.

And Splinter mentioned some of the poets who showed their
love for lovely ladies by running right away from them, and Ouija
didn't think much of that, because you see it didn't give the lovely
ladies any choice at all in the matter. Then Mike White quoted
from a poet named Byron who wrote about a butterfly being pur-

sued, and losing all its beauty when it fell into the hands of the pursuer—probably you know the poem—and Planchette argued that that was foolish and she never liked comparing female character to butterflies anyway. Conserve talked, too, but me and Winifred Jordan we never said nothing. Then one of the men told a awful story about his pa owning two goats that went round peaceable and happy until it occurred to his pa to hitch 'em together with a yoke, and then they spent all their time trying to get apart. No one believed it, (that his pa owned goats) but it broke up the setting. Mike White went home, but the rest started out to breakfast at Mis' Hayses (she keeps one of those One Arm places) and met him and made him go along.

Sunday morning my "pa" Charles M. Sawyer had to dictate his piece for this paper, besides ladling out breakfast, not giving ALL the bacon to Conserve. It was different when Conserve served. Then they bid each other goodbye all over the house, after which, I understand, they did it again at a dining place called the Bird Cage in the Quincy House (like to dine there myself in case it's full of what bird cages often are) and then once more at the dock where the Metropolitan Line Boats go out.

And then, instead of coming home to look after me, I having been some neglected during that hectic week, they must needs troop off to J. Bernard Lynch's office, and all have treatments from Violet Ray Machines, and because they got so braced up they went out to spend the evening with Mike White.

Regular Die-Hards, are they not? Why, even on the way home, they debated if there was anyone who would stand for a call from them at midnight, and decided if Maplewood wasn't so awful far they'd go out and rouse the Parkers! Wonder what the Parkers are like, that they should be considered likely to stand for such behavior? Anyhow, they settled 'twas too far, so they had coffee at Mis' Hayses, and came home and washed the dishes, I think they were dishes from the week before.

And when someone suggested sweeping someone else quoted the man Splinter, who on being told the floor was dusty observed, "Oh, no, that isn't dirt on the carpet. That's only MY ASHES."

If anyone doubts that a puss-cat could have noticed all this and written it out, I'll add the poem Winifred Jordan put in an envelope

115

and pinned to the kitchen door for me one day when Planchette had gone visiting:

Tweet Muver:

> I fot 'at 'ou would 'ike to know
> 'At I is 'onesome w'en
> 'Ou go away an' leave 'our Tat,
> An' jess w'at he do 'en.
>
> 'Ou see, dear Muver, I is dood,
> (I al'ays is th' same)
> But, 'is time, w'en 'ou went away,
> I learned to 'ite my name!

And there was my paw print to prove it. Of course I don't write so kittenish now. Since Epgephi week I'm a wise

TAT.

(*Epgephi*, September 1920)

It pleasures us exceedingly to offer our readers a condensed novel by the renowned Mr. Goodguile. Why pursue the works of this author through Tryouts, Vagrants and National Amateurs, as yet in press, when here is the quintessence? Similar attention is promised later to such of our eminent fictionists as merit it.

FALCO OSSIFRACUS
By Mr. Goodguile

Any form of inquisition into the meaning of this will be fruit-less. Favour me, an' you will, with eternal confinement in a gaol, and everything that I now relate will be repeated with perfect candour.

Again I say I do not know anything at all about it, which is probably why I am making it the subject of this narrative. It is true that I have been for 18 years his closest friend and we have been seen by reputable witnesses near Greenwood, N. Y., Sleepy Hollow by the Hudson, Mt. Auburn, Cambridge, Mass., and Grant's Tomb, Manhattan, but that we possessed tastes mutually morbid or a predilection for graveyards I must strenuously deny.

I seem to remember a weird evening in November. The place was, of course, a cemetery; over the fence peered an inquisitive, waning, crescent moon, and on the fence a vulture and his vulturine a raven and a couple of cormorants remained couchant. Behind the wall I discerned the loud moan of several man-eating sharks, from which I augured that the sea was not above a league distant. A few skulls and cross-bones lay in the foreground, while coffin plates, shreds of shrouds, and mattocks which I instinctively knew apper-tained to gravediggers, scattered around loosely, completed the re-markable scene.

I had, for some time, missed my companion, but as he was most frequently absent when we were together I thought little of the oc-currence. Indeed, the next moment, my attention was arrested by the hurried passing of a completely articulated skeleton, holding its nose, from whence the bright blue blood of a Colonial governor streamed. And this was rather unique, because it had no nose!

Meaning to employ a phraseology which my readers will at once recognize as the common and natural expression of frequenters of tombs, "How's his nibs?" I inquired. Unfortunately a slight nervousness changed the "n" to "r," and the offended object disappeared without replying. I succeeded better, however, with the next bag o' bones, which came forth applying a skeleton hand to the base of a spinal column and groaning frightfully, which was the more peculiar, as it has neither lungs nor windpipe.

"Your pal," came the response, "Iacchus Smithsonia," the name was originally John Smith, but it is always my will that my friends bear a name of my choosing and as cumbersome a one as possible, "is cleaning out Tomb 268."

It was indeed so. In the exact centre of the abode of corruption stood the self-elected subsidiary of Perpetual Care. His shrunken eye sockets, his dropped jaw, as well as practically hairless cranium, proclaimed at one sight a youth who at 15 dwelt far from normalcy, and the impression gained rather than lost by the pennies which, in accordance with a characteristic freak, he invariably wore over his flashing organs of sight. Alone he stood, brandishing the thigh bone of a remote ancestor. I say alone, for the pile of unassorted bones in the corner could hardly be called company, nor yet the half dozen grinning wraiths that floated about in the noisome atmosphere of the sepulchre.

"I am really sorry to have to ask you to absquatulate," he said, employing the choice diction which is so peculiar to we of the educated aristocracy, "but this ain't no place for a feller with cold feet."

As he spoke he pleasantly indicated a ladder dripping with ichor, whatever that is, and bordered by encrustations of nitre. I most wish now I'd made this a poem. As I was unable, through horror, to start at the moment, he went on, "Make yourself scarce, cut sticks, fly the coop, go way back and sit down, 23 for you, advance to the rear, vamoose!" All of which, uttered in the mellifluous tones of unperturbation for which my friend was famed, having no effect on my shattering nerves, he added, politely,

"Good God, Goodguile, get out or I will kick you out!"

At the same time he employed a gesture which in a flash made plain to my understanding the cause for the flight of the second fleeing skeleton.

After that ensued comparative silence. Indeed, I know not how many interminable aeons I wandered stupified through cenotaphs, slabs, mausoleums, urns, icy hands and marble hearts. I do know that I narrowly escaped being bilked of breakfast at my boarding house. The hours are 7 to 8:45 weekdays, and this was of a Tuesday, but not the one the man died of—I strongly desire to obviate any monotony of analogy in this tale.

To my absolute amazement Iacchus was at once discernible as not present. His glass was turned down, as Omar Khayyam recommended, and his Sunday-clean napkin remained folded in its ring as he had placed it the previous evening, cranberry sauce stain outward.

Probably I showed trepidation. I know a few knives and spoons clattered to the floor, a plate shattered the window as it passed en route to the area-way, and my once full cup of coffee flooded the table cloth. My nerves are generally well in hand, I am able to remain calm in the face of any number of ghosts, nor is the miasmal gas of disinterment in the least displeasing to my olfactory organs, but I must admit that seeing my friend's absence, with the odor of Ancient Greece, possibly from frying potatoes, was too much.

Just as I lapsed into unconsciousness the landlady's raucous voice issued as from a necrophagus shadow. And this is what it said:

"You fool, he's got indigestion from a supper of Grilled Bones!"

(*The Muffin Man*, April 1921)

MY MOTHER AS SHE SEEMED TO ME

THE TIMES—THE TIMES THAT USED TO BE

This will be largely from my own recollections—with some references at the beginning to things I have been told. All of it will
seem ancient history to the reader of 1921—when every house does
not have a parlor, or a three-ply ingrain carpet nailed to the "mop"-
boards; when red "tin-carts" do not drive to back gates for rags,
and our kitchen dishes are no longer tin, but agate or aluminum;
when hand organ men do not support monkeys of frayed appearance; when young men use Ford cars rather than top buggies as
implements of courtship. Well, they were happy days, those of old,
though butter spreaders were not discovered, and the only bananas
were red ones. One knew then that the five-year-old child showing
all its leg was safely called "Sonny," and women of 40 hid their age
by dyeing their gray hairs, and then confessed it by never appearing
publicly except in that one good black cashmere. All dress skirts
were six yards 'round, and every clothes reel showed six white
petticoats to each female inhabitant of a Monday. As for the men,
they grew beards and were darned proud of them, fortunes in Gil-
lette razor stock being of the future; their trousers were cylindrical,
as stove pipies, also their Sunday-go-to-meeting hats; neckties were
tied properly once and for all when bought, and after the wearers
got middle-aged and well to do they stuck diamond studs in the exact centres of their boiled shirt bosoms. Everyone had beefsteak and
hot griddlecakes, with no fruit or cereals, for breakfast, and dressed
the beds with pillow shams, and drew up window shades by main
strength and tasselled cords that were always breaking, and presented "Rogers groups" for wedding gifts. Even virtues and vices
have undergone metamorphoses. Novel reading was once a crime,
more specially reading those of George Eliot, because her home life
"wasn't quite correct." Also it was wrong to sew on Sunday, or to
act like the inhabitants of New York, who never went to bed until
11 o'clock, and "ripped out an oath easy as anything." Therefore
men swore only in the company of the like-minded of their own
sex, women being content with wooden damns. But it was quite all

right to buy a ticket in the Louisiana lottery, and most people did for themselves and each of the children. Bath rooms, appendicitis and cathartics had not become topics of conversation in "mixed" company, though some of the stereopticon pictures displayed on marble-topped tables would make the hair of today stand on end. Half-tones had still to drive out engravings, electric cars to displant horse ones, telephones to make morning calls unnecessary, safeties get the better of high wheels, and movies push theatres to the wall. The war was that affair of the '60s and most young men hoped there'd be another, so as to give them a "chance."

About here the world stood when I began to take notice of it and of my mother. She was a young thing, short and slender, with bright gray-blue eyes, very pink cheeks, and a great deal of curling auburn hair. She wore a pretty dress, generally blue, and when she chastised me, which occurred only once and at so early a period that I cannot recall the cause, it was with a blue and gold volume of Mrs. Browning's poems. I have just looked up the book, its contents include those most famous of love poems, Sonnets from the Portuguese. The fly-leaf is inscribed, "Jennie E. Tupper, 1862." My mother always thought a great deal of Mrs. Browning, but somehow I have never cared much for her writings since that day.

Her Family Tree

In wood-colored houses on bad roads radiating from the old Bay Path of Western Massachusetts my mother's ancestors lived for nigh a century and a half before her own advent. None of them came over in the Mayflower, being probably as distrustful of experiments as their descendants came to be, but most of 'em embarked as soon as there was settled going and wolves were not actually at doors.

On her mother's side were the Olds and Oulds from Dorset in England. Dr. Robert arrived in 1669 and accumulated some property as well as 15 children to inherit it. Of the sixth generation from him was my mother's grandmother, Ruth Olds. Families had already begun to fall over, Mrs. Ruth's numbered a mere twelve. Then her daughter (my own grandmother) bettered that by having only two, one of each kind. For me—I am an only child. As before noted, passing years bring changes, and not alone in plumbing and heating systems.

Of my mother's paternal ancestors were the Tuppers, who also came over as soon as there was anything to tie up to. The Tuppers built a house which stood until burned last April on Cape Cod; there the Tupper descendants go every summer and learn things about themselves. My mother would have liked that, but the organization came too late for her to participate. Indeed, this fascinating game of seeking characteristics among progenitors is one of extremely modern development—at least in this country. It gave Jane Tupper Dowe many a hearty laugh. She enjoyed coming on a relative who in the good old days of clergy-worship shocked an entire camp-meeting by baptizing frogs in a sacred pool—or an ancestress who "really enjoyed a big wash if she had a pint of rum." Mostly, of course, one seeks out the best about these by and goners. Jane Elizabeth's grand and great-grandparents were mostly of the New England farmer class, respectable and respected, thrifty yet never rich, well read yet never highly educated, "clever" in all definitions of that word, yet not in the least geniuses.

My mother was born at 6 o'clock on the morning of December 11, 1841, in the town of Wilbraham, Mass. The sun was just showing hints of scarlet in the sky, as her father always remembered and often mentioned. He was but a common farmer-carpenter, yet something of the poetry of the dawn affected him on the day which was also the dawn of life for his only daughter and second child. Seventy-six years later, at the same hour, on March 6, 1919, she was to meet the dawn in another world.

Wilbraham is a small town in Western Massachusetts, on the edge of the famous Berkshire Mountain region. The main street is lined with elms, there is an academy there with beautiful red brick buildings set about on wide fields of green. The railroad is two miles away and a lumbering old stage with rats of horses still forms the only connection with "the Depot." The principal industry of the place is funerals, there are two large and prosperous graveyards to which the dead are brought from miles around, and even from far distant cities.

My mother's father bore the name of Edwin Lombard Tupper, he was ruddy of face, with blue eyes and auburn hair. So also was his mother, both of whom "Jane" copied in these particulars. They were all short of stature and inclined to stoutness after reaching middle life. Her father's maternal grandfather was named David Shield; he was a captain in the Revolutionary Army, and had also fought in the French and Indian wars. He was a man of rather wide cultivation for his times, many of his leather-bound volumes are still extant. He gave his boys classic names—Hector, Mentor, Hiro and so on. His wife was evidently of homelier taste which accounts for a Hannah and a Sally.

From Captain Shield came one strain of the Irish blood which accounted for so much in my mother's work. These people were all long-lived. Captain Shield lived to be 83; his daughter, my mother's grandmother, to 98, and her father to within a few days of 86.

On her mother's side of the house there was another touch of Irish. Her mother's maiden name was Catherine Orpha Moore, and Grandfather Moore was of a branch of the family of Thomas Moore. Catherine Orpha was a real "Irish beauty" in looks, with large blue eyes and soft dark hair; she had no poetry in her make-up, being eminently practical, but there was taste for rhyme as well as reason in the family. Several of her sisters, my mother's aunts, were addicted to the making of "varses" on local happenings. These "varses" used to be tacked up on guide posts with auction bills and other literature; they made the Moore girls quite famous.

Jane's father was not a money maker. He was intensely industrious and of great skill in his line of work; he built churches and beautiful houses, but when it came to collecting pay therefor he was extremely unbusinesslike. No debtor was ever pressed by him, and his partners generally benefited at E. L. Tupper's expense. This resulted in his being famous as a kind and generous man; it also resulted in considerable stringency in his own home. He was always that way. Later, as a farmer, he would bud and graft and sit up nights coaxing fruit trees to wonderful results, but he would not market or sell the products.

Such characters have always been found in New England, despite the fame of the Yankees for trading.

When She Was a Little Girl

No stories are so fascinating to a child as those of mother's childhood. My mother used to reconstruct her life for me, beginning with her first recollection. This was of a sunny day, the house all clean and shining, the kitchen painted a brilliant yellow, Jane sitting serene in a small wooden rocking chair enjoying the peaceful warmth. Somehow this seems typical of the life of one who never failed to find beauty in the most common living.

The kitchen was in a house on Wilbraham Mountain, to which Edwin Tupper moved his family when Jane was just out of babyhood. Wilbraham Mountain is a beautiful and sightly spot, and from her bedroom window Jane overlooked miles of country. Between her and towering Mt. Tom were sparkling rivers, woods that glowed in autumn, acres of fertile fields. She did not care much for these as she grew up. She was chiefly interested in the swiftly passing lights that told her a train was taking happy people to the city. There they associated, of course, with only the great and highly cultivated! Oh, happy people!

Jane's father built his own house on the mountain, calling it done with the upper rooms largely "not done off," as was the custom. Then he went to Brimfield to build a church, leaving his wife and two children to look after a 40-acre farm. I have in my own mind at this moment a mental picture of young Jane, her auburn hair flung to the breeze, her clear voice raised in vociferous remonstrance, while she goes "hell bent for 'lection" in response to the bad news "fence is down and cows is out." It seems that the Tupper family never had company to tea but those pesky cows got out. The pasture was part swale; Jane always prided herself on her skill in leaping lightly from bog to bog without getting bemired.

Her education was well taken care of; she attended the Old Red Schoolhouse, and afterward went to the Academy and "boarded herself" in an attic room of one of the white cottages in the village. Her room-mate was a clever young lady who swore in dead languages when the fire refused to burn, and afterwards married a clergyman. When Jane was 16 she taught a summer school for the satisfying sum of $2.25 a week. She had a "beau" at this time, and with him pervaded the country roads; her headgear being a sunbonnet of green checked gingham.

This "beau" came from the city of New York, and was what might be called a family connection, since his sister had married

Jane's uncle. He was spoken of as a printer by trade, but he afterward became rather well known as an editor; I always felt grateful to him because he presented my mother with a large number
of books that became family treasures. There was among them a
five-volume *Les Miserables*—I cut my teeth on it and have read it at
intervals ever since.

Jane's romances began young—this literary printer was not her
first "beau." The very first escorted her to dancing school when
she was about 14. He, too, showered gifts upon her—or at least one
gift. It is a print entitled "The Lady of the Lake," and portrays a
damsel clad in a red satin waist and full white muslin skirt (over
crinoline) embarking on a water trip in a small boat. She stands upright, apparently going cheerfully to destruction, since her shallop
is provided with neither oars nor rudder. A gentleman in full Highland costume complacently observes her from a screen of vegetation
which the verse says is "brake," but which resembles nothing so
much as the rubber plant which has just been set out for the summer
in our front yard.

This first "beau" became a carpenter, whereby it would almost
seem that he should have inspired in my mother more than common
interest because her life was in a way shadowed by carpenters. Her
grandfather was one, and her father, and her brother. And when she
came to marry she married—not the one who gave her "The Lady of
the Lake"—another! He gave her A Shakespeare Dictionary, getting
up at an unearthly hour one morning when he was "come a-courting" in order to rush out and buy it before breakfast. But I am too
far along in my story—at 16 she hadn't met him.

At 18 she was still teaching school, with a plan—then more
peculiar than it later became—of educating herself and setting up
"a career." She had read about Oberlin, which was the only
college admitting women, and hoped ultimately to study there.
In the meantime she announced to her family an intention of taking her earnings and attending the Westfield Normal. Her father
thought it a good idea, but couldn't help her any because his
partner had absconded with the profits of the church in Brimfield. Her mother did not sympathize, but remarked, "I don't see
why you need any more schooling. You can teach now, and you
better save your money for wedding clothes. You're pretty sure

to get married."

As it happened, her mother was in the right so far as prophesy-ing went. But Jane took her savings and went to Westfield, believ-ing that she would attain Oberlin. She wore prunella shoes and funny dresses. In the winter she tied a "cloud" over her auburn hair, wrapped a Bay State shawl around her shoulders, pulled a pair of old stocking legs over her arms above her yarn mittens, and plunged into the snowdrifts. She attracted no attention because all the other female students did the same.

Well, she had an awfully good time, and ever recalled those school days as the most perfect of her life. Her talent as a writer was recognized; she edited the school Ms. journal, and always read her "compositions" in public. Her boarding place was idyllic in comfort, and there were lots of "boys" in the social circle who took the young lady to Saturday drives after fast horses, waited on her home from prayer meetings, and in winter drew her about town on hand-sleds.

It was while at school that she met William Hilton Dowe, whom she married, but at that time they were not lovers nor was he one of the gallant "boys," but a mature advanced student, intent on Greek and Latin, and already proprietor of his own miniature "academy" in his native town of Charlton. They met—alas for romance!—on a railroad train. He sat on the woodbox, facing the other passengers, and one of them—Jane!—made fun of his boots.

When she completed her Normal course Jane went back to teach-ing. She was very successful and received what was then large pay, "Normal teachers" being few and in great demand. Having the same industry as her father, with the business ability which he lacked, she spent her money wisely yet saved enough for a good "setting out" when she married. She must have been a gorgeous bride. Her wedding gown was a taffeta silk of brilliant blue, her bonnet strings of the same hue were so wide that they afterward made a sash, and her veil of white lace was two yards square and embroidered all 'round.

It was in June, 1864, that Cupid, with his cutomary cleverness proved to young maidenhood the fallacy of seeking a career. Requir-ing only a pre-nuptial agreement that she need never "live on a farm and make butter," she married the before-mentioned William Hilton Dowe. He was cold and logical where she was enthusiastic and romantic, a mathematician where she was a poet, a believer in facts while she was a cultivator of fancies. Yet the seemingly unsuited couple got along well and happily. They went to live in Charlton, "keeping house" after the old fashion in a few rooms of the "up-stairs" in William Dowe's father's house. This was a huge white painted building, set a long way from the road and approachable by its own beautiful, tree-shaded lane. There was a great central chimney, round which the rooms clustered, and a ghost cupboard where once a doctor had kept an actual skeleton in a closet. Strange noises used to be heard in this cupboard o'nights, but the Dowes were used to 'em.

Here, having plenty of leisure, Jane began to write for the press. She sent poetry to the Southbridge *Journal* and it was printed over the name of "Margaret" and excited great wonderment as to the identity of the author. Growing bold she then contributed to the Worcester *Palladium*, one of the literary weeklies that flourished at that period.

My father being ambitious beyond the possibilities of life in Charlton, soon went to Worcester, the second city in Massachusetts, and secured employment with Norcross Brothers, then starting what was to be a great concern of builders. He took charge of a brick church, neither he nor the Norcrosses knowing much about brick, but it didn't fall down, and houses the Universalists of Worcester to this day. Then he went to Springfield and built a stone church and a courthouse of the same material. Stone was also an almost unknown element in those rash young men, but they taught themselves as they went along, and nothing tumbled about their ears, though at one time the courthouse threatened. William Dowe filled his home with books about stone and sat up till "all hours" learning from them.

This home was a little four-room cottage which he bought and then "built on to" in the shape of a large French-roofed house. Here Jane was able to realize some of her ideals, she had her parlor pa-pered in panels after her own designing; she had a beautiful red carpet, and black walnut furniture; she had books, and lace curtains and even a servant girl! In the panels were hung pictures of her own painting, for she was able to achieve another long-cherished desire and "take painting lessons." Her talent in this line was beyond the ordinary, and she enjoyed painting quite as much as writing.

It was at this period that the only child of this couple, I who write this article, came into the world. I was born in my grandfather's house on Wilbraham Mountain in the month of May, which my father, with a wondrous flight of fancy for him, thought might well be mentioned as my second name.

"I REMEMBER—I REMEMBER—"

I now come to the period when—as the well-known Harriet Cox-Dennis would say—"the child's brains begin to sprout." Ignoring science she claims this is a period considerably beyond infancy. Until it happens children are uninteresting little objects. Well, she ought to know. She has three. At any rate, I begin to remember. I think up pictures of our house in Worcester, and how we were always moving from one part to another, and when not moving we used to cut new doors and devise windows, and "put in more plumbing." Of course my father did all this easily, because it was his line; but after his death it seemed to keep right on. Perhaps my mother found it natural to have carpenters around.

First we lived in the "cottage L," and then we lived in the "upstairs part," and next we moved downstairs and "cut through" into the L. Presently the street began to "improve," and burst out into a brick sidewalk, which by some peculiar fancy of the city fathers was elevated several feet above our lot. All the surplus water in that part of Worcester set back into our yard and froze into a most beautiful skating surface, incidentally killing the lovely Norway spruces which my father had planted by the front door, also freezing off the top of a weeping willow, so that it was merely the cheap cheerful kind ever after.

In February, during the coldest of the cold spell, my father died after a brief illness. His death brought sudden changes in my mother's plans. He was about to move to Boston, where the Norcrosses had engaged to construct Trinity Church, of which he was to have charge. My mother always believed she would have "taken up the study of design"—heaven only knows why—but she was always "ramifying out" and did not then look on writing as anything but a passing amusement.

Well, she was left with her Worcester home—and after a short time we moved again into the "upstairs part"—her child, and an income which allowed her to live, modestly, without labor. Then, possibly because it took only pen, ink and paper—typewriters not being invented as expensive tools of trade—she became a writer. Her first attempts were verses in Anglo-Scotch dialect. They dealt with the love adventures of girls called Nora or Molly, whose fate if lucky was mentioned with "heigh-hos," and if the reverse bewailed in "Lackadays." These she sent to the newly started *Scribner's* magazine, predecessor of the *Century*. It had been established with J. G. Holland as editor expressly to encourage American writers.

Strange to say, these verses did not come back! They were accepted by Mr. Holland in appreciative and encouraging letters. They got into print and were copied and bought by composers for setting to music.

My own recollections of my mother at this time tell me that she was still vivacious in manner and graceful of figure. She was fond of pretty clothes and had as many as she could afford. She was also fond of dainty food and we seemed to have more nice things to eat than did our neighbors who were richer than we—more fruit, just then coming into fashion; more summer drinks, more "walnuts and wine," or what they represent. We bought books, besides devouring the contents of the Worcester Public Library, then famous among libraries on account of a librarian years ahead of his time. My mother used to make trips to Boston and visit picture shows, and then Boston's fifty-odd miles from Worcester might have been fifty thousand for all it meant to the women of her acquaintance. There was an Art Students' club in Worcester, my mother wrote a yearly article about their exhibit and became friendly with most of the painters. If anything really fine came to the theatre, which was about once in a twelve-month, we saw it. My first theatrical experience was witnessing Edwin Booth as Hamlet and we saw the Gilbert and Sullivan operas in their first tours, and the elder Salvini when he curdled one's blood as Othello in Italian, despite the incongruity of an English-speaking company.

In our quiet little home every small pleasure was an event, as when the bed rooms were repapered—my mother's with climbing roses and morning glories, and my own with sombre faded fern-leaves. Her liking was always for color. Once she had the dining room done with scarlet walls and a floor painted the same hue. It was a large room with windows to the South and East, so one may imagine the brilliant result. She liked it, and always sat there, till it faded, to write.

We had a large yard which was not in the least like a lawn. There were pear trees in it, and several bushes which brightened the spring with pink blossoms. The flower beds glowed all summer with geraniums, portulaccas, nasturtiums and asters. My mother could have no appreciation for a plant that did not produce a brilliant blossom. In part of the yard was a croquet ground and at one time a target for archery.

Indoors we had our highly appreciated parlor, with a red carpet, a square piano, an "open stove," cherry book cases well filled, a marble-topped table and a what-not. I wish I had them now! But even then they were getting a little old-fashioned, as was our carpet and our hair cloth furniture. It was said, with baited breath that the up-to-date people walked over hard wood floor with rugs, and sat on brilliant upholstery in crushed plush. These glories were beyond us.

My mother taught me herself until I was 14, when I went for three years to a private school approximately a High School. She allowed me to choose my own time during the waking hours of the 24 for learning certain amounts of grammar, geography and so on; also for practising the piano in four installments of 30 minutes each. If I chose amusement for my morning hours I was free to do so without reprimand. I was never subjected to the slightest "order"; the house was as much mine as hers. I selected a most inconvenient corner of the dining room for my doll house and I remember there was objection only when I set it on fire one day and incidentally endangered the larger house in which we lived. (I had lighted a blaze in a cardboard stove to find out what would happen! Having found out, I am glad to report never doing it again.)

One of our great enjoyments was ascending a large hill near us, in order to see sunsets. None of our acquaintances ever went out to see sunsets, but it seemed to me a natural feature in my mother's plan of life, just as it was natural to utilize fine days by taking long walks and "discovering" new streets and lanes in and about Worcester. Chiefly I think of my mother as writing, sitting with some scraps of paper on a book, holding a lead pencil—not very well sharpened—in her hand. Having an inveterate dislike to the regular and normal—despite being a product of that sort of school—my mother never wrote at a desk, but used hers, when she came to have one, as a dressing table. Similarly she would never put a book on a bookshelf, but in a chair. A book on a book shelf was lost to her. If she read anything that was in several volumes she invariably kept the volumes as far apart as possible. When taking notes she generally started on the last page of the note book and wrote towards the beginning. Her poems were scrawled on bits of brown paper from the grocer's, or on backs of envelopes, a brief poem on a dozen pieces, perhaps. These were then rolled up and tied with a tow string. No, my mother was not orderly. Her literary possessions, notes, clippings, Mss., complete and incomplete, came in time to fill barrels. She never threw away anything in the printed or written line, it was agony to her to see a newspaper destroyed, and old magazines or paper novels with half the pages missing had to be sneaked out surreptitiously to the ash pile.

Like most New Englanders, she came from a family of hoarders; my grandmother had a small room literally filled with paper bags and string; thousands of paper bags and all the string that ever came into the house, wound into huge balls the size of a child's head. My grandfather made fun of this, probably because he hoarded old iron. Nails, screws, bolts, hinges, parts of wagons, broken tools—with these he cluttered all the sheds and back rooms and from time to time usurped space on pantry shelves and table drawers in the kitchen. Their daughter, as before noted, preserved anything of possible use in her work.

Each spring of my childhood and girlhood my mother would prepare for the summer's outings. She was intensely fond of the sea, and we generally spent a part of July near the salt water. Sometimes we went to a resort in Maine or Rhode Island and boarded a few weeks; again we visited relatives in the city of Providence and with them made excursions to Block Island, Newport and Narragansett Pier. When the craze for "elocution" set in my mother found time for lessons and became a pleasing reader. In evenings on these summer outings she would be asked to give something of her own, and after the piano playing and the singing Mrs. Dowe's "Nick and

Tarzy" always met with applause. This was a long poem wherein was told an old New England love story. It never appeared in print, though Mr. Holland considered it for Scribner's at one time, finally deciding against it on account of its great length, 260 lines.

After the outing, during which my mother would utilize every experience, every story heard or character met, every moonrise or sunset seen, as a possible basis or background for a bit of writing, then we went to Wilbraham Mountain to stay until frost. There were always two trunks, one was filled with unread books. The "Seaside" library had been invented and proven a Godsend to people like us, of limited means and unlimited appetite for reading. The editions were largely pirated, but this was America's benefit to the English author's loss. So much of our reading was in this form that today it seems wrong to find George Eliot or "Miss Braddon" anything but a pamphlet. My mother's taste for fiction, it will be observed, was eclectic. She particularly liked stories of strong plot, mystery stories, and stories of eccentric characters in unique settings. Wilkie Collins was an intense favorite, she read and re-read *The Woman in White, No Name,* and *Moonstone.* When She dawned it was an episode in our world, and Hugh Conway's *Called Back* was doubly interesting to my mother because she herself had for years been considering a story of similar loss of memory.

Once in her old home in the country my mother proceeded to fill all the chairs in her room with piles of books and Mss., to interleave every volume she read with scraps of paper bearing scribbled notes and often to so load her bed with similar matter that she left hardly space for herself. Yet she never seemed to follow these pursuits to the detriment of any other duties. While abhorring all forms of household labor she was most skillful in their performance. She made over grandmother's bonnet, also the bonnets of the neighbors; she helped in the invariable hot weather job of canning fruit; she upholstered furniture, and she always cleaned the entire house with a slap and a bang before we went back to Worcester.

I suppose I have heard everything my mother ever wrote or thought of writing. She read her poems to me when I was almost too young to know poetry from prose, certainly too young to appreciate love lyrics which they generally were. I used to have hard times trying to reconcile the exceedingly romantic and sentimental performances of poetry people who were "in love," with the very matter of fact manner in which actual young men and women of my acquaintance bought their furniture and sewed crochet edging on things made from "Fruit of the Loom" cotton cloth. It was perhaps this failure to match art to what I saw of life that made me a realist.

When I began to write, which was as soon as I learned the mechanics thereof, my mother in her turn became a listener, always a patient, interested and instructive one. Without thinking the products of her lone chicken anything extraordinary or boring her friends with reports of them, she gave me every sort of encouragement, and treated the puerile performances of a child with just that amount of serious consideration which encouraged me to keep on. We never wrote in the least alike, and in a short time she came to have only intellectual admiration for what I did, with no sympathy at all for its character or style. She wrote largely of the sunny side of life, her poetry was truly "inspired," her verses sang themselves and indeed when composing she often chanted also, to accentuate the rhythm.

I have often spoken of her only as a writer of poetry. As a matter of fact she came in time to write prose also, but never so successfully or so well. Her prose was entirely of New England. Her first attempt in the prose line was a novel about a most unfortunate girl named Margaret—my mother's favorite female name. I think this must have been started long before I was born. I remember it as existing on large sheets of the thin blue paper which was used for foreign letters in days of double postage to Europe. It was a country story; in it were utilized people and scenes of old Wilbraham. There was a humorous chapter, which told what happened at a "regular setting down," and there was a terrible storm wherein Margaret went out and drowned herself. In later years we used this yarn as a basis for jokes, and "Margaret's pool" became a name appended to any gruesome little puddle in a wood.

I think this novel, which was forever being re-written, took all my mother's time that she could spare from poetry, until after she broke by accident into the Irish Verse which gave her what fame she attained.

Shamrocks and Shillelaghs

It was, as Mr. W. Paul Cook notes in his article "Two View-points," about 1889 that my mother's first Irish verse was pub-lished. In 1887 I was married to John T. F. Miniter, a native of Great Britain and a special admirer of Irish literature. We lived with my mother, and she of course had to read all the volumes of Irish poetry with which he swamped the establishment. It seems to have opened a new world to her, one in which she was almost instantly at home.

A few months spent in dwelling on the woes of "Dark Ro-saleen," in admiring "The Green Above the Red," or remembering the glories of "Brian the Brave," had their result in a dozen Irish verses. They were bundled off to "her editor," who was now Rich-ard Watson Gilder. Mr. Holland was dead and the magazine had changed its name to the *Century,* but Jennie E. T. Dowe was still a constant contributor.

She expected that one Irish poem would be accepted; to her sur-prise all were taken and more asked for. Thus put on her mettle she set to work reading more Irish literature, studying the Irish people, and making her own dictionary of dialect. In form her Irish poems always followed the form of some older Irish song, and a dialect word was never used without authority for its employment in just that connection. The little verses that seemed such airy trifles were never put into print without the most careful study. Frequently, when in type, the Century people would telegraph many times be-fore the day of going to press, in order to be sure everything was, as Mr. Gilder once phrased it, "fool proofed and copper bottomed." As a result her poems were never adversely criticized by Irish read-ers, many of whom, indeed, would not believe she wasn't born and bred in "The Ould Dart."

Furthermore her poems were wonderfully original, because she never copied—to do so was foreign to her nature. In the alchemy of her mind the result of reading was transfused, as would Irish life have been transfused had she visited the land of which she wrote. It was their originality that made her verses appeal to both literary critics and the rank and file of readers.

In 1891 our home in Worcester ceased to exist, perhaps because we had put in all the bath rooms and put on all the piazzas we found space for. It was sold and the "curse" with it, to some people who instantly broke ground for a barn in the back yard. My mother also sold most of her furniture, taking only a few things to Wilbraham Mountain, where she went to be with her parents, both nearing 80. And that was how we lost the what-not! I was in Manchester, N. H., working on a daily paper; from there I went to Boston, and similar work on a weekly.

I haven't said much of my grandfather's house on Wilbraham Mountain, which now became my mother's home, but this is merely because its eccentricities deserve a volume by themselves. Indeed I am writing such a one at the present time! My grandfather and uncle had the "improving" craze in most virulent form, and achieved things we never attempted in Worcester, such as a small kitchen with 8 doors and an entire suite of rooms hidden away over a carriage shed and approachable by circumnavigating the swill-barrel and climbing two flights of stairs solely for the sake of immediately going down another.

My mother's spasms of improvements while there were more feminine in character. She re-papered the parlor and made it something to live in instead of a "best room." She opened a long sealed fireplace and gave her father a pleasure he had missed for many years—piling birch wood artistically on andirons, hearing the sap boil out, and then watching the blaze until it penetrated to the farthest corner of the room, which instantly became so hot everyone had to flee. She made the family eat in a dining room instead of from a kitchen table pushed up to a wall.

Hers was not at this time a particularly easy life. The house was hard to keep warm in the winter, there being a great many cold halls and draughty pantries and garrets. Despite his orgies of building—or perhaps because of them—my grandfather had never "had water brought into the kitchen." That performance was left for my own generation. During my mother's residence every bit of water was drawn up from a deep well by a picturesque sweep, then lugged up an ascending path culminating in a flight of stone steps. And at that, in summer you were lucky to escape the drouth.

For about eight years she remained here, doing a great deal of housework, which she despised above all forms of labor; living with very little congenial society, and in the midst of that butter and cheese making from which she had earlier in life asked to be excused. Perhaps because she had proven to herself that it wasn't her life work, she took it quite jauntily. She even made butter and cheese with her own hands, and was immensely tickled when the neighbors considered the results just as good as Mrs. Edwin Tupper's famed products. You see, my mother always accepted what she felt had to be, with good grace. The farm was there, it must be cultivated. Her parents were there and too old to be left alone. They refused to be coaxed from their home, even when unable to 'tend the cows and chickens or keep cobwebs away from that part of the front windows visible to "the passing." My uncle's wife was dead; on my mother alone depended aid in female form.

She managed to keep on writing poetry, and the Irish verse went into the *Century* regularly. She also wrote prose and sold it. *The Youth's Companion* bought a great many stories of boys and old men— principally old men, whom she greatly enjoyed writing about. She sold a large number of stories written for Memorial Days and Thanksgivings to the Springfield *Homestead* and the Portland (Me.) *Transcript*. Having a small boy to study at first hand in her youngest nephew she produced cute verses of child life which appeared in these papers. This was not her best work, but it brought her appreciation from a wide circle of readers. When not writing and cooking she raised chickens, cultivated a garden, and reconciled the varying claims of two old folks, her fiery-tempered brother, her oldest nephew, a bachelor in the 30s, and her youngest, a spoiled child just emerging from babyhood. She consoled herself in her exile by keeping a great many cats.

When she could get away for a few weeks she would come to Boston and we would indulge in orgies of going to theatres and eating at restaurants. Whenever I went to Wilbraham I would have read to me the various literary products she had turned out since I had seen her last. My advice, sometimes given on some point of detail, was always followed, but our lines of thought were so distinct and varying that I seldom felt competent to advise.

Her favorite authors were then Thomas Hardy, Hall Caine, George Gissing, Eden Phillpotts, Jack London, Joseph Conrad; all masters of the vigorous brand of fiction. She bought and studied everything worth while in Irish literature but cared very little for the modern school of Irish writers. Of the writers on nature—Burroughs, Bradford Torrey, Skinner—she was also a student, they were the only exponents of the quiet life to win her admiration, why they did I was never able to explain.

Boston—At Last

In the winter of 1896 my grandmother caught cold and had pneumonia. My mother nursed her through it and she was quite well before spring began to warm up. So well that she insisted on dashing bareheaded from the kitchen to the barn—probably to see if "he" had his hat on! As I think of it my grandmother dressed quite in the fashion of today, but the constitutions of 25 years back wouldn't stand it. She wore socks the year round, tore off the long sleeves from her calico gowns, and was as shy of underclothing as any up-to-date miss of this era. At 82 a March wind got the better of her, and she died in May from that form of heart trouble commonly following pneumonia. My mother took the entire care of her, sitting up through the spring nights with every door and window wide open so that the breathless sufferer might have air. Earlier in life, also later, my mother was extremely timid after dark, heard imaginary marauders with every creak of fence or rattle of tree, but at this time she lived in delightful fearlessness.

This was the first death in the house which my grandfather had built fifty years before, a record which I think few New England farmhouses can boast. There has been only one funeral there since then—that of my grandfather in 1901—and yet but one death after that, of my cousin, whose obsequies were "celebrated," as the saying goes, elsewhere. Eight of Edwin Tupper's great grandchildren are growing up there now; they have torn down the carriage-house-suite and made a summer kitchen of the debris, they have a cement floor to the old "stoop," and they have discovered several places where a new door would be a great convenience. All proving them real chips of the old block.

Not long after my grandmother's death my mother turned her interest in "The Old Homestead" over to my cousin, father of the eight before mentioned—but then only a paltry two—and came to live with me in Boston. It was during these final 21 years of her life that she came to know the friends whose tributes fill the bulk of these pages.

We lived in a five-room flat at the top of a corner house on Berkeley and Chandler Streets in the South End of Boston. It was an
old-fashioned flat—somehow we seemed to have a habit of living in
old-fashioned houses. The parlor had a fireplace as well as the steam
radiator which was obviously an afterthought. The kitchen furniture included a real stove. Also a printing press, known familiarly
as The Proud Prouty in our family circle. My mother did not fancy a
press in the kitchen or type cases setting round on beds and couches,
but as usual she adapted herself beautifully to circumstances. Her
own room had a Southern aspect, and she at once had it done up
with pink paper and a frieze of immense pink roses. Here she sat
behind a window box glowing with geraniums and continued to
write poetry. We went literally to everything that appeared at any
Boston theatre, of which there were then seven and sometimes more
in existence. These included the Museum, now quite forgotten;
the Park and Boston, now motion picture houses; the Grand Opera
House on Washington Street, which vibrated between Shakespeare
and 10-20-30 shows. The Colonial, Majestic, Shubert and Wilber
were neither built nor thought of. There was a stock company, with
Lillian Lawrence for leading lady, at the Castle Square (now Arlington Theatre) and B. F. Keith gave vaudeville exactly as it is giv-
en now, with a boresome thing called moving pictures as a "chaser"
to each show. And no one discerned a sinister shadow on the drama
of the spoken word!

Our life was a pleasant and busy one. In the summer we made
trips to the beaches about Boston, or spent long days in the Blue
Hills or Lynn Woods Reservation. Here we had generally the company of Mary and Harriet Cox, at whose home in Abington we also
visited. Theirs was a fine old mansion, set on the shore of a pretty
pond. Sometimes we would "take boat" for the five-minute row to
a pine wood, there to lounge about, sewing a little, reading more
(generally from authors we preferred—ourselves) and talking more
than all the rest.

Trolley lines were opening up Eastern Massachusetts, and we
tried them all. The open cars of glorious memory made such trips
ideal, and we prized recollections of the rival motor men who bid
for our patronage at junctions by shouting, "Every seat vacant on
my car, and the very best sceneries!" We trolleyed to Providence

and to Worcester, and as soon as the rails were down to Wilbraham. Thinking of her probable preference now I realize that my mother would doubtless have gone always to the salt water, had she been consulted, but as was her comfortable, pleasant way, she said very little of her own wishes, and even accompanied me in my favorite haunts among old graves, though actually abhorring cemeteries and every thought thereof.

We belonged to a club called The Playgoers, which had Tuesday teas when the leading play of the previous night was talked over; and also monthly dinners whereat players were guests of honor. This organization was fathered by Mr. James Henry Wiggin, a delightful old gentleman who had spent his life in preaching, writing plays, listening to music, or entertaining people who did these things; his fund of anecdote was marvelous and he maintained a truly youthful interest in all that was new in art until his very last day. At his fine old home, which was a storehouse of objects symbolizing beautiful memories, my mother became a constant guest. When Mr. Wiggin passed from life his funeral services were unique in that they consisted entirely of tributes to his many-sided character by friends.

"There," said my mother, "that's the sort of funeral I want."

It was the sort she had.

While we lived at Berkeley Street my mother sketched two prose works, neither of which have yet seen the light. One she called "Back o' the Mountain," it was a series of episodes woven about a dilatory old couple who courted for years, playing cat's cradle the while but didn't marry until in the "sere and yellow leaf." She wove into this yarn a great many country tales, humorous or otherwise. It was well thought of by several publishers, but rejected for lack of "a youthful love interest," then generally considered an important sop to the reading public.

The other was a story of Salem in witch times. This last never got completed to her mind, she was always working it over, and buying books to help, and going to Salem to imbibe atmosphere. Labor on these filled in chinks between the composition of poetry and enjoyment. She also had a plan for making a book on "first memories" and collected a vast number. Another scheme of hers had to do with a book on the common soldier of the Civil War, whom she thought neglected by historians. She secured a great deal of valuable matter for this, being given the use of hundreds of soldiers' letters and diaries through the courtesy of the Boston *Transcript.*

I suppose it was one of my mother's faults, to be always preparing to do great things. But it kept her young, she had the youthful trick of looking ever into the future. Then I think, too, she unconsciously felt the difficulties of working in prose, which was not her true medium. For of all the hundreds of poems which she began not a single one was left unfinished.

The Akron Street House

The year 1906 brought us changes. The *Home Journal,* a weekly paper with which I had been connected for 13 years, and which had changed from a literary and dramatic publication with a small hotel department into a large hotel paper carrying a few columns only of "literary stuff" was sold to a knacker. Our flat on Berkeley Street had become intolerably noisy. I decided to give up work and to move.

One day I went out to Roxbury with a real estate agent who showed me a house—not on Akron Street. After saying "no" to its charms, I wandered about the closely built, rather seedy neighborhood and discovered Akron Street. It was "some discovery," as the many people who lost their way coming to see us there afterward, will testify. Akron Street leads up a hill from another street of no importance and ends in a third of even less. This last overhangs an immense cliff in the vicinity of which students of Hawthorne place Hester Prynne in a chapter of *The Scarlet Letter.* There are five large single houses on one side of Akron Street, each set on top of its own cliff, which is faced with Roxb'ry pudding stone. They all have yards, with Norway spruces in 'em, and green grass where it will grow, and shrubs. In the spring the place is sweet with "laylocks" and syringas, and flowering almonds. No. 17, where we came to live, had also a pink hawthorn tree, and a wisteria vine; with plenty of lilies of the valley and violets. You mounted 25 steps, in detachments, before you even reached the front door, which had side lights and ornaments of carved pineapples.

When we first saw the house it was pumpkin colored; afterwards it got painted gray, which presently wore off leaving the original pumpkin, much more appropriate. Inside it was a masterpiece of attempts to adapt modern conveniences to an old-fashioned framework. So that one might almost have thought the Tuppers had lived there. A hall bed room had been turned into a bath room and water pipes, instead of coyly hiding in walls after the general custom, meandered boldly through living rooms, and in damp weather rained perspiration on pictures and bric-a-brac. There had been fireplaces, afterward sealed up, and there were registers which registered not, the furnace being disused. In order to be quite in keeping we put an open grate stove in the parlor and a wood-burning "airtight" in the back parlor, which became my mother's room. We kept china in a real "silk hat" closet, and I had my typewriter in an observatory which was eight-sided and overlooked all Boston and Massachusetts Bay.

It was indeed a charming house, and suited us "to a T." All the rooms were immense except the dining room, which by way of variety just held a table and sideboard and three chairs—not a bit of furniture more. We often packed as many as fifteen people into it! It was papered with Dutch windmills and had a lovely plate rail. The hall excited our friends to envious raptures, the walls were English 'unting scenes in hand blocking. My mother lined her sunny apartment with books and bought an extension table on which to lay out her work, up to then having never enjoyed a large enough writing table.

When we arrived the kitchen had a yellow floor, scarlet walls and a bright blue ceiling, but on finding that it enjoyed the sun all day we did it over in milder tones. Upstairs there were bedrooms in what space the roof didn't occupy, and under the eaves immense runways which were lovely to poke things into—those things one doesn't want around and which are too good to throw away. After we had lived here twelve and a half years the runways were cleared; in the way back parts were things placed there when we first moved in.

I had the front room, under the roof for mine. There was a beautiful North window from which one had a view of Boston strained through the tasseled branches of the Norway spruce. It was here I wrote my one book, *Our Natupski Neighbors*. In the back room John Leary Peltret, who made his home with us when not on the road ahead of a theatrical troop, kept the Proud Prouty press and the type along with his books and the Colt's revolver with which his grand-father, Sheriff John Leary, shot horse thieves and such in California in the days of '49.

Soon after we came to Akron Street my mother had her first se-vere illness. While camping out she stumbled over a tent rope and injured one knee, in which sciatica took possession. For a long and painful winter she lay in bed, suffering a great deal, but always—like Mark Tapley—coming out as jolly as possible. She kept her bed well covered with books and writing materials, and never had a dull hour I am sure. In time she recovered, though she was always obliged to favor herself a bit in walking.

These camping out summers became an important part of our life, and must be described. The scene of our camp was Wilbraham Mountain, where we had acquired the next farm to the one that had been my grandfather's. The house was very old, it had five fireplaces and an immense central chimney. Being rather ruinous we did not try to live in it, but used it as a place of storage for our tents and paraphernalia. We owned the place about 15 years and always had intentions of some time restoring the house and going there to live. As my mother grew older, however, she became less and less favorable to any idea of country life and in the fall of 1918 it was sold. It had done its share of inspiring poetry and providing health-giving outdoor summers. We gave it the name of Meadowbeck and wrote a little book about one summer there, which we called *Fire-flies to Crickets*.

Every summer, whether we camped or not, a great deal of de-lightful time was spent at Maplehurst, where lived our "Cousin" Evanore Beebe. She had five fireplaces in her house, also a tight roof, which we had not. And her spacious rooms were entirely fur-nished with old time furniture, while the walls were adorned with valuable china in bewildering profusion. Add 14 to 20 cats, half a dozen dogs, and all the news of the town via 'phone, and you have some idea of Maplehurst. There was even an immense birdseye maple table which would seem to have been restored solely so that Jane could lay out her work on it.

In those years, just before the Great War, what was this work? For one thing, a novel with scenes laid on the bleak islands of Booth-bay Harbor in Maine. She had spent a summer at Southport, and brought back materials for such a story; also (which was more important), several poems. "In the Shadow of the Sail" was one of these. Mr. R. U. Johnson, editor of the *Century* (for my mother survived the second editor, Mr. Gilder) wrote in accepting it that he would gladly "take 50 more in the same vein." But she would keep thinking of prose—she worked on episodes in the life of a "hoss trader," for which she had studies; also on a yarn about a girl naturalist into which she intended to weave a collection of anecdotes about "tame wild animals."

Then came 1913, and she got on the trail of the Natupskis, for it is to her that I am indebted for that precious family. Their prototypes lived near Maplehurst, they used to wander over and relate their woes to E. O. Beebe, et al., while canny Jane sat on a cricket behind the door and wrote down their talk. In the fall we went home. We had assisted Wilbraham to celebrate its 150th anniversary, and my mother had written a poem, part of which starts off the town history itself. When we got into our Roxbury observatory again my mother read her Natupski gleanings and insisted that I make the matter into some stories. I was not attracted to the characters at first, but wrote the episodes to please her. Then, to please a magazine editor (who lost his job before he could publish them) I wrote some more; and afterward, to please the representative of Henry Holt & Co., more yet. So in October, 1916, there was a book of 100,000 words brought out by that firm and entitled *Our Natupski Neighbors*. My mother undoubtedly was as pleased as if the book had been her own; she was acquainted with every line in it except the dedication to herself which I kept as a surprise.

About this time we began spending our summers in a beautiful bungalow on a bank of the Merrimack, as guests of Minna and Mabel Noyes, though they lived in the "old homestead" (now ashes!) some distance over the fields. Walter Thorpe used to come down for week ends and he—six feet tall and weighing 240 pounds—and my mother—4 foot 10 and about 130—would discuss how to grow thin. Both have done with this world; it seems rather a pity they bothered with diets and cutting out things they enjoyed. Laurie Sawyer and I denied ourselves nothing of the fruit of the land which the Noyes' farm afforded; and Ella Arvilla Merritt, whom we called "Clinging Vine," used to get up in the night and start the Sterno outfit. We had loads of fun and what my mother couldn't make she could laugh at.

In 1917 we varied the programme by a delightful month with the Nelson Mortons at Melrose Highlands and another at Onset. At Melrose my mother had to keep very busy reading up Nelson's books, for she was always one of those visitors who Knight Erranted in a library till its contents were downed. She also enjoyed meals at all hours since Nelson dined at 8.30 A. M., got his night's sleep during the day, and took a 10 P. M. breakfast so as to get to his desk bright and early at midnight.

As for Onset she basked daily by the sea she always loved, and became so fond of the place that on going there now one almost expects to find her lingering among those forest trees that stand so astonishingly with their feet in silver sands.

My mother liked being read to; we generally had a volume on the table and took a few chapters at the end of every meal. With a mind always receptive to novelty she enjoyed the new English novelists—De Morgan, Arnold Bennett, Galsworthy and so on—and the discovery of an author just suited to our taste, such as Compton Mackenzie, was hailed with a whoop of joy. There was no living in the past for her, even though we occasionally fell back on Dickens and Thackery. As for "keeping her mind," well, she tackled Henry James' very last work, including the notes which considerably exceed the book itself, when she lacked physical strength to walk from her bed to her couch.

In 1918 we put in some time in Allston with Laurie Sawyer and her mother, the remarkable and sweet-tempered Mrs. Moody, then hovering round the middle 80s. There was much talk, at this time, of "Charlie and Laurie buying a house." It was one round the corner—20 Webster Street. Our mothers used to peer at it across intervening lawns and gauge the temperature by whether or not the upper veranda door was open.

Neither, I suppose, had any prescience of going to that house for a little, and then being carried forth to return no more.

AND AFTER ALL—

Events are generally arranged so as to justify the old Orthodox faith in predestination. We spent a vast deal of breath discussing whether or not to move to Allston, when all the time we had to move because otherwise it would have been unfortunate for both of us. One of the best features was the fact that the removal compelled my mother to sort over her Mss., destroy a few bushels, and tie in understandable bundles the trunksful that remained. Otherwise the work of her lifetime would have taken several other lifetimes in deciphering. As it is—

I was talking, t'other day, with an editor who had once worked on literary remains, "of which," quoth he, "the one good point was their being written in copperplate." Well, my mother's were written in lead pencil on old paper bags. I shall not allow them to be lost, on that account. Her published poetry, in clippings, fills an immense "extension" case extended to fullest extent, and from that shall sometime come a book.

Our actual moving when the "flu" raged, was attended by many annoyances. Three sets of movers took and then abandoned the job from lack of "lumpers"; and the war board having decided junk collecting to be a non-productive occupation one could not "re-duce" in the way of old sewing machines and magazines as drastically as one would have liked.

None of these occurrences fretted my mother, however. She woke cheerfully on a borrowed cot, to eat a borrowed breakfast from borrowed dishes, and only observed that most of the things we dusted, and slaved for seemed really unnecessary to existence.

When it was finally arranged we had a beautiful little home, with a lot of the things she had wanted, such as pink walls to her bed-room, and the morning sun to shine in; a window of stained glass, a polished floor; an upstairs veranda from which to take the air. She had also the constant attention of the best of friends. But Time, presumably, was ripe. She faded day by day for five months, and died on March 6, 1919.

I have failed egregiously, unless I have made a picture of a sunny-natured person, blessed with a great deal of talent and not cursed with much of what we call "temperament." The last troubled her only in her childhood and girlhood, when a romantic constitution rebelled against commonplace surroundings. After she had settled her life as she liked she found the commonplace people were often lovable, and that the rude farm possessed a picturesque side.

Some of her characteristics were the real old New England sort—for instance, her caution. She never "threw her hat over the house." If a new idea was presented to her suddenly she at once detected and mentioned all possible disadvantages. This once done, the way was cleared for investigating the merits, to which her mind was quite as open. When decided on a line she never felt regrets or played the part of Lot's wife. She never nagged.

Her agreeable qualities were so predominant that she was always being made the recipient of uninvited confidences; as for her ability in securing friends, it is shown in this very tribute to her memory, which was designed by Mr. Michael White, who spent 20 years in admiring her work, and never knew her in life at all, and which is brought to completion by Mr. W. Paul Cook, who met her but twice and thought her some one else all the while!

Of no one might more truly be uttered the trite words, "Gone, but not forgotten." A vivid sense of her personality remains strongly with those whom she left. Of a new made friend we say, "Jane would have liked so-and-so," and in giving ourselves a good time it really seems as if we were pleasuring her just as we used to do.

Most of those writing about her have mentioned her kindness and consideration for all; which she certainly had, but which did not preclude exercising a keen sense of humor and an eye ever open to the ridiculous. Her ironic comments were left for private utterance; however, they were not ill-natured in expression or meaning. I imagine that very few who attain her age are so receptive to novelty as was she. Nothing seemed to have been done better when she was young—except, perhaps, putting handles on wash-basins. She insisted to the last that a wash-basin properly had a handle!

"To the last" describes many of her whimsical remarks. When the bells fretted her by ringing for hours and hours on a certain great day, "Well, I lived through the war," she observed, "but I really did think this morning that the Armistice would be the death of me."

Indeed, her very last lengthy speech was jocular. After complaining that nothing she ate or drank tasted right she observed that all her ancestors lived to great old ages and she was "really afraid" she should do the same, adding, "And won't I be a thorn in the flesh to you!"

It seems, this moment, I wouldn't have minded if she had!

Finis

It is 1921 and everyone says, "What are we coming to?" feeling all the while that they've got there, which is a peculiarity of every present moment and always has been. Skirts are a yard and a quarter round and just cover the knee, and female children ask "What's a petticoat?" as innocently as Grisel asked "What's a father?" in *Sentimental Tommy*. Everybody sews or knits on Sunday, and blames it on the war; and they dance without a single dancing step to music which is noise produced by musicians who are acquainted with no instruments, but use coal scuttles and tea trays. This they blame on prohibition, for which also the war is to blame. And poetry is not rhymed and a play is a picture of one. All the grocers are Armenians, the restaurant keepers Greek or Chinese, while if you buy any dry goods the merchant is a Hebrew, no matter what the name above the door. And still they call it "America." One can get a first-class stenographer for $20 and she will "find herself," but no one is willing to do general housework for $15, even though there is "no washing" and she is boarded and given a suite of parlor, bed-room and bath for her private lodging. A scrubwoman receives 60 cents an hour, and a "dago" digging in the street gets hit by a flying rock and is very indignant because $100 worth of bridge work in his mouth is ruined. The youngest girls, who need it the least, use the most rouge on their faces, but make up for this unnatural behavior by leaving off corsets and facing the world with a figure absolutely unimproved. As for law and order, I have just read in that serious-minded paper, the Boston *Transcript,* a solemn assertion to effect that no person can expect to run an auto and not find himself sometime in the criminal court; and the 18th amendment is constantly defied by our best citizens, who glory in the act. Once they said, "What can you expect from a cat but kittens?" and the next ceremony after the wedding was a christening, but now it's a divorce; only if the separating couple aren't wooing other parties while the case is pending so as to be ready for a marriage when the decree is final we say they are slow, or "what did they want to get separated for anyway?"

But nobody is really surprised at anything; a butcher said rump steak was 80 cents a pound today, and round 65—I remember as a

child gazing with awestruck pity at the one and only girl in Worcester who (it was said) belonged to a family that ate round steak for
its breakfast because it was so large and poor (family, not steak).
And for screening the back porch at 20 Webster Street, which cost
$8 three years ago, and which a carpenter figured on last winter as
a $25 job, he now in this month of May presents his bill, and it's
$70, and he claims he loses money on it at that!

I wish for my mother to enjoy laughing at this topsy-turvy world.
I want her for the more selfish reason of wishing for a listener to
every "good thing" that I hear, a sympathizer in every interest, a
participant in every project. This is a beautiful Garden of Eden we
live in, there are plenty of singing birds and brilliantly blooming
flowers, but encompassing us always is the blank wall of Death.
Sometimes one feels tempted to bite the apple of knowledge unlaw-
ful and escape. All in good time one will, taking along that which
has been acquired here. I cannot believe otherwise when I think of
my mother's life. She achieved much, but was always preparing for
more in the future. That future must exist.

(*In Memoriam: Jennie E. T. Dowe*, September 1921)

THE AFTERMATH

Dedicated
(in Chapter Headings)
to
Howard P. Lovecraft.
Otherwise
to
ALL READERS.

Edited by Edith Miniter

Aftermath: The second crop of grass mown in the autumn;–called also aftergrass, latter-math, eddish, rowen or rowett; and when left long on the ground it is called fogg in some places. *P. Cyc.*

PANTING TIME

Oh, at my first convention, six and thirty years ago,
Things were quite different from now, as anyone should know.
On day the first much merriment it might have had the call,
But those pernicious proxies hung o'er us like a pall;
We got 'em scrambled through at last, we got "our man" elected,
And the millennium was come–or so we all expected.
Then to a love feast all sat down, each one forced to foregather
In the one place where he or she "just really wouldn't rather!"

        * * *

Oh, hark, I hear a pleading voice, "Give me my honor back!"
Jud Russell 'tis, the martyred cause of many a fierce attack.

        * * *

Next one bewildered female lost in Boston streets I see,
A-asking p'licemen where to go, and that lost one is me!

        * * *

The last day comes, and votes of thanks around and round we fling,
To many folks who haven't done for us a single thing.
Then–home so dead for want of sleep that we are scarce alive–
In 1921 this was? No–1885.

Words Are The Daughters of Earth

This publication protests first against being referred to as an "occasional publication." The one before this was rather recent, as E. Dorothy Houtain (she who was a MacLaughlin) and I printed it in 1917 and actually mailed it in 1918. It dealt with the last New York convention. I hadn't read that dic. stuff then and presumed that an *Aftermath* properly described a convention. Now I know better. Those who yearn to read about sitting up all night parties and witnessings of gallant sunrises over the Esplanade must consult Howard P. Lovecraft's memory, or the paper to be issued by and by from Apple Creek, O. Nothing like that here. This is just an *Aftermath*.

Conventions differ, as did members of a once famous family—if you saw anybody who didn't resemble anybody else in the least, you knew (from the resemblance) that 'twas a sister, and ten to one it turned out you were right. All conventions have family features in common, and those who are going about saying they never saw anything like this before, have forgotten some of the others. The present is by no means the first time that success has brought surfeit; and it is invariably the over-indulged creature that snaps at the hand which fed it.

That the so-called "losers" are all smiling jauntily and feeling merry as grigs (whatever they are), while those nominally a-top the steam-roller utter piercing complaints and indulge constantly in carping criticism of those who put them where they are—all this but adds to the gaiety of Autumn, 1921. For holding office isn't all pie; to win out means accepting a load of responsibility and expense—especially expense.

* * *

Professional politicans publicly file expense accounts after a campaign. Such a proceeding in amateur circles would be illuminating—sometimes amazing. "But," someone asks, "is any office in the N. A. P. A. worth it?" Perhaps it can be made so by taking advantage of the psychological moment.

As we all know, the convention followed a campaign in which the office of executive seemed marked as a feminine prerogative. Women have run for the office before. The writer ran for it in 1909 and was elected, perhaps (as I am still being told) because Frank Kendall didn't get to New York. Also because Edwin Hadley Smith did get there and squelched a Wills brothers' scheme to bring him in as a d.h. Jennie Kendall held the office by appointment during more than half of 1913-14. Edna Hyde ran in 1915 and was not elected, her opponent being George J. Houtain. But this year woman was pitted against woman, even the "rumors" being feminine. Marjorie Outwater had the nomination in her grasp from July, 1920, until she voluntarily abandoned the idea. Dorothy MacLaughlin was nominated in January and remained steadily in view as a candidate until she was conducted to the chair by Mrs. Helen Heins and myself on the morning of July 5. Edna Hyde "also ran" from February on. Mrs. Hazel Adams was a possibility often mentioned. Did anything from a superior planet gaze down on us in the first half of the year, and discern an amazing amount of buzzing? If so, 'twas the N. A. P. A. choosing a queen.

Things Difficult To Design

"There was a large and representative attendance," but about all the officers absented themselves. Also most of the candidates.
President
First Vice President
Second Vice President
Secretary
Treasurer
Official Editor
Executive Judges–Three

Nine Elected Officers

Call the roll, except for A. M. Adams, executive judge, "Nobody Home." Are you reminded of that affair in Biblical history, where so many with one accord began to make excuse? They had good ones. First Vice President John Milton Heins, who was also a candidate for official editor, pleaded ill health. Second Vice President Vera Dollman had committed matrimony. So had Official Editor Outwater. Secretary Jeffries sent telegrams and letters describing an awful accident to–his automobile. Executive Judge Kevern was so thoroughly absent that he did not even add his signature to the executive judges' report. Executive Judge Edna Hyde, who doubled as presidential candidate, was supposed to have gone to Washington. "That's All" Adams, at one stage of the proceedings, and with intent to be facetious, implied that she was attending the convention of another organization. Dowdell violently denied the allegation and defied the allegator. Dowdell was probably right. The United convention in Washington seems to have emulated the dodo.

* * *

To return to the National—we must approve of absenteeing. Why otherwise did we elect a first vice president in the far south and a second vice president in Cuba? Especially as Cuba is not a part of the United States or Canada and so Miss Anita Kirksey is eligible for neither membership nor office holding according to the constitution? But no more of this. I want to relate how the convention nearly died before birth for want of a presiding officer. Or rather for want of decision, through too many good possibilities.

Slow Rises Worth

It is 9.45 A. M., Saturday, July 2. Outside water falls in torrents and inside words ditto. James Morton is suggested—able parliamentarian, huge-voiced, steeped in amateur journalistic precedent. No—James Morton is needed "on the floor." W. Paul Cook—he has more than once pulled the organization out of a slough, is indeed referred to as a veritable Messiah by his myriad admirers. He hastily begs to be omitted. He's been in amateur journalism only 25 years, and it's his first convention. George Julian Houtain also wishes to husband his voice for the floor. Charles W. Heins is in that mysterious limbo "visiting non-amateur friends" (however can they do it?). This exhausts the masculine ex-presidents just then in the offing. The clock strikes 10. Billy Dowdell is supposed to be holding himself in leash waiting for the official starting hour, so that he may leap into the forum and make all the appointments. Wildly we rush into the convention hall and (on suggestion of Houtain) put C. A. A. Parker in the chair.

* * *

As his first performance (drat him) was to put me on a committee and send me to an upper room, I only know vaguely that the chair was handed round like refreshments and variously held by Sandusky, Adams, Dench and Heins. When I came downstairs after a two hours' wrestling with what was probably the most baffling secretary's report ever foisted on a perspiring convention Edward H. Cole was presiding and Messrs. Heins, Houtain and even James F. Morton, Jr., were meekly taking their seats whenever he so much as hinted at their being out of order.

*   *   *

It should have been the proudest moment of his life. It certainly was one of the proudest of mine, because I've seen Edward Cole advance steadily year by year from the little lad whom Charles Parker and I took to the Philadelphia convention in 1906, to the cold, calm, collected man who without previous preparation or warning took command of the turbulent elements of 1921. The decisions he was called upon to make were many and "nice," he defined former vaguenesses that have troubled the National Association, and—unquestioned at the time—these decisions will probably govern many a future convention.

*   *   *

Apropos—if anyone really wants to endow a school for any department of amateur journalism I bespeak the fund for a school to train proxy voters. No, you don't need to catch 'em young. The new people, if they vote at all (Rowan White's "Rubber Band" didn't), vote correctly. But your real old timer thinks not to know him augers yourself unknown, and doesn't even sign his name if he feels economical. One man, for instance, signed the name of his paper. Any number wrote over the line, so it seemed as if they wanted Dowdell or Heins for treasurer and neglected the official editorship entirely. A famous New Yorker, once nearly president of the National, clamped his blank to his wife's, and said "Same for Me." James Morton fetched up all his big guns of oratory and delivered a speech on the crime of expecting this man to pause in his well-known pursuit of a fortune in order to properly fill out a ballot! Such a roar of artillery was hardly necessary under the circumstances, but the oldest Morton has nothing for light skirmishing. He failed to convince the convention of the sacredness of a paper clip or that any stay-at-home amateur was any busier than we were with some 140-odd proxies to consider.

To Point A Moral

The proxy committee consisted of Messrs. Heins, Dowdell, James Morton, Cook, Martin, Mrs. Sawyer and myself. It was a perfectly honest and honorable body. I have this on assertion of the presiding officer, who told Mrs. K. Leyson Brown it was. She asked. One trembles at the result had Mr. Cole been prompted by conscience to reply differently.

* * *

Apropos—conscience. Some of the most conscientious people at the convention behaved in such a manner that if Charles W. Heins or I had done so Mr. Leston M. Ayres or Mrs. Helen Heins would probably have said we were tricky. For instance, the custodian of ballots is a very conscientious woman. She has read more Bible history than most of us have forgotten. But she had not read the constitution of the National Amateur Press Association. Therefore she arrived on the forenoon of the first day minus the proxies. Her excuse was delightfully naive. She understood that the Recorder would not arrive until the day of election! After an aghast silence the presiding officer managed to find sufficient voice to inform the well-meaning bar to progress that it was absolutely necessary to have the proxies as soon as possible. One glance at the constitution would, of course, have shown that practically nothing can be done at a convention until the proxies are received, they being the keynote on which is built a N. A. P. A. election.

* * *

Little bits of funny business perpetrated all unconsciously by people who are very, very good—these were balanced by an occasional lack of courtesy in those who truly want to be agents of sweetness and light. For instance that political party which owed all allegiance to the retiring president, actually neglected in many instances to vote for that retiring president as an executive judge. It cast votes for Mrs. Annie C. Ellis and Mrs. Marjorie Outwater Ellis (on the same ballot), but it quite forgot the President who was going out of office. Now, as the result has proven, Mr. Moitoret did not care for the position; like Tim Thrift in 1906 he has "declined the doubtful honor," still it was not the part of the convention to forestall him in this. There were, as it happened, enough people at Boston with a sense of the proprieties to elect him, thus leaving him a free agent in further disposal of the matter. Perhaps he doesn't thank us, but we at least feel the better for what we did.

* * *

My next plan for improving the National is going to raise a howl—that is, it will if anyone digests it, which I doubt, because the N. A. P. A., like all other adult humanity, is naturally averse to studying any plan admittedly for its improvement. I want to put through a scheme for diminishing the size of the organization. In other words, to double the dues and provide for an initiation fee of $1. This would accomplish two things—eliminate (at least largely) recruiting for voting purposes, and provide funds sufficient to pay for the official organ. It would probably make the association a trifle smaller, at least for a time, but the "real stuff" would surely remain.

Round Numbers Are Always False

Saturday may be summed up as "marking time" day. The convention marked time while the proxies were retrieved from Roxbury. It continued to mark time while name by name was droned out of the 40-odd names of new members not considered eligible by the committee appointed to interpret the secretary's report. It being a rainy day this diversion took the place of a trip to Norumbega Park. But finally we did adjourn and get to 20 Webster Street, where beans were eaten and friendships cemented. The proxies, however, hung over the festivities like Damocles' famous sword. Even Heins and Houtain came late to the enjoyment of Mrs. Sawyer's profuse hospitality and the delay was presumed to have some connection with proxies.

* * *

Sunday at 10.30 the first envelope was ripped open and the grind began. It was merely interrupted by a trip down the harbor; it lasted until after 10 that night. That is, seven people perspired and worked while the rest of the convention marked time, with a toddle top. It was obvious that Dorothy MacLaughlin was elected; it was obvious that neither Dowdell nor Heins was absolutely sure of the official editorship.

* * *

Over-discounting robs success of any thrill of triumph, thus it was with the election of Dorothy MacLaughlin. And yet but a few "ifs" would have put naming the next executive in the hands of the convention. The vote of the successful candidate was 98–71 proxy and 27 convention. That of the defeated candidate was 47–40 proxy and 7 convention. There were two scattering votes and 1 blank seems to have gotten by the constitutional rejection of such, by what hocus pocus I do not now recall. Thirty-four proxy votes were, for various reasons, not counted. These were not all, of course, Hyde votes, but they were largely so, for the reason that the MacLaughlin campaign managers were more "on the job" than were their opponents.

* * *

Miss Hyde was obviously cheated of any chance—cheated by her own lassitude in avoiding the convention and many other chances to win popularity, cheated by the carelessness of her campaign managers, who neglected to see that "their" people voted, even when dues were paid and activity records complete. Against such odds even a wave of sympathy roused by attacks on her discretion could not save her. This is a good thing, too, because Edna Hyde would probably have made a very poor president. It is not her metier. Why she persists in running for office is a problem. She excells in numerous other directions. Her fame doesn't require office holding.

* * *

The success of Dorothy MacLaughlin was due to splendid team work, first; and to a winning personality, second. At the beginning of the year Dorothy MacLaughlin did not loom very large in amateur journalism. Starting with the rock basis of membership and office holding in the Hub Club, she was skillfully presented to the National members at large by Charles A. A. Parker during the first weeks of the New Year, in which work he was extensively aided by Laurie Sawyer and the writer, personal friends of Dorothy MacLaughlin for years. Late in February the candidate moved to New York and by pure force of personality won the majority support of the Blue Pencil Club. The latter part of her campaign was conducted from New York, presumably by Messrs. Houtain and Heins, James F. Morton, Jr., being an 11th hour added coadjutor. It was an arduous campaign conducted without any regard to economy of any sort.

* * *

It was successful, but the figures are startling. I cannot refrain from noting my own amazement that under the circumstances the vote was so small. I had looked for returns that would compass the full voting strength of the organization, feeling no doubt that everyone had been canvassed by Messrs. Parker and Houtain—one or both—on the one side, and by Miss Hyde's energetic supporters on the other. And when we come to the official editorship we shall find a vote falling behind that for the two heads!

* * *

Personally I feel that the N. A. P. A. made an excellent choice and that the coming year may, if the powers wish it, be made one of extraordinary achievement. As I said in nominating E. Dorothy MacLaughlin in *The Muffin Man* last April—and which nomination, as every one knows, would have been made two months previous only for my giving the candidate herself the chance promised me for February of getting out my paper on the Parker Press—she is business-like and dependable. The National Presidency requires the expenditure of time and money and she can employ both. She may, if she so wills it, be president of the entire organization, a "United" association that is truly "National." And if she is susceptible to influence it is merely a trait which she shares with most women—and all men.

Studious To Please and Not Ashamed To Fail

With a presidential election largely cut and dried we had to concentrate on something else for excitement; that something else was the official editorship. All candidates for the office came into view somewhat late in the year. Dowdell was generally supposed to have an eye on the presidency, and to be using the official editorship as a stalking horse. John Heins because of youth, had also a hard job to get himself taken seriously. Both candidates were live wires and hard workers, one felt reasonably sure neither would fall down on the job; that there would be a pleasant absence of threats of resigning which had so checkered the last term.

* * *

Now the official editorship of the N. A. P. A. is one of those God-like gifts which may turn out a golden apple, or may turn out a lemon. It may land you in the presidential chair or (lacking contributions) in the poor house. An able official editor may redeem a bad year, and a poor official editor is an old man of the sea to the very best executive. As is well known, the money apportioned to the official organ by the constitution is a mere drop in the bucket to the actual cost, and only men and women advantageously situated as regards the securing of printing can afford to take the office, unless they are willing to accept contributions. And also, it may be added, unless they can secure contributions.

* * *

Under these circumstances it is not peculiar that the office seeks the man or woman. This year the office chased the nominees for months—to have one of the fiercest struggles of modern times develop at the end.

* * *

I have no means of knowing what happened previous to February 21, but on that date I was asked to be a candidate. I declined. Time passed, the New York branch of the MacLaughlin party announced that it would have no ticket. The Boston branch, headed by L. A. Sawyer, Winifred V. Jackson and myself, sent out what we called "The Ticket." On this, choosing "as angels choose," we named people who, without respect to party, seemed ideal candidates. Horace L. Lawson, whose able *Wolverine* has deservedly won him appreciation in high quarters, was named as official editor. More support was instantly offered him than was secured by the finally successful candidate, but Mr. Lawson thought it well to decline for the best of reasons—he believed he would be able to serve the N. A. P. A. to greater effect in some future year. Now at what was presumably about this time the oddity of a Hyde supporter being offered a place on a ticket headed by MacLaughlin was paralleled by an offer which was made to Mr. Heins for a similar position on the Hyde ticket. Whether or not Heins supported the MacLaughlin interests then I do not know, but he later came to do so.

* * *

In mid-spring Heins and Dowdell developed as "regular" candidates, and it was to be supposed that the voting strength of the organization would crystallize around one or the other (but it didn't).

* * *

Young Heins started off gallantly with the support of the old man element. He delighted the Fossils at their annual dinner in April, where he was the guest of L. E. Tilden. He is the "boy with the printing press," whom they have been seeking, lo these many years. Some of the Fossils, be it remembered, do not approve of the National as at present constituted, an avocation of men and women, many of mature age. These doubtless hailed with delight the possibility of a 13-year-old official editor, and only regretted want of a 12-year-old to be his running mate.

* * *

Lack of judgment is peculiarly a fault of youth, so it is not surprising to find it was the chief fault of young Heins, as he has now freely and frankly acknowledged. In the excitement of the campaign he forgot that even the truth should not be spoken on all occasions. Those who recalled the famous controversy between Charles W. Heins and Paul Campbell groaned in spirit as they contemplated a possible replica between a National official and a clever irritant.

* * *

They looked about for another candidate for the office, and several people apparently set their hopes at one time on one man—Charles A. A. Parker. Horace L. Lawson in the West and Michael White in the East were "original Parker men" perhaps, and he was also the candidate of the trio who had earlier in the year sent out "The Ticket." Messrs. White and Lawson issued papers endorsing Mr. Parker for the office. Parker himself was not an enthusiastic candidate. As Sandusky remarked, "He did not try to sell himself." If his election became necessary he consented to handle the office, and with his new printing plant would have been well able to do so. In accordance with the famous "Parker Principles" he would issue the paper absolutely without expense to the association, other than the constitutional sum, and he would invite no contributions. Further than this he intended to ask permission of the executive judges to give the National something really splendid, a monthly paper. Under such a regime the year 1921-22 would at once have taken a place of extraordinary glory in the history of the N. A. P. A.

* * *

At the same time Parker was not anxious to take all this on himself—and who can wonder? It would mean a great sacrifice, not only of time, but also of his own personal paper, which would of necessity have been laid on the shelf. This is the history of an extremely intensive campaign. The actual voting is treated in another paragraph. It resulted, as everyone knows, in the election of John M. Heins, 69 members of the association desiring him. I suppose the one person who heaved a sigh of relief when the election was over was C. A. A. Parker. He was left free to carry out his own cherished plans for the year. His record of 1909-10, five issues of *The National Amateur* issued on time and paid for by the appropriation, remains without present addition. Really, none is needed for his fame.

* * *

William Dowdell, by exercising a very trifling effort, might easily have made himself official editor. He did not exercise quite effort enough, he did not understand the game. A half hour in the convention hall of the Brunswick showed him where he had failed in estimating his opponents. He put up a strong fight and proved himself that *rara avis,* a good loser. After the proxies had been counted and he was found to be 11 votes behind Heins a valorous effort was made by Heins supporters to induce him to accept the office of treasurer—though exactly how the goods were to be delivered, with Lawson on the map as he was, has yet to be explained. The gallant manner in which Dowdell stuck to his guns and refused to throw down his friends "back home" won admiration, and on Monday a convention vote of 23 expressed that admiration during two indecisive ballots.

* * *

On the third ballot occurred one of those things one can hardly believe possible. With the Parker votes removed it became obvious that a tie vote might easily result, throwing the election in the lap of the convention. The idea of not voting evidently occurred to two people, one on each side of the house. The convention vote became 34, the two non-voters declining to exercise suffrage. One guesses shrewdly who they were. Of course the former Heins voter trusted to create a tie. Exactly what happened to the Dowdell voter is a moot question, for an ingrowing conscience is a queer and non-understandable thing.

* * *

John M. Heins was neatly elected by one vote, enabling his fond father to amusingly exult that he was "carrying home the bacon—though on a slender string."

This Was a Very Good Dinner

The banquet was a pleasant affair with one exceptionally fine speech, that of Howard P. Lovecraft, his subject being "Within the Gates," while he was introduced as "One Sent By Providence." And he was much funnier than that, I assure you. He equals anything I ever heard—even the renowned Truman J. Spencer in his active prime on such a topic as "The Amateur Printer," with which he has been known to keep the table a-roar for an hour. Willard O. Wylie toastmastered in slick manner and introduced some novelties, as when—à la Rotarian—each person introduced his or her left hand neighbor; also when he called for "stunts." Then J. Bernard Lynch sang "A Starry Night" to best advantage, with a better accompanist in Miss Ivie than he can usually command; and Miss Gladys Fraze showed that Apple Creek, Ohio, turns 'em out smart and zippy. The Houtain-MacLaughlin engagement was announced, making a pleasing opening for congratulations, and Sonia Green had collected a few nickels as a blind and then presented the president-elect with a literal bucket of flowers, thus enabling Mr. Houtain to make a considerable hit later by saying to people, "Will you have a rose or a flower?"

His Friendship in Constant Repair

Taking advantage of the presence of William Lapointe he was asked to take part in the program, and we listened to a thrilling appeal for more active patriotic work from this eloquent speaker. It was eminently appropriate to the day, but the advice couched therein will of course not be taken by any dyed-in-the-wool amateur journalist. We are narrow in our likes and dislikes, we get out papers for the sake of saying our say, and not for any eleemosynary object. I have no doubt that this will appeal to Mr. Lapointe himself a little later when he has a few more *Onion River Tattlers* to his credit. At any rate, he was able to inspire one listener to the following result.

161

SINGLE TALENT

(NOTE—Mr. Lapointe of the *Onion River Tattler* said at the N.A.P.A. banquet that all the members should write exclusively on patriotic subjects.)

Now, Lovecraft, drop your trenchent pen,
And write no more of fiends incarnate—
Of Delphian dames or supermen
Who courted some far eerie star-mate;

And, Miniter, the day is done
When you, contented with your labors,
Dealt out, for all, the rustic fun
And foibles of Natupski Neighbors.

And Kleiner, too, the Brooklyn Keats,
Must cease his praise of Gladys' eyebrows,
Nor write of ev'ry lass he meets
In measures that delight the highbrows.
Then Loveman of the classic line
Must hush his ancient strains forever,
And with the rest in chorus join—
On orders fresh from Onion River.

For all must make the eagle scream
For pure delight, and never mention
A word of war-time graft, or dream
To doubt a "patriot's" intention.
Old Johnson said, in days-gone-by,
(And Sam I rather think was clever)
A phrase I fain would whisper nigh
The Tattler's ear by Onion River.

Michael White

NOTE—I think the author of the above, in his reference to Samuel Johnson, had in mind the doctor's declaration that "Patriotism is the last refuge of the scoundrel. Printer's Devil.

Elegant But Not Ostentatious

The dramatic moment was when Edward H. Cole, at the close of an address on quite another subject, fished a silver loving cup of severely simple design from under the head table, and presented it to W. Paul Cook, who had been carefully located with his back to said head table. It was inscribed:

Presented to
W. Paul Cook
National Amateur Press Association
President 1919-20
A tribute of appreciation for 25 years' service
in the cause of Amateur Journalism.

A lengthy compendium of loving cup literature might be prepared for N. A. P. A. reading. The flattest "presentation" was, I suppose, that of 1909, when Edward H. Cole was awarded the "Fossil cup." It had already been given to him in April at the Fossil dinner, but the donors requested that he lug it over to New York again in July and receive it once more! By that time one feels that he must almost have expected it. This presentation in 1921 was really truly surprise. One of Mr. Cook's friends relates that a few weeks before convention Cook was heard to remark casually that he was glad nothing had been done to revive the loving cup scheme which Cleveland had side-stepped. He is said to have added that anyhow he "wouldn't want to receive any such gift in Boston." He'd "prefer to receive it in an enemy city."

Well, no city would seem to be that to Paul Cook!

Catch The Transient Hour

Boston banquets appear fated of late to the anti-climax. In February at the conference there was an untoward interruption of what nobody wanted just then—politics—and in July finances were introduced. Taking advantage of "the psychological moment" over $100 was pledged for the official organ and the publicity bureau—William Alcott actually paying $2 in money! Recalling the struggles of Official Editor Outwater last year to induce pledgers to make good on their pledges the sight of real cash was most encouraging.

FOLLIES OF THE WISE

The session next day was important in two particulars. Elaborate provision of compensation was made to the fifty new members whose credentials were unsatisfactory; and Mr. Houtain made a motion that the official editor be empowered to sell space in the official organ, and also to receive additions to the official organ fund, subject to approval of the executive judges, "as the Treasury had nearly $200." (Quotation from officially approved minutes.) C. A. A. Parker then moved to amend that the official editor be empowered to receive an additional sum of One Hundred and Fifty Dollars above the constitutional allowance, the same to be paid in sums of $25 each two months, to be expended under direction of the president and executive judges. Shortly after which Mr. Houtain withdrew his motion!

The exact object of all this I will not attempt to elucidate, the result was excellent. Without any reflection on the present or any other administration, a tendency to utterly deplete the treasury at the beginning of a year should be deprecated. Conventions do love to vote sums, and there's a fatal tendency to play the philanthropist every time a warm campaign brings in a few extra dollars. Robbing the future and forgetting our ever growing list of ex-presidential deadheads is one reason for the N. A. P. A. being so poverty-struck. But I hope this is the last year that the National will find it necessary to go round with its hand out, or to pay its just debts with extraordinary funds however secured.

THE CROWD OF JOLLITY

After adjournment we went to the ball game and to Revere Beach, where H. P. Lovecraft dropped 85 feet and all was over. Until the next evening when we had a mock trial at 20 Webster Street because Messrs. Heins and Houtain considered they had been "swindled" at the banquet (too good so they wanted more, near as I can make out). Then all seemed really over, but before we could turn round James Morton, R. Kleiner and E. Dench were back from a hike that took in Vermont, New Hampshire and Athol, Mass., where Cook reported looking out one evening and finding "three tramps in the woodshed," and the tramps said the loving cup was christened in water. Kleiner then went back to New York and we did think all was over, but Dench went on another hike and came back when we were away and clumb in the window L. A. Sawyer keeps unlocked solely for the grocer's boy, so evidently, though the 'vention lies mouldering in its grave, its soul is marching on.

Very Clubable Men (And Women)

There was no convention bride. But the election is probably legal.

Probably no family was ever better represented at a banquet than was that of C. A. A. Parker. They were all there—even Bunny, the 5-year-old. And demure behavior marked the entire second generation.

Speaking of the second generation, our presiding officer came in late one morning and when asked the reason confessed that it was "not unconnected with an attempted murder." As he had not completed his legal studies it had to be in the family circle. Master Sherman just didn't fancy little sister's eyes, that's all.

One president and seven ex-presidents make a fine front row for the group photograph. Two other ex-presidents—Dr. Swift and Toastmaster Wylie, attended one or more sessions.

"Where are Billy Dowdell and Ernest Dench going in such a hurry?" was asked, and the reply came immediately, "Each fellow is after a detective to help him recognize his wife." Whatever did possess those girls to grow so gloriously tall and then to buy hats almost alike?

C. W. Heins must have had a hunch he and hisn would want to do a lot of writing. He fetched over such a supply of splendiferous red ink.

Toastmaster Wylie may have believed he was convincing when he introduced the lady on his left as "My wife Elizabeth—the best woman in the world," but I bet it was only through politeness that a lot of men folks didn't answer back.

Harriet Cox-Dennis went home after a day and a half and collapsed for a week. Said 'twas hot weather, but I feel guilty because she washed the dishes Sunday morning at my house. Fact, it's a mistake to do such work during convention time. As preventative no more were "done" during the week.

Rumor says that every time any one emerged from the parlor of the Houtain suite he or she ran into a policeman. Fear of this was what made it so hard for many to get out of that apartment, I suppose.

We know now who calls Willard T. Ellis, "Tilt." Practically all the visitors did so, applying the name to every traffic cop they saw. We of the home team assured them that though a big man on the force (6 feet odd in his stocking feet) he wasn't quite so ubiquitous, but "Oh, there's Tilt!" they'd yell deliriously every time they saw a human windmill in a nifty uniform with white suspenders worn outside.

Mrs. Mary Kennedy takes the palm for industry, writing and typing her account of "hungry thirsty hands" since published in the Beacon before echoes of the festivity staged by Mrs. Sawyer at 20 Webster Street had died away.

Miss Gladys Fraze declared it was her ambition to become a virtuous vamp. But I fear that daily letter to the original of a solider boy photo prevented her putting her whole heart into it.

Billy Dowdell is surely some camouflagist. He took my vinegar bottle, poured the brown liquid into several glasses, and Messrs. Heins, Lynch, Houtain, et al., believing it was something forbidden by the 18th amendment, all but drank it. Bet Billy knows how to successfully hand lemons if he ever wants to do so.

Iva Dench's sister is the real Clinging Vine, but Iva became the Clinging Iva round our heart when she came to 20 Webster Street and named Tat "sweet thing."

There is one perfectly truthful paragraph in "Three-Oh-Three," Mr. Houtain's contribution to *National Tribute*. Cat and Tat fight occurred exactly as described.

Sometimes we missed the clever and interesting Mrs. Sonia Green, but as she always explained that she was in her own room "absolutely absorbed in a book" we had to forgive her. At least I had to, the book being *Our Natupski Neighbors*. The same absorption explained (or I hope so) her getting lost whenever she went into the streets of Boston alone. Even when she departed from 20 Webster Street Saturday after the bean supper, with that book under her arm, she got lost. Said she was looking for a taxi—which was about as big a compliment to our part of Allston as asking change for $10 was to the coon.

We did have the politest guests! When Miss Alice Ivie was taken sick Saturday evening she blamed it on the journey here, even though she had just gotten an extended view of the Boston Baked Bean—that viand which so ill agrees with many New Yorkers. Anyhow, we were all made thankful by her speedy recovery.

Laurie Sawyer presented the visiting ladies at 20 Webster Street with gardening aprons adorned with "flowerpot pockets"—all made out of her own head and vari-colored chambray. Not to be outdone in generosity I gave Pearl Merritt a bungalow apron adorned with a grease spot that was a family heirloom. The chambray one inspired Lucie Dowdell, we hear, to give a party. Pearl Merritt, please write.

Nelson G. Morton had the time of his life taking the other side from his brother on every possible point. Any cause, therefore, may say it had Morton backing.

The prettiest picture in "the picture" is back of the president-elect's fiancé. Name it Dorothy Louise Morton.

Ethel Myers occupied the lime-light at one intense moment of the convention, when a huge fly came in the window, and the cockroach then lighting on the dress of Mrs. K. Leyson Brown we all saw a most venemous beetle, and Mrs. Myers being rendered speechless by fright at the spider something awful would have resulted only C. A. Parker bravely snatched the tarantula in his unguarded hand and Mrs. Myers dropped from her handkerchief and the window a dead scorpion.

Mrs. Cole had two good reasons for staying at home, in Master Sherman and Baby Marion Elizabeth, but she gave us two evenings of her sweet and charming presence, for which we were duly grateful.

I only regret that she couldn't have seen her whale of a husband cow the lions with his eagle eye.

H. P. Lovecraft reports going home at midnight of July 6 and "sleeping 18 hours without taking anything off." I suppose if Hazel Adams and I had been there he'd have removed his hat and given it to us to hold. That's what he did when he tried all the soporific stunts at Revere.

Wire received on morning of July 5: "Congratulations, am with you and will help." Addressed "President N. A. P. A." Signed "Doc." Trust that one to play safe.

Rheinhart Kleiner and Howard P. Lovecraft went to the Art Museum on Tuesday afternoon, in an evident desire to see something beautiful. They probably did not know Gladys Fraze was to be at the ball game.

E. A. Rowell arrived just before luncheon Monday and was hailed as "from the Pacific coast." Then he went to lunch and was presented with a check for $11.98. After which he left abruptly. Can't blame him.

Michael MacNamara came also for a brief while, and explained elaborately that he would remain longer only he was not on his day off. It's the way firemen talk before they save anybody's child.

Those who expressed wonder and regret that Mrs. Ellis absented herself from time to time did not know that she was publishing a paper. "Approximately" 75 copies of *The 11th Hour* were done on a typewriter, each containing "practically" the same matter. Such industry deserves a better reward than it got. But why not hire a printer?

Quite like old times Jacob Golden strolled in on the last day, went to luncheon with the bunch, and purchased several foods that he couldn't eat until Edward Cole "fixed 'em" for him. While that was going I harked right back to 1909. But what does he do when he is away from us?

Mrs. Helen Heins was extremely pleasant as met—and that she is clever also was proven by her going home and putting such a lot of barbs on the extremely inoffensive account of the convention which she read us on July 6.

Jim Morton was so sick one morning he just got up on the floor and spent half an hour apologizing because he couldn't talk. Then he recovered and that afternoon talked about a week. We felt relieved, and so, I suppose, did he.

Losses galore reported during doings. Besides hearts and such trash, always mislaid first week in July by amateur journalists, Mosley, L. Sawyer and I lost umbrellas (some were found), Wilber lost a perfectly good hat which he rather needed and which Boston harbor and Massachusetts Bay probably do not need at all. Ritezel lost a fountain pen and spent more than its worth telegraphing for it, Lovecraft deserted a costly and expensive $2.50 Brownie camera and Thomson lost all the minutes because he was too busy being surprised at the way things were going to write 'em down.

Mrs. "Munsey" Jackson, mother of the poet, had a real escort to the banquet. When asked if he did the proper thing she replied, "Well, I'll say he did. Bought my ticket, sent me flowers and upset a glass of water." Regular feller! Name Michael White.

Orvan T. G. Martin just loves to tell at length his experiences over across. When asked "Did you see much of war?" he replies, "I saw enough" and abruptly changes the conversation.

J. Bernard Lynch did more than just get out the best campaign paper of the campaign. He secured the city boat for the Sunday trip, our biggest amusement feature, and even had emissaries posted on Atlantic Avenue so no possible trippers should go astray.

Old timers seeing Albert Sandusky's haberdashery were reminded of Edwin Hadley Smith's famous convention suit only because they were so different. Sandusky says next time he'll not forget to get up early just because he sat up all night. Well, that's a wise crack.

From certain quarters comes the understanding that the writer will be able to "live down" only after a term of years, and C. A. A. Parker "never" the crime of July 4. What is this crime—referred to euphoniously as "it"? Why, C. A. A. Parker knifed himself—cut his own throat—double crossed his own self. Naughty, naughty. Well, 'tis all as it should be. Strange, unnatural, nay, impossible crimes should certainly be deprecated!

EACH CHANGE OF MANY-COLORED LIFE

At my last convention, in July of this year,
The folks expected stayed away (oh, ain't it awful queer?)
On day the first much fun was planned, so furious, fast and loud,
But those pernicious proxies they hung o'er us like a cloud.
We got 'em hustled through at last, we found "our girl" was in,
And now, thinks we, a year of peace is ready to begin.
So to a love feast down we sat, each by and by to say,
"I wish I'd had another seat"—it always is that way.

* * *

Oh, hark, I hear some pleading words, spoke in a voice of pain,
"Please, folks, give me my honor back"—the voice of George
     Houtain.

* * *

And one bewildered female may in Boston streets be seen
A-seeking the convention halls—and that is Sonia Green.

* * *

Comes the last day, of votes of thanks we do supply a quota
All to the folks whose care for us it hain't been an iota.
Then—home so dead for want of sleep we snore from sun to sun—
And this is 1885?—No! 1921!

(*The Aftermath,* November 1921)

THE FEBRUARY MEETING

As President J. B. Lynch called the HUB JOURNALIST CLUB to order in one of the commodious studios at Huntington Chambers on the evening of February 8, he had a right to feel gratified at the large attendance and the "atmosphere" of enthusiasm. The president of the National—Howard P. Lovecraft—had traveled up from Providence; there were also three ex-presidents, Messrs. Morton and Cole and Mrs. Miniter. The entire official board of the club was there, so was the entire Morton family. Mrs. J. E. Gunter was trying us for the first time, we hope she liked us, for we certainly liked her. Other "new" people were the distinguished couple, Mr. and Mrs. Osborne, both well known writers in the professional world; and Daniel S. Lawton, whose work on the *Herald* shows so much promise.

Twelve members were admitted. These included Harriet Cox Dennis of Peabody and Willard O. Wylie of Beverly, who helped to organize the club 33 years ago, and C. W. Smith, who printed the first official organ, the *Hub Official,* as many years back. Miss Adaline F. Norcross, who was present, rejoined following a slight lapse in membership. After 20 years in professional journalism, Miss Norcross is now engaged in playwriting. Another of the new members who was present was Miss Marian L. Carter, editor *Simmons College Review,* and a "double" in charm with her friend Miss Terrill.

"The" feature of the evening was an informal address by Maitland L. Osborne, editor of Joe Chapple's *National Magazine;* a man who is able to talk on both sides of the writing game, for he has been a contributor of both fiction and poetry to the best popular magazines, as well as a critical judge of that sort of thing submitted by other folks for his acceptance or rejection. Of absorbing interest, informative, sparkling with witty references, sometimes cynical and always truthful—the sole regret caused by Mr. Osborne's talk was that it had to come to an end.

Howard Martel turned the mind to another branch of artistic endeavor, with some masterly piano playing; and the club then settled down to enjoying Mrs. Kennedy's delicious sandwiches and cake, with plenty of hot coffee and social chat.

A most thoroughly "worth while" meeting was the comment of both new members and those of auld lang syne.

(*The Hub Club Quill*, May 1923)

THE BIG EVENT

On Saturday evening, March 10, at Hotel Hemenway, in the Back Bay district of Boston, J. Bernard Lynch, president of the HUB JOURNALIST CLUB, looks down on a vista of forty covers, flanked by members "and friends." The club itself looks down on a vista of—one hopes—another 33 years. We may not all be here in 1956, but others will "carry on" even as we are upholding the torch first lighted in 1890. As a starter attention is paid to

INTERIOR DECORATIONS

Bluepoint Oysters on Half Shell *à la* H.P.L.

One sent by Providence is he to fill Sustaining Stations,
They likewise for sustaining we hail from those same Plantations.

Cream of Tomato Soup aux Croutons M.A.K.

Both pink and white blend in a perfect plan
To best result—as with our Mary Ann.

Celery—J.B.L.   Olives—Mr. & Mrs. M.L.O.

Howe'er inclement be the clime   Olives—you have to learn
                                                                              to like 'em
Both bring the best of harvest time. Some folks seem friends soon's
                                                                          you strike 'em.

Fish

It's Lent!

Half Broiled Young Chicken *à la* R.E.B.

Half a chick may the cuisine suit,
But the Club has whole ones,
And each a "beaut"!

French Fried Potatoes   A.A.S.String Beans E.H.C.

One thing's to say of this young man

He "does it brown" when he starts to "pan."

Ne'er let this one
have his fling
He's sure to get
you on a string.

Hearts of Lettuce Salad H.J.C.—Russian Dressing

Hearts of lettuce are bought and sold,
But they can't be bought—the hearts of gold
Of those whose presence tonight's a blessing—
For winsome faces and beautiful dressing.

Ice Cream and Cake, à la "The Ladies"

"Newcastle coals" is still in force,
So, sweet ones, please pass up this course.

Coffee—G.I.M.

Must we drink coffee? Yes, indeed,
Lest law deprive us of our Mead!

Everyone was, of course, felicitously placed, an arrangement easily made possible by there being an equal number of either sex among those present. Attempts—probably subconscious—had been made to clog up the works. One officer brought a female sister, but quite luckily another countered with a male cousin. Three sets of fond parents proudly escorted feminine representatives of the second generation, but to balance Misses Dorothy Morton, Elinor Parker and Geraldine White numerous unattached bachelors—Messrs. Alcott, Lovecraft, Martel, Mead, Dyer, Mosely, et al.—put in appearance. All of which testified to the splendid resources of the club.

The first adventure was a flashlight photograph. One of those affairs everyone considers it a bore to be in, and so nice to pay a plunk to be assured a copy of afterward. Why, the president of the National actually attempted to hide his fragile form behind the massive mould of the H. C. secretary—yet seemed quite philosophical when he was forced to face fire from the seat saved for Sibley. Perhaps because he was so impressed with the subtle compliment of dedicating to him the first course, seeing that he "never touches shell fish in any form." Fish only. Official positions have forced him into frequent association with other shell protected articles.

Formality and the glooms evidently understood they would not be wanted, but we were pleased to note that a recent effort to make the world safe for democracy was not thrown away. Those with dinner coats were perfectly condescending to those with none—no, that isn't quite what we mean. Everyone had a coat of some sort, but some of them had no dinner to 'em, if you get my meaning. Not but what all et and hearty. And I'm sorry I began this important piece of important description, but it runs over from a previous page, which has already been imPRESSed by C. A. A. P. Anyhow, we acted real sweet, even to the unfortunate girl who had lost both her sleeves riding to the festivities in a taxi. Quite a few went so far as to recognize the club treasurer, though most took her for a convention bride when they saw the white satin slippers and the spandy new frock. Indeed, it is rumored that a start was made at raising the usual fund to provide the bride with a piece of useless cut glass, but this was nipped in the bud, probably by the president, who, long our sob story artist, still continues touching.

It must be noted, at the risk of being prolix, that both "Mary Ann" and her sister did their best to look familiar to us, which was especially good of the latter, as it was her first appearance. They actually went to the length of having their hair waved in honor of the occasion; it cost them a great deal of money, and then they went right home and soaked the wave.

Ignoring any temptation to enlarge on the opportunity for inexpensive wit let us pass immediately to the after dinner exercises. Not POST prandial. Mr. Nixon Waterman, the *Traveler* columnist, had his chance at the *Globe* and *Post;* and Mr. Frank P. Sibley, of the *Globe,* his at the *Traveler-Herald, Transcript* and POST; but our own Mr. Albert A. Sandusky of the POST had to eat his words, which was quite superogatory after such a good dinner as Hotel Hemenway provided.

Scratched But Not Hurt

This was too bad—or two bad—first because our Mr. Sandusky is a wiser cracker than any put out by the Educator folks, and because the POST is the only Boston paper owned by a former member of the HUB CLUB, Mr. E. A. Grozier, though the Herald runs a sort of second inasmuch as Editor O'Brien occupied a dormitory at Harvard vacated by James F. Morton, Jr., a former H. C. president.

Scratching a number of our best speakers, even including the writer of these lines, was necessary on account of the musical program by which our Musical Director Martel covered himself with glory. The Harmonique Trio, Miss Harriet Jewell, cello; Miss Doris Dutcher, violin; and Mr. George Coward, piano; pleased us by numerous selections, most especially by a march, "Our Journalists," composed for this occasion by Miss Jewell and dedicated to the HUB CLUB. There was a blithesome solo dance by Miss Marion Hennessey, a vision in pink.

"Three for Jack" Strikes 12

The musical honors went to Mr. Thatcher Clark, baritone soloist; his mellow tones rolled out most delightfully in the droll "Three for Jack," he was then heard with pleasure in an encore, and later he gave us Hawley's "Because I Love You, Dear." "A Starry Night in Ireland," "Rainbow of Love" and "Autumn Blaze" by three club members—Lynch, Wagner and Groves—were on the program, but had to be omitted because Mr. Martel's voice was rendered unusable through grip. Under the circumstances Mr. Martel showed splendid spirit in attending and bringing to successful result the program. Next time we hope for his own sweet notes as well.

Sin-Seeking Cynic

Among the denizens of history who have builded better than they knew, will forever rest the individual who devised the toast list. Of course this cynic seeking sin frightened a few. When Jane Verne Terrill saw

Le Grosse Homme—'Tis said that when an Albanian shakes his head he means yes. Well, we've seen American fellows like that— she shot all her hair pins into space and declined without thanks. Michael White read

Last but not Least—Every dog has his day and the cats yowl all night.

Then he took his dinner pail and went to work, preferring the sweat of his brow to the honey of speech.

But this did not please Edward H. Cole—

Politiculorium—A politician stands only for what people will fall for?

It did not. And he wasted only a few weeks in trying to ascertain what it was all about and sticking to his subject before he realized that that way madness lay. Whereupon, by mercilessly cutting the red tape which in his imagination is so obnoxious at club meetings, he achieved a most excellent set of remarks, wherein were incorporated numerous knocks, a reference to Mrs. Cole and the chapter headings in a volume of Macchiavelli.

ROCKING HORSING

J. Bernard Lynch was toastmaster. Last October we re-elected him president principally because, like the man for whom he himself voted in 1917, he kept us out of war. Presidents on their second terms often lead a rocking chair existence, but that of Mr. Lynch, so far, has been more of a rocking horse one. At least if there's truth in the saying, "Worked like a horse."

He has brought in some twenty new members, and has written to scores of prospectives. His bill for typewriting and mimeographing, if properly submitted, would put the club in debtor's prison until radio stops featuring cat fights. When one promised speaker develops "flu" he phones another and when that one takes an expensive trip to California to avoid addressing us he just makes a well-known magazine editor a club member and at the next meeting snakes him from the audience and compels him to give us the most practical and delightful of lectures.

Some one proposed a vote of thanks to President Lynch, but the idea was abandoned for fear he would think it necessary to go on the retired list, since that often follows the receipt of thanks. Besides, we had made no provision for saying it with flowers. "Joe's" favorite blossom being the piccalily.

BEAUTIFUL BROWN STUDY

Mr. Frank P. Sibley cut short a stay at a hospital in order to be with us. I can't say whether or not he ever gets into a brown study in order to produce those meaty stories of Sacco's hunger strike, now running on the first page of the *Globe,* but he was a study in brown, even to cigarette holder, and fearfully pretty to look at. I liked to look at him, we all liked to look at him when he gave waist bows every time Nixon Waterman mentioned the *Globe.* Mr. Sibley spoke first, and it didn't occur to Mr. Waterman to bow every time he was insulted. This was unfortunate, for now we don't know whether his indentations come at the neck or the knees. One rather imagines at the knees.

Sibley's Simplicity Succeeds

Presenting himself as a member of that profession which is the hand-maid of truth, Mr. Sibley told how he got to Europe as a war cor-respondent by the simple process of saying when he asked for a passport that he had just come from the Secretary of War, without adding that said S. of W. had so cleverly dissembled his love for war correspondents as to all but kick Mr. Sibley down stairs. He also told other illuminating things about journalism. His wit is dry, probably was even before 1919. We are all going to remember him as long as he says President Eliot did.

One secret of Mr. Sibley's popularity was made very evident to us on this occasion. He is generous of effort, had he been getting space rates he certainly gave us as much again as we ran in debt for. Following his regular remarks he teamed right up with Mr. Waterman, as before hinted, and evolved the cutest little sketch. Without any entente with the orchestra or calling the pianist Eddie or anything. All they needed was a musical hat-rack to be good as any other sidewalk artists.

Disorder the Order

About this time the printed toast list went into the discard, only those supposed capable of hitting high places were called upon—or so one likes to think. It was rather tough, though, that not one of the club's board of officers was among the few chosen, when all except the vice president—excused from youth—had been among the many called. Even after Entertainer White had collected his family and went away, there remained the official editor, the secretary and the treasurer. But—oh, goodie!—the official editor has the official organ, the secretary has these minutes, and the treasurer has the *Tryout*. You can't keep a good man down—you can't silence a woman.

THIRD FOR FOURTH ESTATE

Nelson G. Morton represented the Associated Press and himself and the ex-presidency of the National which Mr. Lovecraft is only keeping himself alive long enough to get into, and his revered grandfather the author of "My County 'Tis" and the HUB CLUB idol. This is a relic of 1900, when some bright person said he was that, and he not then a member of the club being as he lived in New Hampshire and sustaining members not discovered as a source of revenue.

After expressing the highly original opinion that his subject "Epistolary Sniping" was his idea of just nothing at all, Mr. Morton described the work of the Associated Press in good, sensible, understandable manner, not forgetting some amusing anecdotes. With the exception of one year when he felt he'd rather go a-fishing, Nelson Morton has worked for the A. P. during all of his career, what he does not know of its working is hardly worth knowing. For it he has even eaten breakfast at 10 P. M. and dined while his family partook of matutinal oatmeal. A topsy-turvy life, he evidences his strength of mind by being no more insane than the rest of us. That is, he writes poetry.

CONSCIENCE AND CONVICTS

Conscientiousness ought to be Howard P. Lovecraft's middle name, but perhaps the "P" stands for probity, which Soule's *Synonyms* says is the same thing. He really tried to make out that he understood his subject "The Bushovik," but if he did it was more than anyone else could say. We got a vague notion that a man named Bush is somewhat in the plot, that Bush writes good stuff—moral:—which Lovecraft unwrites and rewrites, collecting therefor a little cash and great deal of headache.

Sub-title—"A number of Charlestown convicts," says the Boston *Herald*, "have taken to writing poetry." Isn't that going from bad to verse?

This proved inspiring. However far he got lost in the Bush, the speaker invariably wandered back to those convicts. In both places he was excruciatingly funny. He always is, and what part of the fun is due to the speech, and what to staccato utterance and an air of temporarily abandoning Greek for this time only is difficult to decide. That Lovecraft is learned there's no denying, but he can condescend to canaille. He is reading a book recommended by his barber, he let 'em make him president of the National, he spoke to us. Sandusky is right. Lovecraft IS a good old scout.

Nixon, O W'at A Man

Some of us had never seen a real live columnist until we were privileged to gaze our fill at the neat, compact and genial Mr. Nixon Waterman on the right hand of President Lynch at the head table. Once, to be sure, I took on Tuesday the job from which Bert Leston Taylor had been fired the previous Monday, but that was long ago, before Lineotype, when a printer and a machinist were not the same even though the printer did get called a blacksmith.

Mr. Waterman didn't say he was a handmaid of truth, but he bravely acted the part, making no attempt to hide the fact that he wrote poetry. Convicted himself, in short, though he cannily neglected to state whether he knew any more about the Charlestown shack than those numerous committees that keep collecting $10,000.00 every year to investigate it, which according to the *Transcript* is nothing at all.

He not only dares to be a poet, but dares to recite his poetry. He may, of course, have noticed that the waitresses carried off all debris of dinner, anyhow, he took a chance. One poem was about a married couple that got along like the ordinary couple that is married. The feeling of one confessing for the other was reminiscent of a story-heroine in the latest Jane Austen book, who remarks, "I murdered my father at a very early period of my life; I have since murdered my mother, and I am now going to murder my sister." Another bit of verse described a compressed flat. The author evidently had his vitamins the day it was composed.

The High Spots

Mr. Waterman hit these in some free verse entitled "Stockings" where he just socked it into Amy Lowell and Edgar Lee Masters.

And he found many of us at home when he defined free verse as the kind you don't have to pay to get printed.

Mr. Gurdon I. Mead also hit a few high places in responding for "Mine Liebe Mamselle." Hit so hard that more than once he fell down. With a good deal of effort he convinced us that he liked the American girl, but when he was done everybody was too scared to ask for Samoa.

(*The Hub Club Quill*, May 1923)

Fiction

THE VARIED YEAR

QUARTERLY

Vol. 1, No. 1. June, 1902.

TO THINE OWN HEART BE TRUE

The time of sunset was drawing near. The sky was becoming a dull, warm blue, promising of heat on the morrow. The trees cast long shadows, far to the eastward. A mile away the factory whistle blew warningly. A gentle breeze had sprung up from the south. Dusty and sun-wilted flowers lifted their heads to catch the first drop of dew. Close to the grass-grown back road stood the farm house, a wooden structure which was more weatherbeaten than aged. It was built in that style which has a gable roof, short at one side, and stretching to the very ground on the other end. A capacious porch crept under this roof, and presented a distracting variety of colors. Although the red paint had been nearly worn off from the clapboards of the main body, the walls protected by this porch were a brilliant yellow. A green door, with a well scoured brass knocker, opened outward. Between the house and road was a narrow yard, carefully fenced in with a scraggly arbor-vitae hedge, and brilliant with irregular growths of rank grass and flowers. Here were purple and white lichny, flaunting hollyhocks, pink clover, golden-rod, reddish orange tiger lilies, and an immense bed of myrtle surrounding a clump of southernwood.

Lying at full length in this yard, under the shade of a lilac bush, was a diminutive figure with a sharp voice. It was that of a girl, old enough to wear her hair high, and her skirts long, yet sufficiently childish to enjoy lying on the grass, and express no nervousness when mosquitoes bivouacked on her nose, or a company of ants held a picnic in her ear. She was an exceedingly tiny figure, in height and in form alike, with a face of irregular prettiness. The features were of a soberly coquettish cast, her brown hair was of very nearly a like color with her dark skin. Clad as she was in a brown woollen gown with a linen apron, she might have sat for a study in umber. She was anxiously observing her hands, which, although spread to their utmost capacity, were still tiny enough to have satisfied any woman. Yet there was a humorous pucker between her eyes, as she remarked, "Eight fingers, and two thumbs. One broken nail. Two grubbed off short. One cut, mended with black plaster. One scald. One blister shedding skin. Ten scratches. Three black places which won't rub off. Cause, paring apples. Marks of poison ivy. A mosquito bite. Some dirt unwashable. And these are my hands. And Charlie comes to-night. Oh-h-h!"

And a big yawn finished the inventory.

The white cotton curtains, edged with ball fringe, waved lazily in and out of the narrow window above her head. The sight aroused her to action.

"Aunt 'Manthey."

"Wal!" came a lazy drawl, very different from the tones of the girl—sharp and curt, though sweet.

"Make some `apple slump' for supper?"

"Where's th' apples?"

Silence followed. In the heart of the young lady love for "apple slump" was combatting with vanity. Finally greediness ruled and scrambling to her feet she cried, "I'll get them—yes, and pare them too."

"Better be lively," was the response. "It's gettin' on towards sundown."

Standing on tiptoe Camille called in at the window, "Get me a basket. And my hat. I don't know exactly where it is, but it's—somewhere."

A long gaunt arm handed out a rusty tin pail, with the broken handle fearfully and wonderfully repaired with variously colored strings. A limp sunbonnet followed the remark, "You kin find your hat yourself. I've no time to dandle."

With a laugh Camille stuck the unstarched green gingham bon-net on her head, and with the strings waving down her back, emerged into the sunshine. Back of the house was a steep bank, up which she drew herself by clutching the branch of an apple tree growing above, and digging her boot heels firmly into the turf. Green apples from the tree came rattling down into the yard below, greatly disturbing a couple of half grown speckled chickens, which had been pausing before the coop door, and, cocking their heads this way, and that, were apparently deciding between the merits of different roosts. But Camille went on unheeding, only stopping to speak to a lazy white cat, sitting on a stone wall among bittersweet vines, watching for chipmunks, with one eye and a half asleep. Pussy, with a yawn, gave up hunting, and followed the girl in her walk through the orchard. When at length the tree of red astra-khans was reached, Camille looked blankly at the ground beneath. Instead of being strewn with rosy apples, all ready for picking up, there were only a few half rotten ones scattered upon the trampled turf. A desperate shake at the stout old tree was unavailing. Of it nothing resulted but a couple of bruises on the much injured hands. Camille, in her perplexity, thrust her hands into her apron pockets, and whistled "Dixie," in a shrill undertone. Then she arrived at a sudden determination. Flinging the pail over the cat, she climbed to the top of the stone wall near by, and stood while the loose stones rattled down, calling, "Sa-a-a-y! Mis-ter Noble."

Hearing footsteps approaching she hastily returned to terra firma, and said meekly, "I—that is, auntie, wants some apples."

Young Noble was a stalwart young farmer, clad in gingham and tweed, with a broad straw hat, and a rake in his hand. He had a fair though sunburned skin, and a long mustache bitten ragged on the ends. His clear blue eyes and regular features gave him beauty of a commonplace sort. It was mere nothing for him to give the tree a vig-orous shake, which sent the apples tumbling down on Camille's sun bonneted head. She, however, gave no sign of the hard thumps her head was receiving, and picked up the apples with only a tiny smile on her lips as she wondered what somebody else would have done, were he in Henry Noble's place, and she suffering pain. After the pail was filled Mr. Noble inquired, abstractedly, if there was any-thing else he could do in aid, and then went back to his hay field.

Camille watched the erect figure, until it disappeared behind a clump of maples. Then the chick-chick of the mowing machine recommenced, while the girl, leaning meanly against the rough bark of the apple tree, pressed one hand tightly over her eyes, and thus kept the scalding tears from reddening her cheeks. In a moment she looked up, half dazed. Her lower lip trembled piteously, like a baby's, and for an instant she almost gave way to the luxury of pas-sionate weeping. Then she picked up the pail of apples, slung it on her arm, called to pussy, and walked resolutely back to the house, the while training her agonized lips into a mechanical smile.

"Milly," said the aunt, as she entered a dark kitchen, hot with fire, and noisy with the buzzing of flies, "there's a man in the settin' room. He wants to see you."

Camille set her teeth firmly together, clenched both hands for a moment, and then with a sudden catching of the breath, flung off the sunbonnet, and lifted the latch. The farmhouse parlor was wainscotted as to walls, with a whitewashed ceiling, and rag carpeted floor. The open windows gave free ingress to light, air, and flies. The room was furnished with a Franklin stove, now swathed in newspapers; a light stand on which the Bible, a spectacle case, the *Agricultural Weekly* and the *Watchman*, were ranged in precise order; half a dozen cane chairs, a wooden rocker cushioned with patchwork, and a tall clock which mistold the time for many year. It now pointed to half past five, and the man occupying the centre of the calico covered lounge was comparing it with his watch. On seeing Camille he sprang to his feet.

"At last I see you again. Can you imagine what joy it is? Have you not been lonely here? Why did you not allow me to send you another box of novels? Oh, Miss Camille, this is such great, such very great happiness."

This he exclaimed all in one breath, holding her by both hands the while.

Camille looked at him brightly, and drew her hands to herself most discreetly.

"Come, Charlie," she said, "sit down and be sensible. We'll have sup— tea I mean, in a few moments."

Charlie Verry was glad to find that three months' sojourning in the country had by no means altered Miss Camille. She was as saucy, and as gay, and withal as ladylike as ever. And he, poor fellow, pulled his black moustache, and felt that he was more deeply in love than ever.

Twilight came on, the apple slump was eaten, the crickets had set up their mighty chirping, and Camille was standing by the side of Charlie Verry under the willows, down in the hollow from the house. Both were leaning on the railing of a decrepit bridge which spanned a narrow tinkling brook. While they stood in shadow, outside in the meadow a tiny new moon was spreading a few limpid rays. Charlie was holding Camille's hand, and she was absorbed in a slough of thought. Charlie Verry had come all this distance to see her, he would ask her to marry him before he went back, she didn't doubt but he'd a diamond ring somewhere in his lug-

gage—so firmly did he rely upon her saying yes. He had loved her
for years—ever since they first met, a pert miss and a bashful boy at
dancing school. And Camille had always believed she loved him.
The touch of his hand gave her no thrill, and she never thought
long over any words of love which might escape from his lips. She
was always glad to see him, but never felt aggrieved when he might
have unconsciously neglected her. He was always kind and oblig-
ing, he gave her her own way ever, which goes far with a woman.
He was properly humble, and Camille perfectly understood that he
loved her and would ask for her heart in the approved fashion—some
day. And she was by no means in haste for the day to arrive. All
this had been before she had come to Glendale. Now she loved. The
first moment of her meeting with Ernest Noble was burned into
her memory. She saw always the blood red sky, the dripping trees
and turf, and out of the roseate twilight had stepped the man before
whom she had prostrated her spirit. That he seldom spoke to her
made no difference. It was bitter to feel that he refused to enter into
her life in any way, but it did not cure her illness. Ernest Noble was
a young farmer, contented with life and with himself, he was already "keeping company" with a practical young maiden, a beauty
in robust rustic style, whose father's acres adjoined young Noble's
farm. They would doubtless be sometime married—a sort of prosaic
marriage *de convenance*. He was cold and indifferent in all his ways,
practical in everything, rather oblivious to the existence of Camille,
the pretty flirt from the city. But her love, though fed not at all,
grew apace. Each morning she roused herself at the first glint of day,
to crouch behind the woodbine clad window of her room, and bid
Ernest Noble a silent good morning as he drove by on reaper or har-
row. In the dewy evenings she looked up to the stars, and begged a
blessing for him alone. She was most foolishly romantic, despite the
prosaic qualities of her hero. She invested him with few ideal qualities—Camille was clear sighted and a dissector of character—she only
gave him the worships of a tender heart to a strong spirit. Her love
was the deeper because it was hopeless. It was the kind which has
been inspired in some men for women entirely dissimilar to themselves. Only with them it often worked good; herself she could not
change. She would have given her life gladly for him, but there was
no need. He was entirely independent of so insignificant a creature

as herself. To do some great and noble deed, even if possible, would not have aroused any but passing interest in his mind. She was to him but a stranger, he was a god to her. Yet withal she could not feel any bitterness. She knew her own presumption, and smiled over it, miserably, at times. She could smile, and laugh, and play pranks, but all the time there ran through each day an undercurrent of sorrow. She accepted her fate calmly, and it was only at the thought that times would come when she could not even see his face, that she gave way to outward grief. And now Charlie had come for her love. That she could never give him—but she might give him her hand. Life would be happy for him with her as his wife—and he deserved happiness, he was so good. And she—yes, even she would be happier. Life would have more incident, more interest. Charlie would always be kind to her, there would be plenty of money, and no care. And after all, was she not the same as promised to Charlie? Had she not allowed him to love her all these years?

While thus her thoughts were going about in a piteous round, Charlie himself had drawn nearer to her, and had said the words so long on his lips. And Camille knew that the time for her decision had fully come. She paused a moment. Charlie bent anxiously over her, trying to get one look at the brown eyes.

"Charlie," began the sharp voice, now dropped almost to a whisper, "dear Charlie." Then she stopped.

Having made up her mind to be selfish—to prefer ease of life to fidelity—to accept Charlie—yet she paused.

"Dearest Camille."

"Charlie, I—" the words would not come.

"Yes, you mean yes, my darling," and was bursting into rapturous exclamations of an insignificant sort, when she suddenly drew back, put both hands over her face, and cried wildly, "Oh, I cannot, I cannot. Do not ask for me. I must not. Oh, Charlie, forgive me if you can, but you must forget."

And the twilight through which he had been peering, settled into Charlie Verry's eyes, as a mist of agony swam before them.

The long roof covers the same quaint rooms, where through moves another lone woman. Aunt 'Manthey is now gone—a narrow grave encloses all that is left of her narrow life. Camille is Camille alone, and the old house is her only home. Life is very drear and savorless, and she finds it hard to escape growing into a martinet. She has no object in life, but the days pass in some way. Each morning, for twenty years, has she peered through the vines at Ernest Noble. Every night a thrill passes through her heart as she descries the stalwart upright figure following its own long shadow homewards. Ernest Noble yet merely nods to his neighbor, and with his buxom matronly wife Camille has little to do. She feels no jealousy, scarcely any sorrow, all is dull and prosaic, with a little undercurrent of pleasure in the daily glimpses at that adored figure, unbending, stern, indifferent. Camille is very nearly as pretty as ever, but she is dead to all the world. She gave up all to love, and now that alone sustains her. And so the snows drift; and the rains fall, and the red paint is washed in streaks from the weatherbeaten house under the bank, and year by year Ernest Noble walks unthinkingly to and fro, followed by the longing eyes of a woman who could be true to love, however hopeless and useless.

(*The Ideal*, December 1887)

A TRAGEDY OF THE HILLS

Mercy Webster was neither young nor handsome, but she had what was better than either quality in the eyes of her neighbors—she had money. The last survivor of a family whose history had been for many generations identified with that of her native town, Mercy lived alone in the old homestead. She owned her well-stocked farm, she had money in banks and mortgages, in railroad stocks and in bonds. Moreover, as she had heart disease, everyone wondered to whom her property would go at her death. She had no relatives, and in her life she had never been public-spirited, so it seemed ridiculous to think she would will her property to either the town or the Orthodox Church. Attendants at the latter's services saw her there in the ancient red-curtained pew, every Sunday, but she never taught in the Sunday School, or made cake for sociables. She was odd.

She lived all alone, in a great square white clapboarded house, doing her own housework, and managing the farm work with shrewdness. As she was unable to plow or thresh with her own hands, she was obliged to hire a gang of men, and as workmen were not inclined to obey spinster ladies, she generally secured, in the spring, a "boss farmer" to act as her deputy. The "boss farmer" wore better clothes than the others, and did less work, he drew more pay and smoked cigars where they where glad to get pipes full of tobacco. He was a gentleman; they were not.

This summer the "boss farmer" on Miss Mercy's place had been a stranger. He came from nobody knew where, and he declined to tell much about himself. He wore rusty black clothes, fierce standing collars, and a shabby silk hat. His face was round, red, wrinkled, and cleanly shaven. His figure was short and stout. He could drink a large amount of cider without any visible bad effects, and he smoked all day long. His hair was thin, and he combed wisps of it over his forehead, in a vain attempt to hide the shiny baldness. He liked to wear low cut shoes and white stockings, he also liked to make love to all the ladies he met. His voice was low and oily, and in conversation he frequently referred to himself as a "gallant." He laughed a great deal, in a sort of mild chuckle. He was frequently seen reading, and the old valise he had brought with him to the farm, contained little but an accordion and a bundle of books. He knew his business well enough, and could argue the oldest farmers into their own boots, on turnips, potatoes, or whatever subject in agriculture they considered themselves most expert in. There was an idea about that he was more a book farmer than a practised husbandman, and 'Squire Elliott even asserted the opinion that he had never lived on any farm but Miss Mercy's, and that his knowledge of agriculture was one-third book learning and two-thirds cheek. The 'Squire even went so far, after the "boss" had downed him in an argument on Jersey cattle versus Holsteins, as to warn Miss Mercy against her new man, but Miss Mercy was never known to take advice, and besides she had taken an unusual liking to Lucious Benton—"Mr. Lucious" she called him, in her prim way. In the meanwhile the village distrusted him. What had brought him to Edgeley—was it any good reason? Was he not a stranger? In other words, had he not come to town in answer to an advertisement?

It was early in the afternoon of a fine October day when Miss Mercy and her foreman sat in the big dining room, one on either side of the shining mahogany table, a stratum of account books and bills spread out upon it. The year's work was done, harvesting finished, corn husked, rye and oats threshed, and the next day the gang of men would be paid off and discharged. Miss Mercy was going over the season's accounts, to see that no man had cheated her. It was very comfortable in that dining room. A small fire of apple boughs burned on the brass andirons, a tawny cat basked in the glow, the tall yellow-faced clock in the corner ticked solemnly, out of doors the sun shone and the branches of the trees were tossing in a sharp wind. Red and yellow leaves carpeted the ground, the flowers in the garden were dry and dead, except a few hardy dahlias that stiffly held their heads above the general ruin. Apples were all gathered, and the grape vines, torn from their supports and lying disorderly on the ground, showed how reluctantly they had yielded their fruit. Piles of yellow pumpkins lay at every farmer's back door, and wells showed a film of ice in the early mornings. Cattle found little feed in pastures, and the fowls stood around on one leg, warming the other under their feathers. In other words, winter was at hand.

"I don't see but what this is all correct, Mr. Lucious," said Miss Mercy, at length, laying down the last limp leather-bound volume, filled with records of the men's time, all in the foreman's big, sprawling, masculine hand. She spoke a little reluctantly, life was such a too placid affair that it caused her a pang to give up the prospect of an amiable discussion over some slight error.

"The men shall have their money tomorrow," she continued, musingly counting sums on her bony fingers. Miss Mercy was not a bad looking object, as she sat in the genial warmth of her own home, scented with roseleaves from a potpourri jar on the sideboard. Her brown hair was drawn smoothly away from a colorless face with prominent but well-shaped features. Her foot was quite small, and encased in a neat cloth shoe. Her dress, though plain, was of excellent quality cashmere, and there was some dainty old lace at throat and wrists. She was a little prim, a little sweet, and a little sharp in expression. In other words, she was a typical New England spinster.

"I wonder how much the old dame's worth?" thought Lucious Benton to himself, as he leaned back slightly in the rush rocker which held him, and put the tips of his fingers in his pockets, while half closing his eyes. He was loath to leave this snug berth he had made for himself on the Webster farm. He was sorry winter was coming, and that Miss Mercy had no more need for his services. He had been a rover all the days of his life, and all the roving desires of his character had been satisfied years before. He had been a bad man until vice had no more fascination for him, and he yearned to be respectable and good, as a novelty. Since coming to Edgeley he had attended church every Sunday, and really he had found it amusing. He had read the Bible, and found it entertaining, because it was different from other books. He had conversed piously instead of swearing, and found the novelty pleasant. Lucious Benton now hankered no more for cards and drink. He felt a desire to settle down on the Webster farm for the rest of his days. In other words, he was growing old.

So he looked at Miss Mercy and thought, and—thought.

"There wouldn't be any chance for me to stay here this winter, would there?" he inquired.

Miss Mercy shook her head. "The work is all over," she said, "and I only keep a boy in the wintertime to look after the cows.

I cannot afford to hire a man," she added, a smile lighting up her eyes. This assumption of poverty was a favorite fiction of the rich old maid's soul.

Lucious Benton glanced sharply from under his puffy, overhanging eyebrows. Then he nervously twiddled his fingers, and muttered inwardly, "Will I go down on my knees or won't I? She probably never saw a man on his knees asking her to marry him, and she may be taken by my fervency. On the other hand, these New Englanders always distrust sentiment. I guess I'll remain where I am."

So he sat up a trifle straighter, and began without hesitation, "Miss Mercy, you see before you a man who has no home."

Miss Mercy, foreseeing a request to remain through the winter, perhaps on board wages, and knowing that such an arrangement would be advantageous for her, ventured to give an encouraging smile.

"I have travelled largely, and I won't say not without pecuniary advancement. Miss Mercy," continued Lucious Benton, rolling his tongue over his dry lips, "I have never married. I never saw the woman I wanted to marry. That is, never until this summer."

Here he stared boldly and languishingly at Miss Mercy, who blushed, and cast down her eyes, that he should not see the happy light in them. It was her first proposal, and though she had no idea of accepting it, yet the experience was very pleasant.

He went on, "I am worth some ten thousand dollars, Miss Mercy, a small sum, but enough to disabuse anyone of the idea of my having any vile motives in venturing to address you. I—I love you, Miss Mercy, and I want to know if—if you—will—marry—me?"

As he slowly spoke, he possessed himself of one of Miss Mercy's bony, cold hands, and respectfully kissed it. Now, although he chewed tobacco, Lucious Benton was good at the art of kissing, and though he had led a wicked life, he was good at aping a respectful modesty. In other words, he was a hypocrite.

Miss Mercy believed him. Her heart beat with a delightful rapidity, and her mind rapidly went into the future, and planned the happenings in case she should accept Lucious. It made no difference that fifteen minutes before she had had no idea of accepting him. He had not proposed then, and a woman's ideas before a proposal count for nothing after that event. If she should marry Lucious he would always be at hand to rule the hired men, and yet she would not have to pay him wages. He might even decline receiving pay for last summer's work. She would be Mrs. Benton then, and no longer snubbed by matrons. Lucious was smarter than anyone in town, and ten thousand dollars was not a sum to be despised. Her suspicious mind led her to question if he really had ten thousand dollars, and so before she thought she had replied, "Yes, Mr. Lucious, I will marry you, on one condition. I must ask you to prove to me that you are worth the sum you mention, for I promised my poor father when he died, four and thirty years ago, that I would never marry a poor man."

In other words, the pere Webster's dying advice had been, "Massy, don't you be bambozzled by no poor critter. Remember, it takes a fool to make money, but a wise man to keep it. Don't you go to marrying no fool."

Her reply seemed satisfactory to Lucious Benton, for he kissed her hand once more, and glared at her ardently with his round and somewhat bleary blue eyes.

"I will show you my bank books tomorrow," he said.

This matter settled, both seemed in doubt whether to end or continue the interview. Miss Mercy had never been in a like situation before, so her nervousness was excusable. As for Lucious, he had been in like situations more times than he could remember, but the woman in the case had never before been a prim, rich old maid of New England. He could not decide whether to begin ardent love making or to maintain his present distant, respectful demeanor. In other words, he was a little afraid of Miss Mercy.

Finally he said, "As it is a broken day, for work I mean, would you object to taking a walk with me? I thought, if you were willing, we might stroll up the hill road. There are no houses there to be passed, you know, and I saw some very beautiful bittersweet berries growing near the old Lyon house."

Miss Mercy was quite in a flutter of excitement. To walk out with a man was an innovation, but she did want some bittersweet, and, as he had said, the hill road was quite lonely, and it was not probable anyone would see her. Besides, she was going to marry Lucious Benton, and she would have to begin walking with him sometime or other. So, with an exhilarating sense of doing something a little wicked, Miss Mercy put on her black straw bonnet and a fine but ancient white embroidered shawl. The bonnet was her best one, and ordinarily she would not have worn it, but she felt quite reckless on this day, and besides the time of year for straw bonnets was nearly past. Then, with a flush on her cheeks, she made an immediate use of the new fact of belonging to a man, by returning to the dining room, and asking Lucious what she had better do with her money—what of it there was in the house.

"I went to town yesterday," she said, "and drew money enough to pay the men. Then 'Squire Elliott paid me the three thousand dollars which he borrowed sometime ago of me, on a note, and two men whose farms are mortgaged to me happened to call and pay their yearly interest, so I have more money in the house than usual. Do you think it would be best to lock it up, or to take it with me?"

Miss Mercy asked this with a tender air, as if it was really a relief, after long years of thinking for herself, to ask advice.

"I generally take what money there is in the house with me when I go out," she continued.

For an instant Lucious Benton's face seemed to grow rigid, and his entire figure stiffened. Could one have looked through his boots, his toes would have been seen to become fixed in an unnatural position. Then he gave a long breath, and said huskily, "If I were you, I would follow my usual custom and take the money with me, Miss Mercy."

While she was absent he stared at himself half admiringly in the mirror over the narrow mantel shelf.

The last act of Miss Mercy, before locking her front door, was to carefully cover the apple tree fire with ashes, so that no stray spark should fire the house during her absence. Then she and Lucious walked side by side down the gravelled walk, bordered by rose bushes and lank brown lily-leaves, out at the whitewashed gate into the grass-grown road, which led by one way to the village, and by the other to the hills, where no one lived, and the houses had been either burned down or deserted. Miss Mercy carried on her arm an old-fashioned bead reticule which had been a property of her mother's, and at which Lucious somehow never looked. And yet he knew well enough that the much talked-of money was in it.

Up and ever upward the road wound, skirting ledges and groves of pine, its banks on either hand overgrown with weeds and bushes, now a mass of brown and red decay. At length the old Lyon place was reached, a deserted house, long untenanted, with crazy broken windows, a sunken roof, tumbledown chimneys, and a wide open house door, across which a legion of spiders had built webs to catch flies. He respected them, and was of the opinion that it served the flies right to be caught. In other words, he believed that he would have been an excellent spider if he had chanced to have been born into such a sphere of existence.

Miss Mercy and Lucious seated themselves on the lichen-grown doorstep of the deserted house. Miss Mercy was silent, for she was so full of tumultuous excitement over her novel position, that she could not remember to talk. Lucious was also silent. He absently pulled at the yellow bittersweet berries, which grew over a lilac bush by the door, until there was a huge bunch of them in his red, puffy hand. Occasionally he bit his lips, as if they were unpleasantly dry. Quite suddenly he arose and went to the opposite side of the steps, where had been dug an ancient well. The black water was still there, a single white cloud reflected in it from the blue sky above. There was a curb of moss-grown stones, topped by rotting wood. All appliances for drawing the water had long since disappeared.

"These people had their well handy to the door," said Lucious, in a sort of rasping tone, and clearing his throat.

Miss Mercy came and stood beside him, her white fingers resting on the black wood. The sun was quite low, and there was a biting chill in the air. The only sound was the occasional dropping of a nut from one of the tall trees by the road. Lucious looked at Miss Mercy. She was really not homely, and he knew he must begin to be affectionate sometime, so he kissed her.

Astonished at this somewhat unexpected outcome of her walk, Miss Mercy turned, and staggered against the rotten curb. The worm-eaten boards crumbled, and she fell backward into the well. As she disappeared, a cry reverberated from the narrow hole. Lucious Benton, leaning over, stood anxiously for fully a quarter of an hour, gazing into that black water, like a man who looks upon a ghost. Nothing appeared upon the surface of the water. Miss Mercy was gone forever, that was certain. Should he give an alarm? Should he go to the village and tell of the accident? What need? Nothing could bring Miss Mercy to life, and there were points in his own past, which, if raked up, might cast suspicion upon him.

Lucious Benton drew his coat sleeve over his eyes, as if to clear away a film, and then went away, on the hill road. If he followed it long enough it would take him into another state, far away from Edgeley. The last rays of the setting sun cleaved through the frosty air, and lit up Lucious Benton's rubicund countenance—not exactly an unsatisfied one, either. Why should he be unhappy? If he had lost Miss Mercy and a home at the Webster place, yet all was not lost.

In other words, Lucious Benton, as he went away into the cold twilight, carried in his hand the bead bag wherein was Miss Mercy's money.

(*The Fern Leaf*, March 1891)

A SHADOW ON THE WATER

"I am in love with a woman!"

A common enough remark, only this time it was a woman who herself said the words. Behind her was the twilight-colored sky of an early September evening. Before her stretched a sawdust-covered expanse of dirty floor. She stood exactly on the threshold of the country store. The proprietor of the strings of onions, cardigan jackets, plaster of paris images and hunks of cheese, was seated on the counter picking accumulations of dirt out of his fingernails with his thumbnail.

"Come in, Miss Evannalina, and be sure you shut the door," he said.

The woman—who like most New England females might be almost any age above thirty—advanced with a swagger.

"You know most women consider me the scum of the earth," she continued, confidentially. "As a rule, I hate women. Most of their husbands went with me sometime or other, so they're jealous. Then I've lived to be—well, along in years, without marrying. But I'm in love with one. It's Azubah Pine!"

The storekeeper was a small man, with pretty feet and hands, a misfit moustache stained with tobacco, and great black circles around his eyes, which spoke mutely of his dissipated habits.

"Zuby's your cousin Hector's girl," he remarked.

"She's too good for him," returned Evannalina, with a confirmatory nod.

Then she added, "I thought Azubah was going with Jeff Briggs."

"He was, till last night. I must tell you how Hec socked it into him. You know Hec can't stand seeing an animal abused. Well, Briggs came in here rather corned, and as his horse didn't like to stand on the side hill, Briggs went out and yanked the reins seven ways for Sunday. `Stand still, you ——' he hollered. He just went out on the stoop and asked, `Why don't you say the other name?' `Can't think of it.' `Oh, yes, you can,' says Hec, `it's Briggs'."

Evannalina did not laugh.

"There goes my cousin Hector now," she remarked, pointing a brown forefinger at the window. "You know he never speaks to me."

"Why not?"

"Because I never speak to him. And I rocked him in his cradle, too, when I was eight and he was a young one."

"He's coming in," said the storekeeper. "Better stay, 'n I'll give you a knock down to him."

But Evannalina strode heavily out the back door.

"Why wasn't you quicker, Hec?" the storekeeper asked the fresh-faced young man who entered a moment later. "Your cousin Evannalina was in here waiting for you to come and kiss her."

Hector picked up a large paper bag, smacked into it, and then twisted the mouth carefully up.

"Lay that away against the next time she comes in," he remarked carelessly.

II

The kitchen was a dark, unholy-looking place, with ten doors, windows three ways, a closet into which no one ever looked, a glass-knobbed desk where money was kept, and a yellow-faced clock lying about the time. On a range of shelves back of the stove were such articles as a dish of pig mush, an orphaned and shrilly peeping chicken, an empty rum flask, a string of peppers, a file set in a corn cob handle, a bowl of grease, a pie, and a score of browned clay pipes with broken-off stems too short for smoking. An old man wearing a hat with a hole in the crown, sat before the table.

"I suppose," he said, tenderly complaining, "that's meant for my supper, but I'll be etarnally jiggered if I eat it."

"What's meant for your supper?" inquired, in a cracked voice, a little woman with a large stomach and two pairs of spectacles on her nose.

"Dishcloth or two. All I saw since I sat down."

"Now gran'ma," protested Evannalina, "why don't you give gramp his supper?"

"Well, I did ask him what he'd have, and all I could get him to say when I asked him if he'd have milk or meat, was `No, I'll have a tea kettle.'"

"Your gran'mother's getting old," exclaimed the man. "I wanted to pay her back for what she said to me this afternoon. I wanted to talk 'ligion, and I asked her five i-dentical times 'f she thought the wicked would be burned with fire. At first she wouldn't speak, and then at last she snapped out, `No, you old goose, not if they wait for you to fetch the wood.'"

The old lady obligingly laughed at her own joke. Evannalina went to an adjoining pantry and brought a number of dishes to the black oilcloth-covered table. Evannalina was large and rather stout, with a full face, somewhat tanned. Her straight eyebrows and the long hair slovenly coiled at the back of her head were of the darkest brown. She had a way of squinting—wrinkling the skin around her eyes when looking intently at anything. Her hands were well-shaped, and altogether Evannalina was very good-looking in an upright, independent sort of way.

"Here's rice, gramp," she remarked.

That set the old man off again.

"Some like rye, some like wheat, I say rice is the best to eat," he said in a pugnacious tone. Instantly the old lady, who was nodding by the stove, responded, sleepily:

And whatever is the price,

When I eat I wish for rice.

Then there was silence, unbroken except by the nasal slobbering of the old man, as he sucked the rice and milk from a large tin spoon. Evannalina went to a window, and looked aimlessly out. A pair of green eyes and a white frowsy head stared from the other side of the glass. Opening the door she admitted a train of cats, going out herself. She walked under a row of wide-spreading cherry trees until she reached a sagging gate hanging ajar between two rotting posts. Crickets in the grass were chirping loudly. Evannalina had slung over her arm a large black cloak—what was known in her own neighborhood as a waterproof circular. She now wrapped it about her.

"I always did want to take this cloak and go and do something romantic," she thought, with a little curl of her handsome lips. Then, as the wind blew the gate open she took advantage of the accident to slip out into the road. The gate clanged behind her, although no hand had touched it.

III

It was more than the edge of the evening. It was actually night. Over in the west grew a fringe of black trees through which could be seen a brassy sky. One big star and a crescent new moon were visible among the flecks of gray clouds higher up. There was a bar-way looking into a pasture; at the left of the gate lay a tumble-down wall overgrown with elderberry bushes and briars. All around were ferns, frost bleached, and giving off a fresh odor. There was dead silence as far as humanity was concerned, yet the air was full of noises. Birds twittered, crickets and scores of nameless insects seemed to be asking and answering questions. Not far away was a black, wooded hill, dense in appearance, dark at the east, bright at the west, a small embodiment of the world at that hour. Somehow a weirdness hovered over this prosaic pasture.

Evannalina felt it. She leaned on the top bar, looking forward with strained eyes, expecting every moment that a ghost, or perhaps something, would loom up over the wall.

IV

As this was the short cut from the village, it was not long before something did appear. A couple of young people, in whom Evanna-lina recognized a "fella 'n his girl," even before she knew her cousin Hector Shield and Azubah Pine. Azubah wore a light dress, Hec-tor a dark coat. Even in the late twilight which hid her from them, Evannalina saw the black line around Azubah's waist.

"Now, Hec Shield, I'm just going to leave you here." Azubah's voice was soft and rather flat. She spoke very slowly, and she called just, je-ust, and here, he-ar. Evannalina admired this low-toned modulation. She thought it very feminine. Her own voice was that ordinarily possessed only by young ladies who attend schools of elocution—heavy, full, rather gruff.

"That's all right. You can leave me, but I won't be left. I said I'd see you home when I pulled the linch-pin out of Brigg's wagon, and by jupiter hoe-cake, I will."

"Now, how me-an! When Jeff Briggs would have given me a re-ide!"

"Now, I'm better-looking than Jeff, any day. Do you know he always makes me think of a great flannel-mouthed Irishman I used to see in a music hall when I was in Albany? I went there four times, each time they announced a change of bill, yet every time that Irish-man came out and said he was 'Not English, you know, but Irish, you see.' There was no need of his telling of it. There's no need to ask where Briggs was born, either."

"Well, pa will not like to have you come home with me."

"Oh, that's all right. I'm just as shamed of your father as he is of me."

"Hec, please don't come. He'll scold me."

"Oh, all right. Good-bye."

This was unexpectedly sudden, and Azubah was evidently as-tonished. Hector had strode over the ruined wall, and was whis-tling off into the dark path.

"Hec!" she called, tremulously.

"What?"

"Wait a minute."

She came running down the path, and stopped suddenly about an inch from his outstretched arms.

"Let's say good night, Hec," she faltered.

He kissed her several times. Then, when she tried to get away, with a shame-faced giggle, Evannalina heard him remark, "Why, Zuby, you've two cheeks. Don't be in such a hurry."

As if carried away by her feelings, Azubah began to sob.

"Why, you dear girl," said Hector, in a sort of pleased yet sur-prised tone. It was as if he had not expected her to care so deeply for him, as if he was tenderly surprised at this revelation of her love.

While listening, Evannalina's face went through an astonishing variety of changes. First her forehead was wrinkled, then her eye-brows frowned, her lips moved from side to side, she drew her cheeks in, and turned up her nose scornfully. These facial twitch-ings were an unconscious habit she had of working off excitement.

As the couple under the trees, down by the swamp, showed no signs of leaving each other, Evannalina went away, along the muddy road, breathing softly in her chilled fingers to warm them.

She was thinking: "Poor little thing. She does want him bad."

V

Evannalina Shield had frequently recognized the fact that she ought by nature to have been born a man. Her manner of admiring Azubah Pine was essentially masculine. She sat later in the evening in the farmhouse parlor, toasting her feet on the cast iron stove. The parlor had damp-stained paper on its walls, with impossible blue roses and pink foliage for its pattern. The floor was protected with braided and tufted and drawn in rag mats, on which stood a platoon of cane chairs and a table with a "stamped felt" spread. Evannalina sat in the dark, so she could not see the prints of Horace Greely, "Faith, Hope and Charity," "The Lady of the Lake," and "Evangeline," enjoying unprecedented communion of the walls. The door stood open into the kitchen, where Hector, by the light of a kerosene lamp with a pink paper shade, ate his supper.

Evannalina was thinking of Azubah Pine in that style of eye worship which so many men indulge in at certain periods of their life. Azubah's short tendril-like hair, how prettily it curled down on the pink nape of her neck! What wee fragile fingers she had, and tiny pretty features, with soft blue eyes and a pointed chin like pictures of the martyred Dauphin, Marie Antoinette's son. Evannalina turned her gaze into the kitchen, and conjured up the image of that porcelain-like face opposite Hector's, at a supper table of the future. And, naturally, she was led on to making an unusually close observation of her cousin. Hector was big and tall, with broad shoulders, and the hairy hands of a farmer. His hair grew above his forehead in a sort of crest which gave an air of success to his face, otherwise smooth, pink-cheeked, regular featured, and dark brown eyed. Ordinarily he talked very little, but seemed to be thinking.

For two years he and Evannalina, although living in the same house, had not spoken a dozen words to each other. As children they had been playmates, even as man and woman they had never quarreled, but naturally went in each other's company picking berries, gathering cowslips, and to dancing and singing school. Rather suddenly, something over twenty-four months before, Hector had failed to engage Evannalina for the church picnic. Since then they had not seemed to have anything to say to each other. Evannalina had always meant to ask him some time what the cause of this sudden coolness was, but she seldom saw him alone, and, besides, she did not particularly care. Evannalina was eight years her cousin's senior, and she might have been married several times if she had desired. The truth was she liked independence, and all the young men of the town cared too much for their own dignity and for pecuniary advantages to make love in a way sufficiently ardent to suit her.

Suddenly she found, as she sat by the stove, that her heart was beating violently. The rush of blood this physical commotion sent to her head prevented her remembering for a moment what the agitating thought had been. Then, after some mind groping, it came back to her.

"After all," she thought, "I needn't be scared. I'm only going to speak to my own cousin. If Zuby wants him, I'll do my prettiest to help her get him."

And so, in a tone which she tried to make natural, and yet which when used did not sound at all right, she said, "Say, Hector!"

The next minute she was standing on her feet, with tears of anger searing her eyes. Hector had, without answering, gone out and slammed the door.

VI

The old folks were getting into bed, in a tiny one-windowed room just off the kitchen. The old man had already snuggled down under the blankets, from which he uttered a protest.

"Evan'lina, Evan'lina, do come in here. Your gran'mother s' opened the window. I shall be blowed clean out o' bed."

Having got the sash up, and supported it with the sole of the boot recently taken off by her husband, the old lady now plucked determinedly at the top blanket, which the old man held with the grip of both hands.

"It's as cold as all get out tonight," he declared. "I'm sleeping on a tick with one straw in it, and I will have two blankets."

No sooner was the old lady in bed, than she began to be afflicted with memories of unattended-to duties.

"Be any dishcloths hanging back of the fire?" she asked. "If there be, you move 'em now, 'fore you forget it, Ev'lina."

"Yes, Evan'lina," put in the old man, sarcastically, "and while you're about it just take the stove 'n turn it bottom side up 'n pour water on it. Your gran'mam's terrible afraid of fire."

"Wait till you've been burnt out of house and home a few times, Dorias Shield," she returned, nowise abashed.

"Yes, jest wait. Evy, you better get Hec to take the axe and chop down the oak tree. Gram's afraid the acorns from it may fall into the chimney 'n cause a 'splosion."

"Yes, Dorias, but I know one thing. You didn't cover up those pumpkins, I know."

The old man now wanted to go to sleep.

"Pumpkins!" he said, scornfully.

Then he snored.

However, Evannalina had decided to make them a pretext for once more approaching her cousin Hector.

VII

Hector stood on the top step of the series leading from the ground to the "stoop" before the door. He leaned his soft-hatted head against the tree trunk which served as a post to support the roof, his face lighted up by the glow from a briar wood pipe. Evannalina stood a moment irresolutely in the middle of the way between Hector and the door. Then she turned to the water pail and drank eagerly from the tin dipper rusting its life away therein. Not really caring for the drink, she choked herself with repeating, "Say, Hector."

He lifted his eyebrows.

"Say—"

"Well, spit it right out," he remarked, encouragingly.

"I—what do you think, Hector, of asking 'Zubah Pine over here tomorrow night? Would you be at home? You'll stay at home, won't you? We might play croquet if you'd mow the grass; or crack some nuts and make some candy. Don't you think't would be nice, Hector?"

His sole reply was to stretch out his hand and draw her towards him by the elbow. He laid his pipe carefully away in the eave trough above his head, and then scrutinized Evannalina's face as if amused.

"No," he replied, at length, "I can't be at home for Azubah Pine. Miss Rattlehead I call her. I was out with her tonight, and she got stuck in the swamp, but she said she didn't care, it was so romantic!"

Hector, watching Evannalina's countenance, perhaps expected it to show pleasure, as the faces of women who are hearing other women abused, sometimes do. If so, he was disappointed. Evannalina was distinctly shocked and disgusted at this turn of affairs. Tears came into her eyes—for she wept easily—too easily. She was turning away, when he put her cold right hand into his warm overcoat pocket and grasped her left hand in his own.

"If you honest truly want the Pine girl to come, why, I'll stay tomorrow night," he said softly. Evannalina was conscious of a thrill of joy.

"He really likes her," she thought.

She felt his hands—a little hard in the palms from rough work—on her forehead.

"Put that scowl away," he said, pleasantly.

Later in the evening, after the pumpkins had been covered up, and while the cousins stood beside the gate on which as children they had marked their names in penknife scratches, Hector said, apropos of nothing, and yet accompanied by the look of one who speaks with a purpose, "Any woman could make me do whatever she pleased by one little trick—just rubbing her cheek on my shoulder. I saw it done once in a play, and it always seemed to me the most confiding gesture—well—you know—just taking."

Evannalina did not interpret the look, but she made in her mind the resolve: "I'll remember to mention that, sometime, to Azubah!"

VIII

The scent of newly cut rowen, which is like double-distilled odor of June haymaking, filled the air the next morning. Evannalina sat on the rolling upland at one corner of a vast meadow. She was leaning luxuriously against a vast haycock, breathing the voluptuous odors and feeling to her very soul the glamor of the day—a luxurious atmosphere always to be noticed when a warm day follows a period of cold. The sun looked very friendly as it lay toward the westward in a pale sky. Before her was the long expanse of meadow, a tangle of coarse, intensely green grass, tall yellow flags, blue-fringed gentians mirroring the heavens in their upturned cups, and knee-deep in fragrance Hector was mowing a long swath. His blue coat lay on the ground at her feet; each time he came near he took a drink from the flask in his pocket, and bestowed on her a sort of cynical smile. In another part of the field men were loading hay on to a rickety cart, while the horse impatiently pawed the earth. Birds were singing, and just over the horizon was visible—only a red chimney against a blue sky. At length Hector looked at the sun, and wiped his scythe with a tuft of grass. Evannalina rose and began picking the dried briars from her hair and the light pink calico she wore.

"Oh, I feel giddy," she exclaimed. "If I wer'n't such an old thing I would run."

She was really sensitive on the subject of her age, and thought it better to forestall all invidious remarks by making them herself.

"Oh, Hec," she exclaimed, beaming on him, "do you remember when we were children? I used to be jealous of you, and pinched you, so they always sent me out into the chip yard to play. I can remember saying to myself, `Just wait till he's big and I'm the baby, then see how he'll like always being out in the chip-yard.' And once I took you riding in the snow in a box that grandpa nailed on a sled. When I reached the end of the path I slewed you round quick, and off you went. How gramp did scold me!"

"One would think you were old Chloe Lil', by your age," remarked Hector. "Old Chloe Lil', you know, that gram always talks about, and nobody ever saw. I'll race out to the house."

And throwing his coat over his arm, he started on an admirable swinging pace. A game of romp ensued, Evannalina ran and stopped, laughing to catch her breath; got buried in the armful of hay he threw over her head; and at length was rescued from the tottering insecurity of a grass-encrusted bog surrounded by a river of liquid mud. Hector bore her to the railing which had been erected above the brook beside the road, and under the silvery-leaved willows, which, many times chopped down, still showed a determination to exist and grow. She was bubbling over with girlish fun, which did not set awkwardly on her mature years, because it was real fun.

"Oh, Hec," she cried, "listen to that old frog under this bridge. He must have seen that bottle of yours. Hark what he says. It's 'you're drunk! you're drunk!'"

Even at this moment the sun rested on the horizon, behind a stone wall. The light shining through the chinks made the rude affair look, at this distance, like lace work.

It was evening, and she had forgotten all day to send that proposed invitation to Azubah Pine!

IX

"Hec," said Evannalina, "do you believe that tree was chopped off on purpose for a place to hang a milk pail?"

They were standing in the road a short distance below the house. Catching the last glow of the setting sun was indeed a tin pail, inverted over a sacrificed tree. Before them lay a low grass-edged track, leaf-strewn, beside which were clumps of green moss, and great gnarled oaks, leaning to the east because influenced that way by the west winds. Hector was feeling of his cheeks in the meditative way adopted by young men whose acquaintance with razors is but slight. Evannalina could not keep still a moment. She was full of life and energy. She wanted Hector to move faster and think quicker. Why didn't he offer to go down and see Azubah?

"Hec," she exclaimed suddenly, "were you ever in love?"

"I am always in love," he returned, slowly. "The fellows say I'm mashed on every new girl. Well, it's true, only I've no girl now—only you. You're my latest girl."

"No, no," she said, very soberly, as if resolutely putting away something offered. Then, coming to his side, she half whispered, "Hector, when you really fall in love, promise you'll tell me all about it. You will, won't you, please?"

"Yes, dear, I'll tell you all about it," he replied, half putting his arm around her and then withdrawing it.

"And, Hector, I'm going down to Azubah's after supper. Will you go with me?"

"Of course, I couldn't refuse you."

While asking the favor she had softly rubbed her cheek against the rough texture of his coat sleeve. She seemed to do it unconsciously, and Hector was puzzled.

X

With the air of an adoring lover Evannalina hovered about the toilet of Azubah Pine. She had come upstairs without ceremony, and found her friend indulging in what was locally known as "dressing up." Evannalina assisted at the decking out process with pleasure. Azubah looked so very lovely in her blue muslin frock and Byron-like embroidered collar turned over a jaunty silk bow. The little curls about her face—it was all one could do to keep from continually putting one's finger through their rounded prettiness. The earrings twinkled in her shell-like ears, and the bangles on her wrist rang again when she waved her big blue paper fan, on which great silver cupids ran riot. Heavy, dark Evannalina felt as if she would like to take all this fragile prettiness into her arms and kiss it. And yet Azubah seemed to her inaccessible, and like the haughty ladies one reads about in novels. She had forgotten the time when the flaxen-haired girl had flung herself, unasked, into Hector's arms.

"You are perfectly lovely," she gushed, solemnly. "Now run downstairs. Hector is waiting for you."

It was Evannalina's own intention to slip down by the back stairs and run home unobserved.

XI

"Do you go to Corinthians with me tomorrow?" inquired Hector.

What he referred to was church going. It had gained the slang phrase from the fact that the minister had once found his texts for ten months, every Sunday, in this portion of the Scriptures.

Evannalina looked up slowly from under the massive brows she had concentrated on the work busying her hands—the laborious moulding of a mass of dough.

"I thought Zuby was going with you."

"Can't the horse drag two girls?"

Grandpa here thought fit to put his oar in.

"I never thought much of Zuby Pine," he remarked. "Never since I heard of her going to school three miles round to meet Jeff Briggs. It struck me as some like the Springfield feller who went to New York by way of Boston."

"Yes," chimed in grandma. "And she wrote him a letter with 'adieu' in it, and saw him the next day, just the same."

"That was when she was a little girl," said Evannalina. Grandpa, however, had more to say.

"I saw her once," he declared, "walking across lots, and she was so cross-eyed she supposed she was walking in the road. She was singing, too—"

"Gramp, that was her mother," exclaimed Evannalina.

"Anyhow," put in Hector, with a smile "Jeff Briggs' brother visited the school teacher one noon, talked religion all the hour, and ended by kneeling down and making a prayer. The next day he ran off with his sister's money! They're almighty low trash, however you put it."

"Very pint and-a-half folks," laughed Evannalina.

XII

"I can have him if I want him!" This was the staggering knowledge which had suddenly seemed borne in upon Evannalina from Hector. How did she know it? How does any girl know a man loves her, long before he speaks of it, sometimes when he never speaks of it? At the dinner table Hector had worn his usual self-absorbed expression—perhaps thinking of Azubah, perhaps of how he would saw off a bunting cow's horn that afternoon, for all the index of his countenance. Without any warning, he tilted a spoonful of salt into Evannalina's glass of water. When she raised her eyes he looked into them earnestly, as if he were saying, "You and I have a secret understanding."

Actual mind-reading is possible on occasions like these. Evannalina later stood in the parlor, before the high, narrow mantel shelf. She took in her hand a china affair representing a very small bird perched on the edge of a very large nest, in the bottom of which, as in a well, lay three tiny red-speckled eggs. The tail of the bird had been broken off. Unconsciously holding this, she thought, "I can have him. Mine. Mrs. Shield. Folks will inquire after my husband. He will smile down on me the day we are married, while everybody looks. And—afterward. Settled for life. Nobody to inquire about me any more, or wonder when I will get married, or why I don't. A snarl of little children, and gray hairs, scolding if collar buttons break, and nothing to look forward to. I can't."

She thought of the various men she had refused—now married without a broken heart among them, and occasionally looking at her in church, she knew, and contrasting her well-preserved good looks and neat dress with the dowdish, round-shouldered mothers of families by their sides.

Still, it had never been so hard to give up one of these as it would be to give up Hector.

"I cannot do it," she declared, bowing her head against the sharp edge of the shelf.

Then she realized she was holding something in her hand.

"Why, it's a matchsafe, I declare. I never noticed before it was a matchsafe."

XIII

It happened that Evannalina and Azubah sat apart from Hector the next day at church. While he was securing the horse in the shed, they had taken seats in a pew which was filled before he came in. The pews were so called by courtesy alone. They were seats and backs of perforated wood, supported on iron posts. The feet of the people in front were very visible to those sitting in the rear, and as the pews were very high such short people as Azubah were compelled to swing their boots in a way not exactly reverent. The interior of the little orthodox chapel was finished very much like the inside of a neat paper box, with flat daubs of blue and gray. A girl played awkwardly on one of those instruments known as a parlor organ, and Evannalina forgot to sing while looking at Hector. His broad back in a well-fitting coat impressed her with a yearning to possess it, and when he carelessly pushed a lock of hair behind his

ear she wished she was sitting beside him, and that the whole con-
gregation knew him to be hers. There are few things so provocative
of love as to see the lover apart from one, among a crowd of people.
Somehow every woman desires the world to know she has a mate,
and she wants the man more at moments when he seems far away.
Evannalina felt like laughing when she realized that she had lived
beside Hector all her life and had never loved him until twenty-four
hours previously.

Strangely enough, the sermon was on "Marriage." St. Paul had
said it was "honorable." At heart Evannalina was a bit wicked,
however correct her life, for somehow she did not feel enamored of
a condition any Saint had tagged "honorable."

XIV

That afternoon the young people of the town had organized a walk
after early chestnuts. Evannalina had promised to meet Hector and
Azubah at a certain cross-roads at three o'clock. It had been her own
doing that he went after Azubah. In her mind it seemed as if she was
making the decision for Hector between the two women who loved
him. Evannalina really meant to go—she did not feel exactly chari-
table to Azubah. She had come upstairs into her own room with
the intention of dressing for the walk, and instead of doing so, had
thrown herself on the bed in her Sunday frock and boots. The sun
shone with autumnal brilliancy between the faded red curtains of
her window. It was charming out of doors, she knew that. Turning
on one side she could see out, past the slender stem of a tree dividing
the window in two, over past a green hillock on top of which was
a weather-beaten well-sweep, to a horizon edged with apple trees
on which dots of red and yellow accented the gray foliage. Still, she
was rather tired, and inaction was dear to her just then. She thought
she would lie quietly for five minutes, there would still be time to
reach the rendezvous at three. Two flies buzzed sociably against the
sun-heated pane. She thought how warmly Hector had clasped her
hands—both of them—in bidding her good night the evening before.
By closing her eyes she could feel his cordial grip yet. Evannalina
had one of those natures which enjoys such episodes better in ret-

rospect than when passing. Always when being made love to, she had thought impatiently, "Why won't you go away, so I can have time to think this over."

She smiled happily now, as she mused on Hector. Meanwhile the clock struck three!

Evannalina did not mind it at all. She counted the strokes, and then put her mind into as restful an attitude as that previously assumed by her body.

XV

After the inaction of winter comes spring, and following Evannalina's preference for imaginative pleasures to real ones ensued a longing that something interesting might happen. If Hector had only been present at about the hour of sunset that evening, Evannalina would have revoked her own decisions and even promised to marry him. As he did not come until half an hour later, her mood had turned to one of anger. The privileges men have lost by being too late, can only be equalled by those women have lost through showing ill temper.

"I am going to church this evening," he announced. The words struck Evannalina with sinister effect.

"Is it time to start yet?" she inquired, meekly.

"No. If you like we will walk up the road a-ways."

She did like, and they walked side by side in the ante-moonrise blackness. He talked cheerfully, and she began to feel happy, in the grasping way of one who expects to be presently miserable.

"Did you have a good time this afternoon?" she asked.

"Certainly. Zuby forgot to bring her rubbers, and we fellows took turns in lifting her over the muddy places."

Then, after a pause, he added, "Some women make me tired."

He made no reference to Evannalina's defection. She was disappointed. Had not they waited for her at all?

"What's that imp of blackness tagging your heels, Eva?" he asked. "Oh, it's a cat."

He picked up the night-colored kitten, and puffed smoke from his newly-lighted cigar into its face. Oddly enough, the kitten liked it. Evannalina didn't. Her heart sank when she saw him bite the end of that tobacco roll. Hector never remained long when smoking in the presence of womankind.

"Good night," he said carelessly, at the gate. "Don't let anyone sit up for me. I've the key, and I may not be home till late."

He put the kitten into her arms and walked away. Evannalina stared uncomprehendingly as his figure appeared against the sky on the summit of the little hill nearby, and then dropped down behind it. She had half expected an explanation—a coming back.

She put her head on the top of the post, and burst into very miserable tears. The evening, once a time of quiet pleasure, now stretched before her a dreary blank. On returning to the house, however, she saw the key hanging in its accustomed place behind the window frame. Hector had not taken it. There seemed a necessity for someone to sit up, and she looked forward with a degree of cheerfulness to taking part in a further scene before sleeping.

XVI

The house had grown very still. The dropping of something—water from a leak in a pail, ashes in the fire, an acorn on the roof—were the only sounds. Once Evannalina looked out of the window. A sheen of moonlight lay over the earth, the road was flecked with leaf shadows, the meadow looked unusually broad, the clumps of pines on the hill seemed farther away than in reality. Under an arching tree the rickety gate, with its apparently massive posts of plank, took on an appearance of grandeur. It was like a place where something dramatic ought to occur, and the field of cut and bound-up corn on the opposite side of the road was the way for it to draw near, and, fearing the appearance of an untoward object, Evannalina dropped the curtain and fled back to the stove.

The yellow-faced clock never told the time quite right, but Evannalina believed it sufficiently to be aghast on discovering that it was three in the morning. The walls gave those queer cracks one hears and cannot explain in the hours before the dawn, and a long-tailed, sharp-nosed rat started foraging in the kitchen. Both were equally frightful. Evannalina bolted the door, and stole upstairs on tiptoe, glancing slyly out of the corners of her eyes. At the narrow door which belonged to Hector's room she paused. Loud breathing came out in sounds around the door chinks.

"Hector," she said, in a voice which sounded hollow to herself, "Hector."

"Huh!"

It was the sleepy groan of a forcibly roused man.

"How long have you been home?"

"Oh, hours and hours. I don't know."

"You hadn't any key, so I sat up."

"Well, didn't I say you needn't? I shinned up the oak tree and got in over the stoop roof."

Hector's tones were easily identified as those of an offended man, even through the butternut-wood door. Evannalina remembered that he always disliked a "fuss." He abhorred scenes like the average man—she gloried in them, like all women.

She was so exhausted by her vigil that she passed into sleep without any medium of romantic tear-shedding into her pillow. In fact, during her life, Evannalina had not used the feather confidant to assuage her sorrows as frequently as most sentimental girls.

XVII

The next day was typical of fall, with the utter silence of the dying of the year. The brook in the valley, purling over tiny pebbles, sounded like a mighty cataract. The sky was gray, with a brassy band at the southwest. A veiling of yellow leaves kept the grass green. The air smelt of decayed vegetation. Perhaps for this reason horses and cattle nosed the bars through which they were driven homeward, and ate nothing. The air was raw, and the two girls, seated high up on a vast ledge of rock which reared itself beside the road in a place out of sight of any dwelling, wrapped their fingers in their handkerchiefs to warm them.

"Love," said Azubah, airily. "Why love is—is something which lasts forever. One can't help loving anyone who is good to one, you know, and once one loves it lasts always. There are girls over in the graveyard—under the earth, I mean, who died for love. I believe it.

Nora Hammond died just because she couldn't get Hector Shield to go with her—a decline, they call it. I had hysterics at her funeral," added Azubah, proudly.

Evannalina smiled indulgently.

"It sounds pretty, but when you've lived to my age you'll see it's not true. People don't love forever. I just believe that love is caused by continually finding out new features, points of character, faults even, in someone. Just as quick as we know all about anyone, we don't love that person any longer."

"How funny," said Azubah. "You're almost wicked to talk so, Evan'lina. It's awful to be a flirt like that."

Suddenly, for the first time that day, the sun came out, and all the earth was glorified. Against the dense blue-black sky at the east a green hill was chopped off, with a single crooked tree above the horizon.

"There," exclaimed Evannalina, "does it not look as if there was something awful over there? If we didn't know the place, we might go over and see. But we know there's nothing over there, only more trees and the road. Just like old love."

Azubah smiled a simper of vanity.

"You're so much older than I," she said coaxingly, "won't you just tell me whether your cousin Hector is in love with me or not? He was at the house last night, and before he went he took off my slipper and kissed it."

Evannalina stood up, and looked down on the yellow-haired girl. Probably, by her own theory, she had found the depth to her woman lover's character, and so ceased to care for her. At any rate, she felt a determination to become Azubah's rival at that moment. She sharply answered, "It seems to me more like wheels in the head than love."

XVIII

Waiting is distinctly unpleasant, and the woman who waits for man to propose marriage to her, if she has any heart in the business, experiences the tortures of the condemned. Clairvoyants can never read the minds or foretell the future of those dearest to them, and now Evannalina, heartsick and nervous, found it impossible to judge at all of Hector's feelings. All her excuses to secure his presence alone were of no avail. She called him into the back buttery to help her empty the almost used barrel of apples, but he did not come. She followed him into the damp-smelling cider cellar on pretext of holding the candle, but he never looked at her. She was at his side when he went into the barn. He patted the horse's nose, and then climbed up an inaccessible ladder to the top of a hay mow.

The connecting link was snapped. Life wasn't worth living, anyway. It came on to rain in the afternoon, and Hector went away, perhaps to play pool in the village, more likely to visit Azubah. Yellow leaves clung to the trees with a persistency which made Evannalina think scornfully of herself, lingering round a heart that did not want her. "You have got to come down," fate seemed to be saying to her, just as the wind spoke to the withered leaves. The sky was swollen in places, as if bulging with water. A white mist blew aimlessly about the hilltops. Black patches of flies combined with the clinging vines outside to darken the farmhouse rooms. There was lightning once in awhile—it seemed as if nature winked, and then after an interval, groaned.

"In fact," sighed Evannalina, "there is nothing to do."

She had been examining some old letters—not written by herself, but by people now lying dead—letters written in the days when postage stamps were unknown and which were inscribed in one corner with the scrawled word "Paid." Intermixed with these cramped specimens of penmanship were funny silken ribbons of varieties never made now, tying up locks of hair belonging to she never knew whom, and faded flowers with fragrance and sentiment alike dried out of them.

"Sometime my troubles won't be any more consequence," she thought. And this did not console her at all.

"As it will all be the same a few years hence, he might make me happy," she mused, twitching her face impatiently.

XIX

Grandpa Shield had just returned from an infrequent visit to the village. He came gravely in, with his long-tailed coat flapping about

his respectable broad-clothed legs, and his shovel hat well pulled
down over his bushy, snow-colored eyebrows. Without so much as
putting away his gold-headed cane, he proceeded to scandalize his
family by dancing up and down each board in the kitchen floor.

"Do look at that old goose," said grandma. "Get off from where
I've been mopping."

"Mopping! You call swabbing a plank with a dirty rag on a
stick, mopping. By and by, I'll show you how to mop. Now I want
you to listen while I sing:

Oh, all you good people
Married must be,
But first you must sing
Juniper tree, Oh, juniper t-r-e-e!"

"Sit down, gramp," begged Evannalina. "Now tell us who's
going to be married."

"'Tain't going to be. 'Tis. 'Twas an elopement. Zuby Pine, you
know. She that made the wreath of clover tops and hung it to Jeff
Briggs' fence."

Evannalina wanted to scream.

"And Hector?"

"Oh well, Hec only went along of her for fun, I surmise. He
won't care. She's Mrs. Briggs now."

"I want to go to church next Sunday 'n see her come out bride,"
declared grandma, with tremulous eagerness. "You must fix over
my harnsome bonnet, Evy, 'n give my overskirt the hitch you was
going to, against then."

"Briggs was down to the store," continued the old man. "He
was wearing that coat he brags so much about. I tell yer, our Hec
got it on him this time, though. Briggs says, `I wore this coat sixteen
year 'n it's such good stuff the lining was never wet in any rain I
was out in yet.' Quicker 'n wink, you know, Hec steps up 'n spits
on the linging. `'S wet now,' says Hec, `'n it's your treat, Jeff.' You
know Briggs hates to spend money like all get out. `Anyhow I got
your girl,' says he to Hec. `No,' says Hec, `you didn't get my girl.
Nobody'll get my girl only me. If you get a girl 't ain't mine.' Jeff
looked kind o' disappointed 's if he mebbe wouldn't wanted her 'f
he'd knowed that. Minded me o' the time you were a little un, Evy,

'n you come over here a-bawling. `What's matter?' says I. `Wal,' says you, `I'm crying some 'cause my gran'pa's dead, and more 'cause my grand'ma isn't.' Them was your maternal granther 'n granmarm, you know, that you lived with then."

"Now, Dorias Shield, you just get off your good coat, 'n come to dinner," ordered grandma.

"Don't want no dinner. Don't want nothing but to go to bed and kick the bucket," returned grandpa, tired with his walk.

"Well, go 'long to bed 'n kick the bucket."

"That's it," he grumbled, "I always have to work."

"There's no need of your working."

"Well, you holler if I don't."

"Indeed," said grandma with dignity, "I don't holler."

"You did. You told me to kick the bucket, and there's work in that."

Then grandpa grinned triumphantly, and shut himself into the bedroom.

XX

"Zuby's married," said Hector, under the wide-spreading tree above the gate.

Evannalina said she knew it.

Hector, in the half darkness, brought his face very near to hers.

"Do you care?" he asked her.

"I'm sorry she's married a mean fellow like Jeff Briggs."

"I'm not," said Hector. "She can outrank him in meanness any day. I don't like a girl who runs after the men."

Silence ensued. Hector, with the tendency of men to boast of past conquests, was evidently anxious that Evannalina should ask for particulars. Finally he was forced to give them unasked.

"She told me she couldn't live without me. She wanted me to elope with her, because her father wouldn't have me around. I went over the other night and threw pebbles against her window until she got up and dressed and slipped down the front way to see me. I did not want to go, but she asked me."

"You weren't obliged," said Evannalina, rather coldly.

"Oh—well. She was so terribly anxious I couldn't refuse. I agreed to see her again, and then I wrote her a note saying I was busy. She came to the village, got the note, and rode away from the post-office with Jeff on the tin cart. I suppose she thought I'd be all broke up, but you see—! I called on her this forenoon and wished her joy with all the smiles I could gumption up."

All at once Evannalina's wrong burst forth.

"Why do you tell me that you are shallow and that you played Azubah false?" she cried. "You have done the same to me. I have stood a great deal from you, but I will not be flung away without a word."

It was the insane wandering of a nervously wrought-up woman. He stood still with folded arms and watched her weep. Suddenly he bit his lip, and taking her into his arms he said softly, "Why, you dear girl, do you care like that?"

Now that she had obtained what she wanted, it no longer seemed pleasant to have. Her tears were suddenly checked, and she drew herself away. He caught her hand.

"Eva, will you marry me?" he asked, confidently. It was actually the first time in his life that he had asked the question, but he felt no awkwardness, because he was not in doubt as to the answer.

Evannalina opened her lips to say yes, but the intention miscarried, and what came forth was a firm "No!"

"Very well," replied Hector, calmly, "I'm glad you think so. I'm not sorry I asked you, because you can never expect it of me any other time. Kindly let my love affairs alone after this."

Then he led the way into the house.

XXI

Under the gathering frost Evannalina Shield stood on the summit of the hill back of the house. She had been pulling the last of the vegetables in the garden, a big basket of ruddy beets and crackling bean pods rested on one hip under her arm.

The far-away hills were very blue and bold, as she saw them through a gap in the adjacent pasture. The sun was sinking. As it went down, a black line moved up the hillside. The apple orchard in the valley first looked dark, then the yellow glare disappeared from the window panes in the house, the red chimney turned black, next the white horse in the pasture became invisible, the fence was engulfed in the unseen, the woods followedɒfirst the brush and birches on the lower ranges of hillside, finally the timber on the crown. Suddenly she realized that she was standing in dark-ness, and that the path by which she was to go under the trees was hidden.

Hector was walking to the barn, whistling, and clashing the milk pails like cymbals. The boyish sound aroused no thrill in her heart, the brief upheaval of her nature as inclined towards him was entirely over. Without a sigh or any feeling of longing, Evannalina drew near the house. She knew that Hector would presently come in, and that he would not speak to her, any more than he would have spoken a month before.

Grandpa was still repeating his extemporized verses. This time it was:

"The thunder roared,
The lightning crashed,
And knocked ma's teapot
All to smash!"

Some such a commotion for nothing, seemed recent events to Evannalina. She took a drink before she went into the house, from the rusty dipper and the leaky pail. Yes, they had seemed of a good deal of consequence, but the results were actually of very little more importance than her reflection in the bucket.

Really, when one came to think of it, it was very much like a shadow on the water.

(*The Investigator*, 1895)

THE HOMECOMING OF CLEORA

Circumstances are always clever in providing a reason for not doing what one prefers not to do. Thus, for half a dozen years Cleora Wallis had been indebted to circumstances at holiday time. First economy gave sufficient reason for staying from Crissom Centre at Christmas—the fare alone was $2.98, not round trip. Next year, providentially, there had been a kindly chest cold that might have developed into something serious if taken into the country. The other excuses were fully as trivial. If Cleora remembered rightly, the same excuse served two ways on succeeding years. One winter her new frock was too smart, and would surely cause criticism; the year before it was lack of a fresh gown.

The real reason was not untoward circumstance, but Charles.

Nothing had happened to remove Charles from Crissom Centre, yet Cleora found herself there on Christmas-was-the-night-before (Crissom-Centre-ish for the eve of that holiday which we are told comes but once a year). She had left the town at three, and arrived at Crissom Centre at 6.19. The country was covered with crisp, hard-crusted snow; the kind of snow that answered with a crunching noise when pressed by the human foot, and over which wheels creaked dismally. The air was stinging cold, and overhead swam a big round moon that gave an added chill by its long silvery rays.

Cleora placed her handbag on the rear end of a great sled which was being slowly drawn up the mountain by a pair of patient oxen, at the same time declining a seat beside the freckled boy who lounged luxuriously on blankets in the center of the sled, guiding the oxen with demoniac yells. Cleora knew the family failings of the boy's clan. She was not quite ready to answer the questions in a social catechism that should last for two miles of up-hill road. Clinging to a bit of rope that trailed behind the sled, she helped herself perceptibly up the hill, and at the same time escaped interruption in her wholehearted enjoyment of the clear, calm night.

The two miles over, it took but a moment to grab the satchel, shout goodnight to the boy, and, leaving the main road to him, slip and run down a quarter mile of steepness into a hollow, where grew many evergreen trees, tall pines towering above symmetrical hemlocks, that in their turn looked down upon hedges of fir, and which were all intermixed with a few houses, a grocery store and a blacksmith shop. Her greeting at the largest white house of all had been just sufficiently cordial to show she was welcome to come, and still quite comfortingly "offish," so as to give assurance that she hadn't been missed very perceptibly during the half dozen past years. In short, the sort of welcome one naturally expects from New England relatives to whom your only tie is kinship, with naught of kind.

Now Cleora sat by the library window, looking into the wide yard to which the moonlight sifted through the big trees lining the driveway to the barn. Her face was turned toward the street, along which passed an occasional muffled figure.

Returning to girlhood memories, Cleora recalled the fact that this was about the hour when everyone went to the post office, some to get mail, others to see them get it. She wondered if Charles had yet gone by. She trusted and hoped that her unheralded arrival was not generally known.

"It used to take at least an hour for anything to percolate through the place," she murmured, with a smile, "and I've not yet been here thirty minutes."

She had purposely left the student lamp in the centre of the table unlit, lest suspicion might attach to a light in the sitting room at the hour when most folks had a lamp only in the kitchen, where supper operations were under way. Besides, the open fire gave out a bright light of its own, from fat pine sticks and fir cones lavishly thrown on the two big green birch sticks in which the sap sung gaily. In the corner a tall clock ticked gravely, and in a cushioned chair near Cleora the cat was putting her kittens to sleep with a comforting purr.

Altogether, the room abounded in homelike noises, not to speak of the sounds that stole in from the kitchen—the hiss when Aunt Charlotte poured the waffle batter into the iron, the clank with which she brought the iron jaws together, and the thump which followed triumphantly on the toss of another completed cake into a bath of maple syrup.

Still, to Cleora all sounds were overpowered by the persistent and agonizing thump of her own heart. She wondered, idly, why it didn't disturb the cat. She felt that if there was anything in the atmospheric wave idea that it must give pause to Charles, in case he were of those muffled figures that passed the house.

A violent start that set all her nerves a-quivering followed the turning of one figure in at the gate but presently she recognized the limp of Uncle Joseph, and managed to pull herself together so as to speak composedly when he entered the room and inquired why in tunket she hadn't got a light—this wasn't the city, where gas cost like all outdoors. She was even able to make out a very good supper, for Cleora's emotions had for many years been the undercurrent of her life, while to observation she was as placid of nature as is the pond by an unworked mill. She partook of thinly sliced ham, while telling Aunt Charlotte of her day's work in town, she sipped several cups of fragrant tea to an accompaniment of reminiscence contributed by Uncle Joseph, she finished off with waffles, quince preserves, pound cake and ginger snaps, and truthfully declared she hadn't been so well fed for many years.

And all the while she was sick with dread each time Uncle Joe opened his mouth, or Aunt Charlotte cleared her throat. They were sure some time to speak of Charles. Despite the six years of waiting, Cleora still felt unprepared to meet the sound of his name.

After supper she felt comparatively safe. Uncle Joseph read the New York *Sun*, and cussed its politics, before the fire, as he had done for the past fifteen years, regularly. Aunt Charlotte pottered around the kitchen, humming hymns that meant happiness for her, but dolefulness for any who should accept them by sound only. Cleora was free to linger as long as she liked by the window, even to creep into the ice-cold best parlor and shiveringly get a closer view of the village home comers, now going from the post office instead of to it. Perhaps it was the frost upon the window pane, or else the changes brought by years in men's hats, at any rate she did not recognize any who went by. At half past nine she followed Aunt Charlotte's orders, and carrying a small glass hand lamp went upstairs through the frosty hall to where the cosy warmth of a small room, heated by a cast iron "drum" from the kitchen, awaited her. It was the room she had occupied as a girl, and she looked eagerly to see if any of the treasures she had left on the shelf of the large closet "under the eaves" had been disturbed.

"Not one gone," she exulted to herself. "Aunt Charlotte is a good old thing, after all. Here's the doll I had outgrown, but never ceased to love, and the doll's sofa Uncle Joe made for me one Christmas and which never stood straight enough not to topple over when the doll was on it. And here's 'Little Women' with the last chapter read off, and 'Wood's Natural History' as fresh as when Auntie put it in my stocking December 24th about fourteen years ago. Here's—"

Cleora sat down heavily on the well scrubbed floor, gaping at the small envelope that had fallen from between the leaves of that remarkably fresh natural history volume. It bore her own name, in backhand and bad spelling.

"Miss Cleora Walis."

"Charles," she whispered, "it must be from Charles. No one else could have been so ignorant at thirteen.

There were tears on her cheeks as she opened the envelope reverentially, almost as one might a message from the dead. There was nothing in the envelope but a gaudy little silk handkerchief, embroidered with tags and ends of blue and red and green. It brought to Cleora's mind many another equally terrible gift from Charles in school days. Things which it was most unpleasant to use, because of their giving every possible offense to good taste, something that with Cleora came very early; and things that were yet very dear, because they represented so much thought and afterward privation on the part of the giver.

Cleora went to sleep with the little handkerchief under her cheek. When she awoke, in the gray dawn, it was lying far away, on the floor, and her first act was to patter barefooted to bring it back. All her other relics of Charles had been put away long ago, for Cleora recognized the futility of keeping a wound always raw and bleeding. They had so much the advantage of this, however, in that each had received its meed of consideration and caressing. The poor little 'kerchief should not go into that locked casket until it, too, was made a storehouse of memories.

After breakfast Cleora put on Aunt Charlotte's circular, a most unbecoming garment, neither long nor short, and with the sleeves confined by rubber bands that left red marks on the wrists. About her head she wound Aunt Charlotte's scarlet "cloud," and thus equipped she went to the cart path that entered the little grove at the back of the barn. There had been heavy sledding along this path, so the crust was somewhat broken, yet the walking remained fairly good. The woods were gloomy enough, being mainly of pine, while the day was gray, and ending in snow. All things were quite in harmony with the real Cleora, who was not the girl that laughed and joked with other girls at her work in town, or the commonplace creature that raced Uncle Joe at the breakfast table in devouring the flapjacks Aunt Charlotte fried for them as long as they would eat.

For this time her physical self was in a way to match her spirits. Her feet were sodden, and so seemed her heart; she was cold through and through, the great ache in her throat was partly mental and partly the sort of thing to interest a physician. After many years of deceptive cheerfulness there is a positive joy in giving way to absolute misery, and this was the joy that came to Cleora now. Those who knew her general sanity would have recognized it as momentary madness only, but Cleora did not analyze. Always in town, she had been afraid to give away. In the day there was fear of interruption, a sudden wrenching back to everyday existence. In the night there had been always the next day to think about, when Cleora wished to look fresh and well. Somehow the little relaxation of discipline that had caused her to come to Crissom for Christmas had been sufficient to undo all bonds. Cleora forgot her aunt and uncle, she did not remember the Christmas feast left cooking in the kitchen, of the afternoon gift-giving at the Congregational Christmas tree in the afternoon she took no thought, though this year as usual she had sent out a box of trinkets to be hung thereon for those she had played with as a girl, and for their accumulating little ones.

For some time it had been snowing up above the trees, and now the flakes came sifting through the pine needles, and likewise crept in underneath, and whirled around the massive black trunks in a dance before the wind. They clung to the red cloud on Cleora's head, and insinuated themselves into the unprotected spot where gloves ended and sleeves had not begun. They made her feet heavy to lift, and they got in her eyes and clogged her eyelashes. They brought Cleora back to earth with a bound, caused her to give a mental shake, to objurate herself as a sentimental fool, and send her seeking for the path with as much eagerness as she had departed therefrom. It seemed, indeed, as if she had left the path in more ways than one, and would be safe only when upon it once more.

With the return of healthy feeling came a gentle warmth that radiated through her body. Her toes tingled and her hands glowed. She remembered bits of wood lore learned long since, and made her way from tree to tree, in a line as nearly straight as possible, lest she might follow her own footsteps in a circle. Presently she reminded herself that this was about what she had done in her mistaken life.

"A six year circle," she mused, with a smile, "and it has ended where it started, at Crissom Centre."

She reached the path, and for a moment stood questioning which way to go. Then she turned to the right and busily strode in the direction from which she had come. As she came out of the gloom, and saw before her the familiar outlines of Uncle Joseph's barn, with Uncle Joseph himself belaboring a fat cow that insisted on eluding the watering trough toward which she was being driven, Cleora thought that never before had she felt so much affection for the queer old man.

"Been out pickin' posies?" he yelled, derisively; and Cleora gleefully bawled back, "Sure, uncle!"

She went into the house by the back door, peering into the fragrant kitchen before anchoring herself on the braided rag mat by the woodbox.

"Mercy sakes," cried Aunt Charlotte, "you are a sight! Come out here, some o' you in there 'n' brush Cleory off."

Two boys, one small, the other middle-sized, who were obviously relieved at being excused temporarily from their task of filling tarletan bags with popcorn for the church tree, dashed at Cleora with brooms, continuing to brush her even after she had shed the outer husk of clothing. All the irresolution and dread had somehow been left in the dark wood, with a cheerful smile Cleora entered the sitting room, which, like the now-warmed parlor, was filled with groups of children, some sorting candy, to be mixed with corn and raisins, others stuffing the bags, still others sewing them up with bright red yarn. By the parlor "airtight" a group of little girls chattered happily as they strung cranberries and popcorn alternating on long threads. It was such a pretty scene that Cleora regretted having missed any of it, and went back to ask Aunt Charlotte how long they had been there.

"Oh, they began to come about fifteen minutes after you stepped out," returned that good woman. "They're all to be sent home at twelve for their dinners, and after we've had our'n we'll take the stuff over to the meetin'-house, where most of 'em'll be on hand, too, fur the tree. There's your Uncle Joseph driving round, now, with the big sled full of straw, so's to get 'em safe away in the snow."

The scene changed as rapidly as any transformation in the theatre. Uncle Joseph shouted, "Guddap," and Cleora was left sitting by the fire, while Aunt Charlotte in the other room packed the bags and gay strings in a capacious basket. For the first time the visitor assumed the attitude of a well-pleased looker-on, rather than an agitated participant.

"What has come over me?" Cleora asked herself. "I feel so glad for everything. Is something very happy coming to me? Can it be—?"

She dared not carry out the thought, even to herself. At the boy-and-girl stage of life Charles had loved her dearly and she had responded in spite of the traces of a lawless home life which offended her budding taste and caused both uncle and aunt to sometimes have fears for the future. At Cleora's sixteen, during a leafy June, a full-blown romance united the two. Charles was nearer twenty, a big, handsome, ignorant chap, with a vein of poetry in his makeup that somewhat redeemed him in the eyes of youth. Uncle Joseph and Aunt Charlotte have never known, all the village had been quite ignorant of those summer evening meetings in dark corners of the town, of those long strolls through the daisy fields. It had been a romance, pure and simple, with no thought of the future, no prosaic questionings as to engagement rings, or the approval of guardians. To dawdle and dream through the sunny days, and furbish one's clothes prettily for the evening, was a way of living Aunt Charlotte thought natural enough for a girl fresh from high school, in the long vacation. That the evenings were not passed sitting on other high school girls' porches Aunt Charlotte never dreamed. Yet always Cleora sped, straight as an arrow, to the trysting place where Charles waited with loving words, vows of eternal constancy, and great wreaths of wild roses from which he would have cut the thorns, so that she might safely press them to her cheeks, as she loved to while their fragrance was almost intoxicating on the night air.

Just one June out of a lifetime, and yet it had left a memory that like an insistent tune might never be hushed. The end had been one that anyone not sixteen would have anticipated. On the fourth of July, Cleora, looking from the sitting room window idly at noon, saw Charles escorting a flamboyantly attired female "millhand" from over at Crissom Corners to the sunlight dance that was the yearly scandal of Crissom Centre. Almost disbelieving her eyes, Cleora dashed to the yard, and came upon the couple as they passed the gate. Charles, whose face was red, as was not its wont, turned from the sturdy damsel by his side and for a moment looked at little, pale, anemic Cleora with a good-natured smile. And then he went on, after giving her an audacious wink.

It was then the blow was struck that wounded Cleora—for life, she believed. She had never seen Charles again, she had gone where even his name might not be heard. Her letters to Uncle Joseph and Aunt Charlotte had been so worded, as to show Cleora felt little interest in the news of the village. With all this care, recovery had never been complete. Perhaps her strongest feeling had been pity— pity for herself as so poor a creature that even ignorant, unconsidered Charles could not really give her love, and then above all pity for Charles and his wilful mistake in letting his baser nature overpower the better that was his also.

"He was happy with me," she would wail to herself in the middle of those sleepless nights thereafter. "I know he was. I was too close to him to be deceived in that. He loved the romance, the poetry, the appreciation of all that was fine. He meant what he said about ambition and character—else why did he say it? It was by no means necessary. I would have clung to him through everything, had he only asked it. It was not poverty I was afraid of, or an uncouth home. And if he didn't love me, why need he have taken the trouble ever to say so?"

It was a maze in which she wandered, year by year. These dreary questions, to which there was no reply, were forever coming between Cleora and any real cheerfulness. This day was the first time that Cleora had felt able to face the future with fortitude, and to look back with some degree of composure. The jiggly bell that was attached to a rusty wire running from the street door gave a faint tinkle, and just as Cleora thought, "Perhaps I've gotten on the straight path now, instead of back to the beginning of the circle," Aunt Charlotte shouted, "Go to the door, won't you? I'm just busy dishing up dinner, 'n' I guess it's no one only the man who's to play Santa Claus over to the Christmas tree. He was going to come to borrow your uncle's buffalo coat."

Thus prosaically came face to face the two so rudely parted years before—thus did Cleora meet the man whose name she had dreaded, and whose face she had not dared recall in dreams.

All the promise of manly beauty had been redeemed, and there was, moreover, a refinement and dignity in dress and bearing which Cleora dimly perceived at the moment Charles took one of Cleora's limp hands, and then the other. His chest heaved convulsively, and he tried to speak, without succeeding. Cleora, on the contrary, was quite collected. She even said, "How do you do?" and added, "Will you not walk in?"

As in a dream he entered, and thrust his snowy felt hat toward the hat rack. It did not strike right, and fell unheeded to the floor. Cleora became aware that Charles was devouring her face with his eyes. She felt a keen desire to smile inanely and essay small talk. She even began. "A dreadful day out, is it not?" when Charles interrupted her. "It is you?" he exclaimed with a roughness that seemed to proceed from emotion rather than to be still inherent. "It is you, after all. Don't speak yet. I know I'm not worthy of a word with you, and yet I must explain. That day—that girl. It—it was only a ruse, a trick. I saw nothing for you, dearest, but a wretched life of poverty if our love continued. I was uncouth, a boor, your people would never have let you marry me without fearful scenes. And I could not help loving you. How could I help it, and you so heavenly kind? Do you ever think of those awful things I used to send you at Christmas trees when we were school children, and which you never even laughed at, and sometimes wore? No one was ever tender of my feelings but you, and I never loved any other, before or since. Thank me for curing you, Cleora, and sometimes, oh, sometimes remember that to do so broke my own heart."

Cleora looked at him a moment as if he were a stranger, and then became conscious of an awful rage that had engulfed every other feeling. So it had all been needless, her years of misery, as well as her hours of dread since coming to Crissom Centre? This great, blundering, handsome man had known no better than to make her love him, and then to believe that he could end the love by a clumsy trick! And now, very likely, he expected to win her again in a conventional manner. It was evident enough, from his look and dress, that he was no longer an ignorant, an uncouth creature of whom anyone in Crissom Centre or even in town need feel ashamed. All this caused her to feel irritated at herself, disgusted with his density. In an utterly heart-whole and complacent manner Cleora remarked, "I don't believe in broken hearts, and really, I don't think you'll find you do yourself, when you come to think it over. Those salad days are better quite overlooked, it seems to me. I certainly thank you for—much. And now will you not come in and see Aunt Charlotte about the coat?"

Charles drew back his shoulders at the rebuff, as does a man facing an unexpected blow. Then he said, quite gently, "No, I will not come in. Tell your aunt, please, that I find it impossible to act as Santa Claus, and so Uncle Joseph will have to play the part, as was first suggested."

Then he picked up his hat and went away without a single backward glance—though if he had given one Cleora would never have been the wiser. She went into the house, delivered her message, ate a good dinner and took occasion to wrap a certain gaudy silk 'kerchief in paper, to hang upon the Christmas tree for a poor child to whom, as Aunt Charlotte explained, few ever gave gifts.

The next day she went away from Crissom Centre, promising herself to return whenever convenient, since there was nothing now she dreaded in that place. Whimsically she realized that if Charles had come upon her in any of that dreary time when she was passing round and round a circle, ever returning to the starting point, he would have had his heart's desire, and she hers. He came too late, she had struck out upon the straight path, and upon a path on which there might be no turning back.

(*The Pioneer*, December 1903)

HE THAT WILL NOT WHEN HE MAY

A TALE OF CHRISTMAS TIME

It was like a great, wide Christmas card—the country through which Fred DeVoe walked on this afternoon of Christmas Day. Hard white snow, topped with a glistening crust, covered the fields on either side of the narrow road, and the evergreen trees against the pale hillside were literally spangled with icicles, for there had been a freeze after a rain, with no subsequent thaw. The sky was of that deep blue which presages yet more cold weather, and there had been no alleviation from the sun, that was now sinking in a red glory back of the evergeens and the hill. A single house was in sight—its long roof frosted with snow, fringed with ice, and the red chimney with its curling smoke giving just the hint of coziness that was required to perfect the picture.

Fred felt the beauty of the scene, yet thought it proper to sneer, and curled his handsome lip scornfully, while muttering, "Well enough to look at—but oh, how deadly slow to live in."

As he came nearer to the house he heard a clash of milk pails, and voices from muffled-up figures making their way to the barn. Nearer yet, and he caught a glimpse of a white face at an upper window—a face framed in something scarlet, and vanishing quickly. With a meditative expression Fred turned abruptly from the road into a field that was very vast and hollowed out to a pond in the centre. Some sedges and weeds, withered and brown, clogged the edges of the ice, and there was considerable snow upon it also, still enough of the glassy surface was left uncovered to reflect the glory of the sunset and make it easy for Fred to skim half-way around the hill, once he had screwed his shining nickel skates upon his thick shoes.

The ice ended there, but he kept right on skating, going over the crusted snow expertly, though it was indeed rough work for a man who could cut any number of figure eights backward—given good ice and an audience. He skirted about the hill, a good quarter of a mile, and again approached the road, having by the detour avoided passing the house. A spur of the hill compelled the road to make a detour also, in the opposite direction from that of Fred, so that he was not quite out of espionage from the dwelling. He sat on the wall, quietly whistling while the skates came off, and then peered into a patch of verdureless trees clustered nearby. There was, he felt sure, something scarlet that was not of nature's growth, fluttering about the grove. His heart beat violently, but he resolutely compelled himself to pause and light a cigarette.

"It will have an effect," he muttered. "It will show I do not care so very much."

By the time he reached the woods he was seemingly alone; he strode through them, afraid to linger lest he should remember too fully how they looked in mid-July, with twilight filtering through green leaves, and fragrant with odor from the masses of ferns sprouting from the moss—afraid, also, to think what happened there and then.

Beyond the wood was a natural terrace, overlooking more snow-crusted fields, and a winding river, now icebound save for a slender line of black that bespoke the still-living current of water flowing to the sea. On this terrace, leaning against one of the trees as if to gain breath after her rapid run, was the girl with the white face, that face framed and her body partly wrapped by a gay scarlet shawl.

The winter weather, which had put the vigorous Fred into a glow, had acted otherwise with her, for lips were purple, nose was red and pinched, eyes watered, and teeth chattered. Fred felt a twinge of pity, but instantly conquered it.

"Where's your coat and hat?" he asked, "and your overshoes?" he added, looking at her feet in their foolish slippers with red heels.

"I–I couldn't very well get them out, and have f-father ask where I was going," she returned, with a lack of acerbity that showed the ill-humor to be all on one side.

"Yes, if you had any sand," he went on. "Be independent, like I am. `When'll you be back?' my mother always cries when she sees me leaving, and I say, `You'll see me when I come.' And I tell her that every time, too, even when I'm going to the church supper or choir practice, or things she'd approve of, because it keeps her in good training and throws her off the scent when I do want to keep her in the dark."

While he was speaking he had made an attempt to put his arm about the girl, but she eluded him rather primly and with an hysterical, "Don't, please, don't."

He looked as if he meant to argue the point, then suddenly appeared to recognize her mood as helping his desires, for he turned away with a cold, "As you please."

Netta shrank, cut by the words, and then, with a pitiful attempt at playfulness, essayed to smile, while saying, "Don't be angry, Fred. I'm afraid I'm not very interesting today, but I've—I've not been happy, and I couldn't sleep for thinking of what life would be after you had gone."

Fred was coaxing another cigarette to light, turning his back to the girl in order to shield the flame from the wind. Failing to notice what he was doing, she timidly came near and placed her hand upon his coat sleeve. Startled, he lost his concentrative interest in keeping the flame alight, burned his fingers, and dropped the cigarette, which rolled and leaped like a live thing over the crusted snow until out of sight.

"Oh, I'm so sorry," she faltered, while Fred with careful ostentation drew forth the embroidered case—she had made it for him herself during early September—and showed that it was quite empty.

"I'm—I'm always careless," she went on, with abject self-condemnation.

"Oh, not at all," said Fred, with freezing politeness. "Only you might learn the advantage of repose," he went on, with an unconscious imitation of the grande dame manner which he secretly laughed at in his own mother.

"Fred," she ventured timidly, "please let us not spend our last hour over trifles. Be—be a little good to me, Fred, for I'm so—so unhappy."

And once more the tears began to flow.

"By George, Netta, I wonder if you know what a perfect wet-blanket you are to all my ambitions? A man gets deadly sick of tears all the time. It seems as if I never see you excepting you have your handkerchief working. We sneak out from our respective homes and slide off to a dance, and then you mortify me half to death by weeping because I have to do a duty waltz or so with another girl. I write you more often than most fellows think of writing their best girls, and then you have a crying fit because I won't promise to write every day. I come several miles in the cold today, sneaking round through the lots like a chicken thief, all for your sake, and you treat me to another scene. I declare, I'm sick of it. You didn't act so last summer, when we first began seeing each other. My, you had spirit then. That was what I liked you for. Where has it all gone? Where's your self control?"

Netta was beyond speaking, for grief, indeed she did not understand it herself. She had indeed been spirited, flirtatious, full of coquetry and brightness in the days of their early acquaintance, and before those days. "As great a trainer as Netta Brown," was a height of comparison seldom attained in the village, though often cited. The many men whose attempts at being sentimental she had flouted would not have known this Netta, wan with sobbing, pleading timidly for a little kindness. Some natures change utterly, with an acknowledged affection, and so it was with Netta. No sooner had she given her heart to Fred DeVoe than she ceased being the kind of girl he had fallen in love with. She had been an emblem of independence among girls; submitting her lips to her lover, she had likewise given submission of opinions, of mind, of heart, of all life interests. Fred had for some time been in the position of a man who, seeking to gain a modicum, finds himself embarrassingly possessed of a satiety. He was soon to go away for four years at college. He had hoped, of course, that the summer's flirtation would rouse Miss Netta's preference for him to a slightly sentimental degree. What he intended was to enjoy a period of philandering, followed by tender goodbyes. He wanted Netta to write him occasionally while he was away—it would add to his possible importance among other freshmen to receive lots of letters in feminine hands—and to be glad to see him when he returned on vacations. He would send her pretty trifles once in a while, and depend on her to embroider sofa pillows and canoe cushions in the college colors.

Looking for a mere "affair," he had roused a passion. Netta, turned into a drooping, weeping damsel, always sentimental, aroused his pity and then his disgust. She had actually seemed to think that their summertime engagement would be a means of preventing him from following the career mapped out. She was quite ready to elope any time, since she well knew her father "had no use" for anyone bearing the name of DeVoe. With the plebeian ideas due to her upbringing in a common farmhouse, she had implied that the elegant Fred might "hire out" to someone in town. "I am quite willing to live in two rooms," she had whispered one dark night in the wood, when the blackness hid her blushes, and hid likewise Fred's look of horror, for he was quite sure he should never be content with love in a cottage, unless it was a deal handsomer cottage than any he wotted of.

"I don't want to quarrel with you, Netta," he was now saying, "but I do think you might be reasonable. I'm not going to my grave, nor to war. Lots of fellows go to college and leave girls behind them."

"But not so lonely as I," pleaded Netta, "I wouldn't mind so much if I could have a ring, and the engagement announced, and be pointed at in church and on the street as your future wife. But no one will know we are anything to each other, and in that college town there will be ever and ever so many other girls—"

Fred laughed scornfully. "Jealous, are you, of girls I don't know yet and may never know. Well, that's the limit!"

He essayed once more to put his arm about her waist, and was again repulsed. Once more he said "As you please," and this time there came a remonstrance from her, in the whining voice which he abhorred above all else.

"You know quite well it's not as I please, Fred. It's as you will. It's always been as you will, and I must consent. It was your will that made me throw over the man that took me to the party where we first met last spring, wasn't it?"

He nodded, morosely.

"And it was your will that I should steal out of the house last summer, in the late evenings, and meet you in the grove here?"

He lifted his eyebrows and shrugged his shoulders, as of one who might remonstrate, but was too gallant to do so.

"It was your will that I should love you, and I did; and now it is your will that we should part, and I—"

"And you are doing your level best to make our last interview a deuced unpleasant affair," he interposed bitterly.

"Oh Fred—and you've not given me yet so much as a pleasant look—you, who last June would tease for an hour for just a smile and a rose I had worn."

Somehow the vast difference between the brisk, friskily dressed Netta of early summer and the doleful girl now before him, struck

Fred as a matter for ridicule, and he laughed. This was, indeed, too much for Netta's pretense at composure.

She was sobbing now, in earnest, with no idea of appearing collected. Half dead with cold and anguish, she let the tears course unrestrained down her white cheeks, each growing colder as it fell, until it ended in a half-frozen drop upon her quivering chin. Fred would have been heartless if he had not longed, somewhat, to gather her up and hurry her to a fireside somewhere, but his scheme of parting still possessed dominating strength, and under its sway he exclaimed brutally, "Netta, for heaven's sake, dry up and be sensible." Then, when she choked with sobs, he added, "You may not know it, but you are a sight."

And then it seemed as if the very tears in Netta's eyes froze, as well as those upon her cheeks and chin. She gave a cry that was almost one of triumph, the red blood surged into her face, she drew herself up and threw back the scarlet shawl as if the season was once more mid-July, and its warmth oppressive. Her lace-covered neck and chest were exposed to the biting air, and she did not mind this a whit. Her pale blonde beauty took on a vividness that seemed almost supernatural to Fred, too bewildered to notice that it was the pulsating pink of the afterglow that touched her faded hair as with a nimbus of ruddy gold, encarmined her lips and turned her cheeks to seashell tints.

Poised on a hummock of snow she stood for an instant, like a bird meditating flight, then she flew at Fred, and clawed his face, her rage seeming too great for any ordinary expression.

"Netta, Netta," he cried, trying in vain to grab her wrists, and only tangling his fingers in the lace ruffles there.

"I hate you," she was whispering hoarsely, "I hate you! I shall never love you again. You think I am vulgar and low and mean, and so I will be. Go, if you like, go, go, go!"

And she brought both her fists to his mouth violently, leaving blood upon his lips—some from her own mangled knuckles, other from his tongue, upon which his teeth had closed violently. And then she spat with loathing upon him, and turning, ran through the woods without a single backward glance. For an instant Fred was aghast, next he followed her, calling her name loudly, for the first time quite careless of whether or not he was overheard by a chance passerby.

"Netta," he shouted, "Netta," but she never turned. Through the grove, sacred to summer memories, he pursued, dropping his skates, losing his hat, abandoning his overcoat and gloves, and only wincing slightly when an awkward movement brought him into collision with one of the large trees. His only pause was to fill his arms with the scarlet shawl that the girl left tangled in a bush, and again to stoop tenderly for one foolish slipper with a red heel, beside which there was a little break in the crust, proving that its owner had here tripped and fallen. Out of the wood, he saw her again, far ahead, skimming recklessly over the snow crust—now she had fallen once more, headlong, and recovering herself, went on, hobbling painfully, her feet leaving little blood spots on the snow—spots that Fred DeVoe would come back and kiss in sorrow by and by, when the moon would be risen.

For she never turned or listened, though she must have heard his frantic calls. She slammed the door of the Christmas-card house, and though Fred lingered for above an hour, there was no white face at the window this time. Instead he heard a merry tune upon the mandolin that she alone of all that household could play; and he had not even the satisfaction of believing it was strummed for the sake of effect upon him, since he had hidden in the hedge long since, and would have been thought gone had she so much as peeped out.

It was hours before Fred DeVoe returned to the home he shared with his haughty mother. He wandered in the field, and thought himself well repaid for all his trouble when he recovered a few tags of lace torn from Netta's gown by a rude bramble at which she had grasped. He was hungry and cold, but he did not know it; his utter weariness was certainly ample vengeance for all the woe he had caused Netta on days when he promised to come at three, and made her keep unrewarded vigil at that upper window until five or six—and when he had sometimes failed to come at all.

Often he returned to the farmhouse. Once, at half an hour before midnight, he saw a slender figure passing a staircase window. It was Netta, carrying a small lamp. His heart filled with hope, he whistled softly the air of "Kathleen Mavourneen," once selected as a signal between them, but though he knew she heard and though he waited patiently a long time a little distance down the road, there was no Netta, repentant or otherwise, to meet him. Nor was there ever. He heard of her often afterward—she went to a town some thirty miles away, to live with a somewhat prosperous aunt, and from her new place of residence came stories, as of old, concerning Netta the coquette, Netta the flirt, Netta the girl of spirit who would dance all night with one man and then flout him next day. As of old, girls who would be giddy were told that "as trainers they were not in it with Netta Brown."

A man less vain than Fred DeVoe might very well have hoped that all this came from picque, but Netta herself knew better. Once he had, of his own volition, killed her love, all her independence came back; then, indeed, it seemed incredible that she could have wasted days in watching and nights in weeping. Netta thought of Fred very seldom, and remembered their summer's love as she might a brief and delirious illness. Above all, she hated him for the unholy rage to which he had roused her. This moment's passion, during which she had spit and clawed, forgetful of all self-respect, was what put a barrier forever between them, as she thought about it. As Fred thought, it was the one supreme occurrence that had made Netta desirable. The white heat of her anger had served to kindle hotly that which was before but a feeble flame of emotion. The Netta whom he met in the spring fascinated him, the Netta who loved him in the summer and autumn tired him with her meek monotone, the Netta who tore his cheeks and ran away on Christmas Day was the Netta of whom he dreamed while pursuing a weary round of tiresome duties on a farm.

For Fred DeVoe, for some reason unknown even to his mother, gave up all idea of going to college, and "hired out" to the owner of the swale through which he had skated. The neighborhood is dear to him, and he has hope for company. He does not know that he will never have anything but hope.

(*The Scotchman*, January 1905)

WONTED FIRES

"I'm awful glad they's a moon," Clymenia was saying, as she pant-
ed up the path to the house door. "I don't jest fancy thet stretch o'
woods when 'tis pitch dark."

The way was shadowed by shrubs that grew on either side of the
narrow walk, but accustomed feet could not stray.

"Seem's if the grass was gettin' long," she thought, and bent
over to make sure. "Yes," she went on, "and it's dew-wet. I guess
I won't hurt for all that, but feyther ought to keep it mowed down
short. He could use a seckle without hurtin' the bushes one mite."

She was close to the stoop now, and shook her dampened skirts.
As her foot struck the boards a small animal scuttled from behind a
vine-shaded post and vanished underneath the floor.

She peered into the half-light interestedly.

"Was thet a kitten now, I wonder?" she questioned. "Or jest one
o' th' ole cats? Seem's if they'd orter know me. When it's along
towards sundown an' I bring 'em out their vittles I can't so much as
set foot on th' stoop 'thout a whole passel on 'em'll com'n git right
in th' way."

The stoop was too narrow for one to expect to see so much as
a chair thereon. It looked white and very clean in the moonlight.
Even the posts that supported the roof, made from slender tree
trunks with the stumps of boughs left slightly protruding, appeared
colorless, though Clymenia was well aware that really they were
quite brown.

"Th' moonlight's gret on alterin' things," she thought, as she
went into the house. It was so warm a night that she was in no manner surprised to find the door wide open. In the kitchen the cool
night air met with a variety of odors, which Clymenia instantly
distributed within her mind, ascribing the damp to the cellar, the
soot to the uncleaned chimney, the acrid smell to the vinegar barrel
that was ever dripping in the back room and an undefinable tale of
grease to "mother's frying a few nutcakes after supper." She even
thought of seeking a handful in the buttery, but desisted.

"There's pa'n ma in th' little bedroom there," she mused. "I
wouldn't wake 'em up fur a farm with a cow on it. They'd want to

know what kep' me so late. They always want to know. I'll hyper up t'bed 'n not even light a candle."

A sleepy little chirp startled her for a moment, and then she laughed silently, as she murmured, "Ma's canary, o' course, over there in th' corner, hung up so's th' cats can't git at it, 'n sound asleep 'th ma's apurn over th' cage."

With exaggerated caution she lifted the latch and began to creep upstairs, her eyes staring into what was now utter blackness. Her heart beat so that it seemed as if the little house must shake, and when she neared a stair that memory told her always creaked violently she was obliged to pause and gain calmness by thought. Finally she recommenced her silent laughter.

"What on airth's th' matter o' me tonight?" she muttered. "Don't I alwus step clean over it?"

Gathering her skirts about her, she accomplished the feat, and was soonly safely on the top landing. Before her stretched more stairs, going into the garret, and there were three doors, all closed. For a moment she had an idea of entering the large room, over the kitchen. The "spare room" it was, and there, even with no light better than moonlight, Clymenia loved to see her slender figure reflected in the one long mirror of the house, to advance and retreat coquettishly, to smirk, to look stern for a moment, and then to break into dimple-decked smiles—in brief, to rehearse the little comedy that she played during the evening afar down the road, for the benefit of Dick Morehead. It was a fascinating, but dangerous play, and after a moment's temptation, Clymenia decided to have none of it this night.

"Yes, o' course," she murmured, "I remember what Dick says—not to mind 'em, thet their scoldin's can't hurt none, an' thet I'm too big to whip, but somehow I feel frightened just th' same. It's—it's sort of scary tonight, more'n usual, too."

Finding her own room door ajar she hurried down the two steps which gave upon it, knocking her head, as always, sharply against the roof.

"Well, well," she scolded, also as always, "seem's if I can't never g'age thet ole ceilin' right. I can't never seem to git it through my head thet I'm growed up, 'n so I tunk my for-head ev'ry single time I come up here'n th' dark."

The roof did indeed encroach much upon the very tiny room, beginning at a point right above the door, and sloping at an acute angle until within a foot of the floor. Under the eaves, at this point, were two square windows, which had first given Clymenia, when a child, an idea of meaning in the phrase, "A lamp unto my feet and a light unto my path." A narrow bed ran the length of the room, and though the moon gave little light here, Clymenia knew that at one end, where the wall was highest, there stood a chest of drawers atop of which was a looking glass that reflected only in spots, where the quicksilver had not worn off, and this her mother had hung up with a laugh at Clymenia, as she had said, "Here, this is good enough for a young 'un like you, 'n if you can l'arn to dress 'thout gopping at y'urself it'll mean y'ur boun' t' catch a handsome husband."

At the other end of the room Clymenia could dimly see the bulk of the tall wardrobe that held her slender store of frocks. The bed was in disorder, its coverlids dragging on the floors, but Clymenia had little disposition to do more than throw herself upon it, fully dressed, for she had much to think about, and indeed had slept but little in the wonderful summer nights since Dick Morehead had come to help in the haying at Whittier's "down below," and Clymenia had stolen out each evening to meet him by the first bridge in the meadow. Each evening, too, she had lingered longer, their parting had been more reluctant, and her heart had beaten more tumultuously after memory began to busy itself as now, among scenes that seemed continually repassing.

"Oh, Dick," she whispered into the warm soft hands that she had placed on either cheek, in imitation of the way Dick himself had held her face not long ago, "what is to come of it all? By'n by th' hayin'll be over'n done, 'n no one knows if Mr. Whittier's goin' t' keep you fur th' huskin' or not. 'N if he does, then what? You say let well enough alone, n' let's kiss 'n be happy while we kin. I can't somehow feel it like thet, on'y when I'm long o' you. You've nothin', Dick, fur us to live on, 'f we should run away—'n where'd we run to, anyhow, I don't know! You owe more'n your wages this summer to th' academy thet give you your schoolin' last year, 'n they's four more years before you can be set apart to preach 'n have a home. 'N even then I'm mortial sure feyther'll never hear to it, because you've gone to be a Methodist, 'n we're Seven Day Advents."

It was a tangle, with no clue as yet. And so, as ever, Clymenia put aside her grief, and turned to happier thoughts—to visions of Dick, as he had looked in the moonlight, ruddy-faced and gleaming-eyed; or when bending over the muddy pond in the hope of finding a lily or two within reach; and again as he went his separate way down the road after they had parted. She had watched him until he was almost out of sight, and then had turned away her eyes so as to avoid seeing him quite disappear, on account of the old superstition that if she did so he might never come back. "An', arter all," mused Clymenia, "I was in sech a hurry I looked up too quick, 'n there he was jest' a-turnin' th' four corners. 'N wasn't I a silly gilly! I wanted to call him back, 'n did run down th' road a piece, 'n then started to shout, but o' course he couldn't a heard, 'n tomorrow I'll see him again, jest th' same."

And so, smiling in fond fancy of that same tomorrow, even as she shivered with a trifling apprehension, she dropped into sleep. Once she partly woke, disturbed by a sound, and asked herself sharply, "What's thet?" Then, in silent mirth, she replied, "Well, I am a great goose. It's just pa's watch a-tickin' away in th' spare room. Likely enough th' door was on th' jar after all, else I shouldn't hear it so plain."

Some hours went by, the moon sank, and the red ball called the summer's sun arose. It was very quiet hereabout, yet the wakening of bird and plant makes confusion that causes the light sleeper to stir. Clymenia opened her eyes, lay quiet for a few moments, and then quite roused by the prospect of the day's duties sat up exclaiming, "Gracious, I must hurry, I want t' iron thet pink muslin, so's I can wear it tonight, 'n finish th' oak-leafd edgin' f'r my petticoat besides."

A moment more, and the little old house rang with a shriek that was half surprise, half recognition of a familiar terror. The room in which Clymenia found herself was in shape and size the semblance of the one she believed herself to have entered the night before, but in no way otherwise the same. In vain she looked for the rose-bud paper she had, with her own hands, stretched upon the walls, or the frilled muslin curtains she had starched and strung over the long window. A wisp of dirty rag hung above one broken pane. The walls were crumbling. The wardrobe door yawned, showing utter vacancy save for a pile of neatly drilled nuts which proved this to have been the place of a squirrel's winter hoard. The bed was indeed disordered, for the rotten bedstead was covered only with a squalid straw mattress, over which were dragged some torn coverlids, mildewed and stained with the wash of rain from the leaking roof.

With scarce a pause Clymenia rushed into the tiny hall, and flung apart the spare room door. Here was further evidence of decay and change, no furniture remained, the floor had sunken, and a great hole in the wall let in a branch of a tree. Downstairs she almost fell, and saw, with growing horror, that the stair which always creaked, and over which she had stepped so carefully last night, was a yawning hole, the board being quite missing.

As for the kitchen, it was plain why she had felt the night air, for there was no door to close, and no unshattered pane remained in the windows. So close to nature was the room, that a bird pair had builded their nest on a tiny shelf high up in one corner. It was a neat nest, plastered with mud, and above its edge tiny heads appeared, with great beaks opened for food. Mother's canary was gone, why its successors had befooled Clymenia in the moonlight might be plainly understood. There was nothing else in the room, excepting a horrible heap of rubbish in the fireplace. Like a whirlwind Clymenia went through the house, sparing herself nothing. In the little bedroom where she had imagined her parents calmly sleeping, the floor had gone quite down to the cellar, and the plaster was sagging inward until the walls nearly met. The buttery was half crumbled to a mass of debris, and she could actually see the surface of the well which had formerly fed the pump. The spring rains had filled it to the very surface of the soil, and it was covered with a blue scum, mixed with rotting leaves from the apple tree hard by.

On the porch, in the morning sunlight, Clymenia stood, in ever-growing fright. Last night, in the moonlight, had she not been young, of pulsating heart, creeping to her bed after an evening of happiness with Richard, fearful only of waking her parents? Today she awoke and found the house a ruin, the path choked with weeds, wild squirrels running about and chattering from the rooftree, instead of the domesticated tabby cats that she had imagined in the cozy places on the stoop beside the door. Was this the dream, or had she been dreaming in the moonlight? She pinched herself and felt it plainly, she touched the wood and it was rough, therefore she knew herself to be awake.

Turning, Clymenia retraced her steps through the kitchen, up the rickety stair, and into the little room. The looking glass still hung above the dilapidated chest of drawers—at least all that was left of it. Focussing her face until it was opposite a bit that seemed to still possess the power of reflection, Clymenia rubbed it round and round with her elbow, removing the smear and dust of years, and then looked long and anxiously.

She saw not what she looked to see, yet what she saw had been thus for many years.

In place of clear blue eyes, flaxen curls, pink and plump cheeks, she found herself gazing at a section of brown skin marked only by intersecting wrinkles. One eye was visible, bloodshot and bleared. There was likewise a single straying lock of white hair, unkempt, uncared for, with never a hint of curl. By moving Clymenia was able to find a yellowed neck, gaunt and skinny, and a collarless brown calico gown, such as Richard would certainly never have fancied.

The sight calmed her, restored even some semblance of under-standing. "'Tain't jest th' house," she muttered, "I'm a ole wreck, too. How it's come to be, I don't jest da's't to think, but I s'pose there's no help for't. Now what to do—I best go out into th' road 'n calkerlate."

Once in the road instinct led her away from the ruined house without a backward glance. People looking from their kitchen windows said, "There goes Clymeny Clemons, it's a wonder th' almshouse keeper lets her wander quite so free." And one or two old dames, with groping memory, tried to recall somewhat of her history, but only spoke vaguely of Dick Morehead, "more'n sixty years ago a stranger in these parts, who summered pretty good, but didn't winter well."

While sturdily walking in the growing heat of the morning, Clymenia increased in bravery, but it chanced that before long her way led her into one of those valleys that nestle amid mountains, where a creek flows over moss-grown stones between banks shaded by flags and tall lush grass, while untrimmed trees keep out the sunshine. There is a chill in such a place, even on a summer morning. It struck Clymenia at the height of the heart, and while she stood trembling pitifully there came another memory of the night before.

"Pa's watch," she whispered with parched lips. "I surely heard pa's watch. It woke me up, 'n I jest lay still 'n harked to it for ever so long. It was jest as regular 's anything, 'n I counted up to above eighty a'fore I fell asleep ag'in. 'N yet, it wasn't never pa's watch. It was—oh, God, I know what 'twas! I heard it in th' nights long times ago, 'n laughed at th' warnin', but it never failed. Th' time ma 'n I went to set up with gran'ma, granpa's ole eight-day clock's goin' like a good un', I said, 'n ma shook her head, 'n answered `Y' can't hear thet clock in this room, it's jest a-warnin', 'n th' ole lady mus' go b'fore mornin'.' 'N so she did."

Shivering and swaying, Clymenia sank into the muddy road, and lay there for a long time. She had fallen so that her slender, nearly worn out body fitted into a deep rut, and it was almost as if she was already in a damp grave. Lying with the ear close to the earth one quickly becomes conscious of any unusual vibration, and such an one presently stirred Clymenia. As she sat up and mechanically brushed the mud from her arms a second wave of sound passed by, and then a third.

The foliage on the trees grew so low that had Clymenia been standing she could have seen nothing, but as it was she got a glimpse betwixt the sedges of the adjacent meadow, back to where the old house had dominated the landscape for above three-quarters of a century. It would never do so more, the sounds marked its last protest against descending from the standard of a home to a simple mass of rubbish.

Clymenia spoke aloud. "It's fallen into th' cellar-hole," she exclaimed, with awe. "Th' chimney went first, 'n then th' walls crumbled up like pieces o' cardboard."

She looked, for a moment, at the muddy crevice of earth in which she had lain, and was almost fain to settle back forever. A twig moved in a passing breeze, one ray of warm sunlight fell on her withered forehead and roused the love of life that is stronger than love of joy, and remains when even hope is fled.

Clymenia spoke once more. "I thank thee, God," she said in simple gratitude, "thet in thy divine marcy thet was let to come today 'n not last night, when I was there all unsuspecting."

And yet it would have been much better so, heeding the death-watch, than that she should have resumed her hopeless walk to the almshouse, there to remain, a placid inmate, unremembering, unre-membered, for many dreary years.

(*Con Amore*, October 1905)

THE ROOT OF AGE

The girl who was generally called "Here, you," though she had been given the name of Mary, raised her frowsy, aching head from a dingy pillow, and screamed into the twilight.

"What d'ye soy?" she cried shrilly.

From somewhere below the tiny window came answer, "Somethin's come up."

"Don't b'leve it," yelled the girl in reply. "It's three weeks since I stuck 'em into the yearth, and I didn't see nothin' up to day b'fore yistidy."

"Well, come down stairs, y' little chump, 'n see fur y'erself," responded the unseen speaker. "It rained yistidy good 'n hard, don't forgit that."

The girl sprang resolutely to her feet, but the next minute tumbled ignominiously to the floor, striking her shoulder against the bedstead. She did not lose consciousness, but managed to crawl back to bed, and with fierce, ungirlish language address this funny dizziness that had for a long time been growing more insistent, and had now overcome her entirely.

Mary was but ten, but she did not waste tears over her disappointment, having learned long years before not to waste anything. Thus she could make a pretty good stew for supper out of cold potatoes and onion peelings, and never squeeze out a tear unless it would be efficacious in getting her off from a well-deserved whipping. Mary just closed her eyes, and saw quite well the yard below, from which she was kept by the strength of weakness over will.

What Mary saw was a long, flat slice of landscape, set between blocks of sordid buildings in which the making of woolen cloth went on all day long, and from which the smell of grease arose all day and all night. Down each side of this slit ran tenement houses in a pair of long rows. The few unoccupied feet of land betwixt the houses might very well have been sodded, or paved with sanitary granolithic excepting for some spots devoted to growing things, but were not, since "on the corporation" only utility was considered. Flowers represented no practical value, and as for planting vegetables, what was the use when one's time could be employed to better financial result in the mill.

On these warm July days each house door stood open, and each afforded the same vista of ill-scrubbed boarding, with an outlook at another door upon a backyard, where the abomination of the garbage heap jostled the abomination of the full beer keg, always carefully watched over by some member of the family to whom it belonged, brown earth beaten hard by many feet, stretched between the houses, only interrupted by the up-springing elm trees, two in number, that were perhaps tolerated because they just happened to be there, and also because they were more or less convenient for the attaching of lengths of clothes line.

If the Congressman, who was first responsible for sending a package of garden seeds to this place, could have realized the ironic comment raised by their receipt, it would have been an eye-opener to one who thought the "submerged tenth" given to suffering in silence, and accepting any attempt at alleviation with gratitude.

"What d'ye arsk him for?" inquired one hulking youth. The reply roused a round of oaths. It seems that Fred Rousman, the socialist loom fixer, had ventured to write the congressman, reminding that gentleman of the specious promises to aid labor with which he had bought the mill-hand vote before election. The sole response had been the inappropriate package of seeds from the Department of Agriculture. Abusive language of such free character followed Rousman's explanation, that even hardened little Mary was about to creep away in disgust, when a diversion was caused by the entrance upon the scene of the idle lad who had married Mary's oldest sister (still very young) and who since the wedding had found congenial occupation in maintaining a beer keg in his back-yard—both beer and rent being paid for out of his wife's earnings in the weave-room.

For three whole hours this very afternoon Mary had followed her brother-in-law around town, begging him to remember that he had been made the custodian of the family funds, and that supper was still to buy. He had joked with her at the entrance to the first saloon, had been harsh with her at the second, had given way to an appearance of remorse around the corner from the more pretentious one that called itself a cafe, and had promised to come home and hand over a half a dollar after he had "broke a bill and got a couple to brace up on." And hour later he threatened to give Mary "a good kick" if she didn't get on and leave him alone. Furthermore, he added a wholly unnecessary insult to the injury, by applying a bad name to Mary's sister, Marty, his wife. With the canny cuteness of her kind, Mary waited until she was of his sight before she doubled up her fist. Why sister had persisted in marrying him had never been any problem to Mary, since most of the other girls' sisters burdened themselves quite the same way. He was certainly good-looking and could have had his pick of other weave-room girls, had his first choice thrown him over. Mary could easily understand that Marty didn't want to see him snapped up before her very eyes by such, for instance, as the bold-faced Malone girl, who had made eyes at him even since his marriage.

The misdoings of the afternoon, however, went beyond anything in the way of a previous happening.

"It's a dirty mean shame," thought Mary, indignation burning violently beneath her draggled calico frock. "She gave him the whole of a five dollar bill and there ain't so much as a pork rind into the cupboard. It'll be borry off the neighbors, or else go and demean ourselves to ask tick at the grocery, and like as not get turned down, too."

Complete villains being made but by degrees, Marty's husband had meandered homeward while still a quarter remained in his pocket. He was feeling a little shame-faced, and anxious to get "the brat" out of the way while he should square himself with Marty by a few soft words and a hard hint or two as to the bold-faced Malone girl.

"What's the matter?" he inquired, watching the ever-growing group about Fred Rousman. The story of the garden seeds was told even more picturesquely than before. To general surprise the last listener did not add to the indignant echo. On the contrary he declared that the Congressman was all right, and his gift the same. Pretty pictures on the envelopes would do for the babies to play with, and as for the seeds themselves, why not "stick 'em into the ground out there—they'd come up termatuses or something, sure."

And amidst the laughter that followed he actually took Mary by one hand, and grasping the package of seeds in the other wandered to a spot between the elm trees, where the ground was less hard than elsewhere. The onlookers considered it a half-drunken vagary, and went indoors, but when Marty came into the yard—she had been working an hour overtime—she was too delighted at the man's innocent employment to even question as to the whereabouts of the five dollars. Mary was sent running for a pound of tripe and a baker's loaf, with a package of fine cut in case there was sufficient change out of the quarter. Supper was eaten peacefully, and Marty's husband was for an hour very grateful to the scratched up bit of earth and the row of sticks that had helped him to "square himself" for an unusual outbreak. And then he forgot the matter entirely.

Not so Mary, she had been buoyed up by a very unusual hope when the package had been interred, and afterward she waited and watched persistently for signs that the seeds had burst their bonds. As Mary had yelled to the friendly neighbor, nothing at all had happened for three weeks to cheer the long hot days which for the child were full of sordid unthanked tasks. She had not watered the ground with any tears, for reasons previously mentioned, but she had borrowed a few of the oaths she daily heard, and swore often with a pathetic yearning for a happy result.

It was never before that Mary had allowed herself to indulge in any day dreams, but somehow she grew to believe that if only the seeds would come up, though no more than "termatuses," there might be happier days for Marty.

"I can't think what's come to the man," that long-suffering creature would moan sometimes, in the evenings, when they sat in the dark for the sake of coolness, and also to save kerosene. "There he was so good one while—making garden with you an' all that—and now he's actin' like all get out."

In Marty's fond memory that innocent half hour "making garden" was increased to a once regular employment. At first Mary was silent, hugging her newborn hope in her arms. Then she ventured to suggest that "P'raps he'd feel more int'rested when somepin come up." And before long Marty began to share Mary's ever-growing belief that in the wee garden plot lay the future salvation of their squalid little home. Perhaps the hot weather made them both a little mad. Certainly Marty had queer dreams in that awful hour between five and six of an afternoon, when the cheering effect of dinner was worn off, and supper is only an anticipation, when the noise of the machinery and the monotony of the day's round of toil grated on the nerves of all the girls, and especially to those to whom the joy of homecoming was mixed with dread.

As for Mary, she had been picked up one burning noon-tide, "touched by the sun," the people said down in the yard, and had gone to bed, at first feeling a sort of blissful happiness in the privilege of lying still, and in the luxury afforded by a cup of cracked ice left by the district nurse who had made a brief call, and then gone to other patients whose need of her was even more imperative. The sudden rising had, however, undone much of the apparent good of the afternoon's rest, and Mary was forced to tumble back on the pillow which now seemed hot to her throbbing head. Still, she wondered what had sprouted down in the yard. Little as she was acquainted with nature, she realized it was too soon to think of blossoms, yet all the while her mind ran on such vivid blooms as she had seen somtetimes behind the steam-smeared windows of florists' shops. At any rate it would be green—she knew that. And being just come up it might be that brilliant, new green, which the elm tree wore for a few spring days, and then never again until the year after. "Tomorry I'll see it for myself," whispered Mary.

She was wrong. The queerness of her head increased the next morning; and so from day to day she grew "more funny," as her sister said, coming down into the yard for a breath of air in the evening, after she had performed a few house tasks, badly, because so tired with the long day's work in the mill. "And she makes a sight of bother, too," complained the weary woman. "Seems a little too much of a good thing to have to come down here every night, just so's to tell her how that sprig o' weed or whatever 'tis gets on. Grows great, though, don't it?" she added, with an inconsistent air of pride.

The neighbor woman nodded, and then bent ponderously over to examine the thing carefully.

"What is it, after all?" inquired Mary's sister. "I ain't no granger myself, but it looks to me kinder like a squash."

The neighbor stood up, flushed, but delighted. "Squash noth-in!" she cried. "It's a 'sturtium, an' what's more, it's got a posy blossomed right out under th' leaf."

And despite her simulated scorn, for one did not wear one's heart upon one's sleeve down in the yard, Marty eagerly climbed the stairs, and told the glad news to Mary. The child had been rather stupid all the afternoon, but now she seemed revived, actually sat up, and poured out more questions than Marty could answer. At last she sank back happily, making the last query, "When'll you tell him?"

Marty was saying that it must be in the evening, because there was no time in the morning, since she started for the mill before he had even thought of opening his eyes.

"There'll be weeds to be pulled up," said Mary, in an odd little tired-out voice. "And then it ought to be watered every evening. I've seen the super's daughter with a sprinkling can going around hers. Maybe we can fix a can out of that leaky dish with a few more holes punched in. Oh, Marty, do you s'pose he'll be tickled?"

"I just do," said Marty, "if only for the sake of crowin' over Fred Rousman, who said they was no good when they come. Fred's give sev'ral knocks lately about booze 'n folks trying to raise their own rye. It'd just cheer him up great to get the laugh on Fred."

Mary drifted off into something like sleep in the midst of this, and though she presently opened her eyes, she was quite unawake. The room, it seemed, had grown wondrous large, and the walls were gone, so that Mary felt gripped with the fear of rolling off into space. There were things buzzing on the ceiling in the shape of flies, the size of rats. Other objects of swollen bulk obtruded themselves, and seemed to grow and to grow, until their presence was suffocating. One object was dark blue in color, and very pink at the top, and the other was curiously striped. These stripes which were really the chocolate pattern on buff of Marty's old dress, presently began to resemble snakes to Mary, all the more horrible because they lacked heads. She thought to herself that she must scream—then she did scream, louder and still louder, yet the bulky figures paid no attention to her, only continued to usurp the space and absorb the breath out of her very nostrils. Finally she seemed to have screamed her voice away, until she had only strength sufficient to whisper one word, "Marty."

So contrary are things in the land of dreams, that the first real scream came when she thought she whispered. Marty came running to the bed, and was extremely cross when she found Mary, now quite herself, had nothing more than usual the matter.

"Lie there a-soldiering," said Marty, with a brutality such as she had never before shown, "bringing nothin' but trouble between husban' an' wife. You make me tired."

In all life's troubles sister Marty's love had never before failed. Mary could well feel that with Marty turned cold, like other women in the tenement, life would not be worth the bother of living.

"What is it, sister?" she managed to ask in a very wee voice. Marty answered roughly, "That cursed flower of your 's th' matter. For Gawd's sake, you, let me manage my man for myself after this."

"Did you tell him about it?"

"Did I? Well, I guess yes."

"And what did he do?" Mary felt something slipping—slipping into her head, she had to try several times before she could catch the right words for the question as they all slipped round and round in a sort of dance.

"Oh, nothin'," said Marty. She said it several times, and each time the words seemed more horrible to Mary. Finally she began to laugh, and the laugh brought Mary memories of other and similar laughs which she had heard in the tenement—the laugh of Mrs. Goggin as they took her man away in the ambulance; the laugh of Molly McCarthy when, six months deserted by her husband, she had watched her children fighting over a bit of mouldy bread; the laugh of silly little Selma Segstrom because the letter came back from her "fellow" telling her she had better go back to the mill, as he had discovered it wouldn't be "quite covenant" for him to get married for five or ten years.

"Don't, Marty, don't, please don't," she cried, but Marty laughed on, rocking herself back and forth in her chair, and catching her breath at the end of each gurgle with a gasp that might have been heard down in the yard, where now lay uprooted the bit of green which Mary would never see. It would wilt to a mere wisp on the morrow, while tonight Marty's husband wore the blossom in his coat, it having struck him, on Marty's calling his attention to it, as exactly the proper thing to make complete the rig-out of the best he owned, bought for going before the priest with Marty, but now donned because he was going to a dance with the bold-faced Malone girl.

(*Villa De Laura Times,* February 1906)

256

THE EMANCIPATION OF ELIVRA

The wood-colored house stood in a dirt-colored landscape. One imagined that summer might turn the grass green, and give a vivid tint of beauty to even the weeds growing rank beside the door, but now all was dank and hueless, washed with the rains of November, and bleached by December's frosts.

A girl of sallow face, with ash-blond hair and spiritless gray eyes, sat by the kitchen window and looked hopelessly at the birch trees clustered on the opposite side of a road that led nowhere in particular, and so was generally travelled by no one. The girl's dress was of calico that had once been blue, but was now wonderfully similar to the floor boards, which she had just finished scrubbing. She had draggled the skirt in the wet, and then had not removed it for the simple reason that there was no other skirt to put on.

Her stepmother endeavored to induce her to come nearer the fire.

"Just stick your feet into the oven," she was saying. "You'll catch your death sitting there, with th' wind coming in all along th' mop-boards."

Elvira made no reply, and continued to sit by the window. As a matter of fact she would have moved had she heard what her stepmother said, for she was a biddable girl, but just now her mind was having a flight far beyond the confines of the wood-colored house. She was actually trying to view her own future. On one hand stretched a life like the past, as she had been when she reached her fourteenth year, left school, turned up her hair, and began to go into the straw shop winters. It consisted of long hours of work with other girls as dispirited as herself, for a part of the year. The other part was spent in the wood-colored house, helping the stepmother in an almost fruitless attempt to make both ends meet. Elvira presumed the wages in the shop were good enough, but in truth she had never received any personal advantage from them. The stepmother had taken charge of each pay envelope, and had scolded a good deal when Elvira evidenced need of new shoes. Elvira rather lacked imagination, she could hardly understand that presently she would be of age, and that wages then would go to the one who earned them rather than to the stepmother guardian. She did not like Henry Garvice at all, still his entrance on the scene some weeks before had added a good deal to that negative feeling of content which with Elvira passed for happiness. It had been distinctly unpleasant when Henry Garvice held her hand, and tried to peck at her cheek with a pair of tobacco-scented lips, but he had essayed this only once, and had seemed rather abashed at his own temerity at the time. On the other hand there was the comfortable order of stepmother to effect that Elvira had better take charge of her own wage, since she would need it to buy wedding clothes.

Elvira had actually her own envelopes for the past eight weeks, and now the water-soaked pocket of the dingy skirt held forty-eight dollars. Elvira was pleasantly surprised to learn that her labors were worth a whole dollar each day. Forty-eight dollars seemed a great deal of money. Elvira almost regretted that it must go for wedding clothes.

The stepmother was briskly talking of the outfit.

"I'll take you to Greenfield tomorrow," she was remarking, "'n we'll lay it out to th' best advantage. There'll be shoes 'n stockings, 'n a near-silk petticoat. 'N then we'll get th' stuff for a warm wool dress, 'n a But-rick pattern to make it by. We'll have a cut o' cotton cloth, too, 'n some rick-rack f'r trimming. They say th' folks over to Four Corners are kind o' high n' mighty, 'n they sha'n't have no excuse f'r making fun o' your fitout when you 'pear in meetin', or when they pass by on Monday 'n see your clo's hangin' out t'dry."

Elvira was listening now, and indeed had drawn near the fire and put one foot on the broken hearth. The warmth was grateful to her chilled limbs, and the dazzling vision of new dresses was no less cheering. Still, if forty-eight dollars could accomplish all this, why might it not, used for other things, accomplish that which Elvira really desired—a chance to live in comfort, without Henry Garvice?

"Ma," she began faintly, "say, ma—if—if I c'n git a dollar a day e'vry day, 'n if you c'n git a bushel o' taters f'r a dollar, 'n I never eat more 'n one to a meal, why—why do I have to marry Henry Garvice? I c'n git along 'th these old shoes 'f they're patched a little 'n a caliker'd do as well 's a wool dress to th' shop, 'n—'n—"

Her wistful speech trailed off into silence, as Elvira watched the look of stern determination that she knew so well, growing on the face of her stepmother. It was the same face that stepmother had worn when Elvira had been ordered to leave her congenial studies in the red school house and betake her to the straw shop. In fact, Elvira unconsciously associated that look with every faint attempt on her part to assert a feeble independence.

The stepmother did not say much, but what she did say was pointed. Very sensibly she proved to Elvira the fact that the straw shop was liable to "shut down" any time, and for good. As to there being other straw shops—for Elvira actually had sufficient flight of fancy to suggest them—so there were other girls to fill them. A dollar a day would not go very far if Elvira had herself to keep. And then—crowning argument—did Elvira want to be an old maid?

Elvira rather thought she did, but lacked the courage to say so. She was likewise quite incapable of expressing her abhorrence of slovenly, uncouth Henry Garvice, for she knew somehow that her stepmother would not sympathize. Garvice had inherited a small farm at the Four Corners, and he drove a decent horse in a not very ram-shackle buggy. His talk was interlarded with reference to large sums of money—sometimes actually approximating fifty dollars— won or lost at races at the Belchertown cattleshow. He might be uncouth, but so were most men. To be sure, he appeared "close" in money matters, but then—or so reflected the stepmother—that was "better'n being poverty struck." Besides, he was considerably older than Elvira, he would very likely die in the course of a few years, and perhaps leave her "well fixed." The more she thought about it, the more the stepmother believed she was doing well by the girl.

Elvira, now with her feet propped on a couple of old bricks, inside the oven, had taken from her pocket the little roll of bills that made up her dowry, and was fingering it with awe. And just then there was a rattle of wheels on the frozen earth, followed by considerable fumbling at an iron hitching-ring by the door stone. Then the door opened, and Henry Garvice slouched into the presence of the woman and the girl. He was rather tall, with a pale face, clean shaven—indeed, it looked as if no hair ever grew thereon, as if perhaps the meagre skin stretched over the ugly chin and jaw afforded no space for growth. His hair was rather long, and of the color of the mangy buffalo skin coat which enveloped his form. He kept his old plush cap, with ear lappets, on his head, as he sank into the chair the stepmother hastened to place for him by the fire.

His first action was to open the front door of the stove, letting a cheerful glow of hard wood coals, and likewise a good deal of fine ash, into the room. The swing backward of this door was such as to compel Elvira to move away from her comfortable place by the oven, but that he did not seem to notice. Elvira got up and went and sat on the woodbox. She was slightly flustered, and quite forgot to put the roll of money back into her pocket. It fell unheeded to the floor and lay there in the gathering twilight.

At length Henry Garvice opened his mouth, and the stepmother looked up brightly, thinking he was about to speak. Instead he spat into the glowing mass of coals. Then she sank back in her chair, whereat he opened his mouth once more, and instead of spitting, remarked, "Wouldn't Sat'day be a good day?"

"You—you mean f'r goin' t' th' parson's?"

He nodded.

"I s'pose it's good 's any other," commented the stepmother. "Then 'f you don't take any trip Elvi could 'pear out t' church right off, while her things w's fresh. Somehow, I'd know but that's best. When I w's married t' her father we had a trip's far's Greenfield, 'n I 'most ruint my new alpaca through him spillin' oyster stew on th' skirt 's we w's in a eatin' house there. 'N I'd intended t' keep it f'r best f'r at least two year, 'n as 'twas 't had t' last, spots 'n all, f'r a good while longer, 'n be made over f'r Elvi in th' end."

"Yes," said Henry Garvice, with the manner of one who hardly listened, so absorbed were his own thoughts, "seems t'me Sat'day's th' best day."

"Then let's git th' calendar, 'n fix on some Sat'day 'long towards Spring. That'll give me 'n Elvi time t' git her things ready."

Henry Garvice, still having the air of one who heard not, looked vaguely toward Elvira, who was nearly obscured in the steam from the boiling kettle, and said, "Today's Sat'day."

Elvira felt as if other mists than those of the steam were closing in and robbing her of breath. The stepmother expressed surprise.

"Of course you didn't mean t'day?" she said, "why it's most gone now. Besides, Elvi haint got a thing t' wear. She's been savin' up f'r her things, 'n hasn't even got shoes."

"I made up my mind t'day," said Henry Garvice, still heavily pursuing his own line of thought, "that I wouldn't be another day in my house 'thout a woman. You said she could bake bread. Well, I'm tired o' crackers 'n milk. I've eat 'em ever since Marm died, last ha-yin'. I got th' license, an' th' minister over to th' Corners has agreed t' stay to home all evening. 'S a good house, got everythin' in it a woman needs t' do with. I don't ask Elvi t' bring no quilts or table spreads. Marm, she brung a good lot when she hitched to father, I've hern tell, 'n they is considerable wear left in most of 'em yet."

With a sudden dignity that astonished both her stepmother and her lover, Elvira rose to her feet and stood close to the man.

"I will not," she said. "I—I will not—" but the second saying was fainter. "I don't want to."

And then she left the room.

Henry Garvice was, for the moment, actually startled into con-sidering some point of view not his own.

"Why—why, I supposed 'twas all fixed up," he complained, rather fretfully. "You said she said so. I don't want no gal isn't ex-pectin' 't keep house 'n do thin's like Marm did. 'F Elvi don't want 't have me I'll be movin' on."

Both he and the widow had risen and stood confronting one another in the glow from the stove. For some reason the woman began to feel afraid of the man. His manner was mild enough, but there was a tenacity of purpose that she dimly recognized as akin to the loud-voiced tyranny of Elvi's father. The way he kept repeat-ing "Sat'day," for instance, and paying no attention to the need of Elvira's having wedding clothes. And then she and Elvira were so helpless—so alone. They did not even own the wood-colored house. They were terribly in debt, for Elvira's wages had after all but little more than kept them from week to week. If only Elvira was mar-ried the stepmother intended to go away—back to her own people in Illinois. She could work for her board at her sister's, and have, she knew, a good home. There had been enough held out from Elvira's earnings, besides the forty-eight dollars, to buy the railroad ticket.

Henry Garvice was still standing and still speaking of Saturday.

"I may's well say 't now 's any other time," he went on. "I got my mind made up t' git married t'day. It's Elvi first, but if she's bent on not having me, I won't hang round here no longer. I guess 'Mandy 'Twiss 'd jest as soon. Marm always liked her, too."

"Oh," gasped Elvira's stepmother, "that would be too bad, sending you way over there."

Neither she nor the man seemed to be conscious of the humor in this expostulation.

"I guess Elvi's most ready. Jest you wait a minute 'n I'll see."

And the stepmother left the room, while Henry Garvice sank back into his chair, and spat a few more times into the stove. Then noticing that the coals were losing some of their brightness, he went over to the woodbox, and selected a few sticks with which to replenish the blaze. In the meanwhile the girl and the woman, in the icy bedroom, were having an earnest interview. The girl was seated, in the half darkness, on the edge of the poorly dressed bed. The widow saw beside her, and said kindly enough, "It's dretful cold in here."

"I didn't notice it," said Elvira, who had been sustained by her unwonted fire of spirit, though now she was conscious that her feet were like lead and her hands like ice.

"You didn't mean what you said jest now," continued the woman. "An' you hadn't ought t' talked so. He's real mad."

Elvira, by her silence, implied she was desperate and didn't care.

"He says," the widow went on, in an agitated whisper, "that if you won't have him he'll go right off 'n marry Mandy Twiss. Says his mother always liked her. Now, Elvi, don't be a fool."

At this moment Henry Garvice, in the outer room, could be heard to rise from his chair, and cross to the outer door. He spoke a few words to his horse, then came back, and knocked with impatience on the floor with the heel of his heavy boot.

"Gracious," exclaimed the widow, "I must hyper out, or he'll go off in a huff, 'n we'll never see him again. I'm goin' t' tell him it'll be all right."

And she was leaving the room when Elvira, perhaps emboldened by the darkness, grasped her hand and said huskily, but surely, "Ma, you will not. Let him marry who he's a mind to. I won't."

Feeling that fate was about to be too much for her, the widow entered the kitchen, and said, "I guess you're gettin' tired waitin', Mr. Garvice, but Elvi—"

"What's she say?" he asked, with a mixture of eagerness and indifference, the first showing in his eyes, the last in his toneless voice.

To defer the unhappy time of replying, the widow started to light the kerosene light, taking a taper from the twisted few on the narrow mantel, and thrusting it into the fire. The unshaded lamp blazed up in a manner that made the room very bright, but the widow still fussed over it, taking off the chimney with her apron-protected fingers, and rubbing the broken blade of a pair of scissors across the wick as if to straighten it.

Henry Garvice stood still, as if he had abandoned any intention of ever sitting down in that house again.

"Did you say Elvi was gittin' her things on?" he continued. "Parson 'll be home all evenin', but I got t' be movin' pretty quick."

"Well, 'y see," said the widow, "there's her things. A girl can't be married 'thout a weddin' gown."

"I never hearn as my Marm had one," said the man, as if that settled it. "What's she want 'f a weddin' gown? Marm left a real good caliker, she c'n have that. Hadn't been worn more 'n a month or so, 'n one o' th' neighbors started t' use it t' lay her out in, but I didn't have no such waste. I knew 'f I got t' git me a wife 't would come in handy f'r her."

The widow was certainly in the predicament of her life. If she could get Henry Garvice out of the house, and take time to talk with Elvira she knew she could very soon put an end to the girl's new stubborness. But if Henry Garvice left the house, she was afraid he would never come back. Amanda Twiss was a homeless old maid who worked out, and she would surely grab a chance to get a husband with a farm of his own.

In the meantime Garvice was standing with his hands thrust into his pockets. He was engaged in carefully observing his own unblacked boots. First he lifted one, then the other, and mentally calculated how long the soles were liable to last. As he completed the process of observation his glance fell on the floor, where it struck the wad of bills Elvira had left fall half hour before.

Stooping, he picked it up, then saying to the widow, "What's this?"

"My, my," said the woman, nervously, reaching out an eager hand. "That's Elvi's."

He did not return the money, but advanced to the table, where the lamp shed its brightest light. Moistening his finger from time to time he counted forty-eight dollars.

"How's it Elvi's?" he then asked.

"She earned it in th' straw shop, y' know. I let her keep it lately, so's t' buy her weddin' clo's."

Henry Garvice once more counted it, and once more made it forty-eight dollars. Then turning toward the bewildered widow, he placed the bills neatly inside an ancient leather wallet which he took from his breast pocket, and which seemed to contain only a single two dollar bill—probably intended as the parson's fee—at the same time saying, "As Elvi's husband I guess I better take care o' what's hers. Wimmin hadn't ought t' be trusted 'th money. No man would had it lyin' on th' floor like that."

Sudden indignation burned in the widow's heart, she felt very much as Elvira had, she was sorry she had ever made the man welcome. Still, she knew she could do nothing. He had Elvira's money. He would have Elvira—or else Elvira would never get the money back. With a sodden spirit she went again into the bedroom, where the girl still sat. She took the lamp with her, and left the door open into the kitchen, so that she might make sure Henry Garvice did not escape.

The girl blinked at the sudden light. She looked less determined than she had looked, but still her lips were firmly pressed together.

"Elvi," whispered the stepmother, "it can't be helped now. Y' got t' go."

"But I don't care 'f he does take Mandy Twiss," said Elvira, trembling.

"No, nor I neither," said the widow, still in a whisper, "but somethin' else's happened. Elvi, he's got the forty-eight dollars."

Elvira understood that fate was too strong for her. Ten minutes later she drove away from the wood-colored house in the buggy with Henry Garvice.

II

By the light of a September sunset, five years later, Elvira Garvice was washing the heavy and unwieldly parts of a cream separator.

She stood on the rickety porch of another wood-colored house, set squarely in one of the four corners that gave a name to the place that was now her home. It was not exactly a village—just a little cluster of houses, with a white church on the edge of the settlement, and low-lying, unpeopled hills shutting it off from the rest of the world. The land, to be sure, all gave evidence of careful cultivation, and most of the houses were better than that of Henry Garvice. White paint, green blinds, gilded weather-vanes, and front stoops with fringed hammocks swinging thereon were not unknown at Four Corners. The old Garvice place, however, seemed "run down." The chimney had long needed topping off, the roof had been patched until the new shingles were well night as discolored as the old, and all were unable to keep out the rain. Several upper windows were stuffed with rags, and over the front door grew a mass of bushes, proof that what the neighbors said was true—"It ain't been opened since old Marm Garvice's funeral."

When Henry Garvice brought Elvira home she had gone in at the back door, through the littered woodshed. Most of her life since had been spent in that part of the house. Just now she was ending what had been an especially long and weary day. She had risen while it was yet dark, but unlike the woman of the Scriptures, had not looked so well to the ways of her household as she had to the binding of Henry Garvice's field of corn, across the road. She had learned to perform certain parts of farm work with great skill, binding corn being one of her accomplishments. The neighbors wondered to see the painfully slender woman hugging the great burdens of corn stalks close to her bony chest, while her lean arms twisted the withes with slowly exerted skill; as she never complained they supposed she liked to help Henry. Some even blamed her for her evident preference of outdoor work to more womanly tasks. They did not know Henry Garvice, whose tyranny was none the less for being expressed without noise.

There had been some housework, too, and late in the day Elvira had stirred some cream—the churn was broken, and Henry said it was no use to fix it, now the creamery took so much of their cream, though still he carried a good many pounds of butter to town weekly, butter made in the most laborious manner by Elvira. Her hands were torn by corn stalks, and badly chapped by exposure to the chill September dews. Working over and salting the butter was always a painful process, and tonight she had actually hesitated before thrusting her hands into the dish water, frothy with soft soap as it was. Now each movement made her wince, she was glad the hour was late and she was alone, so she could wince without comment. It had been a long summer, filled with much toil. Elvira felt quite broken in body and spirit. Her bones ached, her head was muddled, and she wished for nothing but a chance to lie down and rest. As she put the separator away and hung the dish towels on the line to dry, she made up her mind to slip quietly upstairs and hide herself in the old spare room, where no one slept now, and where she might hope to escape discovery.

She listened an instant at the door which, if open, would have shown her the kitchen. There was a good deal of loud talk therein, she recognized the voices of three neighbors, three of the least respectable and most shiftless neighbors. She also heard, at intervals, the voice of her husband. His drawl had increased with years, one felt that he probably slouched both bodily and mentally. And yet he seemed somehow to dominate the conversation, just as he had dominated Elvira's life.

"He won't know but I'm going out some place," she said to herself. She slipped through the shed, opened a hatchway and let herself into the cellar, and then crept up the cellar stairs into the musty front hall. Here she drew off her shoes, for the second flight had no carpet, and it was necessary to make no noise. The ruddy afterglow crept past the bushes in at the fan light above the front door, falling on the wall beyond with wondrous cheer. Elvira forgot for a moment where she was, while looking at the vivid light. She stepped full on a creaking stair, and felt her chance of escape was lost.

The door from the kitchen into the hall was thrown open and a voice said, "Elvi, be you upstairs?"

She leaned against the wall and held her breath.

Again came the call, "Elvi, be you upstairs?"

"Like's not 'twas a rat," said one of the neighbors, as if trying to placate Henry Garvice, who replied, "No, 'twan't no rat. I got traps all over th' place. Elvi puts new cheese in 'em ev'ry day."

"Mebbe sumbuddy gut in th' house," ventured another neighbor, with pessimistic interest.

"George!" exclaimed the third man, "Let's all go'n see."

Elvira turned and came softly down, putting on her shoes as she came. "'S jest me, Henry," she said, meekly. "I thought I heard a noise, too, 'n went up t' see what 'twas."

Henry made no remark, but waited until she had entered the kitchen, and then closed the door and resumed his own seat, at one side of the battered table, the game being Old Sledge. Seeing them so well occupied Elvira hoped to steal out again, and at least find repose, as she had often done before, on the ironing board, with a roll of rough dried clothes for a pillow. She had risen, when Henry looked up from his hand and said, "Where goin'?"

"I—I got some more work t'do," she murmured.

"Oh, set down."

She sat for an instant, then said timidly, "You want me for any-thing, Henry?"

He thought for a while, then said, "Yes, I want my pipe. I left it t' th' barn."

Without a word Elvira went through the shed and into the hay-scented barn, where a good many animals stood chewing their cuds. She had not ventured to bring a light, but she felt in the darkness of the various ledges and wheel hubs, where Henry was in the habit of leaving that for which she was looking. Once she inadvertently thrust her hand on to a mass of fur, and felt a sharp pang on her roughened hand, and then heard a quick scurry over the floor. She had been bitten by a rat, she supposed—but that was of very little consequence so long as she could not find the pipe. Suddenly she realized that Henry was calling. She hurried back to the kitchen, and was greeted by a loud shout from the three neighbors.

"Ha, ha, ha," they yelled. "Hank's a good un. Had his pipe in his pocket all the time."

He now proceeded, without comment or apology, to clean it with a bit of broom straw. Then he asked, "Where's my tobacco?"

Elvira was ready with it, the flimsy bag having the place of honor on the mantel. Having stuffed the bowl, and drawn a strong breath through the stem, he went on, "Light, Elvi."

Elvi took off the stove cover, as the stepmother had done five years before, and lit a paper spill at the blaze. Henry thrust it one side so hastily that her fingers were burned.

"Go upstairs," said he, "an' git me th' card o' matches outen my vest. I want 'em."

The good-natured neighbor interposed. He wasn't exactly an un-observing man, and he saw that Elvira really looked more weary than usual. "Say," he said, "don't bother your woman, Hank. I got a lot o' matches 'n my pants pocket 'f I c'n git at 'em. Here," and he held out a handful of the sort given away with purchases of tobacco in liberal grocery stores.

Henry did not seem to notice the offer, only to say, "Don't no man lend me matches 'n my own house while I got plenty. In my vest, Elvi, hangin' on th' corner o' th' bureau."

Elvira went silently, and returned with the matches. The men continued their game, even the good-natured neighbor seemed to think he had done all that was necessary by offering the matches. Interference with married couples was not favored at Four Corners. Besides, the men mostly pitied Henry for having as wife a woman who was such a "meaching" creature. Their wives had told them that Henry Garvice needed a woman with some spunk to make him act half decent, and they believed this.

Their hands played and the cards shuffled for a new deal, Henry Garvice paused an instant, and said slowly, "Say, seems t' me some pop corn 'd go pretty good t'night."

"It would so," remarked the good-natured neighbor.

This time Henry did not issue any orders, but nodded slightly at Elvi, who knew what to do. Dragging her feet with weariness she went into the shed for the corn popper, and into the shed chamber for a bag of pop corn. She shelled the corn, which was white, into an old tin pan, then poured into the popper enough to cover the bottom of it. The fire burned gaily; she was just taking off the stove covers to make sure it was right, when Henry turned round and looked sharply into the pan.

"What's that?" he asked.

"P-pop corn," said Elvira.

Henry nodded. "I want th' red corn," he remarked, and then dealt the cards for another round.

Elvira stood for a moment poking the fire. She felt nearly desper-ate. Physical weakness was almost at the point of making spiritual firmness. The red corn was up in the garret, up two weary flights of stairs. And then her hands. The red corn had pointed kernels, each one as sharp as a thorn. It would be torture to shell it. She almost felt as if she could rebel.

Henry was talking to the men. "Red corn's a sight better 'n white," he was saying. "Elvi give me good advice, last year, not to plant no white. I guess I'll take it next time."

Elvira could not combat this grim compliment. She would lose all sympathy in her neighborhood if she proved herself thus ungracious. She toiled into garret, came down with the red corn, shelled it kernel by kernel, and managed by biting her lips to hide the agony as the pricks brought blood from her worn hands. And finally the corn was popped, the pan piled high with fluffy white. Elvira carefully salted it and buttered it, and then brought saucers from the cupboard and offered each of the four men of the dainty. Each received the hospitality after his own manner. The good-natured neighbor muttered, "Thank ye, marm," and greedily filled his cheeks, dropping a good deal on the floor. The second neighbor said nothing, and began to eat kernel by kernel. The third lifted the saucer and seemed to be mentally appraising its value, before beginning to partake of what was therein.

As for Henry Garvice, he pushed it from him with the air of a good man, grieved from the heart.

"Elvi," he said, "I did think you knowed I wanted corn always out'n the yaller bowl."

Elvi felt her limbs giving away with weariness. After all, what could happen if she rebelled? Nothing worse than what she had already experienced. She turned slowly and sank into the rickety rocking chair. She closed her eyes for a moment, as the room was spinning round. She thought she was going to say, "I'm tired. Eat your corn out o' th' sasser and be glad you've got it." She had heard the good-natured neighbor's wife speak thus, once on a time, when that neighbor demanded a clean plate for his pie. She did not, however, say anything, but actually went off in a little faint. Drifting away was bliss, it seemed like going to sleep and still knowing that one did so. Coming back, however, was agony. She was conscious of nausea, of cold, of aches and pains. She opened her eyes to find the neighbors gone, and Henry standing by with a dipper half-filled with water in his hand. The outer door was open, and a cold wind blew in. Her hair and face were wet, as a fact Henry had asked the neighbors to open the door, while he brought his wife to by the primitive method of dashing water in her face.

Her courage had evaporated quicker than the water was doing.

"I–I feel better now, Henry," she said, timidly. She began wringing out her hair, which had fallen down, and putting back the few hairpins.

"Well, that's a good thing," he remarked, closing the door, and resuming his seat by the table. "Now you better go'n git me th' yaller bowl."

And Elvira went.

III

"You hain't acted right, Elvi," said Henry Garvice, vacantly, yet nevertheless with firmness. "You know well enough I'd never have planted that ten acre lot, 'f I hadn't s'posed you'd help in th' harvest."

The woman said nothing. She did not even look from the window at the field of grain, swept into billows by a smart summer breeze, and its golden tints hinting of a readiness for the sickle.

"It–it wasn't quite th' right way t' treat me, Elvi," he went on in an unimpassioned, gloomy voice. "You heard me say I w's runnin' in debt f'r th' seed, 'n you never spoke out. I wouldn't a' thunk it o' you, Elvi."

The woman was still silent. In that springtime of which he was speaking had not her own hopes been lifted far above any consideration of gain? As in a dream she had seen her husband slouch forth in the morning to his work, and back in the middle of the afternoon, for it was now ten years since their marriage and Henry Garvice never labored until twilight, as did most of his neighbors. And he always came to the house with what he termed "a good mouth for pie." She had made the pies, and baked the bread, and scrubbed the uneven floors of the old house, and put yellow soap into the ever-yawning rat holes, and tried to keep out the flies with very little success, because when Henry went to town it always took what money he had to buy tobacco, and he couldn't be bothered remembering a piece of screen cloth.

She had also, at his glum request, led the horse when he ploughed the field, and wielded hoe for hoe with him in a later attempt to keep down the weeds, and she had given him a share of her hard-won money earned by picking dandelion and cowslip greens which went in the big neighborhood wagon to the far-off city, where they were sold on commission, and she wanted every penny of that money, too, had spent it over and over again in thought while groveling on her knees in the damp fields. Yet when Henry had bewailed the lack of a cultivator, and the sad fact that he couldn't go shares with George Lee and Fred Green in buying one, she had silently turned over the contents of a meagre purse—itself testimony to poverty, in its shabby leather and carefully mended sides.

"Of - of course I'm kind o' sorry, Elvi," he went on, slouching in his speech as he slouched in shoulder. "'F he'd a' lived he'd been o' considerable help, I don't doubt. But they're a good many years growin' up, y' know," he added clumsily.

The woman said nothing. She could not, for she was too busy reliving her fond fancies of that growing up of her first born. Had she not seemed to see him lying in the cradle of winter afternoons, when she was ironing, and the old kitchen was warm and cozy, the firelight streaming forth from the numerous cracks in the old stove? And then again had she not noticed how in his second year he loved to toddle clinging to her gown as she went to feed the chickens in the sunlit spring mornings? And by and by she had him clothed in his first trousers and sent forth to the schoolhouse down the road. There he had shot rapidly to big boyhood, the leader of his classes, the pride of each successive teacher. Ere long his school days were over, he was six foot tall and husky—in no way resembling his weazened father or his tiny, work-bowed mother. He worked out and brought his wages to her—his mother—before long the mortgage was paid, the farm that Henry Garvice's carelessness had nearly lost, was once more their own. Then he worked out no longer, but toiled in the fields now visible from the window. They repaid him well, he shingled the roof, and painted the house, he shored up the sinking floors, he bought new furniture, he planted a white rosebush by the door. Above all, he was not ashamed to love his mother. He never called her to work in the fields, and he was a good provider for the house. Henry was wrong, they were no time at all in growing up, she knew the days would fairly have flown had all happened as she had dreamed it would.

And now there remained but empty hopes, a vacant future. On the great white bed that filled the tiny room into which the afternoon sun was pouring, was laid the dead child whose life might have meant so much. He had fought for his life, one could see that by the troubled look of his tiny face. The little hands were clenched, as if he had essayed a contest with fate itself. He wore a time-yellow frock contributed by a neighbor whose babies had all lived to grow up and go out into the world. Beneath him was the patchwork quilt Elvira had sewed on in the previous summer—and with each stitch had gone a thought of how by and by a little boy, going to bed before he was very sleepy, would trace the bright calico stars on their background of dull indigo and chocolate print, and would tease his mother to tell a story of each pink sprig and blue rose.

Elvira looked about, and saw nothing that she had not woven into what seemed the life of her boy, though he had lived such a few days. The old clock with the yellow face and the missing minute hand was to have been a joke, the kitchen floor, sagging toward one corner, would have made a better place for games on that account. She knew the chair that was to have its length of leg diminished to make a seat for a child, and the other that was to have been pieced out for a high seat at the table. The extra woodbox was to have been cleaned out for his toys—when he got to the playing age and the chips would have to go with the stick wood in the larger box. As for those toys, had she not saved each empty spool, even the labels from tomato cans, and the tin tags that came in Henry's numerous bags of tobacco. Ay, and she had filched from Henry a new clay pipe, so the boy might some time make soap bubbles and she had taken notice of certain neighbor children, and had learned their trick of sticking four pegs in a corn cob, and calling it a cow; and of stringing grains of corn alternately with red alder berries, and fastening feathers in a band of string, all wherewith to play Indian.

Yes, everything was ready for the lad, and he had tried to stay and profit by her preparation, but somehow it had been too great a task for his puny strength, and his mother had not been able to help him. She had heard whispers, too, not pleasant for her ear.

"Worked in the hayfield three weeks." — "He's better dead, she'd never have raised him, she an' Henry only scrape along as 'tis." — "Hardly a bit of flannel ready, you notice—she must have known he would not live."

Oh, they meant well enough; they had given flannel and other necessities from their own stores, but they had not understood. Henry had taken her money for the cultivator, but she had felt, somehow, that with the boy in the house Henry would have become different.

He could not have expected his boy's mother to have worked all day in the hot sun—his very words now proved it. He was reproaching her because he realized that if the boy had lived, his meek servant-wife would have been no longer at his beck and call. Elvira felt, too, that she could have been bold had she her child to ask for.

"I know I should have kept my berry money, and all the rest that I might earn. I would tell Henry the boy had to have clothes, and Henry could not deny it."

Even in his short life, the child had done so much for her. There was the matter of the screen cloth, now, which Henry had never remembered. The flies clung to the sick baby's face with grewsome persistence, and quite suddenly Elvira had looked up from her weakly pursued task of brushing them away with a ragged handkerchief, and had told Henry what she wished. And Henry had gone out and borrowed a neighbor's horse, and had driven ten miles to the county seat and returned with the bright pink netting which now protected the bedroom windows. Perhaps he had not paid for it—somehow she did not care at this time, though always before fearful of debt and its entanglements of the future. The flies were defeated and for her child's sake she was brave.

"Seems 'f I always do have the worst luck," the man was saying. "Now 'f that field o' grain panned out th' way I expected I w's goin' t' git me a complete new suit, so's I wouldn't be ashamed o' myself town meetin' days. It's a good while since I h'd new clo's. But 'f I have t' pay out a lot f'r help there won't be more 'n enough t' git a side o' pork f'r th' winter an' keep me in tobacco. I declare, it ain't hardly worth doin' nothin' when you got t' depend on a woman f'r help."

Elvira heard and felt her doom settling upon her. The baby was dead and once more her hope died too. She did not feel that Henry was exactly cruel, but he was never kind. He did not get drunk, or swear, as did some men she knew, but on the other hand he never had times of loving regret and hasty affection, such as sometimes redeemed these other men. He was nowadays less of a tyrant than he once had been, rather he was always lazy, always down in the mouth, always planning jobs of work which he would not do and which Elvira performed. He slept on the calico-covered lounge in the evenings, while she did chores in the barn until midnight. He roused her in the darkness of the morning so that she might milk the cow and get the breakfast and be ready to accompany him to the field after the dishes were washed. And while she washed them he smoked his pipe. In haying time he still mowed the grass, to be sure—public opinion in the neighborhood would not have stood for a fragile woman swinging the scythe—but she tossed the hay, and turned it, and raked it up, and put great forkfuls in the wagon, while Henry drove the borrowed horse, and finally she mowed away in the breathless barn, and if she fainted when it was over Henry hastily brought her to with reminders that he was very hungry and needed supper.

And in the winter Henry always brought forth his tendency to bronchitis as an excuse for not shoveling a path to the barn, or breaking the ice in the brook so that the cow could drink, or indeed venturing forth at all when it was coldest. He sat by the fire and read a borrowed newspaper, while she shuffled in his rubber boots over the crisp snow, and felt the icy winds penetrate her worn shawl thrown over a thin calico gown, and creep up the space between the top of her soggy mitten and her short sleeve. It seemed to Elvira that for many years her life had been one constant round of tasks beyond her strength, each leaving a trail of physical ills. In the winter she had colds on her lungs, and coughs that irritated Henry and left her breathless, and chilblains on her feet, and chapped hands that bled as the spring drew nigh; and in the spring it was a languor no dandelion bitters could cure, and a longing for better food than pork and frozen potatoes; in the summer long hot days and back aches and headaches; and in the autumn she still bound the corn and afterward won blisters at husking.

Perhaps Henry Garvice had been well-to-do when she had married him—she hardly knew, so little had she profited by her new estate—but now he was among the poorest of the poor. The farm was mortgaged for its full worth, food was scanty, the barn was no longer filled with hay, for some of the best fields had been sold; nor with cattle, since no feed for many could be found. In the house nothing new had entered since a day long before the death of Marm Garvice, and the marriage of her son with Elvira. Broken windows exposed their rag-stuffed piteousness to the world, and the roof was simply an enormous sieve. Henry Garvice had married to secure a drudge, but now it seemed very likely he would decide to make her a breadwinner also.

But what was it Henry was saying, as the two sat, the father and the mother, looking at the corpse of their first, their only child?

"He's dead, you know, Elvi. Th' funeral'll be over tomorrow. I can't see, Elvi, why you can't startin 'n help me next week. Ten acres of it, y' know, Elvi. I guess I c'n manage t' cradle 'n you c'n bind. Seein' 's th' funeral's tomorrow we needn't lose much o' this fine weather."

Just then the wind swept through the grain, with a rustle as of finest silk. Elvira had never heard the rustle of silk, but this stirring of the grain made her shiver. Her baby, with all her hope, was to be put into the ground hastily, so that she might the sooner be ready to work in the harvest field.

Once again arose the spirit of independence that at intervals of many years had stirred the dreadful monotony of Elvira's existence. She rose and going behind the bed faced Henry Garvice from across the dead body of her boy.

"It's been fixed," she said, slowly, "with th' parson t' bury baby Monday. Tomorrow—"

"Sat'day," said Henry Garvice stolidly. "Sat'day's th' day I sort o' made up my mind was th' best day. Sat'day—"

What was the matter with Elvira? She was standing open-mouthed, as if listening to a voice from the past. When had she heard something akin to this regarding Saturday? In a wood-colored house, with her stepmother by. And this man—this very man—was saying he had made up his mind to some other happening of a Saturday? Ah, yes, a marriage, a marriage that had brought only misery. Elvira never paused to think that she had often been cold, been hungry, been brow-beaten in the wood-colored house she had shared

with her stepmother. So great had been her unhappiness since coming to Four Corners that somehow her old woes appeared to date
from that other Saturday. And now he had made up his mind to
bury the baby on a Saturday, so as to have next week free for her
to work in the field. It overtopped all he had done, for Elvira felt as
if her baby was hers while it remained unburied, even though she
knew it was dead. He would rob her of two days in its company, he
who had robbed her of youth, of money, of illusions.

Elvira faced him steadily. She said, "My baby will not be buried
on Sat'dy. My baby will not be buried tomorrow."

Somehow Henry was not in the least impressed by her decisive-
ness. His face assumed the look it had worn when he took her forty-
eight dollars, when he had demanded the yellow bowl, when many
another petty tyranny had been exercised over her.

"Now, Elvi," he began, "y' know well enough th't 'f I can't
have your help th' grain'll all go. I can't afford t' hire help. 'N then
the expense—th't screen cloth—"

Yes, he was paying compliments again. He was throwing himself on her mercy, and she could never deny him after that. It was
of no use to rebel. Elvira felt she would be enslaved for life, if the
baby was laid to rest on Saturday. She went into the kitchen and for
a moment stood by the cold stove. Then she turned once more and
looked over Henry Garvice's head to the face of her dead child.

While Henry was yet speaking, paying her the compliment of
showing his dependence on her, she hurried out of the house and
into the shed. She felt it was necessary to work quickly, for was
not the day drawing to a close, and would not tomorrow bring her
baby's funeral, unless she somehow prevented it?

Yes, as she thought, a trifle of white powder was left in the barrel
of Paris Green by the side of the shed. She scraped it off with her
bare fingers, and put the scrapings in a bit of paper. She did this, but
not very carefully, in the bosom of her dingy gown. Somehow she
did not care very much whether or not she were seen. As fortune often favors those who do not sue her, she was not observed by either
Henry or a neighbor. She went back into the kitchen, dumped the
powder into the teapot, then calmly made up the fire and brewed
the tea. Henry had closed the bedroom door and laid himself on the
calico-covered lounge, under another piece of the pink screen cloth,

to snooze away the time until supper should be ready. Elvira toasted bread and even opened one of the few jars of canned berries on the shelf in the cellar way. Somehow this seemed an important, even a festive occasion. At length she said, "Henry, supper's ready."

Henry woke with a start, rubbed his forehead, and shuffled to the table. There were two plates laid, and Elvira started to sit at the place opposite him. Henry looked greedily at the two pieces of brown toast and at the cracked nappy containing the sauce. Then he asked, "Milked yet, Elvi?"

She shook her head.

"'S bad f'r th' cow t' put her off too late," he remarked.

Elvira still sat in her place. She was pouring the tea into the two cups and adding milk and brown sugar.

"I ain't milked yet since—since baby w's born," she said pleadingly.

"I know it," said Henry, taking his tea and sopping his toast therein. "Green's boy done it, but he's gone t' town t'night. I thunk you ought t' be able by now."

Elvira abruptly arose and snatched a battered tin pail from a shelf beside the sink.

"I'm goin'," she said. "I jest as soon go."

She lit the lantern and very leisurely milked the one cow, then added something to her bed of leaves and to the shreds of fodder left in her manger. Further, she visited each hen coop and finally entered the kitchen from the shed, bearing an armful of wood as well as the half pail of milk. She hardly knew what she looked to see, but it was certainly not what she saw. Henry Garvice sat before his untouched cup of tea, with a piece of sopped toast yet in his hand. He looked up as Elvira entered, and his look was strange, milder than it had ever been—or else her own fearlessness made it seem different.

"You ain't drunk y'r tea, Henry," she said, with something wonderfully like a chirp.

"No," he replied heavily.

"I ain't drunk mine, neither," she replied, and went to the table as if to do so.

Indeed, she lifted the cup of her lips, when suddenly Henry Garvice bent forward and took it firmly from her.

"Don't," he cried almost hoarsely. "There's somethin' th' matter o' th' tea. There's been some devil's work. Th' pot's all full o' white stuff. I didn't das't drink none of it."

Elvira stood for a moment quietly. Then she told the truth.

"I know what's th' matter," she said, softly. "Paris Green's th' matter. I put it in."

"You—you put it in?" stammered Henry.

Elvira nodded.

Henry seemed to have nothing to say. He sank back into his chair.

Elvira looked up bravely. "I was real mad," she volunteered, quite cheerful.

Henry Garvice continued too amazed for speech. She went on with her explanation.

"I w's mad about th' baby."

He still stared.

"You said he'd got t' be buried Satd'y. You said you'd made up your mind he'd got t' be buried Sat'day. Well, I made up my mind he shouldn't be buried Sat'day. I wouldn't have him buried Sat'day. Y'know, Henry, you never go back on your word. So—so I had t' do it."

Henry Garvice rose to his feet and moved toward the sink.

"Rense out th' teapot," he commanded, and Elvira obeyed. Then he brought her the cups, and she emptied the contents of both into the drain. Quite without warning he appeared to be struck with the fact that there were two cups.

"You fixed some f'r yourself?" he said to Elvira.

She nodded.

"Why didn't y' drink it?" he asked, still as a man in a maze.

"You wouldn't let me," she cried still cheerful. "You sent me out t' th' barn. I'd jest as soon. I hadn't much t' live for now baby w's gone 'n had t' be buried on Sat'day."

He said nothing further, but with his own hands fetched hot water and scrubbed the cups. The pot, after scalding, he tossed out of doors, into the road, where already lay other discarded household stuff.

"Better not keep it round any longer," he remarked, and Elvira gaily agreed with him.

Then he got a tin saucepan and asked her abruptly if she had any more tea.

There was plenty, it seemed, and she brought the caddy with two teaspoonfuls therein to prove it.

"Make some more," he ordered, and she did so. He sat back in his chair and closed his eyes, not even watching her as she performed the task.

A few minutes later they drank together, each sopping a bit of toast, and sweetening the meal with spoonfuls of the canned fruit. At length, when the meal was nearly over, Henry Garvice once more looked at his wife.

"Elvi," he almost whispered, "'f I'd a' drunk that stuff what w's goin' to happen t' me?"

"I s'pose you'd die somehow," said Elvira, as happily as if announcing the arrival of a sumptuous legacy.

"'N then?"

"I w's going t' have you buried Sat'day."

"'N the baby," he asked, "w's he goin' t' be buried same time?"

"No," she replied, firmly. "I'd made up my mind baby would be buried Monday. Th' neighbors 'd had two funerals in three days."

The meal was completed, the dishes washed, still Henry Garvice sat as one lately awakened from a bad dream. About nine o'clock he suddenly took the lamp and went into the bedroom where the dead baby lay, all unconscious of what changes his brief stay on earth had wrought in his mother's life.

In a moment Henry was back in the kitchen, and he said, as he set down the lamp, "Elvi, I've changed my mind. I guess you better have the baby buried on Monday."

Thus began Elvira's emancipation.

(*The Random Amateur*, March 1906)

UTILIZING A BY-PRODUCT

Every time godfather saw me, he insisted upon being told what I was going to be when I grew up. I wonder that he refrained from making this inquiry on the occasion when he became godfather. It is hardly conceivable that the officiating clergyman could want to know:

Dost thou, in the name of this Child, renounce the devil and all his works?—

and my godfather not, in his turn, demand of me the name of my coming profession, so he could make sure whether I would be able to carry out the contract. Was he not unmoved by my sobs (at five) when, in place of a promised red express cart, he presented me with a yellow wheelbarrow?

"It would be unpleasant," said he, to my mother, "to do anything that should lead his thoughts to the business of a common carrier."

My mother was not without spirit. She replied that she should consider it her duty to suppress the wheelbarrow, as tending to direct my infantile inclination toward the life of a navvy.

It is cheering to reflect that for many years I dashed godfather's hopes by sternly insisting that I would be an organ-grinder. Never pausing to reflect that similar hopes burned in all boyish bosoms up and down the street, and even around the corner, godfather would shake his head and mutter, "Low—low—painfully low." Then he would endeavor to spy out any budding tendency toward higher things by leaving in my way trifles such as books of medical plates, cases of scientific instruments, boxes of colors, and mounts of stuffed birds. Godfather was by way of being president of a freshwater college, which at once accounts for his possession of these adjuncts to learning, and for his absolute ignorance regarding the boyish mind. The general result was what might have been expected. I drew moustaches on the microbes, broke the instruments, attempted to pass the coins at the nearest peanut stand, and proved, by actual demonstration, that the tail-feathers of the birds were not fastened with glue.

Thus, imperceptibly to myself, I grew up, and hardly noticed it, until godfather called one day and asked, "Sir, what do you intend to be when you are grown up?"

He had never addressed me as "Sir" before, so I knew that despite his discouraging phraseology I was no longer in my nonage. As I was aware that a great deal depended on godfather, I should probably have remarked dutifully, "I will leave it to you," but that he made the mistake of going on, sternly, "I trust your taste is for the useful in life?"

I shook my head. Godfather possesses to perfection the art of rendering distasteful anything he may recommend. Of course I had always longed to be useful, even in the days when I had admired the organ-grinder. To make music for little children whose parents frowned upon harmonicas and interdicted drums—this I had considered the highest form of human usefulness. Yet I said, "No, godfather, my taste is toward the useless. Somehow I find it impossible to become enthusiastic over anything else."

Oddly enough, godfather looked pleased. "Nobly spoken, my lad," he replied, rising and spatting me on the shoulder. "The best work of all takes that which the world calls useless and turns it to an object of worth."

I suppose he was thinking of by-products—utilizing the squeal of the pig, and all that—but at the time it seemed to me that his words could apply to nothing but rag carpets. I didn't care to weave rag carpets, rather fearing there might not exist a demand for them in our neighbourhood, which runs largely to hardwood floors and sanitary matting. Nor, when I came to think it over, did I feel much interest in the squeal of the pig. What other absolutely useless objects were there in my immediate vicinity? I had only to turn my glance into the next room to see a number of them.

Girls!

I had always known, in an indefinite way, that girls were useless; I knew, also, that their number was indefinite. Few houses but had some, and on a pleasant evening you couldn't keep your hat on your head long enough to make it worth while to wear it, for meeting them on the avenue. Honestly, my brain whirled when I thought of all the raw material that lay ready to my hand. Talk of the squeals wasted daily in Packingtown, they weren't worth considering when compared to the quantity and girlish uselessness all over our own place. There was a lot of it lying round the house, provided by my sister Sadie, and any quantity more brought in daily by Mamie, Jeannette and Alicia, regular side-door visitors, who were always coming to our house to do their hair, or read their souvenir postal cards, or play on our piano, and whose actions had seemed to me peculiar until I had ascertained, by visual demonstration, that Sadie was always going to their homes to do her hair, and read her mail, and play her Zenobia Waltzes with Variations.

I now seemed in a fair way to achieve something of consequence. I had found my raw material, and had even assembled my parts—for I had Mamie and Jeannette and Alicia where I could find them at any time, and even Sadie was at home more or less, to sleep, and sometimes to eat. Now I had only to settle what the machine should be, and its use.

I presume most inventors will agree with me that this is really the worst of the whole business. To make something is easy, but what to do with what you make—that's the hard part. Watt had steam in his mind ever so long before he added the word "boat," and Benjamin Franklin never developed his electric fluid as he ought. Really, when I came to study my "Lives of Great Men All Remind Us," it seemed to me to be the lot of most inventors to discover the stuff, and then leave discovery of its use for future generations. Now, for an inventor, my interest in future generations was positively lacking. However I tried, I could get up no enthusiasm at all over them. I was willing, of course, to go down to fame as the first to utilize the uselessness of girls, but I remembered how Columbus slipped up on his continent, and didn't even get it named for him, so I decided to be my own promoter, and make the whole thing a close corporation.

Jeannette showed me the way of completion—and that just goes to prove how a master mind can do something with the most thoroughly useless stuff, for Jeannette was probably the most thoroughly useless girl among all the girls I knew. She came in one morning, pretending to hide a few tortoise-shell back and side combs in the least peeka-boo part of her blouse, and seeing me outstretched in the cozy corner, where I find I can best consider the lofty ideas that prowl round me at times, she handed to me a pamphlet in a wrapper, and said something foolish about its keeping me awake until she came back again. Then I suppose she went up to Sadie's room and covered herself with Sadie's face powder. That's what Sadie says she does, and that's why Sadie considers it necessary to go about positively reeking with Jeannette's violet perfume. As I am always interested in anything appertaining to the useless objects of my attention, I opened the wrapper, and found I had one of those cute little booklets claiming to be "a magazinelet of individuality," and having on each page some such matter as:

In case you meet a robber and he takes all your valuables, don't be facetious and suggest that he relieve you of your shoes. One victim did so, and the robber took the shoes.

A man who gets hurt doing some fool thing may get well, but he can never be said to be really out of danger.

After a couple of hours Jeannette reappeared. She had stuck the combs around her head, and her hair looked as if it would tumble down the next minute. It took any girl, Sadie had given me to understand, from three to four hours to achieve this result. Jeannette was smarter than most, she did it in two. I handed her the pamphlet, and asked how she came by it.

"My cousin gets it out," she said. "He's doing great." Then she added inconsequently, "He's my second cousin."

"Indeed," I observed. "I wonder how he thinks up all the things he puts in it? There are sixteen pages, and one to a page. That must be a great strain on a man every week."

"Oh," she responded, "he says he doesn't have to think of 'em, now he's got the thing going. His friends provide them. He goes around with an awfully clever set, and when they say smart things he preserves them. Then all the friends buy the magazine to see if they are in it. His mother showed me his cuffs before they went to the laundry. They were sights."

Doesn't everything seem to carry out my theory that the absolutely useless, once utilized, will prove its own worth? I could hardly wait until Jeannette had finished her prattle and gone to Mamie's house to play ragtime, before putting into active train the ideas suggested by her. In two weeks my prospectus was out; in one month you could buy my magazinelet at all news-stands. I called it *Man Proposes*. That was really clever, because it was all about women, and every girl wanted to buy it. Of course I didn't use my own name as editor. My address was at the printer's, where subscriptions began to pour in immediately. The thing has been copied so extensively, since my idea became known to the world, that you know very well what my pages contained.

The man who fondly believes he was married for love, was really married because the girl did not want to be an old maid.

It was a fool who asked the bridemaid why she cried at her sister's marriage. "It's not your wedding," he said, and "That's why I cry," replied the girl.

The man a girl wants nowadays must have old-fashioned virtues with all modern improvements.

These I got from Sadie, talking to Mamie. Mamie talking to Sadie was more sarcastic, as—

A woman never knows a man until she explains her reasons for refusing him.

No woman really wants to be an angel—she only wants some man to think her one.

Jeannette, however, was my real star. She suggested—

To awaken the dormant domestic instinct in any woman, tell her she looks well in a bib apron.

A simple thing, but mine own. I had the pleasure of seeing it copied everywhere, attributed to Sydney Smith, Mark Twain, George Ade and Anon.

The pursuit of business made it necessary for me to lie in the cozy corner nearly all day long, and so retentive had my mind become that it was not even obligatory for me to employ the method of Jeannette's second cousin. In common with other men of genius I was misunderstood. At times my godfather came and viewed me more in anger than in sorrow, and even mother seemed to be turning from me. My godfather offered to enter me as a partner in a flourishing business of some kind—shoes, I think, or perhaps finger stalls, at any rate it had something to do with extremities. I inquired what were the annual returns? He said he thought that with industry—here he looked at me hard, and mother sniffed into her handkerchief—I might come out at the end of a twelvemonth with a thousand dollars in my pocket. I reflected on the weekly income of *Man Proposes,* and smiled ironically. Jeannette had been unusually foolish of late, and my returns had been proportionate.

I was just polishing off—

Man always claims he desires to make the woman he loves happy, but it is a mark of greater power to make her unhappy.

when there suddenly came before me a vision of Jeannette as she had suggested this. She had been weeping—yes, with tears running off her little round chin, her head had been on Mamie's shoulder, and Alicia had been fanning her. Sadie, for a wonder at home, had gone for the bottle which during the last four years has posed as "my salts." There isn't any smell to it, which in her mind increases its value, since, in common with other girls, she considers that the only thing really interfering with the value of salts, is their objectionable odor. All this to-do about the cousin—second cousin—to whom it seems Jeannette had thought herself "as good as engaged," whatever that may mean, but who had been putting such "horrid things" in his paper that Jeannette had considered it her duty to tell him to leave her forever, whereat he hadn't called for two whole days.

Now that I came to think it over there seemed to me an indication of possible evil to me and mine in this news. I seldom read any other magazine than my own, but now I bought up several of Ford's back numbers and perused them carefully. There was no doubt of it, he was likewise gaining by acquaintance with Jeannette. Else why had he suddenly burst out with—

Speak of the devil, and a woman is sure to appear. Or—

Adam was to be envied in some ways. For instance, Eve never interrupted a fervent discourse on undying love by saying, "Oh, look, Adam, there's the kind of a bonnet I want you to buy me when we are married."

I caught Sadie the next morning, just as she was hurrying over to Alicia's to black her boots, and made a few inquiries.

Being my sister, it was unnecessary to beat about the bush. "I suppose," I said, "that all you girls buy up Ford's magazine in great numbers."

Sadie tossed her head with the air of a skittish cow that sees a red apple on the far horizon—a gesture which she has perfected by much practice before mirrors, and which, I am told, does large execution among the students of godfather's college.

"Pooh!" she exclaimed. "Not a one. We'd as soon buy a dress pattern that doesn't suit our style. We all get *Man Proposes,* because that has nice things about us."

I let her go then. I knew all I wanted to know. Impossible as it seemed, my sister had confirmed me in the suspicion that girls did not care to see the mean things written of the sex. How different from man! Godfather, for instance, subscribed to a clipping bureau the year there was talk of deposing him from the presidency because he was suspected of being shaken in his unorthodoxy—there's a theological branch of the college, of the liberal variety. He used to get his envelopes twice a day, and sometimes the things said were so nasty that they quite took away his appetite for both luncheon and dinner. Yet what man, under similar circumstances, could have refrained from such reading?

I began to reflect—if Ford was losing readers among the young ladies of his acquaintance, might not others also be losing their interest? I made inquiries at the news-dealers'. It was true, they declared, an unaccountable falling-off was noticed in Mr. Ford's brochure. Still, I could not complain, my sales continued to look up! Soon, however, I scented danger in the fact that Jeannette smiled again, and seemed to sport a bracelet in which there was a wonderful something under a plate of gold—something that she looked at forty-seven times a day in order to make sure it had not escaped. Seeking information from Sadie, whom I happened to meet at a dinner party which my godfather gave to a brand new professor and professor's wife, made in Germany and just imported, she said—Sadie said—that Jeannette and Frank Ford had "made up," and the engagement was once more "on." The dove of peace brought forth this olive branch—

A miss is better than a mile if she is pretty.

A woman with beautiful eyes never fears the light.

The head cannot long act the part of the heart.

I was in danger. I felt it in my boots. I must not allow Ford and Jeannette to marry. With inspiration right in the house, there was no knowing what his magazine would become—he might even increase his present inkling of my secret to a full and complete knowledge thereof. If he too began to see the usefulness of utilizing uselessness I was done for.

The following week *Man Proposes* was announced for sale. The next week it was said that the sale was completed. *Man Proposes* had been bought, lock, stock and barrel, by *Woman Disposes*. On the latter I boldly had my own name as editor, publisher and sole proprietor. The news, as you may believe, created considerable of a stir. Godfather was disposed to sulk, until I told him the number

of figures in my bank account. At first he was inclined to disbe-
lief, as he never thought highly of my claims to being considered a
mathematician. He feared I had put the "." in the wrong place, but
inquiry at the bank, where the chairman of the board of directors
had been chief dunce for four years in godfather's college—settled
the matter. Mother was not surprised. She said she always knew
I would "do something to make someone proud." *Woman Disposes*
was all about the men, but so written that both sexes had to have it,
the men for reasons fully explained by my godfather's actions when
he was undergoing accusations of being weak in his heresy, and the
women on the principle that led them to take in the fashions that
suited their style. The subject matter was like this—

To cure a man who is intoxicated by love, woman should make
him take the pledge of matrimony.

Home is where the heart is, and that explains why you see so
many men away from home.

The better a man understands himself the less respect will he
have for his wife's judgment.

Plain knocks for the men, you see, and subtile flattery for the
women. And where did I get the ideas? Not from Jeannette, for the
usefulness of her uselessness had been pretty well worked out. I
hadn't been able to patent her, or Alicia, or even Mamie or Sadie,
and now my fame was such that I got into literary encyclopedias
as dead, and parodists foregathered to batten on my remains. However, I had laid the foundation of my fortune with this by-product,
as a millionaire senator may have started as a people's candidate for
the common council. I was not secure from want, either financial
or intellectual. My material came ready to hand; I had only to take
the things said by Ford and turn them inside out. In order that he
should keep on saying things which I could use in this way, I had
to make Jeannette throw him over. And the only way this could be
done with the assurance of finality was by marrying her myself. So I
did so, after my godfather had promised to give her the equal of half
my bank account as a dowry. I may have neglected to mention it,
but Jeannette, when at home, is my godfather's daughter. I suppose
I forgot to speak of it because she so seldom was at home. But I proposed to her one afternoon at the horse show, and we were married
in the college chapel. Ford was so cut up that he continued to work

the unpopular vein for a long time after we had returned from our honeymoon, so that I got the installments on the house well out of the way before he instituted any change. And even after Sadie consoled him he got from married life only such inspirations as these.

Without esteem for a housemate, love is apt to get lonesome and move.

Can a man ever be said to have a speaking acquaintance with his wife?

If there is no war to test your courage, refuse your wife something she has set her heart upon, and see what happens.

It was no trouble at all to turn these into sentiments bespeaking sweetness and light. Jeannette could always supply the key that made plain what a woman would think about what a man thought about—so different this from poor Ford's crudities.

The most delightsome feature of it all is that Jeannette thinks herself so wonderfully useful. She believes it was her first calling my attention to her cousin's pamphlet that started me on my career, and she mentions to Sadie and Mamie and Alicia, who are still occupied with running about to each other's houses to show their new dresses and babies and similar matters, that I would be utterly lost without her, as I lie in the cozy corner most of the time, "as useless as anything," while she is busy protecting me from bores, and ordering dinner, and discharging the girl, or hiring her. A secret of my useful life is that I never contradict, for that is a form of uselessness which I am sure I could never utilize.

After all, Jeannette's point of view is perhaps not peculiar. I have no doubt other producers of by-products have similar exalted ideas of their value. The pig, I presume looks on its squeal as decidedly useful.

(*The Pioneer*, February 28, 1907)

A BUNCH OF CROCUSES

Unseen of them that pass, and asking not
A wider prospect than of yellow flowers
That nod above her head.
—*Jean Ingelow*

"If I send violets," he thought, "they will be in no manner different from other violets. There's no distinction in a bunch of violets. Carnations—too reminiscent of a local sensation at present. Roses—too gorgeous. Roses in midwinter should only be given to a woman who might rightfully receive diamonds from you, but prefers something more expensive and less permanent. But what is there left? There seems to be nothing left."

All the while he was gazing at a bunch of crocuses, a really big, plebeian bunch, the kind of a floral bundle that a girl in a small town would call a "bookay," and thrust gleefully into a "hand-painted" vase on the parlor mantel.

"Dare I send her crocuses?" he wondered. "Of course I dare not send her crocuses. A girl who has always a bunch of violets against the fur of her muff, a girl who at dinner-time puts against her fair hair one of those `simple white roses' that cost as much as a country girl's Sunday frock. She would perhaps smile at crocuses, at all events she would not understand."

He was standing in the over-heated atmosphere of the florist's shop, but his mind was miles away. It was an early day in spring, a deceptive day, warm when you lingered against the brick wall on the sunny side of the house, but quite cold when you were caught by the cutting wind that lurked around the corner, by the door. Here, against a mass of fresh brown earth, the crocuses were peeping up, bright and cheerful, prosphesying the beginning of a gentler era. From the crocus bed the turf, yet brown, fell away in a long sweep to the fringe of willow trees; under the trees was a little brook that tinkled gaily in an expression of joy at freedom from ice. As far as one looked, there were hills encircling the horizon, hills crowned with stately pines. The sky was blue, the air filled with the drowsy hum of utter contentment from a flock of white hens basking in another sunny, windless spot by the barn. Cattle, for the first time released from the stable, walked stiff-legged over the meadow, seeming somewhat bewildered by this sudden incentment to resumption of summer habits. An awkward calf performed its first outdoor gambol, and seemed amazed at its own length of leg. The cat had forsaken the fireside for sunny corner in the porch, the house dog rushed aimlessly about in pursuit of nothing.

"This is what the crocus means to me," he thought, smiling whimsically. "What would the crocus mean to her? It would mean that the one who sent it lacked taste, that he thought so little of her as to send the least expensive flower in the market."

"What flowers did you decide on?" asked the florist's clerk, perhaps weary of waiting the decision of the customer.

"What flowers—what flowers—?" he was still confused and at a loss to decide.

The clerk persisted. "Were they to be sent," he asked, "with your card, or anonymously?"

"How—anonymously?"

"Well, tomorrow is the fourteenth, Valentine's Day, and we send a great many flowers as valentines, without cards."

This was a new idea, and the customer saw a way out of his difficulty.

"A dozen jack roses," he said, briskly, "with my card, to this address, please. And the bunch of crocuses, without any card, to the same address. You understand?"

Making tea with a teaball is a slow process, but a pretty one to watch if the maker is young and pretty, and there are not too many cups in demand. Maryon Lytton had only three cups before her, she knew that her manicuring was above reproach, she could feel admiring eyes upon her, and she handled the teaball deftly. Besides, there was on the tea table a pink bowl filled with jack roses. Their perfume sweetened the air, their color accorded with Maryon's rose-colored blouse and the wired bow of pink velvet that rose pertly, yet prettily, from her lustrous and fashionably disposed hair.

"The roses are lovely," she whispered to the man who sat nearest. "Thank you so much."

Raymond Vaughn stirred his tea absently, and looked at Maryon and the roses. Of course it was roses that decorated the tea table. He had been right. Crocuses would mean nothing to her. She was a town girl. She belonged to many clubs, she liked to be in town winters on account of the Symphony concerts, when snow came she drove on the boulevard in a fine Russian sleigh behind a pair of black horses, and with a coachman wrapped in furs. How ridiculous to have thought that she might care enough for a man to live with him in a red-brick house perched on a bleak hillside, with only other hillsides to look upon! How futile to have dreamed of introducing her to a community where people drove themselves in cutters, where the servants ate with their employers, where five o'clock tea was an unknown function, where one must eat dinner at noon, or forever bear the odium of being called "stuck up."

He drank his tea, he chatted, he said good-bye and closed the street door with the feeling of one who gives up a beautiful something quite impossible, and therefore provides material for a lifetime's sighs.

After he had gone Maryon thrust back the rose bowl so violently that half the roses lost their petals at once.

"Oh, those beautiful roses," exclaimed her aunt. "Mr. Vaughn's gift."

Maryon rose wearily. "Bother my beautiful roses!" she exclaimed tartly. "I'm sick of beautiful roses and forced violets. I'm sick—yes, I'm sick of Mr. Vaughn, with his eternal well-bred criticism of actors and his everlasting looking at things from conventional standpoints."

"Maryon, I am surprised."

"And I am disgusted. Auntie—auntie, please give me up as a bad job. Forget me. Let me go home. I shall never be a credit to you. At first I felt I was playing a part, I posed, I formed myself on the most conventional models. Before I realized what happened, all Boston— all your Boston and my Boston—took me at my apparent valuation. Auntie, I am homesick. I was homesick the first day I came here; it has been getting worse for the past five years. All things make me homesick. Music speaks to me of nature's own music. Parks are mockeries when I am longing for real woods. I want to hear a crow caw overhead. I don't love gas logs. I can never love gas logs. I want to build a big wood fire out of logs so freshly cut of the forest that moss and ice alike cling to the bark. Time does not cure me. Time will never cure me. Let me go."

"Maryon—think of your chances. Think of the settlement that may be yours."

"Settlement—with Mr. Vaughn, or some similar young man who will want his wife to help him socially, get into a good set, and live in a Back Bay apartment. Never! Listen, auntie, and I will tell you what I want to do—what my heart is sickening for—"

Maryon ran lightly upstairs, and returned bringing a bunch of crocuses. Throwing herself on the floor, she buried her face in the flowers and then looked up, her eyes the brighter for two tears.

"I don't know who sent me these," she exclaimed, "but I feel as I could love whomever it was. I want to go back to the old farm, auntie; I want to run over the fields in the free wind and an old calico gown. I am willing to wait until June for my roses. Yes, I know what it means, auntie. I won't mind the b'iled dinners—in fact, I think I am rather hungry for one, and somehow it has always seemed unnatural for men to call at four and be regaled with tea. I think I shall like to return to a place where they drive over and spend the evening, and you give them doughnuts and cider. What if I marry one of them? He may not know much about musical criticism and the ways of polite society, but at least he will give me the love of a heart that runs honest red blood instead of the cold, blue kind."

"Maryon, you are flippant," said her aunt, severely.

"Auntie, I am giddy. I am going back to be once more Mary Ann."

Next day a train out from Boston took two people to the Berkshire Hills. The man in the smoker thought, "She was more charming than any other. But my chosen life can never be hers."

Then he started to idly stroll through the train. At the door of the second day-coach he paused. There, gazing hungrily out of the window at the landscape, each minute becoming less urban, was a girl. In addition to a handbag and strapped rug, both eminently correct, she carried a partly withered, very untidy bunch of crocuses.

(*The Pioneer*, May 30, 1907)

AUNT ANN'S BED

Young Ann Edwards went into the South room and looked at the bed. (She was 65, but there had been an old Ann Edwards.) The bed, in makeshift location, gave to the South room an appearance of chamber imposing on parlor. It had always given this appearance, though it had occupied the same unhandy corner, and been swept under, for above 40 years. Old Ann Edwards, on getting into it, had observed that it would be only a little while there, she would soon be out and about and able to sleep above stairs as usual. Then she had lain in it 40 years. The rag carpet had been up and down—they had cut out circles where the legs of the fourposter were planted—and young Ann remembered laboriously going over the wallpaper with bread crumb, because her aunt could not be troubled by paper hangers. Otherwise time had stood still in this pleasant apartment, that caught the sun in full force all winter, and was sufficiently shaded by lilacs and syringa in summer.

Only with young Ann Edwards it had not stood still.

She had believed herself pretty chipper when she came east to stay a while with Aunt Ann. She was glad of a temporary rest from schoolmarming, and when she should go back to Minnesota she was to be well rewarded. Well, she had not gone back, but she had a splendid reward. Aunt Ann had left her everything, and that was a magnificent farm, a wide spreading mansion, and fifteen thousand dollars well invested. With it one might be pretty independent. She might travel, or sell the place and live in a city. Her air castles had included both pleasures, while she remembered aunt Ann's hourly doses and diurnal baths. It wasn't the act of a kind niece to wish an aunt out of the world, but toward the last both women had longed for a loosening of their self-forged bands.

"I believe I might chirk up if I only could have a sprightly young girl round me," thought the bed-ridden one. "Ann used to have some life in her, but lately she's as dumb as an oyster and goes about with a face long as her arm."

And Ann, while mechanically performing duties that through much repetition had lost zest, felt that the woman on the air mattress was sapping her health and strength, as she had sapped youth while youth there was to sap.

Now opened new vistas, bewildering in strangeness. She began to plan. Tomorrow to the nearby city, for clothes and a withdrawal of needed money. Then—a summer at the sea? A mountain trip? A few weeks in New York, where there were concerts and matinees?

She began to walk about the room, thinking she was taking a farewell of the furniture and ornaments. How delightfully odd it would be to awake of a morning and not see that worsted landscape which Aunt Ann had wrought in boarding school young ladyhood, and which hung in direct range of the cot that had been set up for young Ann the evening of her arrival from the west.

The bedside table had not been touched since the tray was brought in with dishes after the last meal had been pettishly refused. Ann absently took up the rosebud pattern cup, and remembered how childishly her aunt had rejoiced when vigorous consumption of soup or such disclosed the full blown rose on the inside. It was awful to get like that. She wished she dared smash the cup. After all, why did she not dare? A cheap cup, and all the property was hers. She opened the door that had been so seldom set ajar in Aunt Ann's day, because there was a possibility of draughts even in July. A good many spiders and other unpleasant insects were disturbed in their spring housecleaning by her impetuosity, because a sudden change always means inconvenience to something. Ann sent the saucer hurtling across the yard, it smashed against a tree and fell in fragments. The cup would have followed, but for an interrupting voice. "Why Ann Edwards, whatever in this world! Breaking up housekeeping?"

Ann lacked courage. "I thought I saw a rat," she said. "Come in and let me shut this door. There's an awful draught."

The neighbor entered and was opening a budget of gossip, but Ann stopped her. The ache in her side which had bothered more or less ever since she began lifting Aunt Ann up and down, 15 years back, but which she had never been able to stop and cure, had come on very insistently since the exertion of opening the door. It usually went off with a few moments' rest, but this time it did not go off. Starting from a throbbing centre darts of pain stabbed her shoulder, her bosom, her hip. The caller said, "What makes you so white,

Ann?" and fetched aromatic ammonia, but that effected nothing. Then she said, "Goodness, how you tremble, Ann," and brought brandy, but that was useless. Finally she suggested the doctor, and Ann, beyond speech, nodded. The rural telephone had been put in this house first of all, on account of the invalid. It was used, and Dr. Fosket said he would be over as fast as his nag could trot.

Then came another suggestion, very sensible. "You ought to go right straight to bed. The doctor is sure to put you there. Here, let me help you to undress."

Aided by the kind woman, Ann was soon between the sheets. She didn't notice, so bewildered was she by pain, but the night-gown put on her was one of Aunt Ann's, which lay handily in the embroidered case. Hardly was Ann well covered up, with a hasty soapstone at her feet, when they heard the eager pat of horse's hoofs on the highway, the gentler turning into the yard, a properly dig-nified "whoa," and then Dr. Fosket, letting himself in familiarly, entered the room, tapping his driving gloves on his hand, as he had done any day these 28 years, bar a week.

His remedies took effect with reasonable rapidity; in an hour Ann was easier, but weak.

"When may I get up?" she whispered.

The doctor advised a few weeks' perfect rest—perhaps in June. It was now the first week of May.

"How lucky," said the neighbor, "that you never got round to moving this bed. I should never have been able to tug you upstairs. And now, if you're going to be laid up a while, we better send for some one to stay with you."

Ann turned her face to the wall. In muffled accents she said, "My niece. I think she will come—for a little while. You will find her address in that purple morocco book. Her name is Ann—Edwards—Crane."

"Sure," returned the good-natured woman. "The doctor can take the telegram to the village. And—luck again—here is your cot all prepared for her."

Thus Nan Crane came to the aid of her Aunt Ann. Nan was turned 22; she had a great deal of hair, and the first thing known of her in the neighborhood was that it took her two hours every day to do it up. She performed the task in her aunt's presence, chattering gaily the whole time, much to the invalid's amusement. For the first few months she was seldom seen out, because of close attention at the bedside she had been called to attend. When Aunt Ann was better and up they were to go everywhere. They passed hours planning a glorious making up for lost time.

In a few years Aunt Ann began urging Nan to take what pleasure she might while youth lasted.

"I have every confidence," she would assert, "that Dr. Fosket will have me on my feet before long, but I cannot suppose I will ever be very smart. You know, my dear, I am rather getting on in years."

By and by she ceased having confidence in Dr. Fosket, because he was dead and gone, and in another decade her faith in young Dr. Foster wavered.

"You have kept me lying here so long," she would say, peevishly, "that now I have no heart for getting up. I don't want an active life. If he would only give me something to keep me easy and comfortable I would not complain. I don't believe he's half the doctor Fosket was."

You see Ann—young Ann—was not so pleasant in her old age as her aunt had been. She used to taunt Nan with keeping her out of the way, so things could be "managed," and she made terrible scenes when Nan wanted to marry Dr. Foster, though the niece promised to stay right on caretaking. It was to Nan's credit that she had won the admiration of the only man who ever had a square look at her, but Aunt Ann had so many heart failures and fainting spells whenever the matter was mentioned that both young people saw it would not do. So Nan returned the ring, and began to do her hair a new way, which didn't take so many braids. He kept right on doctoring and didn't marry. Perhaps Nan used to think—when she had a spare moment to think in—that he was waiting.

He was exceedingly helpful to Nan, always. He advised a trained nurse, and from time to time one would air her starched uniforms on this breezy hilltop. Aunt Ann, however, never took to them, and the stay of each was brief. Nan alone never had the footbath too cold, the chocolate too thick. She could read aloud in a voice one could hear (Aunt Ann was deaf but didn't know it). Ann remembered the long novels of Mrs. Southworth and Mary Jane Holmes she had read to her aunt, the old Ann. They had given her a distaste for fiction, and she required much Tennyson and Longfellow from Nan, who grew to dislike any Idyls or any King, and to associate Evangeline's wanderings with hours of monotonous sitting.

It seems incredible, but Ann Edwards lay in that bed 30 years, having gone to it at 65. She ran the gamut of every disagreeable concommitant of sickness, and was by turns domineering, distrustful, capricious, finally senile and disgusting. Nan wore out early. She had become a victim to asthma from close confinement in the dull air, which alone seemed the air Ann could breathe. For five years Nan would tell Dr. Foster it was good she had her aunt to take care of, because it was easy to coddle two as one. The doctor often let his horse stumble at will down the road, while he wiped the mist off his glasses.

"Such a merry girl," he would think, "when I first saw her changing compresses on the sick woman's head. Such red cheeks. She wore a tight-fitting dress that showed her pretty form. Now she is sallow, and what wonder? And I never see her but in a loose house-gown."

He questioned if she owned a coat and hat. Aunt Ann was notoriously "near."

It ended, the long vigil. It had to end. Nan Crane sat upright in the South room, which was now rather too shady the year round, because several unconsidered hemlock saplings had grown to a considerable size, blocking the windows. Ann was never able to bear the noise of chopping them down. Nan felt herself frail, weary, despondent. Physical woe held her fast, she lacked buoyancy to rise above the shortness of breath, the aching shoulders, the throbbing nerve centres which make a natural part of her disease. A little bird, outside, was hopping gaily up and down the twigs. How amazing that anything should have energy to move for the pure joy of moving. Nan dreaded the moment when she would have to get up and take three steps to the cupboard where her drops were kept. She would be better for the drops, but it was such a task to reach them. Well, Samantha would come in from the kitchen if a bell was rung, but even bell ringing was an effort. Besides, Samantha was cross when called from the kitchen. She had been hired to cook, not sicknurse.

While Nan lingered, unhappily inert, an unusual sound broke the summer stillness. Someone was knocking at the side door. Nan was startled. Neighbors knew better than to come there, and for strangers there was the obvious front door with a bellpull. Nan's heart started pounding, but she forced herself up and peered through the hemlock boughs. Who was on the doorstone, wearing pink? Nan softly drew the great iron bolt, and lifted the heavy latch. It was rather disconcerting to feel the matter more forcefully managed from the other side. The latch went up with a jerk, and a strong push sent the door slamming, while creepers gave way, dust tumbled down, and bugs ran in every direction.

Enter youth, in rose-colored linen, a slender form that looked slim in a middy blouse, trim feet masked in ground grippers, a girlish face crowned by a boyish Panama hat. Nan stood panting, her hands pressed on her hips because she often fancied she breathed better so, but her visitor had her in the chair in a jiffy.

"Bronchial asthma," came the staccato utterance. "Here, let me raise your arms. There, like that! Now twist them a bit. Oh, it cannot hurt. Don't be so afraid of its hurting. I see, both shoulders muscle bound. Well, that is curable. Up with them once more. Easier? Knew you would be. The chief thing is to lift the ribs off the diaphragm. Now rest a while."

She laid Nan back as if the woman were a new wax doll, to be cherished. Then pink blouse dropped on a cricket and beamed. She looked the cuddly sort, that would sit on anything that was almost floor, and lie on hearthrugs whenever an open fire was within reach. Her hands had been warm and strong. Nan felt as if gripped by a merciful giantess.

"You have not a blessed idea who I am," observed the girl. "I am the one you have sent a silver spoon to each year since I was born. It's going on two dozen. How long are you going to keep it up?"

"Oh," said Nan, "you are Miriam's daughter?"

"Exactly. Father used to say I looked like her. Of course a stepmother cannot say as to that. She has a hard enough time finding beefsteaks and shoes and a resemblance to papa for her own brood since he left us. That was one reason why, when I read in the paper how you were left by the death of old Great Aunt Ann, I decided to come right on!"

Nan listened to words that seemed to come from a great way off.

"We have always thought," babbled the young person, "it was so beautiful—what you have done, devoting your life to your aunt, and I am determined to see my duty in the same dear old fashion. And so I said to a—friend—of mine who dared to object. It is evident, too, I am just in time. I will have those ribs lifted off in a half a dozen treatments, and get those muscles limbered up, and while we are about it that lump on your right shoulder can be removed easy as anything. Why, auntie, you won't know yourself!"

Nan shuddered.

"First of all, though, I shall put you straight to bed. You have been through a lot of strain, anyone can see that, and what you require is a thorough rest. Lucky enough there is a bed all ready, right downstairs, in this beautiful, pleasant room. And that cot over there will be fine for me. I always slept on one at home, the flat was so crowded, and I shall want to be handy to read to you when you have restless nights. Why, auntie, it will be as good to me as a course in a hospital. And all the time I shall be of service to you. Now do say you are glad to see me."

Nan only sat and stared and repeated two words that the girl interpreted as "My niece." So she said easily, "Yes, that is what I am, of course." But what Nan said was, "The niece!" She repeated it several times. With each repetition her own fate loomed more horrible. She would be put into that dreadful bed by that vigorous young person, and she would be glad to be put there, for it called to her with all the power of rest for the weary. And she would not get up. None of them ever had. She would become an old, bedridden piece of humanity, that had its face washed in the morning like a baby, and lay sticky handed unless someone thought to bring it a rag during the day. It would wear a cap, while all its functions, from sleeping to thinking, would be controlled by medicine. It would do this year after year, until the 20th century waxed to waning. And in the meantime the caretaker—the niece—

Nan bent to pink and white girlhood, clasped the warm paws in her birdclaw fingers, and said, between wheezes, "It is a pity you took this journey. You cannot stay."

"Oh—Aunt Nan! But I am sure you need me. I was so positive when I told that—objecting party—you needed me! And if it is money—papa left me a little. Enough for frocks and shoes. And perhaps

I can get a patient or so for treatments in the neighborhood. Then I can do all the homework. I've been to cooking school."

"Hush, dear, hush! It is quite dreadful to hear you go on so."

"But Aunt Nan, I thought you would be glad to have me, only maybe you didn't send because of not knowing my feelings. Some folks have an idea a modern girl is for self and neglecting home duties. We are not all so, I assure you, as I have assured—others. I am proud to carry on what really seems a sort of tradition in our family."

Excitement, as often with sufferers like Nan, gave sudden freedom and speech. "My darling girl," she began, while tears turned her darling girl to a rosy blur, "you want to be lost. We have all wanted to be lost. You have got to be saved. If you succeeded in putting me into that bed, do you know what would happen? Your hair would fall out, and your eyes would sink in, you would love me, and bear with me, and hate me, by degrees; and I should do the same by you. That is I would love you while you had youth to give me, and when I had sapped it and you were left dry, I would be disagreeable, because I would feel that when you had nothing more to give me I would have to go, and the more useless life became to me the stronger I would cling to it. I would change less than you, being old and wizened to begin with. Year by year I would slip a little lower into bed, and be harder to raise at meal times. You would have rosy cheeks to lose, and bright hair, as well as hope and ambition, and all life of your own. Very likely you might lose the greatest of all—love! Ah, the pink of your blouse is creeping up in your cheeks. I rather think the friend who objected to your coming, wanted to exercise more than a friendly right to object. Eh, my dear?"

The girl regarded a white streak round the lower part of the third finger of the left hand, and murmured, "It was not an engagement—exactly—only an understanding. I would not be coerced. And then he will wait."

"I have no doubt of it. Men do those things. They have more constancy than books tell us. But such waiting is the hope deferred that maketh the heart sick. So you are going, today, now, this very hour, before I get used to you, and feel I cannot do without you. And hurry—please hurry—for I am getting to love you very fast. I think, niece," she added, with a tearful smile at the clock, "that ten minutes more would finish me."

The girl rose and stood in bewildered disappointment. She was almost determined to exercise her will, and have Aunt Nan in bed and under care whether she would or not. It was resolution against nerves, but it was also 21 against 52, and age won. The pink blouse was disappearing through the door when Nan called out, "Wait one moment. There is another thing I must do. All the aunts do it. As you saw, it is traditional. I must make you my heir."

"Oh, thank you," mumbled the girl, abashed. "I—I hope it's a long while before I profit by it."

"Well, it will not be. You are going to benefit today. No, I do not feel a warning. If you truly knew anything about asthma, you know well enough it preserves one to a very old age. There has been enough waiting for dead women's shoes. And not one of the nieces has ever profited by the inheritance. It invariably came too late to be spent in anything more enjoyable than doctor's fees. You are going to spend yours for what a girl wants—I suppose nowadays it's moving pictures and taxicabs. What I can give you will hardly run to autos, because I must keep a few hundreds a year for my old self." "Ah!"

For the girl had plumped herself down on the doorstone, and squealed with delight. "Blessed auntie," she buzzed, "if you can let me have some money, I can achieve the dream of my life, and go to college and medical school. You see Rob—Robert is a doctor, and I wouldn't feel so conscious of his stooping to look at poor me, if only I was trained to stand beside him in every way. Not that he ever hinted, but I always abhorred the idea of being Beggar Maid to any sort of a King Cophetua. And he—Robert—is so brilliant. Why, he performed major operations by artificial light! And if I may learn to follow in his footsteps—be it ever so far behind—"

So ecstatic was the picture that she bounced up again, and so was able to announce the reason for a purr in the road. "Here comes a nice old gentleman, auntie," she cried. "His income does run to autos."

"Old gentleman, indeed," said Aunt Nan. "It's Dr. Foster. The young doctor."

The girl gave one look at her aunt, then dashed in, and deposited on the withered cheek a kiss which felt like a blob of April shower mixed with March breezes and flavored by May flowers.

The machine was now in sight.

"I would like to know," remarked the aunt, "who is the boy in the tonneau?"

"Boy, indeed!" shrieked the niece. "It's Robert. He's followed! After saying he would wait at home!"

The car was parked under the horse chestnut upon which the second Ann Edwards had once smashed a saucer. Nan got a full view of the skillful performer of major operations by electricity, and mentally begged his pardon for thinking him a boy playing hookey from prep. school.

"Go, dear," she whispered, drawing her niece to her side, and giving her a caress that was fresh as camphor, sweet as lavender, and soft as the touch of well-worn damask. "He's sought you. Meet him half-way. That's always best. Besides, I don't think he is the waiting kind."

"All right—I'm off," said the young thing. "If he takes me to the station—and I suppose he will—you may write to me where the spoons go. But have the doctor—the young doctor—your young doctor—get someone to lift your ribs. You won't know yourself. Believe me!"

She was gone. Nan sat a moment looking, wistfully, at the plump bed, so invitingly ready to be pressed by weary limbs. Then she rang the bell with vigor. "Samantha," she called, "have Hiram help you to take down this bed and carry it to the garret. I shall see Dr. Foster in the parlor."

(*The National Amateur,* January 1919)

CINDERELLA SOAPMAN

Just between the September Morn ballyhoo and the Diving Girls' tank, Cinderella's mother said, "Cinderella, don't you want a hot dog?"

"Ya'as, marm," Cinderella replied, all her eyes fastened upon unwholesome pink popcorn and ice cream cones.

Deftly extracting a nickel from her stocking Cinderella's mother pushed the girl in the direction of the booth where a mountainous man announced unctuously, "They're all hot, and they're all fresh, and they're all fried in butter."

Cinderella took one, crushed it firmly in a shell of chalky bread, and stood munching, regardless of the mustard daub on her chin.

Of the 40,000 people perspiring about the grounds of the Middlesex County Cattle Show that afternoon, Cinderella Murdock was probably the gladdest. Others came in autos, spent money to watch Beachy fly, from the grandstand, ate a turkey dinner at a dollar a cover, squandered quarts of chicken feed bucking the knife game. Cinderella had walked five miles to get there, and would walk another five to get home. She was eating her dinner now. She hadn't a penny for a slot. She was very happy. That ma should have let her come, and have given her a hot dog as easy as anything, filled Cinderella's huge frame with quivers of joy.

She finished the dog and licked each finger meditatively. The big man plied a tin shovel among masses of onions softening in olive oil. "Come again?" he asked. Cinderella slowly shook her head, while her eye—the large, intelligent eye of the ox—reluctantly withdrew from contemplation of the food.

"Try a drink? Orangeade, made from juicy Floridy oranges, 10,000 feet underground, and stirred by a section of the North pole. The ladies like it, the babies cry for it, and the old maids say it's the best they ever tasted."

He replenished the glass tank from a bottle of yellow fluid which confessed to containing 10 per cent. benzoate of soda, replaced the chunk of ice it wore like the drunkard in a caricature of the day after, and laid for trade.

Cinderella started lumberingly away, gaping about for ma. Her small head was so much above the crowd that she didn't see a little staggering man until he ran into her.

"Look where yer going," he stuttered, as he picked himself up and carefully dusted his clothes, without paying any attention to the mud plastered on his face. "Cinderella Soapman!"

Cinderella had been for helping him, but this taunt stiffened her rangy frame with sudden anger. Who was it daring to call her "Cinderella Soapman" now she was a grown woman? As a child at school Cinderella had expected to hear, when she passed with her sisters, "That's Minnie Murdock, Bessie Murdock, and Aggalena Murdock, and Cinderella Soapman." She hadn't known exactly what it meant, because her name was down in Teacher's big book as Cinderella Murdock. Now she dimly understood it had been mud slung at ma. Only a long time had gone by since anyone had dared to say the words.

Something—mustard on the dog, or perhaps a rage newly born—ran fiery through her veins. Cinderella slapped the small man with her big hand, opened her wide mouth and loosened remarks.

"Little runt! Come ramming along chock full o'blackstrap up to your gozzle cutting up your didoes. Ef my ma was here she'd give you whatfor."

Cinderella said much more, but it was drowned in the dreadful bawling of the small bully whose nose had been considerably disarranged by Cinderella's blow. A crowd assembled, and even a constable made his appearnce.

"Here, here, lady and gent, what's transpiring?" he asked, in the polite language of fair time.

"She smashed me beezer."

"He called me out of my name."

The constable instantly made a mistake, but justifiable. "How long married?" he inquired.

The man burst into such derisive laughter that he snorted blood over the nighest bystanders. Cinderella buried her ugly face in her red hands and whimpered, "Ma, where's ma?"

Puzzled, the constable decided to run 'em both in. The man, being undersized, was overcome after a tussle. Cinderella, who might easily have floored a couple of constables, came in dismal docility, still moaning, "Ma."

In the crowd that trailed along, delighting in the free show of seeing a woman "taken up," an angular Swede detached himself from the neutral group, and sided with the girl. She was young and unhappy. What mattered that her unkempt hair was the color of greased dirt, and insufficient to hide the wire roll over which it was drawn; that her splay feet clumped along in men's shoes; that her shirt waist was grimy, her skirt fringe-hemmed; that a sallow skin skimpily covered high cheek-bones, was punctuated by a bulbous nose, and bordered by outstanding ears? Perhaps he thought she looked pretty good. He was no beauty himself, but honest and well to do, with a reputation for both.

He came to the side of the constable, gave him a punch and a Fair cigar. Then he nodded backward, where Cinderella followed like a cow bereaved of calf.

"Huh?" asked the constable. "Not your gal, Mr. Anderson?"

Anderson nodded and proffered a second smoke.

"Wall, that's all right. Just march her off. Guess she won't care for witness fees account this feller if it's your treat."

Anderson turned, and touched Cinderella's arm. She put down her hand and stared at her rescuer as if she had found him even more awe-inspiring than the constable. Then she once more opened her mouth and explained.

"I was a-waiting, mister, when by came that chipper, hit my crazy bone, and mouthmauled me. I wasn't carrying on, certain sure. Then the sheriff chipped in and I was cleverly up. Just thought 'twas all talk and no cider, till he started me to the boobyhutch. And to cap all, I've lost ma ma."

Anderson, who understood not a word, did not hesitate to reply. "Have a drink," he said.

And escorting Cinderella to the sacred tables of the Epworth League tent he bought her a pink ice cream soda, a long glass of sarsaparilla, moxie and a bottle of grape juice with two straws. A tumbler of water went with each, and Cinderella conscientiously drank them all.

Then Anderson spoke again. "Enough?" he asked.

Cinderella nodded in blessed repletion. Anderson led her forthwith to the "Sugar Auto," where he invested in wax paper wrapped packages of chocolate. Then he pointed down the line.

"Which?" he inquired.

And Cinderella understood he was offering her Major Morosco, the smallest man on earth, oh do not fail to see this tiny, little man; or the five-legged calf, with two heads, positively two heads and no fake; or the tattoed miracle, done in six colors and seven languages; or the laughing hyena, he laughs himself to death at nothing at all, and you laugh yourself to death at him; or—

"Why, yon's my ma!"

Cinderella's cry of delight reached her mother's ears, above all the din. Mrs. Murdock hurried right up and began to scold Cinderella for leaving the hot dog booth. Was ever such a girl? She's been looking everywhere for her—or would have been immediately. She just went in to see He Eats 'Em Alive, because she met Mr. and Mrs. Hatch from up our way, and they asked her. And what have you got in your hand, Cinderella?

Anderson answered for her. "Choc-let, ma'am."

"Bang up, ma. Have some?" And Cinderella eagerly proferred the box, from which she had not yet allowed herself a taste.

Mrs. Murdock ignored the offer because her entire attention was occupied by the gaunt Swede who had so unexpectedly invaded the family group of herself and Cinderella. She examined his tan shoes, dazzling collar, unbroken straw hat. A leather fob bearing a baggage check told at once of Anderson's line of work and of his having saved to buy a watch. With one hand he rather arrogantly jingled about half a peck of small coins in a trouser pocket. His eyes, real Swedish eyes of deepest blue, challenged the woman silently.

He saw a dumpy little female, fussily dressed in gay attire that tried to be fashionable. Her fat feet were over-running fancy slippers, the henna on her hair had stained the "Robespierre" collar above her jacket. Her cheeks were painted and all the lamp black on her lashes could not make her gray eyes anything but rat like.

It occurred to her that she might send Cinderella home and appropriate this moneyed wastrel to her own amusement. So she smiled and told him she guessed he was awful good. She hoped Cinderella hadn't been and made him no trouble. Wasn't he the Mr. Anderson who worked down to the freight depot? Cinderella'd better go now, the Hatches would take her as fur as they went. They had to leave early to do the chores. She had only chickens, so she needn't hurry.

"No, ma, you no need to hurry," interposed Cinderella. "I'll cutsick, make a beeline and fodder like I'm usted to."

As before Anderson did not understand fully, but he had the answer.

"Come on," he said, and started Cinderella toward the horse sheds where his outfit—piano box top buggy, bay mare, linen duster and six-foot whip—waited. Cinderella tried to see if ma approved, but about 10,000 perfect strangers intervened.

"Wouldn't ma say this was bumkum," she cried gleefully, as they drove out through the large gate obsequeously opened by the same sort of cattle that had so lately been haling Cinderella to durance vile. Then she abandoned herself to perfect bliss.

The way lay through the village square, where "Welcome Middlesex County 25th Annual" waved above a practically empty town. Only the "5 and 10" seemed to be doing a brisk business, the housewives who had seen the show early on an Exhibitor's ticket now stocking up their pantry shelves. Anderson pulled his horse before it, and pointing the whip stock at the windows, inquired, rather eagerly, "Gray—blue?" One window was sombre with muffin pans, teakettles and perforated spoons in gray agate ware, the balancing window was gay with exactly the same articles in a brilliant blue.

For once, Cinderella failed him. "I'd'know," she faltered.

"You cook?" asked Anderson.

Cinderella shook her head. "My ma can cook all around creation. Nut cakes, souse, handrum buff, Togus bread, hot pot. In tomato cans."

"You cook nothing?" Anderson's voice expressed disappointment.

"I can bile taters. And slumgullion. Only 'tain't a circumstance to hern's. Now my ma—"

"All right. Get ap!" And Anderson started the horse at so smart a trot further words were blown from Cinderella's lips. She jounced pleasantly on the cushions and lolled up the hills she had expected to toil over on blistered feet. It was a-many times she had come down 'em with a crate of berries, and puffed up laden with a sack of flour, or some other equivalent in bulky groceries. Never would she have believed in such an excursion as this. Only she called it a carrying on to lick creation.

Anderson drove pretty straight to where the Murdock home was perched among the pines crowning the top hill, only for a detour around the river road, where his own house was a-building. He grew voluble in its description.

"Kitchen, parlor, two upstairs. Eight-foot piazza. Cement cellar. Hardwood floor. Rambler rose. What you like? Red? White?"

Again Cinderella failed him. "I'd'know. Ma says a nice yaller sunflower—"

"Get up!" And they were off, more vociferously than before.

He did not speak again until he drew rein before the dismal cottage that Cinderella called home. It was like her mother in having once been coquettish. Now again, like her, it was rather ghastly. Many of the windows were broken and the chimneys presented a jagged outline against the sky.

Anderson helped Cinderella out, very unnecessarily, and emptied his pockets of various sacks of popcorn, peanuts and potato chips. Then, "Home Sunday?" he asked.

"Ya-as. My ma and the rest calculate to go on a bender."

"We'll ride out," said Anderson with decision, and got into the buggy.

"Goo'by," said Cinderella. "If you meet my ma—"

"S'long!" was all she heard from Anderson, as he rattled away.

Cinderella dragged her dreadful shoes into the house, but it was not entirely occupied, as she had expected, by flies and chickens, the one evading the other. A rather hard-faced woman, so dark and angular it was easy to imagine she had been made from joints of abandoned stovepipe, sat chewing snuff by the table.

"Hullo, Cinderella. Wasn't that Swedish Anderson beauing of you?"

"Broughten me home, Aunt Lou."

Aunt Lou, who was neatly if inconspicuously dressed in lilac gingham, and who owned this house in which she permitted her poor relatives to perch, made an irrelevant comment.

"Land o' Goshen, Cinderella, be them the best duds you got?"

Cinderella essayed an uncouth dance, during which the dreadful shoes fell off her feet, showing toeless socks. "Regular clumpers," she cried. Then she lifted her skirt, and disclosed nothing particular underneath. "My chemiloon went to Ballyhack," she remarked, "and ma bushelled it over for Aggalena."

"Cinderella," said Aunt Lou, "speak up and tell the truth. Did Anderson say anything that would justify an old fool and her money being parted easy as tilly? No stretchers, now."

"Marm?"

"Heavenly day, don't stand there looking so half saved. Didn't he spark you none?"

Cinderella thought a while, then offered, "Atted me to cook."

"And you?"

"Said ma could."

"Dunderhead!" muttered Aunt Lou. Then, louder, "any more side winders?"

"Marm?"

"Any more spooning?"

"We drew around Colton Holler, 'n he p'inted out his bran new housen."

"Take ye in?"

"No. 'Twas all clichy th' paint."

Aunt Lou ruminated, chewing the while like any ruminant animal. Then she remarked, "Well, 't remains to be seen whether you're going to be set above your huckleberry, or left to scuff through a dark, cold world. Listen to me, Cinderella. If Anderson comes to see you don't let him set round this forlorn place. Fetch him right up to mine and you can have the best parlor to court in till moondown, if he's desirous to stay that late. And if he takes you to eating house anywhere don't go letting into the victuals like you do to home, and rec'lect knives ain't used for much nowadays 'less it's something you can't manage without 'em, as beans or pie. And if he asks you to have him don't let the grass grow under your feet, but hyper to Auntie's, and I'll see you've a decent setting out and the ceremony performed in bang-up style."

"Marm?"

"Cinderella, I believe you ain't all stayed with. Wouldn't you like to git married? Have a home o' your own, all complete? And a man to fetch in the groceries?"

"Oh, yes'm! Yes'm!" Cinderella was so anxious to acquiesce that she trod right on Aunt Lou's feet.

Aunt Lou arose, and tied her head securely into a slat sunbonnet.

"Tomorrow," she observed, "I'll get to go to the city. Come next day, Cinderella. I declare it's a burning shame!"

"I will, sure pop," gleed Cinderella, "if ma'll let me."

Aunt Lou turned, let loose an unconnected sniff from her discolored nose, and vanished among sumacs, leaving her grand-niece a prey to so many exciting emotions that she permitted the cats to eat half the chicken dough without interference.

Mrs. Murdock arrived home on foot, and in a bad temper. Cattle-shows were hot, dusty, crowded, impolite, scrooging, expensive and nasty places. Never catch her at another. She'd seen all she wanted of 'em in a lifetime. "You had it pretty soft, Cinderella. I paid your way in and you got a lift home, only you'd ruther go off with that great gorming Swedish pelter than with the Hatches. They was perfectly willing you should ride third on a seat in that narrow carryall o' their'n. I felt meaner'n dirt when I had to say you didn't see fit to wait their convenience. Such awful good neighbors. Always stand ready to let me have a day's wear of M's Hatch's second best shawl if so be it you'll go up and scrub the kitchen floor. And what did Anderson have to say to you so awful private like?"

Cinderella, reduced to tears, faltered out bits of sentiment already poured into Aunt Lou's sympathetic ear.

"Indeed! Indeed! Atted you to cook, and showed you that ramshackle shanty he's having put up, and which I'm told is mortgaged to the top brick of the tallest chimbley. I see his game, and pretty plain. He wants a housekeeper. A good strong girl, that'll get right down on her knees and give his floors a good going over with sand soap. You don't like to scour floors, do you, Cinderella?"

"No'm."

"The splinters gets into your knees and they swell up in wheals. You don't fancy it, do you, Cinderell?"

For once, Cinderella answered less promptly. "I'd'know," she faltered.

Mrs. Murdock was after her in a minute. "You do know, Cinderell," she snapped, "you don't want to stay alone day arter day in that little shanty, whiles he's to work, or larking evenings. They won't always be somebody to talk to like they is up here, with the chickens, and cats, and me and the childern. And he'll come home and rage round 'cause the victuals ain't to his taste. Men do, Swedes more 'specially. Besides, he's probably got a wife in Swedish already. And childern—you'll have a snarl of 'em and—"

"Ma," said Cinderella, gloomily, "if he's Swedish hitched I s'pose the poor little tykes can't be named Anderson. Will they call one of 'em Cinderella Freightman, like I'm called—"

"Shut up!" screamed Mrs. Murdock, aiming a blow of thorough exasperation at the girl, who was quieted instantly, and mumbled, "Yes'm."

The woman, who had been undoing her tight clothing during the conversation, now rose and prepared to stumble upstairs over tangling petticoats. At the door she delivered a final exordium.

"Any time you meet him, Cinderell, any time, anywhere, you tell him out plump you don't want to get married. You hear me, Cinderell?"

"Yes'm," returned the bewildered Cinderella.

Thus we see Cinderella, Aunt Lou urging her forward, for the honor of the family; Mrs. Murdock pushing her back, because she does not wish to lose a willing drudge; Cinderella herself a garden bed of newly sprouted emotions, of which the most vigorous is that long growing perennial, adoration of her mother; Swedish Anderson an unknown quantity, but probably faithful.

Innocently enough, Cinderella next day requested privilege to visit Aunt Lou. Mrs. Murdock, already busy preparing for her own Sunday "bender," had half forgotten any cattleshow happenings.

"G'long," she said, "and stay to supper if so be she asks you. They ain't more'n enough cold corn beef for me and the girls so you'd have to make out with bread 'n milk. G'long. I can do the rest. And if Aunt Lou asks you, you've had a pretty easy day, Cinderell."

And so she had, since she had mopped no floors and hoed no garden, for once. Mrs. Murdock had merely expected her to do all the chores, rub out the family's white P-K shirts on the washboard, kill and dress numerous chickens for the luncheon she would not eat, abstract a watermelon from the Blanchard Bowles estate when no one was looking, and keep the children away from the bottled beer.

As has presumably been observed, Cinderella's strongest characteristics were an unreasoning love for her mother, a meek, yet enjoyable obedience to her demands. That mother had always had it in for Cinderella. Perhaps she owed the girl a grudge for injuring an otherwise flamboyantly asserted reputation. The vine needs the wall whereon to sustain itself, but the oak is irked by the parasite.

Aunt Lou was found presiding over an ungodly pile of boxes, that confessed themselves as hailing from Neuman, the Shoeman, Vera Bonnet's, and Cohen We Clothe the World Too Much for the Elephants. These beasts were pictured as a trademark, vainly endeavoring to dissever a skirt from its binding.

The first order was disquieting.

"There's a-plenty b'iling water in the kitchen tank. Go wash yourself good."

"'Tain't Sat'day night yet."

"Maybe so, but you do's your bid. I got a return check with this mess o'goods if it don't fit."

Cinderella emerged from the kitchen glowing red and rather damp about the edges.

"First," said Aunt Lou and produced fabulously beautiful undergarments all the holes embroidered and some run with pink ribbons, while the price tags announced they had let her in the sum of $1.98 at Smith & Wallace's bargain basement.

"For me?" bawled Cinderella. "Gollypeter, hoy d'ye get into 'em?"

"Considerable of a puzzle? Well, I surmise they pull over. And more shame to me that I've let you grow to a great wallaping girl like you be without learning how to wear things like other folks. Yes, the petticoat ties. And you hitch the bottom of the corset fust off. Now pull that shirt waist down in the behind so you don't get what the store lady called `married back.' Here, the skirt plaquet's just in the place where you suppose 'tain't. Now go look at yourself in the foreroom mirror. And if you should throw a fit fall sideways, for I don't think I could stand seven years' bad luck."

Cinderella came back almost decent looking, with the innocent observation, "Bet my ma is proud of me now, she is!"

Aunt Lou knew not there had been any active attack on her plan of an Anderson alliance, but she was sufficiently wary to say, when the girl prepared, an hour later, to lug her finery home, "Looky here, now, Cinderella, I'm giving you these in return for a promise. Don't show nothing to your ma till you have the rig on for Sunday. I want her to be surprised. No, she won't see the boxes. She's just gone down the road with the Hatches, behind old rackbones. Hyper along, Cinderella."

And Cinderella promised and hypered.

Sunday dawned, such a day as that on which romance was invented. Mrs. Murdock, Minnie, Bessie, Aggalena, marcelled or curled, according to age, starched and primped at all ages, sat out of doors awaiting the cart for the straw ride. They sat out of doors because it was so much cleaner and more comfortable than in. To them appears Cinderella.

"Ma, d'ye know me, ma? Near silk stockings, ma. And patent leathers is killing my feet. And a tunic, ma. And insertings and lace both on my petty, ma. And look at the dinky panties, ma, all sewed to the camysole, ma."

Mrs. Murdock went redder than her rouge, and goodness knows that supplied a sufficiently high color.

"Who—what—not Anderson?" she gurgled.

"Why, ma, don't take on so, ma. Aunt Lou, she gave 'em to me, she did."

"Your Aunt Lou? That stingy old maid, rolling in railroad shares and the best Cavendish from one year's end to another. And all she ever did for me was to put on this corrugated tin roof which nobody can't sleep under for drawing and holding the heat."

"Say," yelled Aggalena, a precocious production, Mrs. Murdock's last contribution to the world's population, "here's Swedish Anderson driving his ball-faced nag."

Mrs. Murdock was equal to the crisis, indeed, her evilly active brain enabled her to instantly connect effect and cause. Grabbing Cinderella by the arm she swept her into the house, moving the huge girl on the familiar principle whereby a fussy little tug is able to convoy seaward any leviathan of the deep.

"Take 'em off, quicker'n billy-be-damned," she hissed.

Half-sobbing in the excitement caused by she knew not exactly what offense, Cinderella obeyed. Mrs. Murdock started to undress at the same moment, ripping open the blouse on which Cinderella had so solidly set the buttons, tousling the skirt Cinderella had so laboriously ironed, trampling her petticoat and chemise into the dirt on the floor. Arrived at the foundation she proceeded to adorn herself with the finery of Aunt Lou's providing. The skirts were a trifle long, but she held them up majestically as she sallied forth, leaving the denuded Cinderella in the squalid room.

The straw ride party came along just then. She boosted Minnie, Bessie and Aggalena into its depths, then smiled sweetly to Anderson, made a couple of the gestures which had done great damage among males when she was 16, and climbed into the top buggy beside him.

"Get ap!" shouted the straw riders. Anderson's horse heard and was off; the noise of the big wagon just behind excited the well-fed animal to a run down the hill. Mrs. Murdock talked her sweetest, and there was a good twenty minutes during which her seatmate could not avoid listening. She had a reputation of always getting what she went after. Alas for Cinderella's chances!

The cavalcade tore past Aunt Lou's, and so the old woman, in a flat hat to honor the Sabbath, hobbled cross lots to find Cinderella, wearing her rags over nothing particular, sitting on the doorstone, purred over by sympathetic pussies, pecked at by ribald fowls, having her cry out.

"Chirk up, Cinderella," cried Aunt Lou. "Never mind losing your beau. There's as good fish in the sea—"

"I ain't cut up 'cause I didn't go a-r-r-riding, Aunt Lou. I stays to home most times. I don't care a hate about giggeting. It's ma. My ma. I've lost my ma."

"Lost your fiddlestick. If you wa'nt about quarter witted you'd know you lost her the very first minute she knew you was likely to be born!"

"M-marm?"

Aunt Lou lowered herself to the door sill and began to prepare a dipping stick. Suddenly Cinderella gave a final jab with her red knuckles, and stood up.

"Gawd, I'm well wamble-cropped," she cried, drearily. "I'm all alone. Maybe my ma did give me whatfor sometimes, but I thunked she loved me. Only Tuesday was four day ago didn't she take me to cattleshow and buy me a hot dawg 'thout my asking? Now I lost her. You done it for me, Aunt Lou, with them boughten belongings. I wisht you was down the well and a stone wall tumbled top of ye and a deaconed veal top o'that. Wisht you was out on a run tiddly o'ice in a boobyhut. Wisht you was treed by a b'ar on a brash branch of a daddock tree. Wisht—"

"Cinderella," interrupted the extensively becursed Aunt Lou, calmly removing her pith brush from her mouth, and using it as a pointer down the road, "ain't the least mit o'use your making such a katowse. Hullo, Mister Anderson. Miss Murdock's been waiting for ye."

"My name's Cinderella Soapman," cried the girl, defiantly. "It allus has been Cinderella Soapman and it always will be. I never had no father. I ain't got no mother. I'm only Cinderella Soapman and everybody points to her!"

As usual, Anderson was equal to the occasion.

"Pretty soon, M's Anderson. Get in. Get ap!"

They drove a matter of a mile before Cinderella's breast ceased to be heaved by surging sobs. Then he spoke again. "Got blue dishes. You like blue best?"

Cinderella's eye—the large, intelligent eye of the ox—turned to her lover with the bovine tenderness hitherto wasted on an unworthy object. His honest eyes of sky color spoke affection to the starved girl.

"Ya-as, blue's peartest," she said.

(*The National Amateur,* May 1919)

NOBODY HOME

The whole kit and b'iling had gone to the cattle show. Sol Russell, halting his little chunk in front of rising ground, decided that, taking it by and large, there was probably nobody home for all of five mile round. Then he cl'kd, thankful that he would get there, in spite of a late start, before early candle lighting.

The delay had been to "deacon" a calf.

Cutting a swathe that made pastured creatures pause in the business of life, which was masticating, and view him excitedly over the post and rider, Solomon turned up the pentway by Gill Nelson's. The wood colored house slept in the September sun, and probably Gill slept also—for the Harvest Moon time would mean late sittings with Gill.

The misshapen hoofs of the little chunk made such small noise on the lamb's-quarter and plantain carpeted road, that Sol could not help hearing the one sound that cut the noontime peace. A most uncomfortable groan, unmistakable, not to be ignored.

Naturally vaulting to the capsheaf of tragedy, Solomon fixed his mind on the cow. Turned into the orchard untimely, and suffering from too much apple juice, as like as not. Twisting the reins about the whipstock he clambered out of the buggy and put for the barn, when a view of bossy contentedly lowing in the yard showed him that guess had been not so bunkum. Then it must be the hens. Pip, probably, or the whites gone looney and so picking the blacks to death. Everything went slantindicular with Gill, and the girl herself wasn't more'n half-saved.

Even as he stooped to examine samples of the half-feathered fowls that were all over the place, a second groan proved that—of all things—the trouble was in the house itself! In the front room, where a flapping screen gave ingress to flies and egress this moment to a sidling and wild-eyed cat.

Summer sunshine warmed the tiny, picketed home-lot, on which the towering Balm o'Gilead tree cast small shade, but for a moment Solomon shivered, and the lot seemed like one in a graveyard, where grass grew in great lush clumps, under the protection of arbor vitae.

"Gill!" he called, licking his dry lips, and trying not to tremble in his throat, "Gill! where be ye, I say, where be ye?"

There was no answer but another groan, yet even that proved of trifling reassurance. Coming closer to the window Solomon peered into the twilight behind the ragged muslin curtain and inquired, "Don't you feel as well as usual today, Gill"

The query, which was almost tender (from Sol Russell) brought no definite reply. But Solomon Russell was not a fool, he put together tags of conversation overheard the last few months on church steps when meeting was letting out and surmised that even if one was an old bachelor one could understand a woman was needed, here, back o' the mountain, in a devil of a hurry.

And the whole kit and b'iling gone to cattle show!

At Slocumb's there was only the old yellow cat on the stoop, at Juliette Pinkney's a likely two-year-old had got out and was foundering itself with sweet corn, and the Perkins house presented a most inhospitable face, with a bull-dog to give it tongue.

So it had to be Mercy Bruill, though she was stone deaf in one ear and couldn't hear with t'other. Anyway, she was reputed to take it out in seeing and to see it all from her neat cottage tucked into the "V" of land so properly termed the Gore. Solomon snatched her from a good meal of victuals which included hot boiled dish, of which he would not have objected to partaking, though without vinegar, so exhausting had been the experience. Mercy did not want to go anywhere and leave her table in the floor, but he threw sunbonnet and shawl her way and tossed her into the buggy like a bag of cider apples. The horse hypered so eagerly back the pentway that, though gone an hour, the groan he met dovetailed perfectly to the one he had left.

Dumping Mercy in the wheeltrack and giving her a shove toward the door, he was off in a hurry around the mountain, well aware there would be hardly enough cattle show to pay for going. Mercy would certainly know what to do, he calculated. An old married widow woman she was, and all of her own in the grave-yard, too.

Public opinion was right. Mercy did take it out in seeing. She hadn't been up here back o' the mountain for a month of Sundays, since long before the abandoned house had been squatted in by Gill, who managed to come around the caretaker, and get it for a little less than nothing. Gill was a cute one, yet after all 'twasn't so much she diddled Hank Waterman out of. Place had been given over to Chuck Will's widow ever since the big drought summer. Advancing warily Mercy observed that since she had last been up there the sixteen double panes of the kitchen window had been reduced to ten above and seven below. The spaces were filled with old hats. She wondered where Gill had found so many old hats. Well, a likely number of young fellows had probably gone home hatless mornings about sun-up.

Mercy Bruill was pernicktiness personified. She had never entered such a looking kitchen in her life. In her wildest dreams—those she had after succotash and strawberry shortcake—she had never imagined one. And there was a smell; a very bad smell. The wood colored house rejoiced in running water, but in no way of stopping it. Something had bunged up the drain, the sink had overflowed, there was a pond in its vicinity, which dwindled off into puddles near the door, where the boards booped up into islands.

Mercy at once put down the disorder as due to this cause, and conceived the idea that she had been fetched to repair it. She could think of no cataclysm worse than a stopped spout, and would never have credited the fact that this had been thus for all of three weeks, since Gill had enjoyed a merry Sunday and emptied all the grease from a feast of pork chops where it would be most harmful.

Casting her white apron to the four winds Mercy shooed the chickens out and attacked the drain with vigor. Grabbing a kettle from the stove she bailed the mess into it with a rusty can, and then bethought herself of the supply and shut that off with a plug hastily constructed from a garment that depended from a chair back. As for the broom it was pretty far gone anyway, being indeed the one with which the abandoning owners had cleaned themselves out the year all the wells went dry. Mercy broke the handle short off and rammed it down the spout as far as the bend, wishing she had a bit of umbrella wire to complete the cure.

All the while the moans of Gill were, to the self-constituted plumber, as silence.

"Will, Will," called the voice from the front room, in the thrill, expressionless tone of the pain racked, "go get somebody to come.

Go ask old Hank Waterman 'f you don't want to. He was always kind o' good to me. And the broom. Some woman'll say I do' know how to keep house. Will, hlep me to get hold o' the broom."

And then, plucking at the ragged sheet which was her only coverlet, Gill fell a-wondering why she had not given the house at least a lick and a promise. Because she had been so languid after long days in the blueberry bush. More likely because she had been sleepy after long evenings dancing at trolley parks.

Trying to rise, her breath went for a space, and then she fell to longing for that garment hanging from a chair back in the kitchen.

"Right there," she babbled, as if the broken rocking chair was listening. "Course I can get to it. So often I've walked the five mile from the Depot and carried a crate o' chicks or a sak o' flour. Only three steps—mebbe four. I washed it good and there's lace on it. Only three-four steps."

Sometimes she stopped to moan, uninterrupted, and then resumed speech. The garment, she thought, had been brought, and she was putting it on. It was smothering her, she could not breathe through its folds, and she beat the air with her fists and gasped a half hour before the moment's semblance passed. And then the drawing of it down. God—would it never draw down? She was tired—she was never so tired before, not even after the two big days at the hop picking a year ago, when Will Glover first picked beside her, and the two had gone to a dance, with never a bit of sleep between.

Once more her cry went up for help. It seemed to Gill that there were sounds in the kitchen beyond the entry, through with the ringing in her ears she could not be sure. But on chance she called and again called—and every call was the equal of silence to Mercy Bruill.

The sun westered and the day drew on the chore time. Mercy, in the malodorous back yard, attacked the spout from the outside. The ground quaked beneath her feet with the results of 40 years' soaking in soapsuds, but Mrs. Bruill was not one to shrink from a task simply because it offered a few disagreeable features. It was all very well for Hank Waterman to give Gill Nelson this house, and perhaps keep her off the town, but she should certainly not be permitted to establish a plague spot and poison the whole mountain.

Mercy wearied herself in the clichy mud, and Gill wearied herself screaming for help and trying to get away from the irritating black curls of hair that were all over the pillow. She plucked them out by handfuls, she was doing this as Mercy Bruill started home-along. 'Twas just getting dark under the table. Mercy left the plumbing in a state of absolute perfection, and entertained no slightest inkling of the real reason for her abrupt introduction to Gill Nelson's kitchen, where she had enjoyed so extensive a vortex of housecleaning long foreign to her own over-scrubbed cottage.

It occurred to some returning merrymakers that the pentway was a short cut and it was getting full time to be home and feed the creatures. Gill was heard by more than one, and in due time a doctor entered the frowsy front room. He was a handsome man, who took two baths daily and was very particular about hygiene in the home. With him came Miss Twiss, one of those delightful district nurses who appear to have emerged from the laundry as Aphrodite from sea foam.

They entered at what proved to have been well-night the last moment of need.

"Convulsions," said the doctor, "I'm afraid we're too late."

The nurse, true to her instincts, even in a crisis, stood at the window manicuring her nails and hoping he'd operate. It would be instructive—and he did look so noble in white.

"But where's the old woman?" he muttered, peering about. "Never knew anything to happen on this mountain without an old woman. And they're clever as the devil, too. Usually give me cards and spades and beat me to it. Quick, Miss Twiss, the aromatic spirits of ammonia. She's going!"

But she lingered until the sun appeared next day, bold and brazen as Gill herself used to appear in the village after a night of riot in freight yard or livery stable. Lingered in agony—even Miss Twiss being thereby a trifle wrinkled in face and cap. Many households were disturbed, lights twinkled up and down the pent way, women escorted by their solemn-faced men folks hastened with offerings of blackberry cordial and tea made from yarrow and stories of the only method that saved a sister's life and now she's an old woman.

Only Mercy Bruill was in no way disturbed. She supplemented cold boiled dish with strong tea, then went to bed gloating, to wake at intervals and chuckle over the feats she had performed. So Solomon Russell found her, breakfasting on red flannel hash. Radiating geniality she stopped her meal, put her teeth in and began to talk.

"Done one good job of work up there back o' the bushes. Real likely job of work."

And so she had. That was the blunder of others being brought down the mountain now, in the undertaker's wagon.

(*The National Amateur*, July 1919)

TARTAR SAUCE

"Hell!" said Warner. Two hours had passed and he had taken no part in the conversation. This consisted entirely of remarks made by his partner, Lindour. Warner felt a right to figure, if only because the subject was his own raincoat.

It was always in the office. No use wearing it home, if it rained, because a fellow changed his clothes directly. And he'd be sure to forget to fetch it back. And he couldn't wear it to the office because it was always at the office, it was. So there you were and it was nobody's business.

As for lying top of the safe, wasn't it his safe as much as Lindour's, and didn't Lindour keep the hooks in their common locker stuffed up with his thin coat and his thicker coat and his real warm coat and his old coat and the coat he wore to luncheon when he expected to meet up with some fellow who went to school with him? Lindour contended the outside locker was good enough for an old raincoat, but it wasn't an old raincoat. Warner had hardly had it on during the four years he'd owned it, and from the outside locker any of the male help might borrow it, thus defeating the object of its possession—to always have a raincoat in the office.

Why, that correct article, Greeley the blond bookkeeper, newly hired at $15 and willing to take on all the work of an $18 bachelor girl in consideration of references waived, pricked up his respectable, pen-laden ears when he interrupted the conversation with checks to be signed. Warner knew well enough Greeley's second and third invasions, on flimsy pretexts, were simply to learn what were the chances of the coat's getting into the outside locker, whence maybe he might borrow it. Wherefore Warner, following his original observation, exclaimed with decision, "That coat stays right there until I say move it. See?"

Such bravery brought down another storm from Lindour, but Warner had the satisfaction of noting a decided change in the countenance of Mr. Bookkeeper Greeley. Warner's position in the house might be midway between chorus and whipping boy, but he could often get back at the help.

Because Warner exhibited so unusual an obstinacy, Lindour suddenly switched to Miss Wilmer, for no sooner did Warner hire most anybody, than Lindour began to devise schemes for getting rid of 'em.

"You like that sort o' thing, y' know, Warner. Me—I can't stand for it. Wasn't raised fussy. 'Course I pay no attention to how the help acts up, but the gosheternal meachin' gets on my nerves. Joe sweeps round her desk and not under. Sure he does. Sure they all do unless you give 'em hellfire 'n damnation today and the fear o' the Lord tomorrow."

"No lady's going to raise hell," observed Warner, in a conversational tone, as—having been a couple of hours in the place—he began to undress for work, hanging his coat on the back of the chair for buyers only, putting his cuffs into the basket marked "immediate," and coiling his collar about the loving cup which stood a monument to the firm's fifth milestone.

"Gotta come near it if she's to make any splash in this office," returned Lindour. "Looking's though you'd been shoved against green paint in white duck won't turn the trick. Going to let her go Sat'day."

And Warner didn't care a darn.

By Saturday Miss Wilmer, while enacting the violet by the mossy stone, had so ably demonstrated her ability to take Mr. Lindour's dictation, and to return his correspondence written out in finer language than he had hitherto caught himself using, that her stay was mentally extended for a fortnight. Her doom was fixed, however, on account of attire.

"Not only meaches, but dresses the part. Puts the whole shooting match on the bum," sneered Lindour. "Every girl child of 'em in white jumpers, and she in a what d'ye call 'em all blooey green, makes me think, Warner, that stationery drummer soaked onto you the summer I was laid up with shingles. On the 15th, 23 for her."

And Warner didn't mind a hoorah in hades.

On the 13th day Lindour went early home, and Warner, as did the first Christian martyrs, improved his brief liberty by playing tyrant.

"Tell Miss Wilmer to step this way," he roared when Joe condescended to answer the bell. Miss Wilmer stepped and he confronted her with, "Where does the `c' go in `peninsula'?"

He was neither ironical nor trying her out. It was a case similar to that of the other poor fool in "Erminie."

In return, he got a treat. Miss Wilmer, the worm, whose second name might have been Patience, who meekly accepted the scorn ensuant on disturbing the symmetry of an office otherwise dazzling as a collar and cuff advertisement; who involuntarily drifted to wall tables in restaurants and invariably moved up in street cars, lifted her eyes and shrivelled Mr. Warner in what he termed the once over. And he ducked. Forgetting she was the last hired and marked as first to be fired; that while she asked but $12 she had been beaten down to $10, that after tomorrow she would be on no payroll anywhere, he ducked. Failing to remember he was the great Warner, who did exactly as he pleased round the ranch when Lindour left him, and who up to the present had kept a raincoat untidily bundled above the safe, he ducked. Her thin lips said nothing, but her blue eyes spoke, in no uncertain manner. "What d'ye think I am," they asked, "that you can pull off a 5,000-word circular that must go to the printer's tomorrow, to ask a fool question about a fool word when Webster's is knocking your elbow?"

It in no way consoled him that in a moment her gaze dropped to its usual resting place midway between the shank and the ankle bone of her interlocutor, and that her lips saved his face by murmuring, "I think present-day authorities now favor the `su.'"

She left the room. She was going away altogether on the 15th.

And Warner now did care a darn and minded several hoorahs.

A $10 a week girl had made him duck, and he should never be happy until a like fate met up with Lindour.

But how to cajole that gentleman into letting her stay? And would it be necessary to give up in the matter of the raincoat?

Unknown wattses of expense were consumed while the janitor fidgeted in the ante-room before there was an inspiration sufficiently devilish. Indeed, Warner had arisen and reached to Lindour's special humidor when striking his arm on a particularly solid book it toppled and gave his toe a glorious thump.

"Good work!" he bellowed and hit the trail. The plan was fiendish.

The next day he was oracular to Lindour.

"About Miss Wilmer. I think she's a gal we better keep sticking around," he ventured, and kept on despite a discouraging, "Oh, you think!" from his partner. "Yes. Did quite some yesterday. Listen, Lindour."

"Well," growled the other, who preferred to do the talking himself even if it meant money out of pocket.

"You know the directory?"

"I know that mutt Johnson gets more money outer us for compiling every issue. Here's his next season's strike right now."

"Wouldn't it be bad to throw him a bluff we got others up our sleeve? Put on anyone at all for a few weeks. Say—the Wilmer person?"

"Fine 'n dandy!" grunted Lindour. "Don't deny she might file and do preliminary stunts. But what happens when your pet falls down?"

"She ain't no pet o' mine. And he'll be starved out and like's not come back at 1911's salary."

"Can't see it," chewed Lindour, and having thus put the kibosh on the plan, began to consider it as feasible. It was a darn shame, he couldn't have seen it first. The directory was his special job, and saving expenses had become his department, too, through much mulling thereon.

Cupidity got him, of course, and he decided to try it on. He could always blame Warner if Miss Wilmer failed to deliver the goods. Warner, in an attitude of watch, look and listen, in some dismay noted the calmness with which the girl accepted such petty obstacles as the darkest corner and a boy everlastingly too busy for fetching $5 in stamps from the post office.

"Gollypeter!" Lindour exclaimed, "I doff my tile to her as the champeen anti-kicker. She went to the post office in her lunch hour, and has rigged up a pane o' glass so her desk's pretty good."

"Way ahead of the printers, too," insinuated Warner, with genial Machiavellianism. "They was always crowding Johnson."

"Favorite scholar!" bleated the other, and went out to find another bramble for his employee's path.

The time came when Warner wondered, after all, if he was as cute and cunning as he had deemed himself. Miss Wilmer kept right on compiling an up-to-date volume from back number information, and never a word of complaint. Lindour was struck of a heap.

"Can't see how the book's coming out if she lets those comps continue to walk over her, but it keeps a-coming. No more idea of control than a fly. They load her up with proofs just when she's due to go home and 'stead o' raising a rough house she sets right down 'n reads 'em. And what have I seen her done? I even seen her on Tuesday owning up to the foreman she was in wrong."

"Maybe she was," was the illuminating contribution of Warner.

"Maybe? 'Course she was! 'Course Johnson was, twelve times out o' 'leven, but you'd never catch that guy taking it from a fore-man person."

The directory came out promptly thirty days late, which was strictly according to Hoyle. Miss Wilmer brought her first fruits to the private office in the shape of another such blue and gold volume as had knocked an idea into Warner's head via his foot. It contained 4,000 pages in nonp. black face, and an appendix of XIV pages done in illegible italic. Both men viewed her as they might a marine monstrosity.

"There's the only darn fool who'll ever read that thing through," was their simultaneous idea.

"Gentlemen," said she, "the directory."

They responded and manfully to the minstrel show opening.

"And I have a confession to make."

Both were all ears.

"It's perfectly awful! I—left out an advertisement."

Lindour experienced absolute bliss. Say it was a cheap $10 ad— or even an expensive $25 one—it would be money in. For of course she was blocked expecting a raise!

"As soon as I discovered it," she went on, "I wrote to the peo-ple—State Bank, Galliapolis, Ind.—and explained. The president re-plied, under his own hand, and said let the same matter go in the next number. He was intending to continue, but he doubles the space, so we need not alter the contract. Of course I said in my letter that I was new at the work, and that I should see my employers did not lose in the affair."

She laid the big book on the table, as a fond mother might aban-don an indulged child in a kindergarten, and went to her unduly tidy desk.

Lindour was quite solemn with joy. "After a while," he chanted, "we can spring a raise on her. Even at $1 she'll be all stuck up
with gratefulness."

"Bah!" intoned the disgusted Warner.

"Bully we got wise to her," Lindour rambled on. "'Member how
Johnson used to ram in an airily listen to the ten million or so kicks
we'd get every mail? He never acknowledged the corn."

"Piffle!" buzzed Warner.

Lindour became almost tearful. "And I'm the soft-hearted boob,"
he meandered on, "to say she's too good for this neck of the woods.
We'd never have known if the Galliapolis contract called for one
insertion or two so the bill was o.k.'d. Make that gal a traveling
salesman and I bet she wouldn't even know how to cook up a fancy
expense account. Say, this world's full o' people 'd just take advantage of a dove-eyed crinoline like that. She's liable to strike the
rocks if she ever leaves here and gets with ginks who ain't considerate. Wonder if she'd switch to a monthly salary? A 48-week year for
us. Think she's stand for it?"

Whereat Warner made the same remark with which this romance
opens, and ruined a perfectly good 25-cent crease by sitting down
minus prearrangement.

His comments were not illuminating to Lindour, but that individual always acted on his own volition. Therefore Miss Wilmer's
wage became payable every thirty days, and she accepted a new
set of pigeon holes with obvious personal pleasure, that contrasted
strongly with the bored acquiescence of Miss Marian Steele whenever
more comfortably backed stenographer's chairs broke the calm of the
private office. She did not even remark their not being varnished.

Warner began to abandon hope. He felt but pallid interest when
Lindour stated, because profits in other branches of the business
were unaccountably shrinking, that it was needful to do stunts with
the next directory.

"Want to tell her," communed he, "that we'd take it as a personal favor if she'd go light with corrections this issue. I gotta 'n idea
for using the old plates far's possible. 'Course if a concern's gone up
the spout we gotta go the expense of a new page, but if it's merely a
matter o' dead directorate or $600,000 off capital, letter go. S'pose
she'd stand for it if I put it to her as man to man?"

"Try it on," was Warner's best, a trifle tinged with anticipation. He watched results, from behind the door. She was agreeing, with her usual air of brisk intelligence united to an absolute docility.

Warner gave her up. Lindour returned singing a jubilate.

"Good gravy. Gawd, what a wife that girl'd make. For a guy like you, Warner," he added, suddenly reminded of an absolute lack of such submission in his own home circle. "For myself, I like 'em somewhat more tartar sauce. You cotton to it, y' know, Warner."

Warner began to believe, not that he did cotton to it, but that it was right there in the office, after all. Miss Wilmer made him duck? Impossible! He had never ducked and Miss Wilmer's eyes had never gotten above the baseboard.

Besides, he still kept a raincoat always in the office, folded untidily atop of the safe. While that symbol remained he was as one whose virtue had not departed.

Due time passed and another directory was launched upon a palpitating world that had been conned into signing advertising contracts by sweet-tongued sirens wearing blue serge suits and working on a 25 percent commission.

"Great little book," purred Lindour, admiringly. "Kills two birds 'th the one stone. Business brung in same's usual, printing bills cut in half, Next issue—"

"Next issue," yelled Warner, brisking up a bit, "has gotta be right up to date. Trifle harder on Miss Wilmer."

He brisked because hope lingers still within the human breast, as per the poets. But what was Lindour chattering about?

"She never has no grouch. Couldn't have put it over with Johnson."

Self congratulation reigned even after complaints began to tumble in. They were expected, up to a certain number; at length they reached such an enduring pile that even the optimistic Lindour got scared at the result of his own scheme.

"Two birds with one stone, indeed," he grumped, as if the novel comparison had been Warner's own. "We're the two old birds."

Think of swans singing before they die, think of those whom the gods love being made mad, think of the Scotch lassie fey ere she is stolen by the fairies, and you may understand slightly what inspiration did for Warner.

"Let's keep the watermillion juice outa our ears," he gleed to Warner. "I can't eat crow. How's your digestion?"

"Rotten," succincted Lindour. "I can, but I'll be darned if I will."

After a gloomy interval, "'Member Miss Wilmer's humble pie 'count of Galliapolis ad?"

Lindour bowed several times like an extremely weary idol. Warner wondered if he'd got to tell the blamed fool. Couldn't he take a hint even with a kick in it?

"I suppose we might get out some sort o' circular," he rambled, when, providentially, Lindour's constitutional objection to being jacketypinch took the words from Warner's mouth.

"My exact dope. Circular, sent every place, apologetic, et al, all due to green help, L. & W. grand ole firm, always deserved your confidence, dear sir, trust to retain it, that's the idea. Jump right onto it, Miss Steele."

"Miss Wilmer like it?" insinuated Warner.

"I guess yes. Why for nit?"

"Well, as she was the whole works it's some backhander at her."

"Aw, Warner, sometimes you make me sick. After all the ways she's accommodated, to think she might cut up ugly on a mere formality. Come to think of it, Miss Steele, you needn't stop whatever you're a-doing to do what I ast you a-tall. It's Miss Wilmer's department."

Warner it was who made a note of the requirements, on the blank page of one of the most profane of the complaints, and stabbed it to the Wilmer blotting pad with the handle of a mucilage brush. Then the partners went to the Exchange Club and lunched in absolute harmony, each being determined to force the check on the other. It rained, and Warner would have taken his raincoat—seeing it might be brough back again in an hour—only Lindour reminded him of it. Therefore he preferred a drenching.

Miss Wilmer came in from a very modest luncheon. Being exactly the sort of girl to put an orphan niece through college she allowed herself only a cup of chocolate and slice of health toast at noon. Her nerves were on the shake, for the last directory had been a dissatisfactory proposition, if only because of the number of errors one was compelled to "let slide." Seeing the note, she read it idly, and sketched the circular in pencil. Then, taking a new pen, prepared a fair copy.

After which came an attack of madness which the girls defined as "queerest ever." She crumpled the notes and cast them into the waste basket. Going to the locker she snatched forth hat and coat and put them on. She dragged a veil over her sharp nose and pinned it tightly as if 'twere never to come off. Turning, she saw the part-ners were back and lighting their cigars for an enjoyable half hour spent in breaking their own rule of positively no smoking on these premises.

Miss Wilmer processioned into their presence, ordered Miss Steele to stop exactly where she was, opened her mouth and para-lyzed the place.

Either she maintained a misery diary or had a marvelous memory.

Speaking in a strident, shrill monotone, that reached from end to end of the establishment, "You're a joke," quoth she. "Like a paper bag, blown up with air. I've heard such terms as `raised the efficiency' and `speeded up' on your tongue, but you don't know the first thing about what goes on under your nose. Item: Joe, for whose integrity I've heard you offer to go bail, has a skeleton key that unlocks even the stamp drawer and the humidor." (Joe swiftly retired into the freight elevator, where he ran himself up and down, in considerable trepidation, the rest of the afternoon.) "As for Miss Peggy Quincy, your Nestor, your Mentor," ("There," thinks Peg-gy, "she's settling with me for advice concerning shirt waists") "she does look, sure enough, like the sort of girl who goes to her hall room, sticks her feet up on the bed, and reads the *Transcript*. I go home and read the *Transcript*. Costs me 3 cents, it's a tragedy when one gets ahead of me. But Miss Quincy, it appears goes out of an evening. She is fond of a certain cafe—The Trowbridge—in spite of your saying no girl can keep a job here who is seen coming out of it! The last time Miss Quincy was there she partook of one olive from her escort's Martini, one slo gin highball, one quart of Muenchinger and one pousse cafe, of which the component parts were creme de rose, kummel, creme de menth and creme yvette. Owing to a Vow she did not drink a cocktail!" ("It's true," whispers Peggy. "Mealy-mouthed little devil. How did she get wise?") "There are others, too, worth Miss Quincy's companionship in your fine little corps. There's one I've heard mentioned as a sweet young thing—a corking good looker—went into a Rathskellar and by actual count drank seven gin fizzes, four Martinis and a Manhattan. She then asked for and obtained a week's leave, with full pay, on account of a sick mother. When she returned you gave her a raise. That same week I was expected to sit up nights with a couple bales of proofs. And I was told if I would come round so early as to walk up the nine flights, because the elevator wouldn't be running, a key should be made for me! Such a compliment! Then you thought there was still some energy left in me, so I heard a speech something like this, 'Miss Wilmer, if you will work a bit harder, and waste as little time as possible in eating, always taking meals at the quickest possible lunch, the firm will'—well, I was guessing at the reward, an honorarium, or staking me to a Niagara trip" (Miss Marian Steele enacted the galled jade successfully) "but the climax of this noble speech was 'the firm will appreciate it'."

She had more to say, but was brought to a quick pause by a peculiar noise. Warner chuckled. All this for Lindour. Why the man should feel raked fore and aft, given nine times nine with the cat, peppered, salted and served up to the queen's taste, left without a leg to stand on, knocked down, dragged out, tarred, feathered and rode in a cart. He, Warner, had ducked at a glance. He believed Lindour, thus riddled with heavy artillery, would never put on side again.

But now she was turning Warner way. That partner could not think, however, that she had a bit of ammunition left. If it was another look of scorn he was ready to meet—nay, welcome it. Her eyes were darned blue and thrilling, and with the element of surprise lacking he shouldn't duck. True enough, it was Warner to whom she addressed herself.

"Silly ass," she jeered. "Laugh if you like. It's you I mean. If that note had not been in your handwriting I should never have balked. Mr. Warner, let me convey to you a piece of knowledge which I accidentally acquired through use of the early key. There's a leak in this office, location near the bookkeeper's cage. You are missing money—not in large sums, but in mysterious manner. You likewise have found premature information as to plans in possession of business rivals."

Lindour resembled a frying fish, and Warner dropped his lower jaw and forgot to pick it up. They had been having just such annoying experiences, but by advice of a private detective, secretly called in and likewise consulted, had breathed no hint of suspicion. The sums taken had been small, indeed it was difficult to be sure if the financial confusion did not result from Greeley's bad bookkeeping. The leakage of plans was more important, and seemed to come even when the partners had not confided the matter to dictation, but left original notes locked in the safe.

Miss Wilmer dragged on a pair of shabby gloves, then spoke again. "Mr. Warner, for your information, not even in the dark ages was peninsula spelled with a 'c.' And not even in this office should you be allowed to keep your coat atop of the safe." She left the place so rapidly she failed to collect the near-month's pay that was her due. She wanted to get away even more quickly, but Mr. Greeley, the blond bookkeeper, was in the elevator as she drew near, and induced the boy to run 'er down without waiting. He was in haste, he said, to get to the bank.

Lindour, confronted with the prospect of rehiring Johnson, at a probable advance, could only taunt Warner.

"Nothing none of us did struck 12," he recorded, "but she had it in for you special. Zowie, what a bawling out! And she's correct as to the coat. No place at all for—Gawsh, what's this?"

Removing the untidy wad of Mackintosh disclosed a hole, and it presently developed that some scientific devil had eaten a chunk from the top of the safe, presumably employing a corrosive acid. Thus it had been possible to "milk" the contents with very little danger of detection. Who was to blame? Well, Mr. Greeley, the eminently correct (and blond) bookkeeper, never returned, and his self-acknowledged, highly respectable address confessed to never having known him. The affair was quite easily understood, even though Messrs. Lindour and Warner did not remember "Greeley's" coming in with checks to be signed, on that faraway day of the great raincoat battle.

To both partners it seemed absolutely necessary the Wilmer girl should be made to return. Their joint motives were—1 percent gratitude, 5 percent admiration for her as a darn smart article, and 94 percent hatred of Johnson. Warner's personal proportion might be distributable differently. While Lindour was getting a line on "W" in the 'phone book, Warner was taking the ink-splashed photograph of the long-departed Mrs. Warner from behind his blotter and thrusting it into the drawer where he kept cigar bands and similar objects of great value.

"To think of the two of us both thinking that peninsula business all this time," he mooned. "Gosh, I guess I like 'em tartar sauce, too."

(*The Californian,* Winter 1936)

THUMBS

Electa Alden taught the summer school that season Edmund Jones started digging. It was on the road to nowhere. Naturally the brisk young schoolma'am strolled that way in the nooning.

Edmund, mild of speech and fair of face, wanted to know what she thought of the location.

"Think it's the last place to set a house," she answered with a promptness that rather took him by surprise. "Right under the hill. You can't see nothing."

Edmund expressed an opinion that there wasn't much to see.

"My eye 'n Betty Martin!" The schoolma'am's colloquialisms would have amazed those objects (on Dinner Rock) to whom she was a precept and example. "Of course there's nothing down this grass grown lane. But there's a sight o' passing on the other road."

And she pointed to the brow of the hill, whence came the com-bined creaking, bellowing (bovine) and bawling (human) that told of a perambulating ox team.

Edmund offered, placidly, a remark to the effect that nobody lived on that road he took any interest in. He looked hard at Electa as he said this, and Electa blushed. She came every morning from the Gore, a good five miles in another direction.

"Well," she said rallying her wit, "I guess it's as good as most trav-eled roads. Starts at the school house and ends in the graveyard."

From ten miles off the whistle at the watershops could be heard bleating a warning of one o'clock. Edmund took up a spade and set a good example to his workmen, who emerged from the bushes with dinner pails turned bottom up. Electa whirled about, vexed that he should be so set in his own way, after her lucid explanation.

"Your poor wife," she exclaimed, "how I'm going to pity her. Never see anything. S'pose you think she'll be proper grateful when you come to your victuals and tell her all that's going on."

Edmund dropped the spade and replaced its insensate handle with the school mistress' fair hand, while requesting her to tell how in tunket he was going to get to know so much.

"Oh, you'll be cultivating that field on the other road, where the house ought to be. Let me go. It's more'n time school took up."

He did let her go, but they had other spirited dialogues, and when the house was nearing completion he induced her to enter, one noon, after the men had taken a half day off for camp meeting.

She admired the elegance of front and back parlors, with folding doors, and thought the kitchen well enough, if small. Then she bounced into a trifling apartment some eight and a half feet each way, and remarked, "Well, just like a man. Rosebud pattern on the butt'ry walls, and not a sign of a shelf."

Whereat he said it wasn't the butt'ry. It was his aim to make a butt'ry from a slice behind the chimney.

"Pshaw, you don't want a butt'ry there. 'Twill be so hot in summer all the milk'll sour."

In Edmund's opinion it would be master warm in winter, then. And he never could abide putting his teeth in frozen victuals.

"But if this isn't the butt'ry what is it?"

It was, he informed her, his bed room.

Electa left without a word. She leaned from the window and made another discovery. One wall was against the earth. It was the sort of a room known as "underground." Such rooms were very good to keep potatoes in, or vinegar barrels; anything, in short, improved by dampness. Poor Edmund, trying to sleep there. It was a pity he wasn't engaged to some sensible girl who would teach him better.

"Let's go up above," said she. "I want something sightly."

He helped her up the unbalustered stairs and she breathed again. There were two beautiful second story rooms, one giving more than a glimpse of the other road. Electa pretended to wonder which the coming Mrs. Jones would choose. She knew well enough where her own choice lay.

Time passed, chestnuts fell where blossomed posies, the summer school was over, and Miss Electa Alden, with parents, was driving over to see Mr. Edmund Jones' new house. Mr. Alden was assessor, he journeyed in the way of duty. His wife came to hold the horse. Miss Electa stuck herself in bodkin, probably to see what the underground had turned out.

Edmund was progressing. He had daubed a great deal of varnish over the finely grained butternut wood of the doors, had laid a two-ply ingrain carpet on the parlors, and hung up some beautiful pictures. One was a "Faith Hope and Charity" nearly life size; another a "Horace Greeley," head and shoulders; a third showed the "Courtship of Washington," with the Custis children assisting. All premiums with the New York *Tribune*, which showed where Edmund stood.

"And now," said the older lady, who wasn't holding the horse because Edmund had put it into the new barn where it was eating its head off, "we want to see the kitchen."

It was shown, also the bedroom. The snuggest little bedroom.

They looked in. Impossible to do more, the four poster filled it. Mr. Alden presumed the bed was first set up and then the house built around it. His wife slipped a housewifely hand between the sheets and shuddered, At the same moment the girl stooped and applied a dainty finger nail to a corner of rosebud paper nigh the mopboard. It was quite ready to peel.

The women exchanged words while the men went down cellar.

"Damp," said Mrs. Alden.

"Of course," said Electa. "It's an underground."

Her mother shook her head. "We must get along," she observed. "It's quite a ways home. I wonder what's keeping your father?"

Mr. Alden was always Electa's father when things threatened to go wrong. Other times, simply "he."

"Come up stairs first, mother," said Electa, leading the way.

"Oh, this is really first class," was the exclamation when the sunny prospect burst upon her. "Go right down and say he must come up."

Mr. Alden having departed to tear the horse from the oat bin, Electa and Edmund were left alone in the front parlor.

Edmund wanted to know how she liked the house, now it was most done.

"Real comfortable and pretty," said Electa, forgetting the kitchen and bedroom and thinking busily of those above stairs.

The parlors, according to his calculations, would accommodate forty people.

Electa raised her eyebrows. Edmund explained that he didn't mean seated. He couldn't sit but fifteen, but he could stand up pretty nigh fifty.

"Oh, a housewarming?"

No, a marrying was what he considered.

"Picked out a lone orphan?" asked Electa, real sarcastic. "Must of. Any other girl'd insist on the wedding party at her own house."

He supposed, casually, Electa Alden wouldn't think of it for a minute.

"Wedding anywhere but the parlor I was courted in? I should say not."

Edmund walked to Washington and hung him straighter in his frame. Then he wanted to know if she didn't like him well enough. Thus brought to bay Electa beat furiously on the new in-grain carpet with her gaitered foot.

"Of course I like you, Ned Jones," she boohooed, "but you're so exasperating."

He essayed to wipe her eyes on his bandanna, and just then Mr. and Mrs. Alden looked in from the buggy, which they halted by the side window. Edmund took his mother's "clasped-hand" ring from his little finger and slipped it on the third finger of Electa's left hand. Then he asked Mrs. Alden to tell him if the ceremony would look prettier before the mantel shelf or under the arch dividing the rooms?

Electa's chin dropped, but she wasn't equal to starting a quarrel right in front of her parents. Dissembling anger at being so neatly outwitted she allowed herself to be handed buggyward by her future husband.

Her parents were pleased at the turn of affairs.

"A real likely young man," said Mrs. Alden. "And of course you will have him finish off those upstairs bedrooms."

"Of course," said Electa stoutly.

He did it without being compelled. The wedding guests found four posters in both apartments, with bureaus and looking glasses quite complete. Electa hung her wedding finery in the wardrobe of the one overlooking the other road. It would be right at hand when she returned from the bridal journey.

The trip lasted a week, Electa 'peared out bride the next Sunday. She wore a new silk, made with a considerable cooperage, and a mantellette bought with her husband's money at Molyneaux &

Bell's in New York city. It was too bad that the minister wasted a new sermon on an audience so largely inattentive.

Electa kept a stiff upper lip, but at nooning got her mother into the graveyard and confessed to being perfectly miserable.

"My dear—I'm sure he's not stingy. This lovely new cape. And he promised to be a good provider—"

"Oh—the house is full of all kinds of sugar. But—I've got to sleep in that underground bedroom."

Mrs. Alden didn't think much of it, but there were ways of getting round husbands—

"Not round Ned. He won't argue and he won't get mad and he won't give in. Last night's a sample. Kept a rousing fire all evening, and when bedtime came said his limb was aching him pretty bad where he hurt it at the raising. When I mentioned a soapstone said he was real sorry but he'd forgotten to provide one. So kitchen bedroom 'twas, though a great piece of paper's loose now and been put up with tacks."

Mrs. Alden chewed meeting seed all the afternoon and was so excessively worried that she even confided in him.

"I declare," she remarked, "I most wish you'd put your foot down against 'Lecta marrying into the Joneses. That young man is sot as a barn."

"Knew it all along," replied the assessor. "Folds his fist over his thumb."

Mrs. Alden shivered. She knew well enough what that meant. It would be dreadful if she that was Electa Alden didn't get along with her husband. And it would be equally as bad if that damp room sent Electa into consumption.

Her health was not affected, probably because she continued to suffer mental martyrdom. Hot nights she lay listening to flies bobbing against the ceiling, wishing for the moonlit airiness of those rooms upstairs. And in winter mornings the room became, to her fancy, a cavern. For she liked to see the sky reddening behind tall trees when she was dressing.

It was such an unhandy place, too, to take care of. She used to shake her fist when she scrooged between the bedstead and wall to whop the tick, and her principles were never satisfied with the way she had to clean the room, from out in the kitchen, just banging round a long-handled mop. And there was something ridiculous in walking over a bed before one could draw a curtain.

For a man whose taste in light victuals was scrupulously pampered, whose shirt bosoms were ironed to an immaculate gloss, and who never heard a cross word at home, Edmund Jones was perhaps the best hated man in town. Electa lived only in hope of things sometime taking a turn. Occasionally her fancy sent Edmund away on a long trip, when he returned he sought the kitchen bedroom and found, that like translated Enoch it was not. She had had it filled with stones and dirt and plastered up. She lay patient, with the hue of death stealing o'er her faded cheek. Edmund, stung by the doctor's warnings, suddenly seized and carried her up to the sunny forechamber, shedding tears of contrition.

Electa was set free in a way of which she had seldom dared let herself dream. Edmund died one winter, when his rheumatism attacked the heart. He passed away in the underground bedroom. The rosebud paper hung in wrinkles on the damp plaster; and the mourners, squeezing about the walls, wept because Edmund was going, also because their feet ached them and there wasn't room to sit down comfortably at their grief. Even the undertaker complained of contracted space. Electa felt grim pleasure in hearing his remarks from the back parlor, where she was supposed to be immured with sorrow and the dressmaker.

Mr. and Mrs. Alden were no more, so Electa took her young sister's youngest daughter Azubah to live out the winter with her.

Azubah, like most young persons, took delight in change for its own sweet sake. The beau she might get while walking on the other road was perhaps not half the catch she had left at the Gore, but he was at least different. Her aunt's house might be the abode of grief, but it was gay to be there because to be there was being gone a-visiting.

"If I was you, Aunt 'Lecty," she advised, "I'd out the seraphine t'other way round, and I'd hang Evangeline where Horace Greeley is, and I'd eat in the sitting room, and take the parlor curtains for the best chamber, and as for the underground bedroom—"

"Well?"

"I'd have the feathers off and see what the floor's like for once in forty years."

Electa felt so too, and the bed was denuded to its cording, then the cording became a length of clothes line, and the posts and cross pieces turned to so many bits of lumber up garret. After which the women yanked the rosebuds from the wall, took the window curtain for a duster and went upstairs feeling the day was well spent.

The widow did not sleep very well, but of course that was because she was over tired. And the moon at the full, too. Yet Azubah complimented her on good looks in the morning. "You're waked up, somehow," she said, "you act 's if you'd begun to live again."

Azubah meant that her aunt was recovering from the first poignancy of grief, but Electa wondered if she had ever lived—her own life—up to then? Edmund had been an awful good man, but it was always his rule. He had cheerfully given her everything he wanted himself.

Now—now—the ideas that crowded on her were intoxicating. Suppose she abandoned this house, as she had abandoned the underground room, and built a new dwelling on the other road? Suppose she stopped calling every cat, whatever the sex, by the generic term of "Rose"? Suppose she ordered turnips planted where onions had always been?

Not being used to intoxication in any form she soon sobered down and decided she would be contented with abandoning the underground bedroom. That was sufficient for the time. It stood for all the rest.

She came to this conclusion just as she folded up the last of the socks Edmund would never need again. Because she was glad he had died and given her her liberty it seemed a matter of justice not to let up on his clothes until they were in perfect order. This being accomplished she went up garret to hunt for something to piece.

It was hot up there under the sunbaked shingles, Electa sat on the crossbeam of the old bed and fanned herself. She guessed she'd have a good housecleaning there when the spring was a little more advanced. Lots of truck Edmund had put away, about which she knew nothing. For instance, what was that roll over behind the front room chimney, on the part where no floor boards were laid? She nipped along the path of plank, and snatched the roll that had been carefully balanced on the lath and plaster.

Wall paper, any quantity of it, carefully wrapped. Lettered in Edmund's hand. "Roses for our room. 1879-1919."

1879—why, that was the year the house had been built. 1919— what did Edmund mean by 1919? It was 1919 now. Unless—oh, Ned. She really believed he meant this to have been hung this very year on the bedroom walls. Forty years married—an anniversary. She had asked him time and again to put on new paper, and he never would—he, so particular about looks, she'd often wondered. Poor Edmund, taken out of the house he had built and loved and left all alone in that graveyard where the other road brought up.

He was a most awful set man, Edmund was; he liked to have his own way, and he liked things always the same way. For herself—she looked down. She was sitting with both thumbs firmly gripped by her heavily veined fists.

"Heavens to Betsey," she exclaimed. "I'm exactly that way my-self. Now however did I get so? Has it come from living forty year with a sot man?"

She couldn't tell exactly, but she went down and told Azubah she was going to new paper the kitchen bedroom. No, not pine cones on the wall, or a stripe even if it would make the ceiling seem fur-ther off. She had some rosebuds. Yes, very much like the old ones.

Azubah grabbed the excuse of paperhangers being round to go a-visiting her sister, whose family had recently been added to. It wouldn't be as care-free as here, with a funeral lately over and no man to cook for, but at least it would be a change, and beaux were everywhere.

When she got tired of it over there and came back she found her Aunt Electa had gone to sleeping among the rosebuds.

"It's well enough upstairs, but that eternal passing, on the other road, is awful disturbing," confessed the relict of the late Edmund Jones, "and then when you've slept forty year in a room it gets to seem the only one you rest good in."

Azubah voiced a hope she'd never have to live forty years in any one house. And if cruel fate did prevent a person from up stakes and moving, at least one might switch beds.

As for that underground bedroom, wasn't it infamous through-out the family as dark, damp, unhealthy, unhandy, cold and hot at wrong times, airless?

"To go into it now—it's beyond me. Why, I thought you could do as you liked?"

"I can," said Electa, short as piecrust. "I've found out that's what I like."

And again fisted her thumbs.

(*The Californian,* Autumn 1937)

DEAD HOUSES

Miss Bachelor sits on her piazza and worries about the neighbors. They absolutely refuse to worry about themselves, but keep right on living high under inherited mortgages, selling slices of whatever the mortgage doesn't blanket, and drawing one hundred dollars principal from the savings bank without even considering whether or not there is a dividend due next month.

"Touching the principal" was once one of those things native born New Englanders did not do, but nowadays only Miss Bachelor observes it as a rule. Even I have used up the twelve hundred dollars from the sale of the Hathaway place. But then I had the excuse of Sallie's—that is, my mother's—last sickness and funeral. And no memorial yet to my father who passed away in 1875; though I did send for circulars and carefully considered pink granite in comparison with a native boulder and riveted bronze plate. My mother's remains were cremated, at her earnest desire. She wished, too, that they might be scattered under a rose bush. Some day I may get round to it....

Miss Bachelor acquired the worrying habit with the property from her aunt and uncle. She has told me how they used to look, every winter morning, when she wasn't more than fourteen, for signs of smoke from the Edmands house. I judge this was one of those story and a half affairs, with front door on one side, large parlour, kitchen in ell, bedroom downstairs choked to repletion with one bed; two rooms upstairs, fore one finished off. The Edmandses must have cultivated a flower garden, for the cellar hole is now a perfect mass of bloom. Fleur-de-lis in the spring, and forsythia, snowballs, flowering almond; then petunias of every hue, self-seeding from year to year; in August a tangle of hollyhocks, wisteria in the second flowering and Bouncing Bet, not yet overpowered by wild grapes or bittersweet. Huge lilacs and syringa bushes waste sweets in May, when the straggling grass is gay with pansies that are not yet quite violets, and fragrant with lilies of the valley.

There is no possible way of finding out what kind of folks were Birdie Edmands' forbears. Judging from the worst of them, because of the foolish "Birdie," one must still reflect that she probably bush-

eled the name over herself. Didn't my mother change austere "Sarah" into frolicsome "Sallie"? Girls never had latchkeys then, or
parked their stays, but they did as they liked with their names,
achieving an "ie" when possible. One reckons on those forbears
being thrifty, since the property passed to Birdie unencumbered.
Birdie was a woman of fifty-five when she came to dwell in sight of
the Bachelor mansion. She had been married, but didn't live with
her husband. She had a daughter, who had been brought up by
"his folks" down Philadelphia way. Birdie was a harridan, her face
looked like leather, her neck was all strings not tightly hitched in
place, like a worn-out violin. Her hair was a wig, but she refused
to wear caps. Earrings that weighed a ton, pulling her lobes all out
of place, the piercings regular gashes. Stockings not well gartered
(they thought a lot of that in those days) and funny clothes.

She took the house and sent for her brother. He was her husband's brother and scandal ensued, though not immediately, because he was a school teacher. According to legend a fine upstanding
man. Knew Greek and Latin perfectly and had cyphered through
all the arithmetics. Took the West Holly school several winters and
held it through the term easy as old Tilly. He also had been unhappily married and was supposed to have endowed his wife with
all he possessed before he came to batten on West Holly and his
sister-in-law.

One has to imagine the degringolade. They had entirely gone
to bad when Edna Bachelor came to West Holly from Wisconsin
sometime in the '80s. I presume that at first Birdie got him a seven
o'clock breakfast of coffee and griddlecakes before he trudged the
mile and a half to the school which Miss Bachelor afterward taught
with such success. At night Birdie would have a good supper, with
picked up salt fish and potatoes, or ham and eggs, and apple pie to
follow. What Birdie had done to earn a living in the great world
I don't know, because Miss Bachelor doesn't know. Probably she
worked in a factory, because she dipped snuff. But legend says she
was able to cook—after a fashion.

First she would come to cutting out the pie. No time to make a
pie, because all the afternoon she was lost in dreams. Let him eat a
raw apple. "An apple a day keeps the doctor away." Quote it to
him. Just for this her brother-in-law would decline to pay his board

money. And Birdie, too inert to fight for her own, would clap on a mortgage rather than ask him for it.

The mortgager was Miss Bachelor's uncle, Jasper Bachelor. Tight-fisted odd fellow, yet always ready to lend anybody he knew something on anything. His character exemplified by his being exceedingly conservative, yet his trousers always improperly buttoned.

By and by the man was no longer asked to take the winter school. He sat at home and read old books. He became a miser. His tendency to being slightly near was approved at first, thrift being considered a pretty good thing, but in the end he carried it too far. Even his sister-in-law considered that he carried it too far, using beef that must be left in the swift flowing brook twenty-four hours before boiling; buying every diseased sheep and every fowl that keeled over from unexplained pip. Perhaps people in cities ate such carrion, but the average inhabitant of West Holly was fussy and didn't approve of even bob veal.

He'd steal, too, would that formerly moral schoolmaster. Miss Bachelor's uncle caught him more than once at the Bachelor pork barrel.

Before sinking into final inertia one desperate attempt was made to win back fortune by boarding town poor. To its everlasting disgrace Holly was one of the last towns that gave up farming out its paupers. Birdie and her brother-in-law took an old woman who wasn't quite right in her head. They curled her hair, painted her face and dressed her in fancy calico with ribbons. When drunken blatherskites came along the road from the Ramson quarries Nance was pushed out of the front window and taught to lisp ribald songs or to simper invitations to stop and bait.

There was always rum in the cellar; when the poor fools were sufficiently stupid they were left alone with Nance, who was supposed to rob them of all that was left. Business well designed, but not always well paid. Sometimes Nance fell in love with a pretty boy, and helped him to hide his money until he could sober up and sneak off. Beaten with sticks she would wimper for days, so that no bully, however far gone in liquor, could find her congenial for a spree. Tramps, lacking everything except vermin, stormed the house and had their will of all therein, from pantry to spare bed. Nance died. Preparation for the grave showed her to be a mass of disease, probably of long standing. Waves of horror started at the house on the byroad and extended even to Faculty Street, where the Academy professors lived. Pious matrons licked their lips and sent the children out of the room till they finished swapping remarks—"She sat in one armchair a month without getting up"—"Light minded, even a dying. Let any old tramp pull her about and giggled fit to kill."

—"A burning shame to allow such goings on. Selectmen deserve to be turned out of office."

They were. The new board refused Birdie and her brother-in-law another pauper, thereby depriving them of any visible means of support. Summers they secured a lean living by picking berries, boiling greens, and surreptitiously milking neighbors' cows at pasture. Winters they hived in, a pile of potatoes in one corner, of windfall apples in another; mice busily weaving in and out of each. Come spring the two emerged more emaciated than before, more fantastic in distorted features, more determined never to do a stroke of work.

There was scant sympathy for the pair in West Holly. Ruthless logic told other men and women that but for the saving grace of labour they might be quite as miserable. They had sweated in hayfields, and grown rheumatic in weeding dew-wet gardens; and sat up nights with sick calves, had planned to make the black cow's coming in match the red cow's going dry, so as to keep up the supply of butter that was turned for sugar and flour at Holly Depot. No reason why Birdie and her brother-in-law should not have done the same. Not a physical disability, so far as anyone could see. Started with a farm as good as most and better than some. Education, too, that should have kept him, at least, from evil ways. Of course nobody'd really see them starve, but once you began taking them things they'd never scratch round at all.

Second growth birch now encompassed the house, and lilac bushes grew to the eaves. The chimney alone was visible, and that only from the garret window of the Bachelor mansion. Edna Bachelor, vigorous fourteen-year-older, had come to visit her aunt and uncle for a few weeks. She has remained over forty years. She had then, of course, no slightest idea of what lay before her. Daily, as she climbed the garret stairs and yelled to Aunt Ruby, "Yes, I see smoke," she thought of her home in Wisconsin, where the land was neatly divided into quarter sections, and one might walk in comfort for miles on stout fences.

The crooked roads, the piles of uncemented rocks termed "walls" with untidy bush-filled corners, the old wood-coloured houses like that at the chimney of which she dutifully spied—how she despised them! Her father and mother had grown up in next town to Holly, had married there and accumulated all their family except Edna before they went away. But they had gone, and to the great middle west, where there were deer and real Indians and acres of fertile soil, perfectly flat and glowing with the most exquisite blossoms.

Where people, too, were not so queer as in Massachusetts. Edna had never known any able bodied adults who had lost their grip, like the woman and her brother-in-law, about whom she heard so much that she was consumed with curiosity to see them, and hoped daily that a dead chimney would make reason for a family visit.

Even Great-Aunt Sylvy, in the Bachelor "other part," didn't set down to her daily deception without being relieved as to Birdie and her brother-in-law. Then grunting, "Well, s'long's they've got a fire...." she would grab her pack of cards from a hiding place ingeniously contrived back of the endpapers in an ancient Bible, and seat herself to cut-throat euchre with whoever could spare an hour for play. This feverish pursuit of dissipation ended only with the arrival of darkness and the threatened arrival of Great-Uncle Siah, Great-Aunt Sylvy's husband. He always spent his winters chopping off; he would as soon have had vipers in the house as a pack of cards. Half wakened from her gambler's dream, Sylvy descended to the cellar, armed with a hatchet, and chopped off a section from one of the many chicken pies frozen on the hand-shelf. While this melted in a spider a dozen huge potatoes were flung in the oven, and the fire brisked up with a handful of chips. By virtue of which energy Sylvy felt perfectly justified in despising Birdie and her brother-in-law.

Miss Bachelor tells this sordid tale to me, as we rumple our slightly modish gingham dresses in hammocks on the piazza, but I seem to have most of it tucked away in child memories. My grandmother wouldn't have much to tell when my mother and I made our summer visits the other side of Holly Mountain. A fortnight's steady talking would exhaust our folks and even the people of Back of the Mountain, which grandmother invariably misnamed Back of the Bushes. She never thought much of the people Back of the Bushes. They might have bigger farms than any on the Mountain, and redder barns, but she didn't think much of them. They held a Christmas tree in the Methodist Church every year and gave the men folks present of overalls and jumpers. Jasper and Ruby Bachelor were my grandmother's first cousins, as well as first cousins to each other. She didn't think much of them, especially she didn't think much of Ruby, who couldn't get anyone to marry but a first cousin; and then got a hired woman to do her housework while she rode round with her husband helping him fool greenhorns in horsetrades. Grandmother occasionally condescended to visit these relatives, and related with horror the order of their household, whereby help, family and company sat hugger-mugger at the same table. Grandmother's seat, the one time she stayed to dinner, was next to a great big nigger! She had a silver fork to eat with, but all the same she felt insulted.

Somewhere in her story of Back of the Mountain there was sure to be mention of Birdie and her brother-in-law. With the usual child's propensity to concentrate interest on a detail, I was struck with the hiving in, the entire living in a single room. I knew how houses went to pieces; several were doing it right on Holly Mountain. Bricks flew off the chimney, so that it was all jagged as looked at against the sky. People talked about borrowing a ladder and driving over to Eastfield for some mortar and pointing it up, but it was too much work after all and never got done. The shingles on the north side rotted, the roof leaked in a dozen places. There were old pans all over the garret floor to save the chamber ceilings, but after a while the pans leaked too. Well, the chamber windows got blown in by winter storms and cracked by hail; and anyway glass doesn't stay set without puttying up every three or four years.

Ceilings sagged, wall paper came off, lath showed its form behind plaster as ribs under the skin of a consumptive. Underpining bulged, and the parlour floor was unsafe to walk on. At any rate, why keep up a great lot of fires when there had to be one always in the kitchen?

Just such a house-death was consummating right under my grandmother's nose on the Mountain which so set itself above Back of Itself. Hathaway's house stood about the length of a loud shout from the house which my grandfather, Robert Shield, built for himself on the Mountain road when my mother Sallie Shield was about six years old. It hadn't always been the Hathaway house; it dated way back in the last part of the eighteenth century, when they piled up an immense chimney of field stone and huddled a house around it. There were two downstairs bedrooms so small that one stepped directly onto the bed from the next room; there was a flight of nearly perpendicular stairs, there was a north room, and a south room with a south door, and a middle room of no possible use except to go through. Upstairs the eaves reached the floor on two sides, and each pair of large windows was flanked by little square windows of four panes. These lighted rooms so low that no adult could stand up in them, therefore they were inhabited by the children, and even the children, after getting to be eight or ten, had to go crouching to bed, in the attitude of first class conspirators bent on vengeance.

Tradition said the house had once been white with green blinds. After I came to know it the colour was that silvery grey peculiar to wood that has been long exposed to wind and weather. There were no blinds. I suppose the Hathaways burned the blinds up before starting on the fence rails. Grandmother never liked the house. She complained that it was "stuck in her own porridge dish." The only view from Robert Shield's was to the north, and it's a fact that one sees the Hathaway house first, before the winding Chicopee and the building on Mount Tom with window panes reflecting light like diamonds.

Owing to a misunderstanding of the soil Robert Shield was obliged to dig his cellar quite up to the northern—that is, the Hathaway—line. Everywhere else along the forty-rod road front was a swale or ledge. Grandmother considered it disgusting to spit out of her bedroom window on to her neighbor's land. She didn't see John Hathaway in the future, constantly coming hard up to Robert Shield and selling a strip of real estate, so that long before the death of anyone concerned the line would have moved up to Hathaway's south door.

Before the Hathaways there was Joseph Burlingame, and before that Benammi Peters. Benammi was not exactly a shining light, though he did live on the Mountain, and not back of it. He sold

Robert Shield a farm without mentioning an ancient widow's dower which clouded the title, and which Robert was called upon to pay after he had finished building his house. Benammi also kept town paupers; he put up a shackly ell to keep them in. He was quite a moral man, so far as the female paupers were concerned, but he got into trouble through running George Reynolds five miles a day after a buggy hitched to a fast horse. The reason was laudable, to stop George from having fits, but it was not a true remedy. George continued to have fits, but Benammi did not continue to have George. That ell was never used again except as a catchall for the succeeding owners. In 1905 I had it torn down.

Both house and farm were in the best of condition when John Hathaway paid a fancy price for the place in the days of farmland boom after the Civil War. How gladly he turned his back on the paltry ten acres and rickety house which his father had left him. That estate was too small for a farm and located too far from the city of Eastfield to ever become a part of the settled district. The fool that bought it from John Hathaway thought that sometime it would be cut up into lots. John Hathaway thought he knew better!

Of course John Hathaway was wrong, and later realisation of his faulty judgment was his tragedy.

At first, though, all went well on the Mountain. Burlingame stock, acquired with the farm, was strong and fertile. Burlingame land produced big crops. The Burlingame house had a tight roof. John Hathaway's children were not all born, and his aged mother retained a few hundreds of her own which she lent freely. Presently Robert Shield proved glad to give ready money for the slices between the two houses. When the youngest Hathaway boy was born my grandfather paid fifty dollars for an addition to his door yard worth about five dollars at prevailing Mountain prices. On the arrival of Rosalie Hathaway an attendant nurse reported that first there wasn't so much as a handful of meal in the house, and then there were layer raisins, oranges and plum cake. Between these conditions Robert Shield had purchased what was ever after known as the forty-rod strip, extending from road to woodland, including a delightful little mowing which he called the Hathaway lot; including also a "right of way" through the Hathaway lane. This last, as a thoroughfare short but sweet, I do not consider can be outdone in romantic beauty by anything of a similar kind in the wide world. There's a baby brook running across it, spanned by a bridge of natural stone, there is a charming curve up hill that pretends it is going thirty miles to a haven of delight, there are trees from which fall tiny red apples to be baked without coring and eaten without sugar. Raspberries and blackberries abound in the hedgerows, wild grapes hang garland-wise from otherwise useless trees, there are winding corners for cozy sunning in on cool afternoons; and at the end a barway just precisely like the ones which the happy lovers meet at in pictures.

Grandfather would not have been so ready to buy but for grand-mother's nagging. He said he wanted to stop her mouth more than he wanted to even the line. She kept right on nagging. Not only, said she, did he pay too much, but with his usual carelessness he bought subject to a mortgage. That the mortgage was held right in the family, my father having loaned the twelve hundred dollars to John Hathaway, made the bad bargain no better in grandmother's talk. She "believed in no family in business." Besides, one never knew what might happen. Sallie might die and Hilary (my father) marry again and what with widow's thirds and maybe a lawsuit there'd be a pretty mess. But that's just like you, Robert Shield. When you built that church in Brimfield....

Grandfather went out rather quickly and asked of the chickens in the dooryard who, in the name of goodness, he could trust if not his own son-in-law? He had heard that complaint about the church in Brimfield before. So had I, though its construction so long ante-dated my birth that Sallie, my mother, was barely seven when it happened.

Perhaps this was the time my cousin Charlie and I asked gram an impudent question.

"Seeing's you don't like grandfather a-tall," we began, "why did you go and get married with him?"

Whenever the inquiry was put, I well remember her glare at the pair of us, who would thus invade the veiled source of her affections.

"Robert Shield was a very handsome young man," she observed, and shut us up.

How did John Hathaway manage to get himself into such finan-cial scrapes when this was a time in which all farmers made money? Well, John Hathaway never was a farmer, not even a "gentleman farmer." He had supposed that buying a farm well stocked, barned and machined, would automatically provide him with skill. In this he was as much out of the way as he was lacking in vision of the growth of Eastfield.

A peaceable man, low voiced, gentle mannered, he was the very moral of inefficiency. Never would he assert his rights, whether dealing with other men or with nature. Let weeds put in a claim to a crop and that crop was theirs. Yet the man was always at work, wandering from field to field with a hoe on his shoulder, dressed in threadbare clothes, his hat drooping as his head drooped. Perhaps he was not very strong, yet he lived to an extraordinary age, always discouraged, often undernourished.

By an irony of fate he had been a butcher in early life, and after his fortunes declined used to be called upon for all the pig sticking in Holly. By daybreak he would arrive with his instruments of taking off. By noon the huge carcasses hung from trees, and Mr. Hathaway, looking like a boy who had outgrown his strength, was accepting a plate of fried hog liver at the dinner table. Liver, being most perishable, is the first part of the hog eaten. John Hathaway dined on it six days in seven throughout each autumn for forty or fifty years. That alone might have given him a discouraging view of life.

His good looking children refused to be educated, refused to work. They were not dissipated. They sat around the fire, too lazy to drive to the woodlot for anything to burn. My grandmother caught them burning fence rails, and these they were too lazy to saw and split. One end of the rail was thrust into the stove, when that burned off a simple shove replenished the fire. The eldest son achieved fame by bringing home a wife one day. She was twelve years old and her trousseau consisted principally of dolls. She nor they stopped long. Her father took her home on her complaint of having nothing to eat but griddlecakes without butter or molasses. Two other sons declined to go a-courting; finally a pair of energetic Scotch damsels came up from the factory settlement and courted them, bore them away to work, made successful men out of them. This is a fact! People on Holly Mountain always considered it the most amazing performance of the century.

There was a good honest daughter who married respectably and went to Eastfield, but before long she came back a poor widow burdened with children. There was another son who died of a fever, nursed by my grandparents for weeks after his own father and mother declared themselves "all beat out" with a few days of sitting up. And there was Rosalie. She had long fair hair and distinguished herself in the village school by being able to put her fist in her mouth. She got married in a fearful hurry to a funny little fat boy who frequently went on the town winters. Come spring, if the town declined to honour his recquisition for canned peaches and new clothing, he'd get mad, pile his furniture in a wagon, and move right out of the poorhouse where he'd been enjoying free quarters. His work was generally cobbling. He called at the door, stuck a few patches to shoes with a coat of blacking, collected fifty cents and hastily moved on. In a few years he and Rosalie had lived in all the ell parts and "underground rooms" of all the tumbledown houses in Holly, Hansom and Palmer. They had a good many children, some of whom lived. Most of them were born in the north room at her father's. Rosalie hated to hear a baby cry, so she bought soothing syrup by the dozen bottles. Whenever an unmarried girl would listen she issued warnings against getting married, illustrated by tales of her husband's inconsiderate treatment. Perhaps she told the truth. The town has supported her for years in the State Hospital for Insane. Her oldest daughter is there, also.

John Hathaway's life represented a series of abandonments. His farm ran in natural terraces from the road to the wooded hillcrest a half mile away. Every year some upland ceased to be cultivated, until there remained only a tiny strip of garden between house and wilderness. The herd of cows dwindled to one; yokes of oxen and spans of horses came to be represented by a limping nag. Instead of filling several barns with hay, he mowed barely enough to carry these animals through the winter—sometimes not enough.

From paying the interest on the mortgage in money he came to paying it in kind. That is, my grandfather would take John Hathaway's apples and try to sell them so that Sallie, my mother, should not lose. When I was grown up John Hathaway had stopped paying in anything. There was as much back interest due as would swallow the mortgage.

"You take the darn thing," said my mother to me. "Maybe he'll give you some attention. Call on him, give him a good scare."

I never scared anyone in my life. I was quite as averse to fighting for my own as was John Hathaway. My mother did not know this. Because I was positive in speech and would argue in favour of my own opinion on any theory until black in the face, she went to her grave believing I was a noble fighter. But how sinking was the heart with which I tackled the job of getting blood from a stone.

Indeed there was something more than ordinarily appropriate in the trite comparison. I went there on a day of stone, a bloodless day. All the inferior granite formations that underlie Holly Mountain came to the surface and stuck out. The only melting of the leaden sky produced an occasional snowflake, and these lay unmelted where they fell. I approached the south door, which had for a step a piece of field stone big as a middle-sized gravestone. The front door was one of the things the Hathaways had abandoned. Trumpet creepers thrust their tendrils into every crevice, leaves sprouted from the key-hole. I imagined it would never be pried open but for a funeral.

The widow-daughter let me in, her hands steaming. She had become a washerwoman, and when a New England woman takes in washing she is about at the last strait. We went through a narrow passage from which the wall paper had been worn at shoulder height by years of rough treatment. In the south room there seemed to be gathered all that was left of the once complete furnishings—a bit of ingrained carpet, the painted bureau of one bedroom set, bearing the cracked mirror of another, one stuffed chair in black haircloth, a threadbare footstool in red brocade, cane chairs that did not match, a beautiful tip table which they probably did not value.

Old Mrs. Hathaway sat flabby and mumbling by one window; under the narrow wooden mantle blistered by heat from ancient fires, two massive young women were doing each other's hair. They were the widow's daughters. I was amazed to find them so nearly grown up. Their hair was wonderful. It lay on their shoulders in great heaps of pale brown, ending with no diminishing of thickness far below their waists. On a wooden chair was displayed a regular beauty shop's apparatus of large tooth combs, white backed brushes, barrettes and pins in the gold celluloid that approaches tortoise shell.

They glared at me from under beetling brows, those girls about whom I knew nothing but that they bore Bible names—God knows why. My presence did not abash them, they kept right on combing, but they seemed to sense that my coming somehow endangered their comfort.

The widow apologised. "My daughters...driving from the Street musses 'em so...have to brush and comb...every day...they go to the Academy...Naomi, don't forget your algibbery..."

So she washed that they might pay Academy fees. Their grandfather's old blind mare used her little remaining strength to drag them six miles daily down and up the Mountain.

John Hathaway wandered in and sat down with the air of a man never in the place before. His clothes were faded to a yellow hue, his black coat quite green in the back. He never wore blue denim, like his neighbour farmers, he was always just about so shabby, but never patched. He had a long, melancholy face, his lips drooped, his chin whisker was sparse, as was also the dark brown hair on his head, which resembled an uncovered skull. I managed to tell him I owned the mortgage. He said, well, my mother was getting older, perhaps business was too much for her! Then he drifted, somehow, to the difficulty of farming in a Western Massachusetts winter. He told me about the ten acres and the house which he had sold so unadvisedly before buying on Holly Mountain, and how inconsiderately Eastfield had grown out and over the property once his. All sorts of handsome houses there now, whole streets of them. One street called Holly Road.

I got up to go, without mentioning interest. I determined to quiet my mother and my grandmother with some sort of a lie. In the presence of the Bible-named damsels I felt the need of a more thorough grooming. I did not live in a mortgaged hovel, but my hair was not as theirs. Nor my nails. (For they had produced boxes and begun manicuring.) It was not pity that moved me, it was a desire to escape before their eyes spied out all my physical deficiencies—for instance, the mole on my left shoulder, which kept me from decollete evening gowns.

John Hathaway followed me into the dooryard, but even in that comparative privacy I couldn't dun him. I pitied him now as the victim is pitied in the rural play when the old squire comes to foreclose. Threaten him as Sallie—my mother—had said to threaten! Tell him to pay something or pack up and get out? Well, she hadn't ever had the courage to do it, I noticed. The snow helped me to vision a creaking cart drawn by the blind mare, passing through the barway in a driving storm. The cart bore a few blue chairs and nondescript tables. Old John Hathaway held the reins in his trembling hands. He did not look back. His wife, a gibbering imbecile, sat beside him, her crazy bonnet falling more awry with each wobble of her palsied head. The widowed daughter, in rusty weeds, crouched under a patchwork quilt. With her two small children. I made them small, for effect.

John Hathaway was telling a story.

"Life's different in its deal to different people," he remarked. "I was struck particular when my brother came out to see me this summer. We hadn't seen each other for most twenty years. `Well, John,' says he to me, `how you making out?' He could see I wasn't making out any too well. But things have always come easy with him. In fact, he's never known what it was to do a real hard day's work in his life. I told him so. Says I, `Ben, you've never known what it was to do a real hard day's work in your life.' Now I'd never known anything else."

I shook myself free of fancies and inquired what this comfortably situated brother did for a living. Presumed he had a sitting down job—was what we had begun to call a "white collar man" some twenty years later.

He was a carpenter!

The whole family seemed to me warped, just as I suppose I seemed warped to them. I rested after sending John Hathaway a carefully typewritten description of his indebtedness. I learned afterward that he was struck of a heap at the "printing" and never really believed the document had any bearing on his personal affairs. This seems fantastic, but in 1895 there was probably not a typewriter in Holly. The changes wrought by time! That puzzling paper was written on a Smith-Premier with a double keyboard. Now I can't buy another. They don't make them anywhere.

In the winter of 1903 most of the Hathaway family had pneumonia. A sickness like that, running from bed to bed, was reminiscent of the old times when Fred Hathaway raved with fever and Gran'ma Hathaway was some time a-dying in another room. Then my grandmother used to go over and watch, while my grandfather kept himself awake reading John S. C. Abbott's *History of the Civil War* in two volumes by his own kitchen fire. At exactly midnight he loaded a wheelbarrow with pies and firewood cut out stove-length, which he pushed creakingly to the solace of his spouse.

The widow's daughters, name of Blodgett, having had the fore-sight to sometimes attend the Union Church at Holly Depot, were rescued by that body and given district nurses. They recovered, with hair intact. I caught Naomi raspb'ring in my pasture the fol-lowing summer, with it down. John Hathaway, probably more or less neglected, died and was buried months before I knew about it. In fact, there was a neighbourhood conspiracy to keep me in the dark. It turned out successful because by this time my grandparents were no longer in the next house, but also dead and buried beside my father in the Dell.

It is my present conviction that nobody liked me in Holly. I've often wondered why. The place pulls ever on my heart strings, and I'm one of the scant half dozen shining lights emerging from its gen-erally dun-coloured history. But nobody cares two cents except Miss Bachelor, and she also had a hard row to hoe. She lived in town ful-ly forty years before they ceased thinking of her as a squatter. Those Blodgett girls always bulked big; perhaps because their common ar-rogance gave great value to occasional acknowledgment of favours. The widow and her daughters were encouraged to remain in the old house, where they certainly had no rights at all. They were helped to buyers for all they could strip—fertilizer, hay for bedding down, siding off the tottering barn. They wrenched the corner cupboard loose and sold that. And I always wanted a corner cupboard! Tak-ing refuge in the Washington Tavern, where almost anyone might hire a few rat-infested rooms, they declined to give me the key.

Miss Bachelor drove me down to make the request for it. The day was a magnificent one in June; long grass, ready for cutting, but not cut, concealed clustered wild strawberries that tasted like essence of fine weather. The younger girl sat on the incongruous porch with which a French Canuck had ruined the front of the Washington Tavern. Her hair was down, it had just been washed.

Anticipating the worst and assisted in doing so by instructions from a city lawyer who magnified every legal act until it was some-thing worth charging twenty-five dollars for, I was planning to make what is called a foreclosure by entry. Miss Bachelor and I, in her smart top buggy, were the head of a cortege. Three teams, each bearing a selectman, they had first to listen to a refusal of the key; then they were to assist us in breaking the door. About half an hour after defying the whole of us, the widow Blodgett weakened, and came panting up the hill, bearing the object of contention. It looked like the kind of thing one could get up a large quarrel over. A Yale lock might be safer—one could have picked this with a hairpin, but as a symbol...

We instantly spread through the house, Miss Bachelor, the eighty-year-old auctioneer who would presently foreclose the mortgage by a sale to the highest bidder; Ambrose Almy, intending to bid, and myself. The auctioneer announced that he was born there, being a son of Benammi Peters. As a boy the future auctioneer had crept up those perpendicular stairs and bumped his head on the lowest ceiling of one of the four tiny rooms. Before doing either he washed his feet in an Indian stone trough, which was found to be still in existence, and nigh the well.

Ambrose Almy declined to bid when he heard me start at twelve hundred dollars. His limit was a thousand dollars, and that was indeed more than the ruin was worth. I returned to Miss Bachelor's piazza after a successful foreclosure, with the place mine. I could do exactly as I liked with those five fireplaces, that staircase the model of the one in the Hancock-Clarke house at Lexington, that mammoth doorkey. I was jealous of my rights and much resented well-meant advice to put up metal ceilings and beaver wallboard. In my mind I restored the house without an anachronism. With a pang I now remember being very short with my mother, who wondered if it wouldn't be possible to have a central hall and a gallery with doors around. She was ever romantic and impractical. I brutally convinced her that even with the wonderful fieldstone chimney removed it couldn't be done. And that chimney went only over my dead body.

I need not have been so fierce, because all the alteration the house experienced during my regime was shearing off the "ell" built by Benammi Peters, and pulling the floorboards from an upstairs room to floor a tent which was set up several seasons in the meadow back of the dooryard.

Miss Bachelor told me the story of Birdie and her brother-in-law's grewsome ending during some one of these visits. We discovered that it must have been about the era of her peerings for smoke from her uncle's garret that I first met her on the road to Holly-Back-of-the-Mountain. She had on very striped stockings and was riding a diamond frame bicycle. She had begun to teach the West Holly school and her oldest pupil, a youth considerable her senior, was walking by her side trundling another wheel. All Holly told with horror how on Saturdays Edna Bachelor in pants took the boy picnicking in faroff graveyards. Being hard pushed for excitement Holly tried to make a scandal of such goings on. I looked at the Bachelor girl with rank curiosity, unknowing that we were to be united by a thousand ties—even by the fact that her aunt and my grandmother were mutually worrying about neighbours. For while Ruby Bachelor was saying of Birdie and her brother-in-law, "Well, there's some smoke, so anyway they've got a fire," Elizabeth Shield was peering Hathaway way at nightfall and observing, when a dim light showed, "Anyhow, they've got kerosene."

One morning, after a snowfall like that in Whittier's "Snowbound," no smoke came from Birdie's chimney. Uncle Jasper and Aunt Ruby harnessed up and Edna Bachelor packed a pail with freshly cooked doughnuts and went along. Certain odours, she told me, always brought the picture of that dreadful front room where Birdie's brother-in-law lay on the floor as he had fallen fainting while trying to niggle a tree trunk into something the stove would burn. Birdie, bedridden, was in the stupour that solaces starvation. The house held nothing eatable—absolutely nothing. Yet the undertaker who prepared the man for burial—for the brother-in-law died in an hour—reported his body as exhibiting no physical defect. Reported also a money belt alive with vermin and containing several thousand dollars in dirty bills. Birdie was able to take sustenance in the form of doughnuts, and lived for two weeks. She inherited the money which the brother-in-law had died holding out on her, it went to her daughter, from down Philadelphia way.

The daughter put up a white marble gravemarker in West Holly cemetery, which still attests to one virtue of "Birdie Edmands—A Good Mother." Reward, I suppose, for the inheritance!

Plenty of people stood ready to buy the Edmands place and live in the house, because land wasn't then the useless possession it is now, and no house is haunted to folks with common sense. But communications sent Philadelphia way received no response, and the building rapidly fell into its own cellar. I took Miss Bachelor's dogs and went up there one day in May, when we wanted a great mass of flowers with which to decorate her house for the Holly Street Women's Club. The lilacs and syringas were like trees and waterfalls of bloom; birds fluttered about, bees droned in the matrimony vine, and I found such a blessed little green dooryard, with turf like best quality velvet, that I wondered how it had been kept, year after year, unseen and unappreciated. From the tameness of the birds I judged that I was the first visitor in a long time.

Across the road was a bit of wood, where the trees grew far enough apart to let sunshine to the ground, which was covered with moss and Princess Pine, partridge vines and maiden hair fern. On this sunlit afternoon it seemed the happiest little corner that the earth might know. Sitting on what had once been a step and looking at about the angle from which poor old Nance had cast her blear-eyed blandishments, I suddenly realized that very possibly the daughter from down Philadelphia way had done the best thing in letting the old house be buried.

My own course had been so different. I had glowed in pride of possession, yet I hadn't been much more considerate of my old place than John Hathaway had been of his. I had stopped the mowing of hay until the proportion of weeds grew to prevent salability. Ignoring the rotting roof I had painted the old clapboards green one summer because that was better fun than hiring a man to shingle. Paint made the neighbours wonder, and the storekeeper at Holly Depot exclaim at my extravagance because green was the most expensive hue on the colour card. I did keep the windows protected by shutters for fourteen years, but I let them be exposed by an Eastfield realtor who took an option. Whereupon the prismatic panes, sixteen to a sash, instantly became broken, though there was hardly a boy in the neighbourhood.

Yes, I had wonderful dreams. I used to stop an hour or two on my way to Miss Bachelor's and dream them. Another coat of green paint, window boxes with geraniums, striped awnings. My mother wanted a piazza to the north, where the "view" was, and a markee on the lawn which would gently incline in the same direction, and which, in the present tense, was an orchard of wormy apple trees. I allowed her these, and we encouraged one another to believe in a high wall of field stone along the front where there was now nothing in particular, not even that last resort of a lazy man, a Virginia rail fence.

Sometimes I drew plans. Like Dorothea, born Brooke in *Middlemarch*, it has always been my fad to draw plans. I made the smallest bedroom into a pantry, the other and the passageway I threw into the south room. A quite unauthorised dormer window turned the open space at the rear upstairs into something real useful. We were probably a good deal like John Hathaway, because I have no doubt he too was always making improvements in anticipation. Miss Bachelor pretended to believe in us. She said she knew exactly the man to construct that cementless wall, only we must hurry up and employ him because he was very old, and with him the art would die so far as Holly and vicinity were concerned, barb wire being as highly considered there as it was in Brussels in 1914. She also promised me a four-post bedstead, the real old corded kind, when I should start furnishing.

I was terribly vexed, all these years, by people who implored me to sell them the place, or at least to let them live in it. One summer I actually came upon a "squatter," who had moved into the south room with the bedroom set and crayon enlargements that he had inherited from his parents. An uncle of mine, having been burned out of one home and ejected from another, insisted on ridding me of the squatter, and having done so moved in himself without so much as a yea or a nay.

Clack-clack went tongues, approving of his cheek, telling me how much better it was for the house to have an occupant—"keep out the damp"—"keep up the insurance." Probably true, but my interest in the place was gone forever. I had loved the position of dog in the manger; to think of the rooms as absolutely mine, waiting for me to straighten their floors, plaster and paper their walls, whiten their ceilings, and bring them to life with furniture. I could forgive the Hathaways, even though the Blodgett girls were down in Holly Depot, combing their hair over the books of the town library and refusing anyone the new novels until they'd finished reading them themselves. I could not forget my uncle, whose evil habits were giving the house a bad reputation, and who wintered a hunting dog boxed in under his bed.

"Besides," said my mother, "now he's got into the house there'd be no getting him out. He'd insist on living with us." She knew him, she was his sister. He died in the house after five years' residence, paying no rent, leaving a last request, that I should not attend his funeral. But I did, and saw him put into the grave minus regret. Yes, even though it was my mother's grave wherein he was interred by a series of mistakes rather characteristic of Holly, a town in which a funeral seldom comes off without leaving material for a funny story.

I was glad enough to sell the property to an Irish lawyer in Eastfield in 1918, for the last part of my ownership was often vexatious. Once a city man who bought at the back disputed my deed of "eighty rods more or less from the Mountain road so called" because that considerably overlapped his equally vague "eighty rods more or less from the road to the Street so called." We spent a day in the woods along with surveyors and fence viewers. It was in beautiful April, we stayed until a silvery moon shone out, turning the paper birches into dancing visions, and making cart pathways of glory. My neighbour on the rear was finally convinced concerning the line, but he never paid for the wood cut on my side, and I caught an access of asthma from which I feel the effects to this day. At another time I went into fussy conference with a company that bought everything to my north, and hoped to develop by selling house lots at two hundred dollars per acre. Would I sell my woodland for a thousand dollars and let them pay me by building a bungalow in the huge upland pasture that always seemed to me like a Socttish highland out of literature? I sat an entire forenoon on the ledge which stood for my possible piazza. Before me was a wondrous view all green and brown, to be scarlet and yellow in autumn. Streams were blue in streaks and silvery; toy houses thrust impertinent red chimneys from nosegays that were actually oaks and maples; floating clouds made bits of shade out of which the emerald-hued fields emerged as jewels newly polished. In my ears was the soothing voice of the promoter. There would be an avenue—nothing so cheap as a road—paralleling my north line, with just one row of dwellings between my property and it. Then I might build another row, and construct another avenue—he called mine a street—and with 'a couple more lines of dwellings on t'other sides of our thoroughfares we had possibly provided for the needs of a twelvemonth! Say a couple hundred homes, several two-tenement. Some growth for a mountain where a dozen families had comprised the entire population even before the halcyon days when George Washington Browne's father's house hadn't been torn down and the Almy house and my uncle's burned up.

Ambition did not pause here, either. Another road—which he called a boulevard—would traverse the crest of the hill. That was why my woodland was wanted, also other woodland, and even sacred Hunting Hill. What a view, lady, what a view! Right slap up to it, nigh my projected bungalow, there was to be the public park; bandstand for Saturday evenings, dancing floor, tennis court, shrubbery, flower garden. Just for the people who bought our lots—perhaps let the natives in. Nobody else, nobody from the factory settlement down at the Depot.

Of course he was a good talker. Otherwise he would have been in some other business. I saw myself playing tennis in that exclusive park; yes, though I had never played tennis in my life!

Possibly some of this stood a chance of coming true, for several thousand dollars were spent in laying out the "avenue" and constructing a huge concreted reservoir top of the hill. This last specially interested the natives, who even laid aside the constitutional aversion of farmers to walking so as to go and inspect the thing. They told their wives the tank was big enough, but what in tunket was the use of a tank with nothing to put in it? They knew well enough how their springs went dry in the summer, and the same thing would happen to the fifty springs which this deluded company had bought for a big pump to work on.

John Hathaway and Robert Shield used to drive their cows to the river, but a concern would look pretty funny chasing two-three hundred gents and ladies!

So just for want of a little advice which any farmer's wife could have given, the Sunrise Development Co. ceased to function. Their advertisements disappeared from Eastfield papers, their avenue faded from Holly Mountain. Last time I saw it 'twas a streak of rank weeds marring an otherwise good and grassy pasture.

The final avaricious eye fixed on the place during my ownership was the fishy one of Jim Welch. He leaped upon me out of a void, assailing me with telegrams, long distance 'phone calls, special delivery letters and legal documents sent registered. Immediately afterward he arrived in a huge auto, when the following conversation took place:

"Mrs. Julia Gurrelamo, a rich New York woman, has taken a fancy to your house. She would like to buy it."

"I'm not anxious to sell..."

"Well, she is to buy. Only, until June, her money is tied up... United Fruit..."

(This was August.)

"I suggest that she call on me then and talk it over..."

"She never calls on anyone. She's very old. She would like to lease..."

"I don't care to let..."

"Twelve dollars a month and no privileges. Except starting to make repairs. You wouldn't mind if the roof was shingled this fall? Inspect the work, of course, as much as you like..."

Was this man insane? This is his actual conversation. He was fat and fussy. I discovered afterward that Mrs. Julia was his own invention.

"I guess I prefer to sell," said I.

"Option of buying next June. Price five thousand dollars, two hundred dollars forfeit if bargain not completed. Rent in advance. Three months now. Check for thirty-six dollars."

He waved it in my face.

"I ought to consult my mother."

"All right. Where is she?"

She was visiting friends twenty-five miles away. We drove out and fetched her home. Agreeing 'twas too good to be true, we decided we had better accept and bank the check instantly.

Jim Welch lived up to his bargain, all but the shingling. By June he stopped paying and we heard he was head over ears in the purchase of an abandoned hotel in South Brookfield. What he got from the attempted deal with me I cannot understand. I suspected a rumoured trolley line up the Mountain or a traced vein of the Shortmeadow sandstone quarries, but Miss Bachelor laughed me out of any explanation so sensible.

"Jim Welch," she said, "is a dreamer who's able to concrete his fancies because he does business with his wife's money."

Seems inadequate, but after all I know no better explanation.

In September the Irish-American lawyer of Eastfield paid me twelve hundred dollars cash and took title. His wife, a dainty little creature all American, interested me by her frankly confessed sentimentality. She and Mike had longed to live on Holly Mountain ever since they had done their courting number Sundays up and down the road. Were they, I asked myself, among those warned off the homelot in the days when I had camped back of the old house? I almost gave her the ten unused "No Trespass" signs left from the dozen which I had extravagantly caused to be printed at the office of the Hamson Chronotype. Then I bethought me of the couple who once paused under the darling old cherry tree in the front yard. Such a wonderful old cherry tree, loaded with the most luscious red cherries. The young man climbed it to pick her some, and she stood below with full pleated skirt outspread to catch them—for we wore full pleated skirts then. The couple did not know that old cherry trees have very rotten limbs, and that the earth around old cherry trees often becomes a metropolis of ants. He fell at about the time she started to run, clutching at her shoulders. Their ignoring of the No Trespass signs was adequately avenged. They might so easily have been the purchasers that I refrained from presenting the signs.

"Come and see how beautifully we shall do the old place over," said she.

That was nice of her, I thought. Exceedingly nice. In the summer of two years afterward I spent one Sunday afternoon in the front yard. There was no hedge or fence or wall. Automobiles loaded to the gunwales with folks and lunch ploughed by, each sinking nearer the hubs in the flinty dust peculiar to the region. The yardful played a betting game on number plates. Somebody always lost and he brought the others out glasses of the worst homebrew I have encountered—up to now. There were raisins in it, but it was not wine; neither did the obvious presence of hops cause it to resemble beer. It was not palatable. It was not even intoxicating. Everyone present drank it avidly.

The house had been painted white, and I did not like it at all. Perhaps because there were no green blinds. And the windows!

Was it for this that I had preserved the sixteen panes to a sash for fifteen years? Even though a few glasses were broken, others had been left, prismatic and intact, and the frames had been quite perfect. All, all were now gone, stupid modern double sashes taking their place. Indoors—metal ceilings in patterns like those dreadful ones artificial stone is so apt to assume, and beaver board walls. Wide planks ripped up and "hard wood floors" laid.

I saw no faintest trace of fireplaces, nor did I venture to inquire just what was their fate. As for decorations, there were no old books, no pewter, no blue plates, not even the ordinary and so easily acquired flowing blue. I peered out of one of the abominable windows. Where were the towering lilacs, the unique black currant bushes, the walks bordered by golden glow?

"We have had the yard trimmed up a bit," observed that Irishman's wife, whose breeding in a New England family was certainly wasted. "It was dreadfully shaggy."

I recalled the glaring white, the absence of greenery. The trumpet creeper was gone. No matrimony vine cascaded between the front windows of the south room. Something had happened to the famous white rose at the southeast corner. I had sold the house to the kind of people who would chop down a tree because its leaves choked the rain gutter.

When I go to see Miss Bachelor I pass the place sorrowfully, for it is never any better than on that day. Perhaps it is worse, for they live there the year round, and there is a clothes reel in the side yard. I think of the Widow Blodgett handing her white linen to bushes, or spreading it on the grass. The old house tries to look reproachfully at me from the ugly modern windows, but does not wholly succeed, being pretty well smothered by new plaster board. As they have kept it in good repair up to now and promise to keep on doing so, I see little chance for a change.

I am apologetic, even contrite. A charge to keep I had, and I allowed it to escape my care. Restoration in accord with its time is to a dwelling as new blood to a sick man, but cosmetics and violet rays will not revive a corpse. Birdie's daughter from down Philadelphia way had better understanding than I. A dead house should be buried.

ca. 1920 (*Leaves,* 1938)

Devoted to amateur journalism and
good literature.
By EDITH MINITER,
147 Summer Street, Boston, Mass.

ABOUT THE EDITORS

Born in 1948, Ken Faig has been writing about H. P. Lovecraft since the early 1970s and was a founding member of the Esoteric Order of Dagon (E.O.D.) amateur press association in 1973. He founded his Moshassuck Press in 1987 to publish specialized works by and about Lovecraft and his associates, and published two large collections of work by Edith Miniter (1995, 2000) and *Susan's Obituary* (1996), a novel by Lovecraft's uncle Dr. Franklin C. Clark. He has made a specialty of Lovecraft's family background and published a genealogy of Lovecraft's branch of the Phillips family in 1993 and (with collaborators Chris J. Docherty and A. Langley Searles) a monograph on Lovecraft's paternal ancestry in Devonshire, England in 2003. He is also very interested in Lovecraft's participation in the amateur journalism hobby, and has been editor of *The Fossil*, the quarterly journal of the history of the hobby, since 2004.

Sean Donnelly is assistant to the director of the University of Tampa Press, where he is also editorial assistant on the literary journal *Tampa Review*, a contributing co-editor of the series Insistent Visions, and an associate of the Tampa Book Arts Studio. He also collects supernatural and fantastic literature and mystery/detective fiction from the late 1800s to the 1950s, with a special interest in the pulp field. His previous books include *Willis T. Crossman's Vermont: Stories by W. Paul Cook* (2005) and *W. Paul Cook: The Wandering Life of a Yankee Printer* (2007). He is also the author, with J. B. Dobkin, of *The Peter Pauper Press of Peter and Edna Beilenson*.

The book was typeset and designed by
Sean Donnelly at the office of the
University of Tampa Press
Tampa, Florida.